*Claire stopped and
slowly forced herself
to focus inside . . .*

6/07

The stillness within her rippled, shifted,
and adjusted uneasily.

Everything in her work room was too quiet.
The colors were soft, the windows draped
against the bright morning Montana sunshine.

But the container of ruby beads gleamed
bloodred.

They seemed dangerous, holding her . . .

She drew aside the window's heavy drapery.

And she wasn't feeling friendly toward the
big, brawny man who was walking toward her
home . . .

CAIT LONDON

AT THE EDGE

AVON BOOKS
An Imprint of HarperCollinsPublishers

AVON BOOKS
An Imprint of HarperCollins*Publishers*
10 East 53rd Street
New York, New York 10022-5299

Copyright © 2007 by Lois Kleinsasser
ISBN: 978-0-06-114050-1
ISBN-10: 0-06-114050-3
www.avonromance.com

First Avon Books paperback printing: June 2007

Avon Trademark Reg. U.S. Pat. Off. and in Other Countries, Marca Registrada, Hecho en U.S.A.
HarperCollins® is a registered trademark of HarperCollins Publishers.

Printed in the U.S.A.

10 9 8 7 6 5 4 3 2 1

*The Aisling triplets' stories began brewing years ago
and I am so glad that they are now coming to life.
Lucia Macro, (my editor); Carrie; Liate;
and the rest of Avon Books' wonderful people
have my gratitude and appreciation
for their confidence and support.*

————————————

Prologue

"I'M SO SORRY. I WOULDN'T HAVE GONE IF I'D SENSED THEY were coming for you. I'm sorry I left you. I'm sorry for what happened to you."

From her study, Greer Aisling watched her ten-year-old daughters in the garden below. Surrounded by Washington state's lush coastal flowers and herbs, the triplets seemed to be like other children, each green-eyed with a bright cap of fiery hair that matched their mother's.

But just returned from their two-day abduction, the triplets' faces were too pale for children who should be lively in play. The girls had been unusually quiet, communicating without words, using only a soothing touch or a knowing look. They'd been sheltered from the curious and sometimes cruel outer world. Now, after being torn from their safe home and plunged into a nightmare of testing, they would never be the same. After two days of intense examinations by doctors, parapsychologists, and scientists, they fully understood how unusual they were—psychics, born of a psychic mother.

Greer, a widow, had been traveling away from home to work with the police, to find a missing boy. She had thought her daughters were protected. As a world-famous psychic, she had understood the scientific interest in her children and taken safeguards to protect them. Their friends and tutors were carefully selected, and she worked very hard to get the girls out into everyday circumstances, like visits to the grocery store, museums, or family vacations in national parks. On those occasions, she was always there, monitoring them as they interacted with others.

And yet, while she was away, they came—the doctors and parapsychologists, the psychologists whom she had prevented testing her children. Their beloved housekeeper and caretaker hadn't been prepared for the onslaught of child-care authorities and doctors, the invasion under the ruse of checking on the children's welfare. Whisked away from their home and placed in a clinic to be studied, the triplets were enveloped in a nightmare of testing; their extrasensory perceptions and their psychic links to each other had been probed.

She glanced at the sensors blinking quietly on the wall; the new, ultramodern alarm system would detect any intruders. And from now on, until her daughters left her care, Greer would work from home. . . .

It had taken Greer two days to get them safely back home, but the damage had been done. After exposure to the outside world, her daughters now knew how unusual they were. Greer braced herself against the wave of anger consuming her. A quick, sharp look up from Claire, a special child who could sense emotions of others, warned Greer to be careful. The tests had proven her to be an empath, something Greer had known almost from the time her daughters were born. Greer had soon learned that she had to protect Claire from herself; a mother's link was stronger than any other. Her anger and fear could trigger Claire's own, too fierce and terrifying for one so young.

Greer forced her anger down and smiled at Claire as she blocked her intuitive daughter's perception. Claire's clairvoyant powers had been triggered by the trauma, and now her psychic antennae were much more receptive, especially to her mother.

Greer's fist gripped the sleeve of her robe, crushing the gold Celtic pattern of the cloth. She could not stop the future and its grip upon her unique triplets.

She studied her three unique daughters, each with an individual, developing sixth sense, each linked to the other—and to her.

Firstborn, Leona's dreams were of the future, just terrifying bits that a child could not interpret . . . but her talent would become stronger. And as Greer had once done, Leona was certain to fight her precognitive ability.

Middle-born, Tempest was a bold rebel, an adventuress already. Every day was a new challenge for Tempest, who could hold an object and "read" its history.

Last-born, the "baby," Claire was the most vulnerable. She was also the peacemaker, the one who listened and gave comfort. Claire's ability as an empath would bring her pain because the outside world held cruelties and savagery; she would feel the dark emotions of others and be terrified. Generous and caring, she would want to take pain away—but then it would become her own.

In the garden, the triplets locked hands and stood looking up at Greer. Claire's perception of their mother's anger had been transferred to her sisters—all without a word. The delicate psychic probe Greer felt was the result of their joined powers.

They'd learned that much in those horrible days, that they were stronger when linked. And they were testing her.

She smiled gently and, with a skill much stronger than her daughters', blocked the childlike probe.

Another wave of anger caught Greer, the need for

revenge, a mother striking out at those harming her children . . . She knew ways she could reach inside the people who had taken her daughters. . . . She knew how to bend them to her will. . . . She knew how to make them do things they didn't want . . .

Suddenly in the garden below, Claire's expression changed to fierce anger, and her slender body trembled, her small fists tight at her side. Her green eyes had changed; they flashed gold in the sunlight, reflecting her anger.

Greer pushed down her emotions, steadied them, focused into a level plane, and Claire relaxed slightly.

As her senses developed, Claire would be even more vulnerable. She would need more peace and isolation than the world would allow.

And as sensitive as she was to her sisters and her mother, eventually Claire would have to live apart.

Or she would be influenced by their emotions, and would never have peace.

One

_____

Twenty-two years later

"I SHOULD GO TALK TO HIM, BUT I REALLY DO NOT WANT to," Claire murmured to herself.

From her kitchen window, Claire watched the man standing in front of the house next door. Hunched against Montana's bitter January wind, he seemed alone, his collar turned up, his hands in his jacket's pockets.

He stood so still amid the ghostly white snowdrifts and stark, leafless trees that he seemed a part of the landscape. Snow covered his knit cap and shoulders now, but he hadn't moved. He stood facing his aunt's house as if he were facing memories and bracing himself to enter it.

Claire had recognized Neil Olafson immediately; she'd seen him many times as he'd visited his aunt. There was no mistaking that tall, powerful body, despite the curtain of snow.

A warning tingle at the back of her neck caused Claire to reach for the telephone before it rang. That special tingle told Claire that one of her older sisters was calling. The triplets and their mother rarely needed the ring of the telephone to know family was calling. Their psychic link was stronger than electronics, and Claire's senses instantly picked up the identity of the caller. "Hi, Tempest. Neil Olafson is over at his Aunt Eunice's house now, and he's been standing outside, just looking at the house for some time."

"Mmm. Dreading to go in. You should go to him, Claire."

"I know. He really needs someone now. He looks so alone."

"He *is* alone, you know that. He's lost all of his family, according to what Eunice said. It's the right thing to do, Claire—to walk over there, say a few comforting things, then leave."

Claire inhaled slowly. She still had her family and could afford to comfort a grieving man she'd seen but never actually met. In fact, she'd avoided meeting him for five years, preferring her solitude and her work.

Tempest was unrelenting, an older sister nudging a younger one. "You know you should. He's standing out there, lonely in a freezing blizzard, dreading to go into his aunt Eunice's home, and he's all alone. You were her friend, and he knows it. Just remember to protect yourself. You know how to block other's energies from you. You can protect yourself when you try really hard. Just go over there and do it, then you're done."

"I've managed to *not* meet him since I moved in here. So I just walk up and tell him that I'm sorry his aunt died?" Claire was only prolonging the moment. Her reluctance was genuine, but so was her affection for the elderly woman who had just passed away. Tempest was right: Neil Olafson looked as if he really needed someone else standing near him in that snowy cold mist, someone to share his love of his aunt.

A gust of wind tossed the snowflakes in front of Claire's window; they churned slowly, almost like elegant dancers, before settling onto the layer of snow on her window ledge. To see better, Claire wiped her hand against the window glass, clearing it of the fog her breath had created.

Open on the cold glass, her hand paused as she thought of her friend, an old woman who had died at Christmastime. Claire continued looking through her window as she steadied the pewter hummingbird that dangled from its suction cup on the glass. The cheerful little bird seemed at odds with the blanket of snow draping the trees and Eunice's little house.

Her sister, always in tune with Claire's emotions, sensed her hesitation. "You need to help him, and you want to, so just do it. You'll regret it if you don't. He's alone, grieving, and you're elected. Eunice would want you to. You'll be okay, Claire. You're stronger now, but you also know how to block the feelings of others better. You've had enough practice. You deal with people all the time."

"On a necessity basis, Tempest. I'm out here in the-middle-of-nowhere Montana because I need solitude. I'd be drained and exposed to everything if I dealt with people every day. This is different. It's emotional. He's grieving. You know how dangerous that can be to me, especially when I'm missing her, too. I could take his emotions, his energy, into me, and they'd be magnified by my own, and—"

"You'll be fine. You've gotten better at protecting yourself. And wear the brooch I made you. If you feel you're in trouble, focus on that. We all have one, and we're all together. Love you. Truly, I do. Get back with me about what happens. You can use me to get rid of any upsetting energies. And I want to know what he looks like up close," Tempest advised, before the connection closed.

Snowflakes swirled around the man as Claire replaced the telephone.

How often through the years had the older woman peered through her own kitchen window and waved back at Claire? Or toasted her with her morning cup of tea?

Claire had missed the morning ritual, just as she was ending her all-night work session, and Eunice was rising.

The big man hadn't moved and stood like a shadow in the bluish white mist. Claire understood that this time was different; this time was Neil Olafson's reckoning, to face the truth of a loved one's passing. He would be wrapped in memories of his aunt Eunice. Since her death, he'd come only once, just after her funeral, staying but an hour or so.

Claire placed her hand over her heart, where the warm, fond memories of Eunice rested. She inhaled sharply, her heart twisting just that bit as the memories tightened within her: the little tea parties they'd shared, the way Eunice had always wanted her to meet Neil Olafson, her nephew. *I worry about Neil. He'll need a soft hand when I'm gone. He's been through so much. . . .*

The secluded valley was so quiet that Claire could almost hear the snowflakes tumble down her window's glass.

Listening to the quiet inside her, that special quiet place that made her so different from other people, Claire could almost hear the boughs of the juniper and fir bend with their burden of snow. She could almost feel the serviceberry and wild rosebushes crack with the weight.

In that quiet place where only Claire wandered, Eunice's words echoed from the past:

Neil hunted for his son, just a baby, only six months old when he was taken years ago—but they never found

Sammy. . . . It took the heart clear out of Neil. . . . When I'm gone, he'll have no one. . . .

Under the weight of snow, a branch cracked suddenly; it plummeted to the snowdrifts in front of her window, startling Claire. She shivered, despite the warmth of her home and sweater. She weighed the cost to herself if she went to Neil now. Grief could come slyly wrapped in the ache for other loved ones. Just as she still grieved for her unborn daughter, Neil would have that emptiness in his heart, magnified by the loss of his aunt.

Claire understood how Neil must feel: As close as she was to her sisters, the loss of any one of them—or perhaps her mother—could tear out her heart.

She stared down at her knuckles, bone white beneath the skin, then suddenly pushed back from the counter. "Okay, that's it. He does need someone, and I'm elected. I know how to protect myself. I've learned a lot in these five years. I'll go talk to him."

That warning tingle signaled another call from Tempest, and Claire reached for the telephone. Linked by psychic ability and as a triplet, the ties were strong. Claire knew exactly why Tempest was calling again. "Okay, Tempest. I have to get ready now. I'm going over."

"You'll call me later? I need to know that you're all right," Tempest worried.

"Yes, I'll call."

"As soon as you can. Hold that brooch I made in your pocket and think about how each of us wears one like it. I love you, baby. You'll be okay, you're a lot stronger now."

"Sure. Talk with you later."

Claire dressed carefully for the weather; she tugged up her snow boots, slid into her quilted coat and, after arranging her earmuffs, drew on her hood. She slipped the familiar brooch into the pocket of her coat, gripped it, and found the prick of the pin.

She tested the sharp point with her finger, just enough to experience the slight pain that would keep her safe. The prick was only a backup, just in case she forgot to focus as her mother had taught her. She repeated the protective mantra she used on the occasions she needed to block the feelings of others from her: "Stop. Think. Focus. . . . Build a wall around myself. See it in my mind. . . . I won't let his grief come inside me. I won't."

After she'd lost her baby, she'd had to learn stronger ways of protecting herself from absorbing the emotions and sensitivities of others. Standing a distance away from others was one method, focusing on that protective mental barrier was another. And then there was creating her own physical pain.

When she stood on her front porch, the fierce bite of the wind stunned her. At the end of the roof, an icicle cracked and plunged down into the snow, startling her. Claire listened to the slight crackling of the brush and noted the dull gray sky before slipping on her sunglasses.

In bright daylight, the snow could blind, but on a snowy day, she needed her sunglasses for another reason—that of protection, a silvery barrier between her and others. The earmuffs helped; they served to muffle sounds, tones that could be detected easily by her psychic antenna. She gripped the silver brooch in her pocket tightly, found the tip of the pin with her finger, and started to make her way through the three-foot snow to Neil Olafson. She would do this for Eunice, try to comfort him a little, then she would retreat to the safety of her home.

He didn't turn as she came near. He just stood looking at the front door as if he hoped it would open, and Eunice would be there.

"I'm sorry," Claire said, when she stood that careful, measured three feet away from him, a distance that helped to protect her from the energies of others. Though she'd seen Neil Olafson at a distance, he was much taller than she'd expected, and gauging by her own five-foot-nine height, he was at least six inches taller.

She couldn't see his face, or maybe she didn't want to see the grief hidden between the black knit cap and the high collar of his peacoat. Her sixth sense could grasp not only feelings and emotions, but an expression.

The snowflakes swirled between them, and she wondered if he'd heard her above the howling of the wind. He didn't move, his workman's boots braced apart in the snow. Then, suddenly, he turned to her, and the wind caught a strand of dark waving hair, taking it away from a harsh, weathered face.

Beyond her sunglasses, narrowed light eyes caught her, held her, reminding her of a wolf pinning his prey. At close range, but with snow falling steadily between them, that broad face, that blunt nose and strong jaw held the look of the Norse heritage Eunice had described. Light eyes flickered, and the set of his lips hardened, the lines deepening around it. As his gaze ripped down her, then back up to her face, she noted the snow clinging to his thick eyebrows and the dark stubble of his jaw.

The snowflakes seemed so fragile against his weathered skin.

One tumbled down to his lips and melted, unnoticed on the hard contours. Claire mourned the boyish grin she'd seen from her windows, a man teasing his elderly aunt and causing her to laugh. His breath stirred the snowflakes with steam, and his voice was deep and raw with anger, cutting through the wind. "So now you come out. Claire Brown, isn't that your name?"

When she nodded, he added roughly, "Took Eunice's death to bring you out, did it?"

He turned back to the front porch, as if waiting for that door to open. The bitterness in his tone stunned her. But then, grief sometimes brought anger, and Claire struggled to remain calm—she couldn't get upset, because too much emotion could take her to a place where the pain of others became her own.

"She loved you," Claire began, and fought to remain calm.

"You don't have to tell me that."

He was like that wolf, captured in the silver brooch she held, fierce and dangerous, but as a man, he was wounded and striking out at those who had come to help. Claire closed her eyes as she waded through the incredible sadness surrounding him. Eunice had said that he'd lost other dear ones, his parents, and his son had been taken, and now, divorced from his ex-wife, he was horribly alone. Then, anxious to do what would have pleased Eunice and to return to the safety of her home, Claire stepped into the grief they shared. "I'll miss her."

"I'll bet." His tone had changed to sarcasm, holding the anger and the frustration that couldn't be helped because Eunice wasn't coming back. A cord worked in his throat, tensed in his jaw. "You didn't even go to her funeral. I'd think a friend would do that, wouldn't you? There were few at her funeral, not a good show after all the charity work she'd done. You should have come, Claire Brown, if you were a friend, to see her off."

Eunice had described a playful boy inside the man, but he was gone, replaced by a man who had been through the worst of times. Claire could have eased him with just a touch—if she'd been skilled enough, but then, she preferred not to open herself to that sixth sense, keeping it outside her. Twice, she had been too open, too vulnerable and receptive, and twice, her senses had been triggered, sent to a higher plane, where she received every emotion and physical sensation near her. "I was there, but not to say good-bye. A part of her will always be with me."

"I didn't see you," he challenged.

"Later. I was there later, at her grave. We talked. I'll be going to see her again. I thought we'd have tea—in the springtime. I'll be digging in her lily of the valley bed, and planting a start near her grave, if that's okay."

"Her funeral was a damned pitiful thing. Not even my brother came," he said, his breath erupting into the eerie silence.

Her instincts told her to help him—as an empath, she could with a touch. But that would be leaving herself open to take his pain, to add it to her own. Instead, Claire stood that careful distance apart, the tip of the pin just at her fingertip, and waited for him to speak.

"I turned off the water and electricity when I came—before, just after she . . . died. She looked a lot like my mother. They were close as sisters could be, my mom and Aunt Eunice, always were," he stated suddenly, releasing a bit of his pain to the freezing wind. "I should get the snow off the roof, the weight could . . ."

If any one of her sisters had died . . . Claire's finger found the pin's sharp tip and pressed against it, a reminder to block his grief from her. "Yes. I was going to do that, but—"

He turned to her suddenly again, his breath shooting at her, those light eyes pinning her. "What's with you? You've lived here for five years, and we've never met. When I stayed with Eunice, I saw your lights on all night, but the house is closed and dark during the day."

"I work at night and I like—I need privacy."

"That's what my aunt said. She liked you. She said you make pretty purses. You gave her one. She liked it. It had irises, her favorites."

When Claire had spotted the purple irises in the silk fabric, she'd known immediately that it would make a perfect handbag for her neighbor. "It's too cold, and you've been standing here a long time. Maybe you'd better go in."

Neil turned back to the house, studying it, but he didn't move. "Yeah. Maybe."

Then, as if avoiding the moment of entering that tiny white house, he scanned the gray sky, the falling snow. "Why are you wearing sunglasses?"

For protection, a small barrier between us, because I could absorb your pain and I can't allow it to double with my own. . . . I could become too open. But instead of answering him, Claire said, "I'd better go. I just wanted you to know that I'm sorry. She was a good friend."

"Your only one, from what my aunt said. She said you were a loner. She came here because she was grieving for my uncle and needed some space to heal—she stayed. I guess you came here for a reason, too."

There was the opening for conversation, just that pause to give her the chance to talk. *He didn't want her to leave; he needed the presence of another person.*

Claire didn't answer. "It's good out here."

"Uh-huh. Good for kids to grow up here. I always thought—"

His lips clamped closed, as if sealing away the wish for his son, the baby who had been abducted and never returned. Claire understood only too well, the ache for her own baby growing within her. "I'd better go."

He shifted a little, and snow tumbled from his shoulder down his coat. "At the last, I wanted her to stay with me, close to medical help. But she wouldn't leave.

When she didn't answer my morning call, I knew something was wrong. I found her. Hell of a Christmas present. And you didn't come out." His words were like mallets, spaced and bitter.

That morning, when Eunice had failed to stand at her kitchen window and toast Claire with her morning teacup, she had known. . . .

"No. I knew when I saw you hurry into the house, and later when the ambulance arrived. But she knew her time was coming, and she wanted to pass in her own house, among her things. When she told me how she worried about you being alone after she passed, I knew her time was coming."

His, "Did you?" was too sharp.

"So did you," she said softly, pressing the brooch's pin a little harder, focusing on it, instead of the man. "You're angry now, aren't you? Angry because she left you. That's a normal reaction."

Neil sucked in air as if bracing himself to move on with life. "I'll be back in April. It will take me that long to close down my shop in Great Falls. I'll be setting up here."

"Living here?"

"Working here, too . . . building a workshop."

Claire stiffened and frowned. *Eunice had said something about her nephew making campers.* "A shop" would mean noise and people, and both would be an intrusion to the solitude she required to survive. "I hope you don't. Eunice loved the quiet here."

Neil turned to her again, that challenge in his voice. "I'll be sinking everything I have into new equipment and building a workshop here, so I'm not likely to change my mind. Are we going to have a problem over this? I inherited Eunice's place, and I can do what I want."

Claire's emotions simmered slightly, and she pushed her momentary anger down; Neil was hurting inside, bristling at the person closest to him. Claire refused to get caught up in his emotions, to let them enter her own. She focused on the wolf's-head brooch in her fist. "I hope you'll reconsider."

He peered at her. "You're not even going to ask what kind of business, are you?"

What exactly had Eunice said? That Neil made "cute little campers"? A shop would mean an invasion of noise and people . . . traffic passing her house. "Eunice said there are always a lot of people around you. There's no social life here to speak of, except maybe a cafe and a tavern in Red Dog—that's ten miles from here. You won't like it out here. It's very quiet and remote. I doubt your Great Falls friends would want to drive this far out to visit you."

"I like people. Don't you?" Neil asked suddenly.

Claire braced herself against that blast of simmering anger, but she recognized the source: In his grief, Neil wasn't likely to be reasonable, his anger flashing at her. "Mr. Olafson, I think we're both a little overwrought right now. So this probably isn't going to be the time to discuss your plans. I'd better go."

"You just do that. Is there anything I can do for you while I'm here? Clear your roof?" He scanned the amount of snow covering her roof. "Can I wrap any pipes for you?"

"I've winterized my home, Mr. Olafson. And I can clear my own roof." Claire instantly regretted the bite of her words; she pushed away the slight anger trying to snag her senses.

"Just asking, ma'am. I know Aunt Eunice cared for you, but I wasn't asking to adopt you," he said too softly, as he studied her. Snowflakes clung to those dark lashes, curiosity lurking in his light eyes.

"I should be going. Again, I'm sorry about Eunice." In a hurry to escape that penetrating stare, Claire forced herself to turn and work her way back through the snow to her front porch. She stamped her boots, then swept them to remove the snow before stepping inside her house. Inside, she bent to remove her boots, tore off her coat and sunglasses, and tossed them aside as she hurried toward her kitchen window.

She folded her arms and watched Neil move inside the house. Seconds later, lights appeared in the windows.

For five years, she'd enjoyed this quiet little valley, and now Eunice's nephew was set to "set up shop".

Claire struggled to calm herself; she lined up the reasons Neil would probably not make good on his plans to move—and work—next door to her. "He'll change his mind. Eunice said he likes a lot of people around him. He's just going through a grieving time now. He wants everything to remain the same, but it isn't. He'll realize that placing any kind of shop out here would mean a change of lifestyle. He'd have to—"

She watched Neil emerge from the back door and walk to the shed where Eunice had kept her tools. He'd made that same trip through the five years that Claire had lived next door, as he'd come to care for his aunt's home.

"He'll change his mind," Claire repeated as she watched Neil emerge with a ladder and carry it to the house as easily as if it were a small limb. He braced the ladder against the house and, carrying a broom, moved up to clear the roof of snow. Clumps of snow that could break the strongest roof began to fly into the cold, gray air.

Claire turned from the window and hurried into her workroom; she sat in her chair, her arms around herself as she rocked. Snug in her home and with minimal contact with others, she'd been safe here for five years after the trauma of losing her baby.

She'd found the perfect spot, a little house next to an elderly woman's. Claire had managed to support herself by creating designer handbags, to surround herself with beauty, the quiet connection with nature that soothed her sixth sense. In front of Claire's home was a small meadow where Native Americans had come to dig camas roots; in spring and summer she could watch the deer graze amid the layers of morning fog. Her herb garden was a joy to tend, and past her small backyard, box elder trees, serviceberry, and wild rosebushes provided a base for the pines and fir that had been planted by someone long ago.

The setting was perfect for her, an empath who needed quiet and nature to exist peacefully.

Even as a child, she hadn't wanted her inheritance, that sixth sense that set her and her sisters apart. As an intuitive, she could feel too much of what ran inside others, the darkness, the anger, the pain.

The trauma five years ago had opened her to those and other horrible emotions as the hospital's staff had cared for her. She'd been "opened," exposed to the gamut of raw human emotions; they'd come inside her like spears.

And that trauma had sent her psychic senses into high gear, a second time. Each time—as a ten-year-old and when she'd lost her baby—her perceptions grew more intense, making her even more sensitive than before.

Claire squeezed her lids closed, then rubbed her eyes, trying to clear away the memory of how Neil had looked—bitter, grieving, hard. And most of all, alone. Somehow, she'd caught his emotions, but then, anyone could see his expression, even in heavy snowfall.

He'd lost everyone dear to him, and from what Eunice had said, his brother was estranged. How horrible to lose a child, a baby as she had done, but never to have closure over a stolen child. . . . The ache would be endless and consuming.

From the harsh look of Neil, he'd gone through hell, searching for his son, and now he'd lost his aunt, a tie to his mother . . .

She reached to pour a calming cup of tea and the slight throb of her fingertip surprised her. Claire looked at the small prick where she had pressed against the brooch's pin. She brought her finger to her mouth, sucking it slightly. Then, as a comforting affirmation, she whispered, "He's just upset now and wanting to keep Eunice's warmth for a while. But he'll decide against moving his business here. A man like him is going to want people around him, neighbors, get-togethers, not miles from the nearest town."

Claire shook her head as terror skipped through her—she'd been so safe. Her intense need for quiet and solitude wasn't normal, but then, as a psychic, bred from generations of the same DNA, she wasn't normal at all.

Neil got into his pickup, started the motor to warm the cab, slid off his gloves, and sat staring at his aunt's house. The cold emptiness clawed at him. He should have insisted that she move in with him; he should have visited more often.

The defroster had begun to work on the windshield, and he could have driven away. Instead he sat, waiting for the warmth that came to his body but not to his heart. He automatically reached for the thermos and poured a steaming cup, cradling it in his hands. Perhaps he was only delaying leaving a home that had once been filled with life and was now cold, but he thought of Eunice's friend, the reclusive woman next door.

Between the hood of her coat, those large sunglasses, and her chin tucked into the raised collar of the bulky coat, Neil had seen little of her face. The steam of her breath and the snowflakes between them blurred her nose and the soft, full look of her lips. Her cheekbones were sharper, slanted a bit, indicating a lean body.

He swiped the passenger window and looked at Claire Brown's house, the shades on the windows closed as always. "So I've met you at last, Claire. I know what you came to do. It must not have been an easy thing to leave that house after five years and come over here and talk with me. Aunt Eunice would have liked that. But then, as her friend, I guess you knew her pretty well. I'm sorry I wasn't in the mood to be receptive to sympathy, but thank you."

Neil looked at his aunt's house, the empty rocking chair on the porch moving a bit in the wind. How many times had he come here, sometimes in snowfall as heavy as this? But now the windows remained dark, and his aunt wasn't standing in the doorway, welcoming him. "Good-bye for now, Aunt Eunice. I'll take good care of your house. My son would have liked it here. I always thought that someday—"

Someday, little Sammy would be eating your ginger-snap cookies and—

Neil started the windshield wipers and gripped the steering wheel, putting off the moment when he must leave. Then, bracing himself against the ache for his son, Neil put the pickup in reverse and backed out of the driveway.

As he passed Claire's house, he glanced at it and spoke to his aunt. "So she came to talk with you at your grave, huh? You would have liked that, a little private moment with a tea-buddy. That was nice, I give her that. She's an interesting woman, your neighbor, Aunt Eunice, what I could see of her between that coat and those sunglasses. She seemed to want to keep her distance, but then I guess I wasn't very pleasant. Like you said, losing her baby probably twisted something inside her, and sometimes it takes time to heal, if ever."

Neil doubted that he would ever heal. Death of an elderly woman was eventual and to be expected. The abduction of a child wasn't, and Neil would never stop looking for his son.

Two

_____

Four months later

"I COULD HAVE DEALT WITH HIS JUST MOVING INTO EUNICE'S house next door, but setting up an intrusive business, a noisy machine shop, is another issue," Claire murmured to the little pewter hummingbird attached to her kitchen window.

As she looked toward her new neighbor's place, Claire finished eating her apple. She shook her head as she walked to her workroom. "I've read about residential zoning and fights with businesses to keep neighborhoods quiet with less traffic, but I never thought that anyone would want to set up shop out here."

At seven o'clock in the morning, the sound of a chain saw ripped through Montana's rural countryside and into Claire's quiet home. Outside her workroom, the morning was gray and cold; a few snowflakes swirled around her window. A recent warm wind, a "chinook," had melted late April's layer of snow, leaving only pale patches amid the small valley's brown weeds.

Box elder trees and a big oak separated Claire's

home from the neighboring small white house, but the trees and the brush did not buffer the chain saw's annoying sound. Claire caught glimpses of a big man dressed in a black knit cap and a red jacket holding that chain saw. Puffs of blue smoke from the machine mixed with the light snow, and a tree crashed to the ground.

Neil Olafson had made good his plans to return.

"That man knows how to ruin quiet." Claire closed the window's heavy, light-blocking curtains and adjusted her headphones; she turned up the flowing sound of the ocean and let the rhythm settle gently into her body. After a typical all-night work session, crafting her designer bags, Claire was determined to ignore the chafing noise next door. She intended to calm herself and sleep, as usual, through the day.

She carefully placed plastic over the lady's handbag she was creating and smoothed it with her hand. An artist pleased with her work, Claire let the textures and colors flow peacefully through her. This design suited the name of "Date Night," with its black and red beads glittering beneath the plastic. A gold-and-black-braided silk shoulder strap would set it off, perfect for a woman's dressy evening wear.

With a sense of artistic accomplishment, Claire glanced at the unique bags lined up on her shelf, each covered in protective plastic. For her sister's shop, Claire had chosen her new "Claire's Bags" collection to be the A- and V-shaped bags, with a few of the small shoulder strap design. One of a kind and priced from hundreds to several thousand dollars, Claire's designs each had special names: "Orchid," a fragile watercolor-type silk, a very delicate wide bag; "Razmataz," a tapestry tote with bugle beads, beaded fringes, and a round black handle; "Bliss," feathery bag in pink; "Shy Me," a small perfect "hip" bag, done in a sturdy, subdued, quilted fabric and ribbons.

The chain saw's noise suddenly cut through the peace Claire had wrapped around her.

The handcrafted bags required Claire's absolute concentration—but that was difficult with her new next-door neighbor. Neil Olafson was set to ruin everything Claire loved—and needed to survive.

"Only a few more finishing touches, and you little piggies are going to market—if my new neighbor will stop causing such a ruckus. And backwoods Montana was so quiet, too—before he took over Eunice's place. Now it's nothing but trucks and noise and men yelling," Claire said as she straightened her work area and neatly placed the scissors and fabrics away.

Okay, so she was grumpy and out of sorts. In February, Neil Olafson had turned down her offer to buy Eunice's house, sent through a local real estate company. In March, he'd come to clear away the broken limbs around Eunice's home and work on the roof.

From her window, Claire had seen Neil haul a new metal ladder from his pickup and place it against Eunice's house. After a time inside, he appeared to climb that ladder and move easily over the pitched angles, a big man, wearing a workman's tool belt, comfortable in his strength and skill.

With legs braced near the brick chimney, and the old chimney pot tucked under his arm, he'd looked at Claire's house. Neil had grinned and waved for her to come over, but she'd closed the curtains firmly.

Now, her mind locked on that boyish grin—irritating the turmoil within her—Claire slid the drawer holding the beads back into its big wooden cabinet with a little more force than necessary. The cabinet, once used by a frontier druggist, shook slightly, the beads and buttons inside the individual drawers rattling. Hanging on one wall, the colorful feather boas fluttered as if disturbed.

But then, Claire was disturbed. Had she really expected her safe little nest to remain the same forever? Even when she understood that Eunice would pass someday, and a new owner would take her place?

In an attempt to focus on peace and harmony, Claire lifted the bags' protective plastic and picked up a quilted drawstring pouch. "Puff Mama" was perfect in a retro red swirling tapestry. She studied the bag critically; it was a good basic design—with a few changes here and there, fringes and buttons and handles, it would market well as a "Claire's Bags" trademark style.

She replaced the bag and studied "Matador Sling." Subtle stripes with an elegant beaded matador defined the A-shaped bag. His scarlet cape swirled and turned into a ribbon that circled the bag.

Claire frowned as her fingertip traced that scarlet ribbon; it seemed almost like a trail of blood—

She shook her head; the man and the noise and commotion next door were getting to her, and she wasn't letting that happen. Claire carefully replaced the protective plastic and yawned. She was ready for a little yoga to stretch her taut muscles, a little meditation, then bed and sleeping through the day.

She turned off her CD player and removed her headphones. The heavy curtains of her home blocked the sun's rays and unfortunately, also buffered the sound of the birds. Claire listened intently for those first calls, leaning into them—

The chain saw revved again, startling her.

She took a deep breath and replaced her earphones, turning up the volume on her CD player. She had tried to be reasonable; after all, Eunice had spoken well of her nephew. The CD's ocean sounds weren't calming Claire; she turned off the player and settled in to brood about the changes next door.

Behind Eunice's house, the new large cement pad and the skeletal framework defined a very large building.

Claire held on to the hope that maybe all the noise was just temporary, and once Olafson was finished and inside his shop, her part of Montana would be quiet again.

A heavy-duty truck ground to a stop at Eunice's, and the chain saw died.

Men were unloading and stacking more lumber. Someone had turned up their radio, and the beat of country music sailed through the tree-and-brush buffer between the houses to Claire. The beat was loud enough to make her window's tiny pewter hummingbird dance against the glass.

Claire removed the suction cup from the window and placed the handcrafted hummingbird to safety. She took a deep, steadying breath to breathe in the "good" and exhaled, trying to push out the "negative."

Then a man yelled loudly, "Hey, Fred. Put that over here."

Claire released her breath, and the feather boas fluttered briefly again. She smoothed them with her hand. The turmoil in Neil's backyard grated on Claire's nerves, but she tried to focus on one point: Peace might be restored once the building was finished.

Hopefully, the leaves on that big old oak and the brush would thicken quickly and offer a noise buffer. She wished more pines and spruce would shoot up overnight, and Eunice's nephew would go back to wherever he came from. Or just maybe Claire could swing enough money to make another buyout offer—

Right now, though, she had to calm down. She was

tired, and she was angry—not a good place for a psychic to be, even one who fought to keep it locked away.

In an attempt to calm her senses, Claire settled into her workroom again, letting the familiar environment enfold and comfort her. The old farmhouse with its hardwood floors suited her, a spacious bedroom converted into her workroom. The colors were muted by soft lighting, with high-intensity lights near her individual work areas. As with the rest of her home, heavy curtains and thick liners blocked out the sun's intrusion.

Her worktable, with its cutting mat and fabric guide, stood in the center of the large room. Her portable sewing machine and serger waited like old friends on her workbench, lining one wall. Folded fabrics—cottons, velvets, linens, silks, faux fur, leather, and suede—were neatly stacked on her shelves, and patterns of plastic canvas to be used as lining for her designer, one-of-a-kind bags, waited for her scissors and pins.

On one wall, several wooden drapery rods served as spools for rolls of fabric, and a variety of feather boas hung nearby.

They drifted a little as she passed, welcoming her like soft little arms reaching out to her. Her threads—metallic, polyester, rayon, embroidery—waited for her to choose them, almost like eager children, waiting to play.

Near her rack of threads, a tray of beads caught the dim light from the window, and, drawn to the glittering colors, Claire picked up a handful. Resting in the palm of her hand, the beads caught her, and she studied them, an idea for a new handbag brewing in her mind.

But the ruby beads trickled through her fingers back into the tray. Claire frowned slightly because the beads reminded her of drops of blood.

The tiny matador's scarlet ribbon had also reminded her of blood—

"It's because I'm uneasy. Noise and commotion upset me, that's all. The beads mean nothing. Unlike Mother or Leona, I don't have the ability to see into the future. . . ." Claire held very still, letting the quiet of her workroom circle her, protecting her from the noise next door.

As her mother had taught her, Claire stopped and slowly forced herself to focus inside.

The stillness inside her rippled, shifted, and adjusted uneasily.

Everything in her workroom was too quiet. The colors were soft, the windows draped against the bright morning Montana sunshine.

But the container of ruby beads gleamed bloodred.

They seemed dangerous, holding her.

Claire shook her head. The noise next door was upsetting her more than she realized, and that unwanted sixth sense was stirring ominously.

She drew aside the window's heavy drapery to watch the men start trimming away the branches from the fallen pine tree. The stark, leafless limbs of the other trees reached into the bright sky like open fingers, and the men moved beneath them, hauling limbs and brush into a center pile. They were clearly experienced with chain saws, moving deftly around the fallen tree.

With a whoop, Neil Olafson raised a hatchet and hurled it; after a series of revolutions it hit a tree and stuck deep into the trunk. There was that disturbing boyish grin again as Neil talked with his friends; she reluctantly admired the ease with which he seemed to move among them—an ease she had never had, could never have, she corrected. Claire supposed she could expect lumberjacks in rural Montana, men dressed in plaid flannel shirts, boots, and jeans—some with the Western hat, of course. The chain saws died, and Neil reached into a picnic cooler and tossed cans to the others.

"Show-off." Claire remembered Eunice's description of Neil: "Loves to tease and he always has a pack of friends around him. He helps them, and they help him, give-and-take." Neil probably needed those friends now, helping him build the shop. Momentarily, Claire envied him, the connection with others outside her family, the freedom not to limit friendships with others, not to weigh the danger of them to herself.

Suddenly, a woman came out of the house; she yawned and stretched and leaped from the porch into Neil's arms. With long, black hair and a shapely body in a tight sweater and tighter jeans, the woman latched her arms around him and kissed him.

He grinned and carried her to her small red pickup. He stood and talked with her for a minute, bent down to kiss her, then shut the door. When the pickup drove out of his driveway and past Claire's house, he turned to Claire and waved for her to come over. He'd done the same in the last four months, but she'd never responded.

Claire closed the curtain. "As if I would."

At least he hadn't pushed the point, hadn't called her, or come to her home. He'd respected her privacy that much, anyway.

Claire pushed down the annoyance building inside her; she well understood the dangers of becoming upset. When she became upset, Claire could be very vulnerable and open, where the feelings of other people moved into her, as if they were her own.

How often had her mother warned her after she'd been traumatized five years ago? *Concentrate, Claire.*

*Think, Claire. Stop and think, and focus . . . build a
mental wall around you. None of their emotions are
your own. In your mind, see that wall getting higher.
Find something, wear something, and center in on
it. . . . Keep the others outside you . . . outside
you. . . .*

Claire studied the Celtic-styled ring circling her finger. When she needed to interact with others, she sometimes focused on the ring, turning it slowly around her
finger. She'd intended to give it to her daughter, that
tiny part of her body, and bonded already at just four
months into Claire's pregnancy. After she'd been taken
to the hospital, she couldn't focus, and she should have
protected Aisling. . . . She should have had more control; she shouldn't have been so open.

*It was a time of her weakness. A time that had
shamed her—when she couldn't protect her unborn
baby from herself, and she'd lost control.*

She looked at Neil, standing amid a group of men.
*Had he lost control when his son was taken? Life with-
out closure could be horrible. . . .*

Men yelled and whooped next door, and the crash of
a falling tree cut into her terrifying memory.

Claire struggled back to the annoying present—it
was going to be another long, noisy, annoying, and
frustrating day.

And she wasn't feeling friendly toward the big,
brawny workman who was walking toward her home.

As Claire watched Neil Olafson stride toward her
home, the warm prickle at the back of her neck identified the caller. Holding the curtain aside, Claire traced
his path as she spoke to Tempest on the phone. "He's
coming over here right now. I suppose he saw me looking at him while he gave his girlfriend her morning
send-off."

"You did the right thing by going to him when he came back to Eunice's that day. I know it cost you. But I know you felt for him, too. You're like that, even without your psychic sense—you're kind and good, probably the best of us. . . . What's he look like up close in the daylight and without his winter coat and cap?"

Claire studied the length of Neil's stride, the way those large steel-toed work boots were eating up the distance to her front porch. "The same: big, rough, that broad kind of Scandinavian face, a lot of jaw. Midthirties, maybe. You know the outdoor kind—big shoulders, little brain. He needs a haircut. Looks like a lumberjack."

Tempest, a sculptor, was working at the verbal image. "How tall?"

"He'll fit under my front porch. Maybe about six-foot-four or so. I'm not going to answer the door, so we can keep on talking quietly."

When Neil came close to her front steps, Claire closed the curtain. "I'm okay, just frustrated by all the noise next door. He's building that shop, a big building. They have bonfires almost every night since he moved in last week, and this guy has a camper or two—funny-shaped little things—and a flatbed trailer. His pickup needs a muffler, and I don't think any of his friends know how to talk below a bellow."

"You're upset, and that's not good for you. I think you should move closer to one of us." Tempest spoke with the authority of a three-minute-older sister.

"You know how we upset each other. We need the distance to function normally, or as close as we can get to it. If we were close, we'd always be dealing with each other's emotions. You in New Mexico, Leona in Kentucky, and Mom on the Northwest coast is just close enough."

The loud rev of the chain saw ripped through the

morning. "Good God, what was that?" Tempest asked sharply.

"Chain saw at his place. . . . But he's on my front steps now. It's the first time he's come over here."

"You need your rest, Claire Bear. You know how dangerous it is for you to be tired . . . you're more susceptible then. You could go talk to him about keeping the noise down—or try to work out something with him. You managed before."

"I suppose it is unreasonable to expect the same quiet as when Eunice was alive. It's just that—"

"That you need to protect yourself, like I do with my gloves," Tempest stated grimly. "Mom protected us as best she could, but we always knew there would be a time when something could happen—like to you, something traumatic—that could throw our senses into high gear."

Claire thought of the hospital's staff, converging around her, the panic and terror enveloping her. Her intuitive senses had absorbed everything, too much, swallowing her, and in her terror and panic, she'd lost her daughter. *I'm so sorry I couldn't protect you, Aisling.*

"Neil seems to like people and from appearances over there, they like him. He couldn't be totally resistant to some kind of adult dialogue. I'm going to try anyway to make him see how much I would . . . appreciate his cooperation in keeping down the noise. I thought I would just put something in the mailbox in front of his house." Claire cradled the telephone between her shoulder and head, ignored the brisk rap of the door knocker, and tried to focus on "Date Night."

Just bits of tapestry and cords, a bit of bead, fringe, and fluff added, and they were perfect for Leona's vintage clothing store in Lexington. "It's been one week of nothing but noise and people. Eunice was so nice. I really liked her. But her nephew has had trucks hauling stuff back and forth . . . big, loud trucks. He bangs away over there all the time, and now there's a whole herd of men taking down that bush-and-tree barrier between our places."

"Men," Tempest stated flatly, in a dark tone that said her love life wasn't going well.

"Want to tell me about it, Tempest?"

"Oh, it's just— No, I don't. You've got enough problems with whatever is going on over there. Let me know if you need help with him."

Claire had a fleeting image of Leona, Tempest, and Greer set on rescuing her from the hospital nightmare. Once they saw her terrified and strapped to the bed, hellfire had begun. But before that—twenty-two years ago—Greer had arrived at the parapsychology clinic to rescue her triplets. The descendant of a Celtic seer and a Viking chieftain, and an incensed, protective mother, Greer had simply raised pure hell. "No, thanks. I can manage. I wouldn't want to go through you three getting worked up again."

Tempest chuckled softly. "You know us so well, baby."

After the call ended, Claire stood still for a moment, curiosity tugging at her as she heard movement on her front steps, the squeaking of a board protesting a heavy weight. While she didn't want to absorb the emotions of others, understanding Neil Olafson a little better might give her an advantage in reckoning with him.

Claire realized that as an empath, she was naturally curious. But, on the other hand, she wouldn't be fully open, and she could close herself later, protecting herself. It was only logical. Just a bit of harmless psychic fishing might help get what she wanted—peace and quiet. Maybe the noise was just temporary. Claire eased toward the front door and placed her back against it.

The board on the porch creaked again as Claire opened her senses to the man on the other side of the door.

She'd felt his impatience, his frustration when she didn't answer his knock. Fine, let him be frustrated; she was not obligated to answer the door, not for someone who was clearly set to call her out. An argument would only leave her vulnerable.

Still. To deal with Neil, she had needed to know more about him, and since he was within a few feet . . . Curious, Claire had moved closer, flattening her back and hands to the door. Instantly, a storm of fierce impatience hit her.

He'd noted and appreciated the big metal rottweilers that Tempest had created to guard the front porch. Neil considered the sharp fangs snarling at him and wondered why she'd chosen the guard dogs instead of the usual rooster-and-hen sets, or maybe some cute little cat statues?

Because her ability ran more to emotions and sensing, rather than specific word-thoughts, Claire had received a hot blast of impressions. Neil's had been rough, masculine, abrasive. *He didn't have time to deal with a silly woman, an annoyance. She'd either have to adjust to the noise and the traffic, or she'd have to move.*

Oh, she would, would she? Claire inhaled sharply and crossed her arms, her own anger rising.

He'd have to cut down that big oak tree, good for firewood when seasoned, maybe get some good lumber out of it—good for a camper. . . . Still, the woodsy look appealed to some buyers. . . . He needed a good woodworker under contract. . . . Profit. . . .

That big oak between their properties was gorgeous,

filled with acorns for the wildlife, fiery leaves in the fall—and he wanted to cut it?

Neil's emotions and intentions were blurred, but Claire had understood them: Annoyance returned and to Claire's sensitive psyche, it felt like sandpaper. He knew she was inside, and probably not as sweet as Eunice thought.

A gentle sweetness slid through to Claire, thoughts of a boy hugging a woman and loving her. Neil had loved his aunt deeply.

Then his thoughts swung back to Claire, the recluse, the pain in his butt. *Two old maids drinking tea together. . . . Or maybe some kookie drug addict, brewing the stuff. . . .* Impatience snagged at the air around Claire, Neil's emotions reaching her. *What the hell was taking her so long?*

He was chilled a little, his muscles ached, and inside him . . .

Inside him was a sweet ache, a long heartbreaking search. . . . His son would have liked Eunice's house. . . .

Claire remembered how Eunice had showed her the picture of a six-month-old baby, Neil's son, who had been abducted years ago. The loss, and the lack of closure, had torn Neil apart.

A wave of Neil's impatience came again, overriding the brief tender ache. Masculine, harsh, abrupt, his impatience riffled the quiet shadows of her home.

He needed sex.

Sex. His primitive need seemed to churn and simmer inside Claire. She tensed, bracing herself; she did not need to be inside a macho, peace-disturbing, caveman's elemental need. Or his medicinal need for sex.

His need for sex pounded at Claire. Because she had opened herself, she could feel sensations of the person closest to her, her own body reacted; it softened and moistened in response, a riveting, primitive hunger rising within her.

She hadn't prepared against the onslaught of that raw hunger, and it held her in its grip for a heartbeat.

Shaken, Claire quickly moved away from the door, just those few feet to close the elemental link, and waited until his heavy footsteps crossed her wooden porch and down the steps. She drew the curtain aside and watched Neil Olafson move toward Eunice's home.

Then he turned suddenly and stared back at her, as though he could see through the glass and the curtain and had found her.

She didn't like his wave, just that taunt to tell her that he knew she was inside and watching.

After settling her raised sensations—one of which was irritation—Claire remembered that horrible ache inside him. It had just been a skip in his emotions, not even a heartbeat, but Claire had caught his pain. A part of his heart was missing, waiting to be found. *His son.*

She placed her hand over her own aching heart, because she knew what it was to lose a part of oneself—she had lost her unborn daughter.

Claire had just reached the kitchen when that odd trickle ran up her neck. Claire reached for the wall telephone before it rang. "Hi, Leona. So Tempest called you and told you that Eunice's nephew was on his way over here."

"I'm surprised he's waited this long." A businesswoman who wanted none of her mother's powers, and yet the triplet most like Greer Aisling, Leona wasted no time. "No, she didn't call. I know you're about finished with this collection of bags for my shop. Tell me about them. I can't wait to see them in Timeless Vintage.

They'll look great, darling little things, mixed with dresses in my shop window."

Claire filled her teakettle and placed it on the stove as she carefully described her latest creations. She smiled as the tense ripples coming from Leona eased slightly. Set on profit in her vintage clothing store, Leona was excited about Claire's unique work and good sales. "I should have the bags ready for shipment soon. You'll have them for your summer displays. They'll go great with your vintage collections, lots of beads and tapestry, cute little spiraling handles, fringes. . . ."

"I'm getting all giddy, just picturing them. You're trying to distract me, and you knew just how to touch all the right buttons," Leona noted with affection. "You're so good for us all, baby, definitely more gentle and more feeling—the natural kind, I mean, apart from our blasted inheritance. I just worry that—"

"Worry about profit and markup. I'm going to charge plenty for these 'Claire's Bags' designs. One-of-a-kind cost plenty, no 'sister' discounts, so don't even try that with me," Claire teased. Then on a serious note, she added, "I'm fine. Really. I know my limits, and if I can't handle anything, I'll call in the cavalry."

The memory five years ago momentarily tangled between the sisters, then Leona asked softly, "Promise? I'll never forget you in that hospital. They were getting ready to ship you to the—"

"Funny farm?" Claire supplied, hoping that her tone was light, while horrible flashes leaped back at her. That nightmare had pushed her psychic sense to a higher, more vulnerable level where she was a human receptacle for every emotion of anyone close to her, devoured within a storm of emotions not her own. As a residual aftereffect, they had shimmered deep within her. It had taken painful weeks of determined focusing to exorcise emotions that were not her own.

Leona was instantly sensitive to the dark hole in Claire's life, when she'd been terrified and helpless, a time she couldn't erase. "I'm sorry. I shouldn't have said anything. I guess this is why we're better apart—too tuned to each other, lapping over on each other."

"We'll never be truly apart. That old DNA family tie, you know."

Leona's rich laughter curled over the lines. "Just that bit of unexpected spice when least expected. You always make me feel better. But then, you're probably just preparing me for a price hike."

"Now, would I do that? Leona, these bags might be a little late . . . maybe next month. The noise next door is really distracting—"

Leona was indignant. "Not for another month? But that's the end of May. I need them *now*. You mean, it's that loud that you can't work? Now *that* is serious. And I'm worried about you. You need your rest, Claire, and if you're not getting enough quiet, then—"

"You're getting really upset—"

"Yes, I am." Leona was a fighter, and she was getting angry. When she did, her dreams would start to stir, and that wouldn't be good. The visions of a clairvoyant weren't always pleasant.

"I can manage this," Claire stated firmly. "I'm just lacking a little sleep. But I'm fine. Really. I know that it won't be easy, and maybe my expectations for a little quiet are asking a little too much of an ordinary neighbor, but this one is building a commercial workshop. I just have to find a way to get Olafson to keep the noise down."

Leona stated that one visit from their mother should do it. "Mom would look right into his soul. She could tell him when he last had sex and when he polished his shoes. He'd be spooked and run with his tail between his legs."

Claire pictured Neil's face as he had walked toward her home. His expression had been distracted, but purposeful. He hadn't looked like a man who could be easily "spooked," and he had been thinking about sex.

She shivered slightly as she remembered absorbing that need and her response to it.

A chain saw sounded, men shouted, a heavy-duty delivery truck passed her house and Claire quickly ended the call with her sister. Leona, on the alert to protect her "baby" sister, could be deadly and upsetting. She needed to tend her business and Claire was determined not to involve her family.

When the call ended, Claire poured the hot water into her teapot. The steam rose, fragrant with alfalfa mint, and she let herself dream of what it would be like to be a normal woman—one who could move easily amid others, without protecting herself so fiercely, without their emotions consuming her.

She'd fought what she was and yet "It" remained. Claire could feel her senses stirring inside her; the gift from that ancient Celtic seer was always there—waiting—no matter how much she pushed "It" back. But the walls of reality were thin for psychics, and cocooned inside her safe home, away from crowds, Claire had managed—until lately.

While her sisters had touched base, one call was missing—their mother.

Anticipating her mother's call was distracting, because when Greer Aisling did not call, that meant she was working very hard, through a very big problem.

Beyond Greer Aisling's lawn, the Pacific Ocean waves crashed against the rocks, layered with gray stone, mica, and tiny red garnets. The ocean wind bowed the weaker trees, distorting the shape of the pines and the pool of water in her birdbath rippled ominously, the birds coming near, but never landing on the rim.

She inhaled sharply, bracing herself against the emotions rippling within her—anger, frustration, a mother defending her young.

Gifted were they? Or were the triplets really cursed with powers they did not want? At thirty-two, the triplets still fought their powers, trying to be normal. Normal? Her daughters shared Greer's psychic blood, each in a different way. Even as toddlers, their unique talents had emerged:

The first of the triplets, Leona, had been terrified of her insights into the future.

The next was Tempest, a too-curious rebel, passionate, even as a child. She had to wear gloves, for if she touched the wrong object with her naked hands, she would feel its past, the light and the darkness. Psychometry was not always a kind talent.

Then Claire, the intuitive, the empath, the most vulnerable.

"Be careful, Claire. I feel it stirring. I would stop it if I knew how. Protect yourself and stay away from large bodies of water. You're most vulnerable there."

They were in contact now, reassuring each other, the elder sisters checking on Claire, an empath and the most vulnerable.

In rural Montana, amid thousands of acres of dry wheatland, Claire should be safe, shouldn't she?

Greer's fingers tightened on her arms, digging through the caftan and into her flesh. Five years ago, those quick, bright flashes of nonreality had leaped at Greer as she stood in her kitchen: In her mind, she'd seen Claire pregnant and entering the bank, she'd seen the masked holdup men and the terrorized crowd, she'd seen her daughter's shock as she absorbed all the emotions battering her—then in one final, terrifying flash, Claire had collapsed, to awake terrified in the hospital—

But it had been too late to stop her daughter; Claire was already en route to the bank—her living nightmare was about to begin.

Greer ached to hear her daughter's voice, to know that she was safe. What kind of mother couldn't call her daughter to see if she was all right?

The answer came back in a blinding flash—a mother who feared that contact with her daughter now could harm her.

In his new home office and too restless to sleep, Neil Olafson ran his finger over the plans for the first camper-trailer to be built in his new workshop. Small, teardrop-shaped, weighing around six hundred pounds and easily pulled, the interior's design and the chuck-wagon-style outdoor kitchen could be easily customized.

A movement in the night caused him to ease aside the lacy curtain; a tall, slender woman walked toward the mailbox at his driveway.

"Three o'clock in the morning is an odd time for a delivery," Neil stated quietly to himself, but then his aunt Eunice had already told him that his neighbor avoided daylight and people.

Claire Brown seemed so solitary, so lonely, a slender woman pinned by the moonlight, her stride long and athletic. His instinct told him to go to her, and curiosity made him wonder what she looked like without her bulky coat and hood, what caused her to avoid the day, to hide behind her home's curtains.

But drained from the previous day and respecting his aunt's cautions about his neighbor's privacy, Neil waited until Claire had started to walk down the road, passing her home. Then he retrieved the note she had placed in his mailbox.

Inside, her handwriting was feminine, precise, the message was brief:

Dear Mr. Olafson,

Please stop making so much noise and leave the tree and brush barrier between our property. This has been a quiet area. Eunice would have liked the property to remain so in your care.

> *Thank you,*
> *Claire Brown*

"Sorry, no can do, Ms. Claire Brown. I've put everything I have into building that workshop and buying new equipment. I'll do what I can so far as the noise, but it isn't easy at this stage. I'm setting up a business, not just a home, so there is going to be noise and people. I can't just ask people—who have helped me get started—to be quiet after they've worked so hard all day."

In Red Dog, a small one-street town, southeast of Great Falls, word had gotten around that Neil had inherited Eunice's property and that he was setting up a camper business. Old friends and the curious were bound to turn up; in fact, for the sake of his business and word-of-mouth advertising, he welcomed the people coming now.

Neil yawned, thought about the layout of his shop, the cost of the metal roofing, then crumpled Claire's note and tossed it into the trash.

Behind her window and from what Neil had seen of her in the snowstorm, Claire Brown had a pale oval face wrapped in an easy-to-read, displeased expression— he'd invaded her turf, and she wasn't happy about it.

"Too bad, Ms. Brown. But I'll do what I can." He

stretched and rubbed his shoulder, punished by that showing-off hatchet throw yesterday morning. He noted the framed picture of his son and picked it up. The hollow ache within Neil swelled as he studied his six-month-old son, the photo taken just before he was abducted. Where was he now? Then—Was Sammy alive? Neil's hand trembled as he carefully replaced the picture. "I love you, son."

Neil placed Claire Brown's request at the bottom of his attend-to list and managed to get a few hours of sleep before six o'clock that morning. And then the day began all over again, filled with workmen and new friends coming to help.

Someone brought the makings for sandwiches at noon, Neil ordered several pizzas for the afternoon, then, after their day's work, more of his friends began to drop in. As usual after a hard day's work, the men and women settled down to the bonfire and grilling brauts in the backyard. Glenn Fitzpatrick took up his guitar and began to sing and play.

Neil was certain that Claire was watching, and not very happy; he thought about taking food over with an apology for the noise. But the next couple of hours were tied up with a wiring problem, then the crowd began to leave.

The next day, a couple of friends who already had his Model A Teardrop pulled in, with the offer to help. Neil helped settle the campers, and with the concrete slab ready, the men and women worked on the building's framework, their children playing away from the construction.

With unseasonably warm weather, and in the tradition of campers, they sat around the bonfire that night. Early the next morning, they started the shop's siding.

After their day's work, another pickup of men came to help, and Neil set up overhead lights to work a few hours before calling it a day. By ten-thirty, the campers had settled into relaxing around the bonfire, and Neil walked over to Claire's house and knocked on the door.

No one answered, and Neil used the odd door knocker again, louder this time. He noted the wolf's head set into a woven Celtic design as he said, "I know you're in there, Brown. Come out, come out, wherever you are. Look, I'm sorry about the noise and commotion now, but there's really no way to avoid it. It's your call on how you want to handle this neighbor business. You're invited on over to my house. We've got enough food over there for an army. You don't need to bring anything."

He glanced at the life-size, snarling, poised metal rottweilers; from a distance, they had looked real. While some people placed Chinese Foo dog statues at their doorways for protection, apparently Ms. Brown had a taste for the more menacing. "Hey, nice sculpture work."

The curtain at the window moved just that bit, indicating that she was definitely in the house; the lady was obstinate. "Okay, have it your way. I don't have time for this. I just wanted to let you know that after we get done with the building, the noise and the traffic will settle down. I think we can work out some kind of co-existence. I'm open for suggestions, but right now, there's not much I can do about it. Some of these people have given up working on their own places to help me set up. I can't just run them off because you're sensitive to noise."

He waited, but Claire Brown did not respond—or open her door. Neil's impatience rose as he glanced at that door knocker and at the rottweilers. "Okay." He sighed, before walking back to his friends. "Like I said, have it your way. You don't want to be friendly—fine. I'm not pushing you."

From now on, Neil promised himself, he'd leave her alone. A mutual truce—or standoff, whatever Claire wanted was fine with him.

Three

THE ELECTRODES REACHED OUT TO HER, WANTING TO ATTACH.
Machines with gauges stared at her, waiting for the response of her body to stimuli. Hands in rubber gloves probed her body. A needle plunged at her. . . . Her sisters were somewhere else. Were they being tied down and hurt, too?

Where was her mother? Why were the strange people doing this? Why had they taken her from her home?

"They" were curious and wanting to see inside her mind, see what made her different. They terrified her, and she was only a ten-year-old girl. . . .

"They" wore white clothes, but she was a woman now, and their anger, lust, greed, and hatred burned her in fiery jabs, the belts wrapped tightly around her wrists and ankles, and there were bars on her bed.

She fought the bonds, screaming in terror as the people dressed in white circled her, their emotions invading her mind, the bright lights overhead blinding her. . . .

Claire sat up in bed and closed her eyes to the bright strip of May sunlight that had slid though the joining of her bedroom curtains.

She gasped for breath, felt the sweat cooling her body, the nightmare's terror still wrapped around her. Would it ever go away?

She carefully pasted herself back together, a piece at a time, just as she had done so many times in the five years since her last trauma. She rubbed the almost-invisible scars on her wrists, a constant reminder of her time in the hospital. But there had been another time—

"The Blair Institute for Parapsychology," Claire whispered darkly, the name imprinted on her forever. Under false pretenses, the ten-year-old triplets had been taken from their home while their mother was away, to be examined by doctors. It was then that Claire really understood and feared what she was—an empath, a human antenna tuned to receive the sensations and emotions of others. Only now, after her second experience with terror, her empathic sensitivity had grown, and waited to consume her, to toss her into a maelstrom of others' emotions—if she let it.

Claire rose suddenly and jerked the heavy curtains of her bedroom closed, as if she could seal away that horrible memory; she sat on the edge of her bed, forcing the last of the nightmare away.

A glance at her bedside clock told her it was noon, a time when she usually slept peacefully after a night's work.

Her sanctuary had been disturbed, and she was definitely stressed. As a result, "It" was awakening inside her, that empathic inheritance from an ancient Celtic seer; "It" had grown stronger with each shocking and disturbing episode in her lifetime. . . .

Claire could deny it, block it, and yet it came back.

The loud, steady bang sounded over the hiss of Neil's welding torch.

He turned away from building the metal base of the camper and glanced through his helmet's visor to the woman standing in the shop's open double doorway. She tossed the rubber mallet she'd been using on top of the barrel, and Neil knew that the event he had been anticipating, actually to see Claire Brown's face clearly and hear her voice without the wind howling, had come.

On the first day of May, the bright afternoon sunlight outlined Claire's body as she stood in there. Without the camouflage of the snowstorm when they had first actually met, and his unsettled emotions after his aunt's death, Neil settled in to study Claire Brown. The bulky garment draped around her shoulders ended at just past her hips; the rest of her was all leggy jeans. A triangle of sunshine spread through those long legs that ended in high motorcycle boots.

From the shadows of the cape's hood, those large silvery sunglasses stared at him. Neil turned off the gas to his welding machine, lifted his helmet away, and momentarily relished the moment. From her hands on her hips, that rigid set of her shoulders, Neil instantly knew that his neighbor had come to make her point about noisy businesses in previously quiet neighborhoods.

Those long, slender, pale fingers dug into the soft drape of the cloth, and Neil realized that she was probably nervous, too.

"Oh, hello, Claire," Neil said more smoothly than he felt. He hadn't seen her fully since that day in the blizzard, when he'd seemed so alone—then Claire had appeared, her voice soft and concerned in the cold, howling wind. He had to see her up close, this woman who hid by day and walked by night, and Neil walked closer.

When she suddenly turned aside, looking around the

shop, Neil noted the temper framing her tightly compressed lips. In an impatient movement, she swept back the hood. She was wearing red target-practice earmuffs, and the fiery tendrils around her pale face caught the sunlight, the big sunglasses shadowing most of her pale face. Her cheekbones were as sharp and slanted as he remembered, her lips as full and feminine; her chin had that edgy, clean-cut look that went with her oval face. "You've been here eleven days. I thought the noise and crowd would settle down. It hasn't."

Mirrored sunglasses flashed at Neil as he walked to the picnic cooler and took a can of soda from its ice. Closer now, he was surprised by the long, thick, dark red braid crossing her shoulder and flowing down the cape.

At her shoulder, a silver brooch gleamed as she moved. Neil popped the can's tab. If she'd have a soda, he could get closer to her. "It has. Drink, neighbor?"

Her "No, thank you" didn't sound exactly friendly, but then she hadn't made any neighborly effort either.

"I can see you peeking around those curtains, you know." He wondered about her eyes and why she only walked at night—did she have some sort of sun disease? Those big, mirrored sunglasses picked up his reflection and followed his movements. He rubbed the ache in his back and settled into a lawn chair, propping his boots up on a box. Then he spoke loudly, "Can you hear me with those things on?"

"You're curious about me." She moved impatiently into the shadows, away from the double doorway, as if the sunlight disturbed her. "You're not taking me seriously, are you? You're seeing me as a curiosity, are you, Mr. Olafson?"

"Call me Neil. And I already knew you were— interesting—from my aunt's description." He raised his drink in a toast and turned the ball cap he'd reversed for the helmet around to the front. If she shielded her eyes, so would he. He wanted to see just what had eluded him. The slant of her cheekbones caught the dim light, and from what Neil could see of her face between those big sunglasses and that cape, her lips—

The shape of her lips interested him—not a soft full shape, but rather wide and firm, like a woman who knew what she wanted and how to take it; he wondered briefly what they would taste like, how they would move beneath his own. His curiosity was fleeting, because Ms. Brown was definitely not the friendly, cuddly type. She ran more to the hard-case-hermit blend, and Neil preferred easy friendships.

On the other hand, Claire Brown—his only neighbor—could annoy him by just not answering her door for a neighborly invitation.

When her lips tightened, Neil shrugged. "I was hoping you'd come over and we could talk. I thought you might like my aunt's china tea set . . . she liked having tea with you. And I think she would have appreciated you coming for a private chat at her grave, too."

He was still surprised, and grateful for the small tribute Claire had paid at Christmastime when others couldn't be bothered to attend Eunice's funeral. For all his aunt's donations to charities, the times she had helped her church, few had attended the ceremony, and that nettled Neil. But then, his own brother hadn't attended either.

"I'd love to have your aunt's tea set, something to remember her by. Thank you. But for now, I really think it should remain in the house she loved so much." Claire seemed to be considering the camper-trailer he was building. "This is a camper? It's small."

Neil glanced at the skeletal framework of the camper,

no more than a metal base and one axle upon which he'd build his first camper in this shop. A sense of pride ran through him; he'd worked hard to get a good name in the business, the word-of-mouth kind that didn't take expensive advertising dollars. "My base model and best seller, a sweet little model. This model sleeps two people comfortably. It's light enough to pull easily, around six hundred or so pounds when finished. Custom work in the chuck-wagon kitchen could add a few pounds, then if the customer wants, I can add frames for privacy and canvas awnings for shade, but they would add more weight—depends on the customer's needs."

Claire's sunglasses flashed in the shadows and pinned him. Her next words weren't a question, but an accusation. "It would be different if you were just moving into her home, but do you really think that Eunice would want some factory set up here?"

"She would have recognized the necessity, I think, of living close to my business. She came here to grieve for her husband, my uncle, who died years ago. Aunt Eunice never got over his death. Then my parents—her only sister and husband—were killed in an accident. She wanted her property to go to me, and it's handcrafting, not a factory line."

Claire walked toward the camper base, studying the shape as she circled it. That thick, dark red braid ended in the middle of her back and gleamed as if alive. Claire's feline movements caused it to sway slightly, the tip curling and reminding Neil of how a cat twitched its tail when studying its prey. Tiny fiery tendrils caught the dim light, and, fascinated, Neil wondered what her hair would look like loose and around that pale face, softening those edgy cheekbones. He wondered what her hair would feel like in his hand—warm, rich, silky?

On the other end of the shop, yards away from him, her mirrored sunglasses suddenly turned and flashed at him. "I do not like to be dissected, Mr. Olafson. How long does it take to build one of these things? Will it be quiet after this one is finished?"

Neil took a long drink of the soda. "Depends on the custom job. I build them myself, one at a time. It's a little noisier than building a purse."

"One-of-a-kind designer handbags, Mr. Olafson," she corrected tightly. "They pay well, and crafting them is my only income. Since I can't work with all this noise over here, you are endangering my income, and I was here first. You've become a real problem for me. In the five years I've lived here, and you came to visit Eunice, I didn't mind you slamming your pickup doors or calling out to Eunice, or periodically helping her repair her home. I expected all that, and I was prepared for the same from anyone who took her place. But setting up a business here, a noisy one, is something else. So . . . you intend to continue hammering, sawing, that sort of thing?"

Neil took his time; he lifted the can and downed the last of the root beer; he crushed the can in his fist before tossing it into the recycling bin. He was enjoying this skirmish too much to be annoyed. If Claire had come out to play, he was more than ready. "Sometimes."

That heavy cape did not hide the sudden lift and fall of her breasts, the gleam of that big silver pin on her shoulder, as if she were angry.

"I'm not angry," Claire stated suddenly. "It doesn't pay to be angry. And I do not want that big oak tree cut down. Some of the animals around here depend on it. It's bad enough that you're cutting down *my* privacy and noise buffer and the berry bushes that feed the deer and birds, but now you want to cut down that beautiful tree."

Neil frowned; he hadn't told anyone that he planned to cut the tree, to harvest the wood and clear more space for a display room and office next to his shop. He stood, picked up his inventory clipboard, and pretended to skim it, as he asked casually, "What makes you think that I would cut it down?"

The shadows around Claire seemed to still. "Anyone can see that big old oak provides habitat and shade and—"

Neil tossed the clipboard aside; despite his intention to keep their discussion friendly, his own irritation was developing fast. "I didn't ask for a lecture. I just wanted to know why you would think I might cut it down?"

Claire held her breath; suddenly aware that because she was upset, nervous about talking with him, she'd left herself open to his feelings— He was grieving for a lost child, a son who would love to swing from that big oak tree. Every time he looked at the tree, it reminded him that he'd lost his son. . . . She could feel the slight waves of his pain stirring within her, and she had to get away.

Neil needed closure more than he needed anything else, his ache for his kidnapped baby reaching out to her.

He was a "family man" according to Eunice, and now his arms and his heart were empty.

How awful if her mother were to lose her children— how awful for any parent.

Claire's impulses told her to place her hand over his heart, to ease him as an empath could do, but caution told her that he wouldn't understand—a woman, touching a man, looking into his eyes and absorbing his pain.

"I'd better go," she stated as she started to move by him.

Neil's hand on her arm stopped her, not hurting in its grip but firm enough to hold her still. Through the heavy woolen cape, his big tanned hand was an intrusion, his thoughts and feelings too near her. "No, my eyes are not injured," she stated.

He was taller by several inches and big enough to block out the rest of the spacious shop. He seemed to be blocking out *everything*, moving into her senses. She *knew* he was taking in the green weave of her cape, the handcrafted style of the silver brooch at her shoulder, comparing it to the Celtic design of her door knocker, and wondering if the dark woodland green matched her eyes. She *understood* that more than anything, Neil wanted to see her eyes.

Claire held her breath as a swallow dove from the sunlight into the shop's shadows, then out again as Neil stood closer and studied her face. He was amused, the lines fanning out from his eyes, deepening. At close range, his hair was crisp and in dark waves, shot with lighter streaks that marked a man who enjoyed the outdoors. A deep, half-moon-shaped scar marked his cheekbone, and he bore his Nordic heritage, broad cheekbones, a blunt nose, and a mouth that liked a smile, like the one tugging at it now. He'd been a taunting, playful boy, and that boy still lingered in the man, despite the tragedies that had touched his life.

They stood on some kind of isolated plane where she could feel—sense—his heartbeat, almost in sync with hers. . . . She should leave, she should protect herself, but something inside him, something hidden snagged an edge of her senses, holding her still.

Claire closed her eyes as she waded through that incredible sadness—he'd lost other dear ones and struggled with guilt. *What guilt? Why should he feel guilty?*

Neil's deep voice interrupted Claire's brief journey through his grief. Surprised, she tensed and shook her head, clearing it. "I'm sorry, what were you saying?"

"My aunt said you were like that, sometimes jumping into a question before it was asked. She said you were a very feeling person, that you could sense a person's mood and give them comfort. You did that for me the day I came here—when it was snowing so hard. You came out to tell me you were sorry about Eunice. I'm sorry I snapped at you. I—was feeling a little raw just then. . . . Maybe feeling sorry for myself, and that's not something I like to do."

Neil had loved his aunt, and the sweet memory clung in the air around him, scented of Eunice's gingerbread.

This close, the spicy scent of his aftershave mixed with that of a workingman, of gas and oil, the sunlight trapped on his flannel shirt and jeans. Claire's sixth sense picked up that Neil was waiting for her do something, anticipating— And he was enjoying the feel of her as a man enjoyed touching a woman!

But then, what could she expect from a man who thought about sex so strongly it could leap into her and become her own desire. He would be hitting on anything nearby. Unfortunately, now, that was her.

And she was responding sexually, the damnation of an empath opening herself up to explore this man, to seek an advantage she could use to dislodge him. She'd gotten too close, too much inside him. Rather, his energies had come inside her, and suddenly she was reacting. . . .

Claire shivered and pulled herself away from the sensual heat curling around her, through her.

Neil's head had tilted, and his curiosity flicked briefly within her. "You just flushed. Are you feeling okay?"

She felt all wound up and soft, as if she could leap upon and devastate the first man she came upon—unfortunately, that would be her irritating neighbor.

Dealing with her untrained curse, trying to use it before she had full control, had just backfired.

Immediate sensual hunger wasn't like Claire at all; she forced herself back to focus on her own emotions, which was a mistake. She was feeling very feminine and desirable and—

She'd been unsuccessful in blocking his energies, and they were definitely sensual. His energy was so strong that it was messing up her internal "reads," emotionally and physically, heightening them, sending them off-kilter!

"If you leave the tree," Claire ventured cautiously, as she focused back on preserving the tree, "your customers' children might like to swing from it. That would keep them busy, wouldn't it? Some of the limbs are quite low. They might even like to climb—"

Neil's dark memory slashed into her, a boy pushed by another, falling through air and landing in pain, that half-moon scar an open wound—

"Let me go, Neil," she said quietly, using his first name and a haughty tone intended to remind him of Eunice's proper schoolteacher reprimand.

The ache for his child palpitated around Claire; Neil had searched for his son for so long, so many disappointments. And he was reminded of his son by every little boy he saw.

She felt flames and his terror; Claire felt the grief of Neil-the-teenager for his parents. . . .

A heavy darkness enfolded her, weighing her down, and she knew it was guilt. . . .

Why did he feel guilty about those deaths and the abduction of his son? Claire must have been quiet too long, because Neil's fingers slowly opened and released her; he crossed his arms as he stood looking down at her, his head tilted to one side as he studied her.

"What's with the sunglasses? You said your eyes are fine."

Still tangled in the sensations coming from Neil, aware that her absorption of his energies had become tangled with her own internal sexuality, Claire answered with a breathless statement: "I like my privacy."

"You have your reasons. I'm sorry I asked."

Claire closed her eyes, grateful for the safety he had just offered her. "I—I wanted to tell you that I appreciated your consideration . . . not forcing the issue of meeting me, in those five years since I've lived here."

His eyebrow lifted. "And? That's not going to change. I understand you want your privacy—I respect that."

A muscle moved in his jaw where the skin was rough and scented of shaving lotion, where the tiny scars of shaving nicks remained. "I think we can work things out, Claire. I know you have a problem with noise and disturbance . . . maybe I could install some sound-proofing here, or at your place. That's one alternative. There are probably other options from residences that disagreed with businesses in their neighborhood. For what it's worth, I have displays in other places, so only a small percent of customers will be coming here. Like I said, I'm open for suggestions."

"Thank you. I'll . . . consider that, but I can't think of any right now. I need to go." Shaken by the kindness wrapping around her, by Neil's obvious consideration, Claire turned and was only a stride away from him when the sensuality coming from Neil wrapped around her, almost like seeking hands; she felt them stroke her hair. Then his curiosity, laced with strong, dark masculine opinion, slid into her: *Classy, sweet, terrified of men. . . . What had happened to her? Why was she holed up out here in the middle of nothing? He mourned*

*the life she could have, an attractive woman like that—
what a waste. . . . He wondered what she looked like
when she smiled . . . she should learn to play and not
take life so seriously. . . .*

Claire turned to stare at Neil, but couldn't state
aloud the curiosity she had detected from him. She'd
been able to pick up sensations, energies, feelings up
to this point, but what she'd caught from Neil now
seemed more telepathic— *She was picking up his actual words, just as she had that day when she'd pressed
against her door, fishing for an angle to use in dealing
with him.*

*She'd thought those were emotions, energies, needs
coming from him, but they were partial thoughts!*

Neil's arms were still crossed, his ball cap shadowing
his eyes, and his grin softened his face. "I'm picking up
pizza tonight. Come over, if you want. I'll save a slice
for you. There won't be a crowd here. You'll be safe
with me."

Safe? When her body was reacting sensually to his?
Claire backed away a few feet, just enough to get out of
empathic range. "No, thank you. I've had to change my
working schedule already to accommodate yours, when
it's finally quiet over here."

Neil's grin widened, those lines deepening around his
face just as she'd seen when he'd teased his aunt. He
enjoyed watching her back up and away from him and
moved closer, his hands hooked into his back pockets.
"Life's a bitch, isn't it?"

The grin eased as she backed farther away, and he
added softly, "I don't know about cutting down that
tree yet, so we'll see how it goes. I think we can get
along. Let me know if you have any ideas about how we
can help each other out. Meanwhile, you're welcome to
visit anytime."

Neil stood, hip shot, considering her, that broad face shadowed. "On second thought, I'm driving into town and meeting some friends at the cafe. How about it? Want to go along? Run some errands . . . pick up some groceries? If you don't like a lot of people around, I could manage a quiet dinner."

"I'd rather not. But thank you," she stated firmly. She was too sensitive now, tuned to Neil, and somehow she wasn't able to block him entirely. She'd have to work on that.

His grin was back. "Just thought I'd ask. It's the neighborly thing to do."

Claire turned and walked toward her house, but she sensed him watching her.

At three o'clock in the afternoon, the day was already dimming, the stark trees spearing up into the over-cast sky. In the small meadow, mule deer—Montana's "mulies"—were grazing, blending in with the shades of brown native grasses. Still simmering from her encounter with her neighbor and unable to sleep, Claire watched Neil's heavy-duty pickup truck drive past her house toward Red Dog.

He waved, and his grin flashed behind the window; it said Neil knew she was watching him from behind her curtain.

"Irritating jerk."

Who was she irritated at? Neil or herself? Whatever psychic energies had sparked when near him, Claire didn't want them. He had upset her, and she was off-balance and must have seemed to be even more odd than she already was.

By habit, when trying to settle herself into working, Claire brewed a pot of tea and placed a relaxing CD into her sound system. She tried to push away the nagging thought that just being near Neil could send her senses scrambling.

She sat at her worktable, turned on her lamp, and removed the plastic covering from "Date Night." Locked in turmoil, she hadn't been able to complete it. She lifted the evening bag and shook it gently; the beaded fringe was just heavy enough not to tangle badly. Claire considered the gold cordings braided with black for the shoulder strap. "You're going to love this one, Leona."

Claire began working, hand stitching around the bag. Absorbed in the fine work, she lost all sense of time, then, taking a breath to flex her fingers and to stretch, settled back in her chair.

In the shadows of her workroom, the high-intensity lamp caught the divided tray of buttons and beads on her counter. Claire hadn't replaced the tray, and, in a tiny compartment, the red beads caught the light and sparkled like fresh drops of blood.

Uneasy with that thought for the second time, Claire frowned as she heard a truck pull into her driveway and pulled aside the heavy curtain to see a delivery van parked in front of her house. She recognized the van that usually brought her supplies, leaving them on her porch. At seven o'clock in the evening, he was running later than usual. The uniformed driver reached behind his seat, grabbed a package, and checked the address.

"Ah, my new handles. Black and natural bamboo, here I come—" As usual, she waited until the driver was walking back toward the van before she opened the door, taking the package inside.

Excited about the handles, Claire set the package on her table and frowned. The package was too light and her supplier's return address wasn't noted, nor hers. She began to open it carefully . . .

A rush of hatred and pain hit her like a physical blow, taking away her breath. And yet, no one else was in the room. When she turned to her front door, the man was already inside; she hadn't taken time to lock the door. . . .

His fist stunned her momentarily, then he was hurting her, and she was fighting for her life, his hands clamped around her throat—

Her knee shot into his crotch, her hands clawing at his face. In pain, he yelled furiously and momentarily released her. She tried to run to the kitchen and out the back door, but he grabbed her blouse, tearing it—

She managed to get to her workroom; she reached for her scissors, but still fighting the man, she accidentally caught a tray of pearls and the one of red beads. They spilled around her like red, glittering raindrops as she went down on the floor, the man stronger and filled with hatred— His energy tightened around her, pulsed like a wave of fire through her. Obsessed by Claire, he had to hurt her before she died. She needed to know pain. His eyes glowed with it. *He wanted to rape and kill her.*

Then a length of beautiful gold cording wrapped around her throat, tightening.

Such rage, focused entirely upon hurting her, on making her pay—for what?

"You tramp. You've slept with other women's husbands. You don't deserve to live!"

Choked and unable to speak, Claire's hands hit at him, and the struggle toppled a heavy pottery lamp, hitting him hard. He abruptly released the cord around her throat. He seemed stunned, staring blankly down at her. He shook his head as if trying to clear it, his hands pressed to his head as if trying to squeeze the pain out of it. He seemed confused, standing and shaking his head as he looked down at her struggling for breath. "I—lady, I don't know what—"

He looked at his hands as if they didn't belong to him. Then the man ran from her workroom, his footsteps taking him out the front door and down the porch; the van's motor revved and tires spun . . .

Claire turned her head slightly, saw the ruby beads resembling drops of blood, another and another tumbling from her workbench, hitting the others and rolling aside.

Then she slowly gave in to the safety of the darkness falling upon her. . . .

After dinner at Red Dog's Lincoln Cafe, a few drinks at the Watering Hole Tavern, and a discussion of last summer's fires, Neil picked up pizza. Life alone had taught him to pick up food for the next day's convenient reheating and with the pepperoni pizza scenting the pickup and country music on the radio, he considered it a good, productive day. Life was generally okay, purring along with hard work; and then he'd had that sweet little interview with the interesting, unsociable Claire.

Neil admitted that she had a point: Residential homeowners had a right to expect some kind of quiet; a workshop and customers were logically not a welcome addition to a neighborhood. Whole territorial wars had been fought on the issue. In her place, Neil would have a problem with a shop next door, too. Still. Finances and necessity worked toward the establishment of business and home at his aunt's, and he'd had little choice—plus he wanted to live in her house, to keep close the remnants of his loving aunt.

Claire had mentioned preserving that big tree, wanting to protect it, and he hadn't said anything about cutting it down. How had she snagged that idea even though he'd never voiced the thought?

She'd come out for the first time during the blizzard, when he needed someone. She'd come over today, and they'd had their first actual dialogue; maybe that was a start for working together on their problem. Then, if he were truthful, Claire Brown interested him. *She'd known the instant his curiosity rose, and she'd moved away from him, the color in her cheeks rising, almost as if there was something happening between them.*

Neil shook his head; his instincts had told him that there was a certain softening of her stance, a certain sensual awareness of him. That contradicted her need for privacy, and Eunice had said that in those five years, Claire Brown had not had male visitors.

It was around nine o'clock. Montana's big moon hovered over the sprawling wheatfields, and a coyote crossed in front of his truck. The rural sights were familiar and comforting. He'd lived with Eunice for a couple of years after his parents' deaths, and Neil had driven the distance from town to her house many times. He'd seen the same lights in the night, picked choke-cherries for his aunt's jams in that thicket many times. He'd crossed lifetimes since his parents' house had burned, and his life always seemed to circle back to this place.

Neil reached for the letter on the seat beside him and tucked it into his shirt pocket. His ex-wife wrote often; Jan still hoped that somehow, after eight years, their son would be found. . . .

Neil watched the great horned owl spread his wings across the moon, lifting into the starry night. His son should be with him, looking at the same magnificent creature. Every minute of his life, he would ache for Sammy, his baby abducted eight years ago; he'd never stop hunting for word of Sammy. . . . "Sammy, where are you?"

Near Claire's home, Neil glanced at the take-out

carton beside him and decided that since he was a "good guy," he'd drop tomorrow's lunch off for his neighbor—just to see if she'd open that door. Apparently a night person, Claire would be awake at nine o'clock and probably working on her purses.

"Handbags," he corrected, using her term. Neil smiled at the memory and noted the deer at the side of the dirt road. Startled by his pickup, they leaped into the brush and the lifted, pale flick of their tails labeled them as white tail deer.

His mind swung back to his irritated neighbor. Claire Brown's first move was pretty memorable, that big green cape had emphasized her pale skin, that edgy feminine jaw. The long red braid was a surprise, the way it moved sensuously around her body. Neil wondered what her hair would look like, free and bright in full sunlight, if the reddish tendrils and dark red braid matched blue eyes or gray or green.

If he delivered the pizza, just maybe she'd come to the door. Just maybe he'd see the color of her eyes or her hair loose, although that braid was pretty sexy, sliding around her body.

In short, Neil wasn't ready to call it a day without another exchange with the somewhat crusty Ms. Brown.

Neil didn't notice that the door was partially open until he was standing in front of it. He glanced at the ferocious metal rottweillers, poised as if to strike, then at the unique brass knob. Handcrafted within a swirling Celtic design, the doorknob was a little heavier than usual, and the brooch she'd worn earlier held that same arty look. But then the lady wasn't an everyday variety, was she?

He glanced around the quiet yard; he hadn't passed her on the road, but she could have walked somewhere else, and the door hadn't latched properly. He could leave the pizza just inside the door, but then he'd miss seeing her again, wouldn't he? "Claire?"

Silence answered, and Neil called again, before pushing the door wider. He could hear her furnace running, yet the house seemed cold—but then it would be, right? At the first night of May, with a door open on a chilly night, the wind picking up and rattling the dry leaves, something was definitely wrong. "Claire! Answer me, or I'm coming in."

The moan was soft and chilling, floating out to him. Neil switched on the living-room light, noted crumpled package wrapping paper, the empty box lying on the floor. A small table lay turned on its side, magazines scattered around it—"*Claire!*"

Neil righted the table, placed the pizza box on it, and moved cautiously into the next room. Apparently it was her workroom, spools of decorative cording lined the bench, a digital camera, a computer setup, a clipboard nearby. A big wooden cabinet with drawers dominated one end of the room. The high-intensity light hit a wide pool of beads, the plastic trays on the floor.

And then Neil saw Claire's bare feet; he hurried around the big worktable to see her lying on the floor. . . .

Too pale and too quiet, Claire lay amid pearls and glistening red beads. Her blouse had been ripped open, exposing a white bra; her left sleeve was torn, bruises ran along her upper arm as if she'd been manhandled. Her hair spread out around her head, lush dark red waves glistening with pearls and red beads. One hand lay at her throat, and the other gripped a length of gold cording. Her swollen cheeks and lips spoke of a vicious attack.

A bead slid from her pale forehead, rolling on the floor toward Neil's muddy boot, the tiny sound echoing as loud as thunder in the room. "Claire," he whispered, the terror in his throat causing his voice to thicken.

Her hand fell from her throat to lay palm up and still, and then Neil saw the bruising at her throat—a solid mark of the cord.

He crouched beside her, fearing the worst, fearing to touch her, and the telephone was ringing. . . .

Four

―

"DON'T . . . DON'T—" CLAIRE'S EYELIDS FLUTTERED, HER bruised throat working as she tried to talk.

Neil feared to move her; he could worsen her injuries. "I've got to get help—an ambulance, honey."

No sound came from her, but fear widened her eyes. She shook her head, her hair rippled around her, and the telephone continued ringing. "Phone— Tell Tempest . . . I'm all right."

Claire's hand reached for his, her fingers digging in as her eyes pleaded with him. They were shimmering with tears and an odd shade of gold. "Tell my sister that you did not hurt me. Tell her you are not the one."

Neil did not question that a sister would call at a predetermined time. He simply held Claire's hand as he reached for the telephone.

Before he could say anything, the woman was yelling fiercely, "You bastard! You hurt my sister. I'll kill you. There's nowhere in hell that you can go, that I can't find you."

Stunned for a moment, Neil was about to tell the woman where *she* could go, to get off the line so that he could call for medical help, when Claire's fingernails bit into his hand. "Tell her," Claire whispered raggedly. "Tell Tempest."

Caught between the woman cursing him, who somehow knew that her sister had been injured, and Claire's frantic expression, those gold eyes—or were they green?—begging him, Neil spaced his words carefully. "I didn't hurt her—Tempest. I'm her next-door neighbor. I just stopped by to drop off some food for your . . . sister, and the door was open. She didn't answer, and I came in to find her. My cell phone isn't with me. If you'll get off the line, I'll call an ambulance—"

Fear widened Claire's eyes, and her body trembled.

Momentarily quiet, Tempest rallied fiercely. "Do not call an ambulance. I repeat, *do not*."

"Someone just beat the hell out of her, lady. She needs help."

Claire shook her head slightly, and her fingers tightened on his arm. "You. I want you."

Tempest caught the words. "She trusts you, you jerk. Don't you dare let her down. You stay with her until one of us gets there, got it?"

This time, Neil shook his head. His instincts told him that Claire needed medical help, yet here he was, battling his best judgment against two women. Tears squeezed out of Claire's eyes; the silvery trail slid down her temples into that tangled lush red hair. He smoothed a strand away from her cheek and found it clinging to him. "No, I don't get it. She's going to an emergency ward, one way or another. We have a pretty good clinic in Red Dog."

"*No!*" both women shouted at once.

Then Tempest asked cautiously, "You're Eunice's nephew?"

"Do you actually want to chat when an ambulance

could be on its way? You're tying up the line . . . but yes, I'm Neil Olafson, Eunice's nephew."

"Let me talk to her. Claire can talk . . . I heard her. Just do it."

"Dammit." But Neil placed the telephone beside Claire's ear. He moved another strand of hair away and found it damp, but then, so was her cheek. Neil jerked a tissue from a nearby box and carefully patted her cheek dry, but the tears kept sliding down that pale soft skin. Her eyes, now a dark shade of forest green, shimmered with tears.

Neil carefully eased her torn blouse over the bra. He couldn't hear what Tempest said, but Claire whispered, "Truly, I am okay. I'm just bruised—and then I . . . he was filled with hatred. It burned. . . ."

"Burned?" Alarmed, Neil hurriedly looked over her face and body for burns. He couldn't see any burn marks on her, no singed clothing.

"Tempest knows what I mean. But no, Neil. I'm not burned how you might think." Claire squeezed his hand briefly, her eyes searching his face as she spoke to her sister. "Yes, Tempest, I can trust him. He's upset now and worried, but he'll do what he has to. Yes, I'll call you—call Mom and Leona? It won't do anyone any good if—"

Neil took the telephone. "Listen—she's in bad shape. I'm no doctor, and she needs to file a report with the police—"

"Sorry, buddy. My sister said you're okay and you're there, and you're elected. Stay with her . . . I'm north of Edmonton, Canada, stuck in a snowstorm. With luck, I'll be there by early morning. Just make sure she calls us when she's feeling better. And *do not call the police*. We'll handle it."

"You? You're not even here—how the hell can you handle—?"

The line clicked off, and Claire studied Neil. "It will be okay," she whispered gently. "You'll do fine. Please don't worry so."

"You would if you could see yourself. This is serious, Claire. What if you have internal injuries? A broken rib can puncture a lung. You could have been—"

"That will be Leona," Claire whispered. "Answer it, please. Tell her that I am okay."

Neil breathed deeply, fear pulsing at him. "Claire, you're hearing ringing in your ears, and that could be serious—"

The telephone rang once, then again, before Neil realized that Claire had anticipated the call.

"That's my other sister, Leona. Tell her not to worry, that I'm fine."

How could she know the exact identity of the caller? Neil answered with his name, just in case the attacker wanted to check in on his handiwork—and maybe drop in for a repeat performance. If he did, Neil had a nasty little present waiting for him. "Neil Olafson here. Who's this?"

"Where is she? I've been calling for an hour, and she hasn't answered. She's usually there and working. What have you done to my sister?" a woman's crisp voice demanded.

Apparently, Claire's sisters knew how to pick their moments, each calling within minutes of his discovery of her. Neither sister seemed that sweet; it must run in the family.

Neil glanced at the blinking message machine; Claire must have been unconscious since—

"Around seven," Claire whispered.

Neil tried to adjust. Had he spoken to himself, wondering about the time? He cautiously repeated what he'd told Tempest, and in Lexington, Kentucky, Leona was evidently frustrated by airline schedules. She demanded to speak with her sister.

"I'm just fine. You're not coming, Leona. Tempest will be here soon—you know her, not much is going to hold her up." Claire frowned slightly and closed her eyes. "Please do not worry about me, Leona. Please."

She glanced at Neil, who was studying her critically and wondering if he should take her to medical care, despite her wishes. "No, you won't. . . . Yes, I was talking to Neil. Don't come, Leona. I don't want you disturbed—"

Neil frowned; of course Claire's sister would be "disturbed" by the attack. "Disturbed" was an odd choice for loving siblings, but then Claire could be off-center after the attack. . . .

Claire managed to convince Leona that she had everything "under control." "You shouldn't get upset, Leona. I'd blame myself if you got back into it again. You've worked so hard to close that door and start a new life."

"It?" What the hell was It"? What "door"? Neil wondered. Claire was unconscious; she could have been raped—she needed medical attention.

When the call ended, Claire focused on Neil. "Don't worry. You're wondering if I was raped—I wasn't. . . . I'd know. I'm very much in tune with my own body, and I'm okay. You're undecided as to what you should do. Do as my sisters and I ask for now? Trust me?"

She was "okay"? How would she know? Trust her? Shouldn't the question be, trust him? What if he didn't get her to medical attention, and she died? Her dark green eyes followed him and suddenly flashed to gold as he eased what was left of her blouse to cover more of her bra. "You have to see a doctor and get X-rays, Claire."

That odd shade of green returned to her eyes. "Nothing is broken. I'm just bruised—and upset. I shouldn't have been so careless."

He started picking the beads and pearls from her hair, using the time to decide what to do. If he had any sense, he'd ignore her wishes and get her to medical help.

"Please?" she whispered, and Neil damned himself; he knew he'd do as Claire asked.

She awoke to the pain and the darkness and the man sitting beside her bed, staring at her, trying to dissect her, trying to understand. The small chair didn't fit his tall muscular body; it creaked as he bent to ease her hair back from her face. His thumb stroked her temple, the workingman's texture rough against her skin. "Claire?"

A rush of anger hit her, sucking her breath away, terrifying her. Then she realized that she'd absorbed her attacker's anger. Claire focused and slowly pushed his rage away from her. She closed her eyes, breathed deeply, and concentrated on her healing technique: *Breathe in the good, exhale the bad.*

Claire felt the anger within her dimming. She opened her eyes and found Neil still watching her, still sitting beside her.

"Lie still," he said quietly. "You're okay. You've just been dozing. Don't move."

In her bedroom's shadows, the soft lamplight did nothing to soften his harsh face. Grim lines cut into his weathered skin, his jaw dark with stubble. His brows were dark, though lightened by the sun. Strange how a line of sun gold bordered the tops of his eyebrows.

That sun gold ran in almost-imperceptible streaks through those deep brown waves and ended in flecks, like sunlight riding the ocean waves.

In the shadows of his workshop and with the protection of her sunglasses, she hadn't noticed anything but the humor in his light eyes. Now they were the color of smoke and steel, the dark centers mirroring her pale face.

Somehow, Neil had managed to get her into bed and ease her with tablets, just aspirin from her medicine chest. His energy bounced off the walls and into Claire; she sensed his emotions: Neil was fearful, certain that she should have gone to the town's clinic.

A ripple of fury circled her briefly. It was Neil's, a different sensation from the other man who had hurt her. Neil's sensations were those of revenge, of showing another man how it felt to be abused.

Neil had seen her bruises and was angry with the man and wishing he'd called an ambulance. . . . If she died, he'd . . . Wishing he'd had the bastard in his two hands right now—and she didn't want her sister to be "disturbed." The choice of words was odd for a curious woman who didn't want medical attention. What was she hiding?

"Don't worry," she whispered through dry lips. She reached for his hand—big, rough, and warm, it curled around hers. She moved cautiously through the layers of his concern and frustration to the sensations of good and safe.

"I wouldn't like it if you died. Not while on my watch," Neil stated darkly, as his other hand smoothed her forehead. She'd seen his strength, at odds with his gentleness now. She felt his fear as flames licked at his parents' home, the helplessness of a teenager, restrained from entering the house, the guilt that he hadn't been home when the fire started.

"I know. You've had enough death around you. You were only a boy, and you couldn't save your parents. But I'm all right. Ah . . . if you can, could you please think pleasant thoughts now? For me?"

"Pleasant thoughts? Now? Why?" he rapped at her. On her forehead, his fingers paused, then continued their soothing gentle stroke.

"Meditation heals."

"Yeah, sure, okay. New Age is great, but it isn't a medical checkup. Why didn't you want to see a doctor? You could have something broken, or internal injuries."

"I'm just bruised, that's all." Claire had already used her senses to sweep her body. Surface bruising, nothing more—but shreds of the man's temper lingered, a residue of fiery pricks. Claire focused away from the man's hatred of her. She was lying in her own bed, her own scents mixed with Neil's masculine ones. And she was wearing only her bra and panties. "My clothes?"

He shrugged, but his expression was wary. "I thought you'd be more comfortable without your jeans, and your blouse was torn quite a bit. There was blood on it. It seemed the right thing to do, making you more comfortable—if you weren't going to a clinic—which you really should."

Neil leaned closer to study the marks around her throat, turning her head a bit. He was angry, his gray eyes glinting like steel, and Claire was picking up his emotion with the shards of the other man's rage. But Neil's touch was gentle, despite the roughness in his deep voice. "I've undressed women before—just not under these circumstances. Listen, don't get all worked up about your modesty. I'm just here to help."

"I'm sorry if I've insulted you. I'm a little upset."

" 'A little?' Lady, you deserve a whole lot." A line had appeared between those dark brows, the ones beside his lips deepening grimly. Claire missed the warmth of his smile, the teasing boy within, the man who enjoyed life.

That big broad workingman's hand slid through his

hair, making it stand out in peaks. "Dammit. You've been attacked, lady, and you don't want to see a doctor. How the hell am I going to take care of you if something is really wrong?"

"You're upsetting me," she stated unevenly. How could he know that it was critical he become calm, so that she could heal from the onslaught of hatred and pain? "And I'm so tired. Think about being a boy and Eunice's gingerbread. You liked it, didn't you?"

Neil's frown was quick and puzzled. "I did. She told you that, didn't she?"

Eunice hadn't told Claire, but Neil wouldn't know how a psychic could snag thoughts and emotions, absorbing them. "Please?"

"I don't get it." After a deep breath and the puzzled shake of his head, Neil did as she asked: *He was a boy again, stuffing gingerbread into his mouth, happy and eager for the day. . . .* The soothing motion of his fingers began again. . . . The peace of darkness called to her, and Claire floated into it.

"I knew something was wrong. I felt it, and I did nothing. But if I'd called Claire, I would have only upset her more. Our connection is too strong."

Greer Aisling stared out at the night, the moonlight creating a trail over the black Pacific swells beyond her window. *Claire, the most emotionally sensitive of Greer's children, had been violently attacked.*

Tempest's and Leona's calls had confirmed that Neil Olafson, her neighbor, was attending her, something that Claire probably wouldn't like. But his care, right now, was probably better than the heightened emotions her sisters could bring with them.

Tempest was calming herself as she drove southward from Canada to Claire in Montana. An expert traveler, and usually not waylaid by problems, Tempest would soon arrive at Claire's.

Meanwhile, Claire needed quiet so she could heal. She trusted the man. Claire's instincts were always true, when she was near that person. An empath could quickly sort dangerous intentions, but the attack had been too sudden—why?

Greer had sensed no warning, no vision-flashes of Claire's attack, just the unease, the sense that something was about to happen. Yet the attack had obviously been planned, the usual delivery van arriving with the empty box and distracting Claire. Someone had a reason to go to the effort of researching Claire's habits and to get the van and uniform, and to hurt her. The man had struck quickly, before she could sense and brace for danger, and then he'd unexpectedly apologized. The apology didn't suit the vicious, planned attack. *Why would the attack be so carefully planned and executed, then the man had seemed as if he didn't know why he was there—and he'd apologized? Why didn't he know what he was doing?*

Greer rocked herself, small comfort for a mother worrying over her child, no matter if she were fully grown and on her own. Greer continued reassuring herself: Neil was staying with her, and from his description, he would be strong enough to defend her from another attack.

Why would anyone want to attack a recluse whose only conflict had been with her neighbor over noise? *Neil Olafson was definitely not Claire's attacker. . . .*

It all came down to motives, Greer decided, with the experience of one who often worked with detectives. *Motives? Whose?*

Claire could sense Neil's emotions: the frustration, the impatience, the uncertainty and the curiosity.

She ached all over, her throat tight and dry. . . . Claire forced her eyes open to find Neil's concerned, uncertain expression in the shadows of her bedroom. She wrapped them around her. Familiar shadows, good shadows—she was safe here. . . . "I'm not going to die. I'm not seriously injured."

Was that her voice? So raw and uneven?

"Lie still . . . take it easy. You've been dozing again."

"Is it morning? Have I slept that long?

"No, it's only midnight."

Neil's emotions tumbled around her: He'd had time to question how an injured woman could make sound judgments. He should have taken her to Red Dog's clinic anyway. "You're probably a little off-center now. You don't know that you're okay."

"I just know."

She turned to him, the big man sitting in the chair, his jaw dark with stubble, his face lined with fatigue and worry. "You look so worried. I'm sorry for this."

His anger exploded around her, sharp, frustrated. "Why the hell didn't you let me call an ambulance? And how is your family going to handle getting this guy?"

"We just will." Claire didn't want her sisters or mother to see her now; the repairatives she had planned would take a few hours to smooth away the worst of the bruising. "I don't want them upset. Tempest is coming. It wouldn't be good if Leona and Mom came."

"What the hell!" Neil exploded and rammed a hand through his hair. "Good for them? What about you? You should see yourself. You're all bruised—"

Claire knew she had to react quickly, to diffuse his emotions and protect herself. "Pretty, am I? Colorful?"

When he stared blankly at her, Claire knew she'd successfully channeled his anger into confusion. He was trying to shift mental gears, worrying that she might have a head injury. "You can go home now, Neil. I'm just fine."

"I've been watching you closely, but we should call the delivery company and see who was driving that van."

"Please don't call them. I couldn't take an interrogation now. I just couldn't."

"I'm not leaving you, and for now, I won't call the delivery service. I don't get this whole thing. Someone broke in— Did you know him?"

Her head ached as she tried to remember. "I can't place him. I remember a nice man, though, someone struggling really hard with life and trying to change. This man wanted to hurt me."

"Bastard. Do you have any idea who would want to hurt you? Or why?"

The tiny scarlet thread from the matador's cape and the glistening ruby beads had made her uneasy, but she'd never been receptive to warning signs. But trauma could change psychic ability, opening and shifting it to other facets. She was already too sensitive, the man's residual anger mixing with Neil's, and she just couldn't bear more. "I don't want to talk about it anymore."

"So, just forget it? No charges, no medical checkup, just go on as if it never happened?" he demanded.

"I *know* that it happened, Neil." Claire sensed that he was loaded with questions, and he wasn't stopping. "My sisters usually call. You're wondering about that, aren't you? Why they both just happened to call? Their timing just happened to coincide— You're not going to cut down that lovely old tree, are you?"

Derailed from his questions about the attack on her and her reaction, Neil frowned. "You pick your times, don't you? How am I going to refuse you when you're all beat-up?"

"My mother didn't call, did she?" Claire asked softly. If Greer Aisling did not call, that meant she was working—and probably trying to find whoever had hurt her daughter. . . . And it also meant that Tempest and Leona had reported everything.

Claire's slight frown hurt. Something was very wrong. As a clairvoyant, Greer's ability to sense flashes of the future and her strong attachment to Claire should have warned her about the attack. But just as with the bank holdup, Greer hadn't sensed anything until it was too late— Leona's unwanted precognitive gift might have told her, too—and she would have alerted Claire.

But the attack had come without warning to either clairvoyant closely linked to Claire. They could usually sense an uneasiness before it occurred, and Greer, the more developed psychic, could pinpoint details.

This time was different. Unprovoked, a man had attacked Claire, and Leona had called immediately after. Greer would have been informed immediately, but she hadn't called.

Claire shuddered, her body icy. At least this time she hadn't been exposed to the hospital's nightmare, absorbing every emotion, the problems and pain of the people around her. She was safe, and a good, if argumentative, man stood guard over her.

Neil watched Claire doze, then he stood, impatient and furious with any man who would hurt a woman. "Anger won't do, Neil," Claire whispered drowsily. "You're upsetting me, and I'm not strong enough to fight. . . ."

Fight what? Him? "I'm not going to hurt you," he stated unevenly.

"I know. You couldn't help what happened to your parents. You shouldn't feel guilty. Don't blame yourself. . . ." She sighed softly, then drifted back into sleep.

Neil stared down at her. *His parents? His parents' accident?* But then his maternal aunt Eunice would have told Claire about the death of a beloved sister, wouldn't she?

Restless, Neil moved out of the room and walked into Claire's living room. Neil lifted the package from the floor. In her brief description of what had happened, Claire had said she was just opening it when she had been attacked. Neil studied that package and wrapping carefully; it was only a shoe box wrapped in a paper grocery sack, and there was nothing in it. *But it was a good enough fake to cause Claire to get excited, to forget to lock her door.*

He placed the package on the table and studied the rest of the room: An aqua afghan lay across a cream-colored, comfortable sofa; a stream of framed pictures crossed the top of a polished chest. A sound system and CDs finished out one corner, and a large overstuffed chair matched the couch. A reading lamp stood nearby with a basket of magazines beside it. Neil flipped through them—women's life, craft and clothing sales catalogs.

Since music and movies might reveal more about Claire, Neil sat down to study them—orchestration, New Age, Celtic, all without lyrics. Her movies were "girly," humorous and cute, nothing "heartwarming" or "tear-jerking" that other women might prefer. Everything was smooth and cool, just as Eunice said Claire preferred her life.

Neil stood and ran his hands through his hair. *Why would any man want to attack a woman like that?*

And how could he have known she was alone at exactly the right time? Had some lunatic been stalking her, waiting out there for just the chance to— Why, dammit? Why?

Evidence of a male visitor wasn't anywhere in the house, yet according to Eunice, Claire had been married and divorced; she'd lost a baby. What had caused her to back away from people and life? Five years was a long time to heal—but then, it had been eight years since his son was taken, and Neil still hadn't healed.

Then, Claire was obviously artistic, and maybe that talent required solitude.

Neil walked to the framed photographs on the chest. Clearly a mother and daughter grouping, the three younger women resembled the older one, each with a different hairstyle, but the same bone structure— slanting cheekbones, edgy chins. The sisters could have been the same age, dressed differently. One would be Tempest and one Leona.

In one, the mother stood, heavily pregnant and wrapped in a man's arms, smiling up at him. Another photograph was of a man, blond hair windblown as he worked the rigging of a sailboat. Another photograph was of the man alone, with an ocean behind him, his feet braced apart on the deck. Daniel Bartel, a man, had written on the photo.

In another, the young girls stood in a row; each grinned at the camera and held a Happy Birthday balloon, cakes on the table in front of them. Their pink T-shirts read, LEONA FIONA, TEMPEST BEST, CLAIRE BEAR.

Neil frowned and turned the photograph to the light. Each cake had seven candles. *Triplets—the women were triplets. . . .*

He recounted what he knew of Claire, trying to make the pieces fit: She was a loner, working at her craft. Her eyes were green and she didn't need sunglasses.

She had told him to answer the telephone before it rang. Coincidence? She had said her family called regularly, hadn't she? And then, a recluse wouldn't have many callers, would she?

Neil walked quietly through the house, noting everything. The kitchen was homey, filled with hanging dried herbs, a teakettle on the stove and teapot nearby. The entire house was small, quiet, and feminine. Nothing was expensive, the quilt on her bed handsewn, and unlike Eunice's, Claire's home was uncluttered. Neil pushed aside the kitchen curtain, surprised at its weight and the extra lining, and found the view of his house, backyard, and shop. Why the sun-blocking liners on the curtains? Why did Claire walk only at night?

Returning to the living room, Neil studied a shelf lined with small pewter fairies, obviously the work of one artist. A small earthen bowl held a collection of unique, handcrafted silver jewelry. The Celtic design of a gold headband was unusual and evidently antique; but it hadn't been taken.

Theft didn't appear to be the motive for the attack, rather it was sheer rage.

Large and intricate, a silver brooch formed into a circle bore a woven, interlaced Celtic design, a heavy pin attached to it. Either Claire was a collector of the design, or someone was fond of giving them to her.

Neil moved into her workroom. He'd straightened the rest of the house, but now he bent to collect the pearls and red beads that had been toppled.

A tiny pearl bead rolled in the center of his large callused hands, as delicate as Claire seemed to be now, with all that mass of red hair framing her pale face and striping the white pillowcase.

Neil shook his head. A woman alone in rural Montana should know better than to leave her door unlocked, even in her excitement to open a package.

Why didn't she want to report the attack?

Neil stared at the ringing telephone. Earlier, Claire had known it would ring before it actually had. Neil answered, and Leona started talking immediately, "Now get this, cowboy. Don't you dare leave my sister. I was already on my way, despite what Claire said, but now I'm headed back to Kentucky. Once I was on the road, I had time to think. I don't agree with Claire, but if she thinks Tempest is the best one, then okay. I can make Claire nervous sometimes, and she doesn't need that now. Don't you dare leave her, and do not—I repeat—do not let her get anywhere near lakes, rivers, that sort of thing. She chose that place carefully so as not to be near those."

These women needed keepers. Why would Leona make Claire nervous? No lakes, rivers, "that sort of thing?" "I'm not going anywhere. But she should see a doctor and file a report. There could be fingerprints on the box and paper. This guy needs to be caught."

"We 'women' seem to manage just fine on our own. Our family will handle it."

He'd heard that line before, and now he was certain that the women needed someone to do their thinking for them. Neil decided that since he was elected at the moment, he'd try to help in that area. "Exactly how? He came in so fast, Claire didn't know what hit her. She was unconscious when I found her, and she could have broken bones."

"She'd know if she did. She knows exactly how her body works, how her blood feels flowing through her body. In short, she can almost see inside herself. Look, cowboy, we've been doing this for a long time—taking care of each other, and we know how to do it. Don't try to play big daddy to a herd of helpless women. Believe me, we're not. Just be glad that our mother isn't coming. She can be a real witch when she gets worked up."

Neil took a deep breath. If the daughters were any indication of the mother— He tried to remain reasonable. "Has Claire had threats? Anyone stalking her?"

"Not that we know of." The electric silence said Leona was cautious, slowly framing her words. "Could you just please try to be, well, nice, and think nice thoughts until we get there?"

Neil had reached the end of his "reasonable." "Hey, lady, I am 'nice,' and what the hell has *thinking* got to do with anything?"

On the other end of the line, Leona's long sigh indicated that she was tired of dealing with someone whose intelligence was just above that of a door. "Okay, just try to feel good about yourself when you're around her. Could you at least do that?"

"Oh, I feel good about myself. But I'm not about to be pushed around by your clan. By the way, I saw the pictures and that birthday cake. You all look about the same age."

"We are. We were born three minutes apart. I'm the oldest, and Tempest was next. Figure it out."

Neil shook his head. He'd known that Claire was going to be trouble. Now it looked like trouble came in threes.

"You can go home now . . . I know you must be tired. I appreciate everything you've done, but I'm fine, and I'd really prefer to be alone."

"That's not going to happen." The big man seated in her workroom chair didn't turn away from her computer.

At two o'clock in the morning, Claire stood at the doorway, after a long, bracing shower. She had taken her time beneath the water, turning her mind inward and focusing on healing. Wrapped in her short toweling robe, she was still a little sore but felt somewhat better.

She finished brushing her damp hair as she studied the man in her chair. Unprepared for the blinding overhead light, Claire shaded her eyes and carefully marked off the three-foot distance she wanted to keep from him.

Ordinarily two feet was a good gauging distance, but Neil's emotions were stronger right now and required more space between them. She tightened the belt of her robe and braced herself to evict him.

From his brooding, dark look at her, Claire knew that an angry storm lay just beneath the surface. Neil was sitting in his boxer shorts, on *her* office chair, his bare feet propped on another, and tapping away at *her* computer's keys. The steady hum of her dryer indicated that his clothing was in *her* laundry. The male invasion was unsettling, and she couldn't afford that now. "I'm fine—really. Surely you must have things to do."

His statement was abrupt: "You should be in bed."

"I couldn't sleep. I'm used to being up this time of night."

"I'd think a woman who just got worked over like you did might want to take it easy." He turned back from the computer screen. "Can't find any break-ins listed locally, no attacks. Red Dog is a boring little area, except for a few bar fights. . . . There's an upcoming Blackfoot powwow. They usually put out a good feed with buffalo meat, and I like the fry bread. I like to see the kids dance in costume."

Claire took a moment to adjust to the big powerful man dominating the very feminine room. The hot pink feather boa around his muscular throat snagged on the stubble of his jaw. It ran down his tanned chest, tangled a bit in that wedge of dark hair, and crossed over that six-pack stomach to end at his shorts. The contrast of soft and feminine against Neil's tanned and muscular body was almost comical.

If she were in a laughing mood, the pink shade of his boxer shorts would set her off.

She tossed her hairbrush to her worktable in the center of the room. That was just great. A man, entrenched in her home and wearing a hot pink boa and pink shorts was all she needed to make things just peachy-keen. Her head still throbbed from the blows, her frown caused the bruises to hurt slightly, and her whole body felt like it had been hit by a truck. "My sisters will be here—"

Neil had watched her slow, pained movements, his gray eyes shaded, his lips tight and grim. "Not until later this morning. Tempest checked in a couple of times . . . I told her you were resting. She seems to be more of a sweetheart than your older-by-six-minutes sister, Leona. Tempest is fighting bad weather up in Canada. Meanwhile, I'm here. How are you feeling?"

"Like *not* chatting. I'll be fine, thank you. I promise that we'll talk later. I'll call you periodically if you want. Please leave."

Claire rubbed her temples where remnants of the man's rage flickered. She shouldn't have been so abrupt with Neil; he was only trying to help. "I appreciate everything you've done, really I do. It's just that I prefer to be alone."

Neil scanned her face and down her short robe, then abruptly exited the computer. He sat back and folded his arms behind his neck. The boa seemed almost alive, a feathery wave caressing his body. But then, Claire wasn't in the best of moods, and her perception was definitely off. And she couldn't stand it anymore— "Your shorts are pink. Isn't that a little unusual for a Western man?"

"Could be. I didn't know that washing a red blanket with my underwear would turn them pink. But I don't think that's the important issue here. You are not fine. You look like hell, and I'm not leaving until someone is here with you. If you want something to eat, there's pizza in the fridge, but I can't find anything else to fix for you, no canned soup, nothing fast or prepared. Now, that's just not right. How about some toast? Your homemade bread is good, by the way."

"If I eat, will you leave then? I really do need to be alone—please." Claire absorbed the flick of sensual interest—and amusement—as Neil's study lowered to her robe, tracing it over her breasts and down to her legs. But then, he'd undressed her, hadn't he?

"Well, you're not going to be alone. I said I would stay until Tempest got here, and I am. Leona decided Tempest was the best for the job. . . . You're embarrassed. I guess that's what you're getting all rosy about. We went through this before—I needed to see if you were injured, and I undressed you. If you're offended, I apologize."

Claire considered what she would have done, under the same circumstances; after all, her bra and panties were a little more than some bikinis Neil had probably seen. At no time had he done anything suspect. "I suppose that was only reasonable. Would you please take off my boa? You look really silly in it."

"Well, Claire Bear, it's like this: I'm a modest kind of guy. And my clothes are in the laundry, and I didn't think you'd want to see me in the buff, or just my shorts. And I didn't think you'd like me sitting around in my dirty work jeans."

Claire took a heartbeat to adjust from the childhood nickname. Then she wished she could have stopped her body tensing, the uneasy movement of her hand to smooth her messed hair, or the blush on her cheeks. "I'm uncomfortable with you here, and you know it."

"Uh-huh, but that doesn't change the fact that I'm not leaving until your sister turns up." That hard mouth curved a little, the amused lines beside his eyes deepening. With his hair curling a bit around his forehead and ears, he had the teasing look of a boy.

Then his glance at her throat brought a savage darkness, and her perceptive senses latched on to it. Instantly, the resulting headache was painful. She was too weak to successfully block him—and she was also too tuned into receiving his thoughts. Claire rubbed her temples with the tips of her fingers. "Please think about good things."

"Your sister said that. What does it matter what I think?"

There was only curiosity in Neil, not arrogance; Claire knew that he simply wanted to understand. "Because it matters to me. You're very easy to 'read.'"

"What do you mean, 'read'?"

Claire didn't want to him to know that at close range, she could feel everything that rode inside another person; that sometimes, she could absorb their stress and pain, the problems of their life—if she wasn't careful. Her barriers were down now, her attacker's residual rage still irritating her, and she was too receptive to anything around her. "Your expression. I mean, your face is very revealing, and I remember how his was and I—"

Neil shook his head and stood. He tossed the boa to her worktable; the feathers clung to his hips momentarily. Without that softness, Neil's body was hard and defined, rippling muscles beneath the skin as he braced his hands flat on the table and stared at her. "You need to report this, Claire. This guy could be after other women, right now. There's no way you should wait for your sisters. Sure, having family around at a time like this is great, but the more time that is wasted, the less chance of catching him."

"My family will handle this."

"I'm getting a little tired of hearing that." His fist hit the worktable, jarring it. Then, as if remembering that other hands had misused Claire, Neil braced his open hands on the table again—a calculated move to show that they weren't moving, they weren't hurting. "There's no way—unless you've got serious legal pull in the family—husbands, maybe? Did you have an abusive husband, Claire?"

"Paul was kind and gentle."

"Sure, and you divorced him because of that." Neil's sarcasm rang through her workroom. "You've got scars on your wrists and ankles. They're almost gone, but I saw them. He tied you down, didn't he? Then worked you over?"

"Paul never did any such thing. It's none of your business, but we had our differences." Paul couldn't understand, and he'd had enough. Even if their baby had lived, Aisling would have deepened the rift—because she would have inherited psychic ability from a long line of women mystics.

But Neil had noticed the scars from her time strapped to the hospital bed, and he was pushing for answers. "If you want to keep this private, if you've got some record or something and—"

Maybe she was still affected by her attacker's rage, because Neil was nudging a temper she'd never known. "Of course, I don't have a record. I'm not an FBI transplant, and I've never committed a crime in my life."

"So, you women think you can handle this—you don't know this guy, and he almost killed you? Did you ever think that he knew just the right time to come, that

I'd be gone if I did see something wrong? Hell, maybe he's been watching you for days. It's easy enough to do with binoculars from anywhere around. What if he decides for a replay?"

"We can handle it." The triplets had handled lifetimes of dealing with their oddities, hiding and refusing them.

He'd moved closer, breaching her safe three-foot perimeter; Neil's emotions pulsed heavily inside her, a blend of curiosity, admiration, a male appreciation for the scent of her hair; the flow of his feelings caught and bound her still.

When he touched her hair, Claire jumped and turned, her senses catching Neil's emotions. *He regretted surprising her, because now she probably feared any man's touch. Too bad.*

"So you make these, huh? These bags?" he asked quietly, watching her as he eased back a little, folding his arms over his chest so that he might not frighten her.

Claire absorbed a wash of Neil's apprehensions and curiosity: *He feared that she might always be terrified of people. . . . Someone had really done a number on her. He wondered if she had been attacked before, if that was why she was a recluse.*

She reached for the telephone again and regretted the impulse, because it hadn't yet rung. Claire noted Neil's grim, narrowed stare at her scarred wrist and pulled her sleeve over it. "I'm fine, Tempest. Yes, he's here, but I want him to go home. I do not need him here."

"I promised them I would stay. And if this guy comes back while I'm here, he's getting a dose of his own medicine," Neil warned quietly. But his frown, the way he looked at the telephone and then to Claire and back again, said he'd noted that the phone hadn't actually rung.

"If you could just tell him that he could leave, Tempest, I'd be fine. I'm not a baby, you know— Oh, give up that 'baby,' last-born business. You're only older by three minutes and Leona by six. Yes, I am getting a little peeved. My *neighbor* is standing here in his pink shorts, he's already done his laundry—"

"And yours," Neil added. "There was blood—"

Alarmed, Tempest yelled, "Blood?"

Neil took the phone from Claire. Little ribbons of his emotions reached out to trap her; they were male— harsh, impatient, and frustrated—as he spoke. "Look, her lip was split a little. It bled. I used antiseptic on every mark I could find—a few scratches, nothing more— used some ointment she had in the cabinet, used a frozen bag of peas on her cheek to keep down the swelling. I did what I could, but I still think she should go to the clinic and get checked over."

Neil's gray eyes locked with hers, and that big wide hand rammed through his dark brown waves, rumpling them. "She's stubborn, she's mean, and contrary. In contrast, I keep my word. I'm sweet and easy-natured, and I'll stay here until you get in. Slow driving? Just be careful. Yes, I'm staying."

Claire sensed Tempest's passing sexual interest, and Neil's smile was sexy and knowing. "Uh-huh. Look forward to it, Tempest. Meanwhile, Claire Bear can be as nasty as she wants. Yes, she is a little miffed by me staying here. If she weren't hurt, I'd be enjoying myself."

When he replaced the phone, Neil leveled a challenging look at Claire. "Problem?"

"Only that you . . . have . . . invaded . . . *my* home."

Neil placed his hand on the top of her head and waggled it gently as she frowned up at him. The sensations from him were friendly, boyish, and pleased with himself because he'd gotten to her, purposefully distracting her from reliving the assault.

"Since you're obviously not going to rest, let's have a little three-o'clock-in-the-morning snack, shall we, Claire Bear? And then you can tell me all about yourself, Tempest Best, and Leona Fiona." Neil Olafson was actually looking forward to meeting her sisters. He was confident that he could handle any woman with ease. Women just naturally liked him.

Claire allowed herself one small, slightly grim smile. But then, Neil hadn't met the rest of Claire's family, had he?

Five

———

CLAIRE GLANCED AT THE KITCHEN CLOCK—IT WAS FOUR o'clock in the morning and several hours since her attack, yet remnants of the man's rage still simmered deep within her.

Neil stood at the sink, and the presence of another man in her home probably wasn't helping her to settle completely.

She looked down at the torn blouse she had retrieved from the trash, smoothing it with her trembling hands. The material was faded and comfortable. But even the little rosebud pattern seemed ugly. Poor little rosebuds, they'd never be the same. Would she?

Her body and muscles ached from fighting the man; she looked at her arms, studying the bruises, already much lighter than when Neil had first seen her. Why would anyone hate her that much? Was it possible, as Neil had first suggested, that the man could have studied her movements? Or Neil's, to choose exactly the right time?

Suddenly, Neil turned to her. He threw the dish towel aside and folded his arms. "What's with you? I thought you wouldn't want to see that blouse again, since you're not planning to report the attack. You should really rethink that."

Tempest would want to hold the blouse. Claire folded it and placed it inside a brown paper sack. She folded the top over once, then again, wishing she could close away that segment of time last night, when . . .

Neil watched the slow, meticulous movement of her hands. "I don't get any of this," he said finally.

"No one asked you to. You don't need to be involved." But he *was* involved. He'd found her after the attack. Uncomfortable and nettled because Neil wasn't leaving her, that he was committed to staying, Claire shivered. "I would think you'd have better things to do than to hang around here."

Neil moved right into that, his sarcasm hitting back at her. "It seems the thing to do, since you were all beat up and all. But hey. I could have just left you there on the floor, barely conscious, and gone home and watched TV. Instead, a bunch of really irritating women start bossing me around."

He'd been kind, caring for her, and he was right—she was off base, but then, nothing was *on* base. To hide her embarrassment, Claire rose from the kitchen table and began clearing away the dishes. She sensed Neil's need for coffee so that he could better cope with a bunch of willful women—one in particular. "I don't drink coffee. You can go home if you want that."

"Did I *say* I wanted coffee? You've been trying to get rid of me for the last hour. I promised to stay with you, until your family arrived, and I am *not* leaving."

Neil regretted his curt, angry tone. He didn't like the frustration he was feeling, and he didn't like thinking that a man would want to hurt a woman. And he wasn't certain that these women knew what was best for Claire, like dismissing proper medical attention. On top of that, he'd been wishing for a strong cup of coffee, and Claire had picked that up without his saying anything. The whole thing was downright upsetting; here he was involved with a nest of women fearing lakes and rivers and—as if there were a lot of them around in basically dry wheat country. And he'd heard all the "We'll take care of it" he wanted to hear.

On top of that, every time he came too close, she eased away, though Neil supposed that was logical and natural for a woman who had just been mistreated by another man.

He stared at Claire, who was obviously uncomfortable. But then, a loner would be uncomfortable—especially one who had been attacked—and unused to anyone in her space. "Okay, I was wishing for a cup of strong coffee. I need it to keep up with you and your sisters. I got the feeling that either one of them could hurt a man where it counts."

Claire sensed that despite his words, Neil's urges ran to something else—like holding her in his arms, like stroking her hair, like comforting her. Those sensations rippled over her, and Claire fought to hold them back; she'd already experienced her body's response to his. . . . She couldn't get tangled in his needs; she had to protect herself. "I really do appreciate what you've done, but I'm used to being alone. I've been trying to get rid of you because you're in my way. I have work to do, and I'm certain you do, too."

"So you just intend to go on as if nothing happened? As if you're *not* all bruised and shook-up?"

"Tempest will be here in a few hours and I need some thinking room to recover. You're taking up that room. I can manage, really. Quiet and relaxation is what I need now, and with you here, that's not going to be possible. Please understand my need to be alone."

"I understand that I'm not leaving until someone is here to take care of you. She's driving hard, but slowed up by that bad weather. It could take longer than you think for her to get here."

"Meanwhile, I'll be just fine." When Claire reached to place the dishes in the sink, she came too close, and Neil's need to kiss her, to taste her, stunned her. She turned slowly to look up at him. "I don't think so," she whispered unevenly.

"Think so—what? Think what?" he asked quietly, those dark gray eyes locking with hers. His gaze slid down to her lips, and before Claire could move away, he bent to brush his lips against hers.

It was so easy for him, a man who enjoyed women and life— Her body ached from one man's harsh hands and now another wanted to hold her. In that heartbeat, Claire couldn't think, absorbed by the needs of her own body—to be held gently, to sink into slow, thorough lovemaking, and to place yesterday behind her.

She held very still, sorting through her senses. Right now, her emotions were swinging everywhere, from fear to needing comfort to sensuality. She had just gotten a good old-fashioned sexual jolt from Neil, and it had become her own.

But making love with Neil would open doors that she'd closed forever. Claire moved away, staring at him, still absorbing that banked male hunger that had run warm inside her veins, his needs stirring hers.

"I was going to kiss your cheek—to make it better," Neil stated lightly. "I missed."

"You want to make love to me." The flat breathless statement left her before she could stop it.

His eyes flickered, but never left her face. "What kind of man would I be, wanting to make a pass at you now? No, I'm wondering if you've ever been in a camper before. You ought to try camping sometime—it might loosen you up, or at least get you out of this house. What happened to you? Why are you living out here?"

She knew he'd lied but didn't challenge him. "I have a right to live where I want."

"Bull. You're out here for a reason. The way your sisters worry about you, they're overprotective of you. They seem more ready to deal with people, and you aren't. You're playing hermit out here, because someone really hurt you . . . or you wouldn't be so hard to get along with. Maybe the guy who hurt you was the same one, maybe you've been running from him, and he found out. And just maybe, you're protecting him."

"And I think that you should get out. Of course, I've never seen him before. I'd have a name, wouldn't I?"

Neil wasn't being put off; those steel-hard eyes pried into her. "Fear can close lips. This time could just be a sampler, and next time, he'll do the whole job."

He tugged her earlobe and watched her cautiously move back from him. "I'm not leaving. Sorry, no can do. I promised your sisters."

"Oh, boy. You are really, really enjoying this."

"Well, you know, lady, a man's got to do what a man's got to do." His fingertip tapped her nose lightly. "And you—you should go back to bed and get some rest."

Soaking in her tub later, the lavender-scented bath salts easing her body, Claire listened to Neil's deep voice and his chuckle, which sounded as if coming from her living room. She got out of the tub and opened the door just a bit to hear him. "Okay, I'll tell her, Tempest. I'm looking forward to meeting you. Yes, Leona has called. No, I haven't left Claire Bear, but she's not happy about me staying here."

Claire frowned as Neil chuckled again. "Uh-huh. She can get nippy. You know, I'd rather have that right now than her retreating inside herself. I know she's upset, and I'm a likely target. I can take it. Later."

After a moment, Neil's deep voice rumbled, the tone clipped and businesslike. Claire listened carefully: "Mary Jane, it's Neil. Sounds like your message machine is full—better dump it. I know you're in Missoula overnight, but I just checked and got your message. I'm tied up tonight, so that's not good for me. When you get this, don't bother to call. I'll check with you later."

Neil replaced the receiver and turned to see Claire moving swiftly into the living room. She walked straight to Neil, then bent to take the phone plug from the wall. "You're not calling your girlfriends from my house, and I'd appreciate it if you didn't discuss me with my family."

He noted her expression: she was steamed, those gold-green eyes glaring at him. Okay, well, he'd rather have her a little angry, focused on disliking him, than remembering the attack. He smiled blandly and thought how great she looked, all flushed with anger and from her bath, and smelling sweet. She looked a hell of a lot better than when he found her. She could use that anger to paste herself together and file a report.

In a red sweatshirt and jeans and bare feet, that fabulous rich long hair twisted into a high, loose knot on top of her head, Claire pointed to the door. "I'm not filing any report. I've had enough of you. Out."

Neil noted that her movements were quicker, her face no longer swollen. Whatever magical thing she'd done in the bathroom had worked, but he wasn't leaving. "Give it up, Claire Bear. We're getting along so well."

"If you think that, then you aren't very—"

She closed her lips and tried to move away from his hand as it cupped her jaw. Neil turned her face, inspecting the bruises. "You heal well. Very fast. But you need more rest."

"Relaxation does that to me. I need peace and quiet now—alone. And I'm used to staying up all night, remember?"

His emotions tangled in Claire: He liked the feel of that pale smooth skin beneath his fingers too much. The way her green eyes slid into angry gold excited him, and he just had to nudge her to see what she would do. In contrast to that, a little uneasy wave of guilt came from Neil because only a jerk would make moves on a woman who had just been attacked. He promised himself that he would walk the fine line between distracting her and irritating her too much.

At odds with Neil's dark frustration, Claire also sensed that as a male, he was appreciating how she smelled. He'd missed that, the fresh smell of a woman, and Claire did smell really, really good, like flowers and honey and woman, the deep kind of scent that could fill a man's nostrils and start him simmering.

Claire moved warily away from Neil. He noted the tensing of her body; she'd just purposefully moved away from him. To him, the distance seemed almost calculated, as if she were pacing it off. He understood: She was skittish of men after the attack. Or was it something else? "Since you're not going to rest, we might as well talk. It might do you good. Want to tell me about your divorce—the reasons?"

She seemed stunned. "No. Why?"

"It's logical. It seems like a topic, something we might have in common, a way to spend the time until your sister arrives. That is, if you're not going to sleep. Why did you divorce? I'm divorced, you're divorced, and that's a topic we share. Most women usually have a lot to say about their exes."

"I'm not 'most' women. You still think that my ex-husband might have a hand in this, don't you? Paul wouldn't think of such a thing. I haven't asked you about yours, have I?"

Clearly the cause of Claire's divorce wasn't open for discussion and she had turned the focus to him.

Neil considered the slow disintegration of his marriage. Jan and he had drifted apart after their son's disappearance and all the emotional turmoil that went with trying to find him.

"I'm sorry," Claire said softly. "I know that was difficult for you."

"What? Talking about my divorce? It just happened."

Claire nodded as if she understood everything about him. "I know."

"Eunice told you, I guess. Jan and I were so tied up in finding Sammy that we didn't realize for a couple of years that we weren't the same people. One day we just sat at the kitchen table with nothing to say. And we both knew it was over, as simple as that. We're friends. She's married to a good guy, has a couple of kids now—boys. Now let's hear about you."

Claire shook her head and walked toward her workroom; she closed the door and the subject of her marriage.

Neil studied that closed door; Claire Brown wasn't sharing. He bent to replace the telephone plug just as it rang. Claire picked up at the same time as he, and Neil recognized the caller's businesslike tone as Leona's. "Claire?"

"Neil."

"Yes, it's Claire." The woman on the workroom's extension didn't bother to shield her impatience. "Get off the line, Neil."

"Maybe Leona wants to talk with me. We've been getting along great." And maybe Leona had something to say that she didn't want Claire to hear, maybe something about what sedative to give her? Maybe he wanted to ask the same.

"You're obnoxious, Olafson." The hiss of Claire's breath caused him to smile.

A businesswoman addressing the point of her call, Leona said, "Claire, I'm worried. You usually pick up the phone—"

Before it rings? Neil silently finished Leona's sentence and frowned. He replaced the telephone, allowing the women to talk privately. Leona was right, Claire usually picked up the telephone before it rang from either sister. And the mother that he'd heard was concerned hadn't called. Strange, that a loving mother wouldn't call to check on her daughter at a time like this; Claire's sisters had no doubt relayed the information.

The workroom door suddenly opened, and Claire frowned at him. "She wants to talk with you, Olafson."

"Thanks, Claire Bear."

The door slammed shut, and Neil reassured Leona that Claire was recovering perfectly, in fact rapidly, her bruises clearing. He reported that she was a little peeved at his presence, but otherwise, no problem.

"I think she's really mad. My, my. I didn't know my little sister could have such savage feelings." Leona's tone seemed pleased. "My little sister is focused entirely on you. Good work, Olafson—distracting her, huh?"

Neil decided to keep the conversation light. If he were truthful, he'd say that Claire confused the hell out of him. "Uh-huh. Women usually like me. I have no idea what her problem with me is."

Leona's rich laughter was encouraging, but her warning was quiet and dead serious. "Keep her away from large bodies of water, Neil. And crowds. No clinics or whatever you have out there in Montana. Claire picked that place because it had neither. She needs quiet and solitude to heal. Tempest will be there soon."

"If you say so." That was the second time that Neil had been warned about keeping Claire from large bodies of water. He wondered about that and something else: "Your mother hasn't called."

"It's best that she doesn't, but Mother always knows everything. She's really upset, and she's working hard at—" She broke off. "It wouldn't do for her to call Claire now," Leona ended ominously. "We'll handle everything. And thanks."

It wouldn't do for her to call Claire now. Neil wondered how a mother could be upset, but not call her daughter, and be working too hard to check in on her. These women were as easy to understand as other galaxies. He'd be better off doing something he understood. Neil noted the kitchen's dripping faucet and set to work. Then, in the tiny box of cheap hand tools, he found unopened packages of dead bolts and began installing them on the front and back doors.

He'd noted the unique doorknobs before, a twisting Celtic design, interwoven around sturdy brass or glass knobs. Eunice had said that Claire's sister Tempest was a metal sculptor, and if this was her work, she was very good.

Because the dead bolts were new, Claire had difficulty in opening them to hurry outside and away from Neil. Her little struggle with the locks could have been amusing if not for her desperation.

"I'm going for a walk. No need to tag along," she stated briskly as she fastened the odd wolf's-head brooch on her shoulder, closing her cape.

"It's six in the morning. After a night like you've had, don't you think you should take it easy?"

Her answer was curt. "No."

"Okay, then. Let's take a stroll." Neil wouldn't be that easy to shed, not with Claire's attacker possibly waiting to jump her again. Neil grabbed his jacket and walked beside her; he moved to block the sweeping cold wind from her. Since Claire evidently was set to ignore him, the lift of her chin proud, naturally Neil needed to push his presence. He certainly wasn't letting her retreat to brood by herself.

"Nice day, huh? Take in that air. In another hour or so, it will be another bright, shiny day. Great for camping. See what you're missing by walking at night? With this kind of weather, I'm expecting good sales this year." When she was silent, Neil talked about how his campers, the 1930s styles, were regaining popularity because of their light weight and ease of towing.

The tight set of her lips and her tense jaw, the way she walked faster said that she wasn't happy with his presence. At least she was focused on getting him out of her life and not on last night's brutality.

A pickup neared, and Neil drew Claire to one side of the road, his arm protectively around her stiff body. His son would be about the same age now as the boy in the truck—around eight or so.

Suddenly, Claire turned to him; her expression was softer than moments before. She pressed his hand at her waist. "It must be awful."

"What?" The ache inside him eased slightly.

"Losing a child before you really knew him, or played with him, or watched him toddle. I don't know what my mother would have done if anything would have happened to any one of us."

Neil frowned slightly; it was strange that Claire had picked up on that thought, just at the very minute he was missing Sammy.

The ache for Sammy rose and swelled and hurt. "I'll never forgive myself for letting that happen. It was my idea, going camping with our son, doing a little business at the same time. Jan didn't want to go at first. I could have gone by myself, but oh, no, I wanted to show off my son. If we hadn't gone, Sammy wouldn't have been taken. I should have taken Sammy walking with me. He liked being outdoors in the sun. But Jan was really tired when I left, and he was a little cranky from teething. I thought they could both use a nap."

Neil shook his head, the emptiness and guilt growing inside him. Sammy would have loved Eunice's place. "My fault all the way. Maybe I missed a cue from the people who were there—everyone was investigated thoroughly, but nothing turned up. Ifs and maybes all come back to my fault."

Claire nodded slowly. "I understand."

Raw emotions took him turning on her. "You couldn't possibly. What if I somehow missed the only ransom note from a kidnapper, and Sammy paid for it?"

She moved closer and removed her sunglasses, her gaze meeting and holding his. In the daylight, her eyes were cool and green, her voice was soft, melodic, and seemed to wrap around him. "Everyone needs closure. You're missing a part of your heart, and it can't heal."

Of course, she'd know. Claire had lost a baby. "Look, I'm sorry, Claire. I shouldn't have come at you like that. You've got enough to deal with."

On his cheek, her hand was warm and soft. The ache in Neil's heart seemed to ease; he felt lighter as she whispered, "You had to tell someone. It was burning inside you. I'm glad I was here to—to listen."

After eight years of quiet guilt, Neil didn't understand the momentary lightness as Claire touched him. But he didn't want Claire inside his private, gnawing hell and removed her hand.

"You have his picture with you, don't you?" she asked.

"Always. In my wallet. It was taken just before we went on that trip."

"I'd like to see it."

Neil obliged, holding it up to the daylight for her to see better. As always, his thumb ran across the plastic protector, a caress he wished he could give to his son.

She searched his face, taking in his features. "He looks like you."

"I suppose."

They continued the walk in silence, but Neil brooded about his son. He hadn't kept Sammy safe.

But Sammy wasn't the first one Neil loved and had let down horribly.

Six

—

NEIL HAD NEVER SEEN A WOMAN WEARING GLOVES EAT pizza.

After driving all night, Tempest had arrived at nine o'clock in the morning. "Sorry I took so long, Claire Bear. The roads were hell," she said, around a mouthful of yesterday's pizza as they all sat in the living room.

She had the same dark red hair; the short, spiky cut emphasized her slanting green eyes. Tempest's were a little darker, her jaw a little more square, but the sisters definitely shared the markings of their mother. Shorter than Claire, Tempest's body was more curved and athletic-looking beneath the black leather bomber jacket, sweater, and jeans. Her personality seemed more open, more reflective of her emotions.

She moved restlessly, a physically active woman who had been driving too long. The ornate, Celtic-looking cuff-bracelet at her wrist wasn't off-the-rack, and neither was the intricate little handle tucked into the back of her black jeans. That handle was curved and led into a leather sheath.

Neil doubted that sheath served as a lipstick holder; Tempest had the look of a woman who knew how to take care of herself in the worst of situations.

That silver belt buckle at her waist looked like it could do some damage, too, if the center prong came out of that heavy circle.

The contrast of the two red-haired women struck him; they seemed so different and so alike. Neil listened intently to the sisters' subdued conversation. But there was something other than tender looks and soft touches passing between them, and for a caring older sister, Tempest seemed almost cool, very controlled for the situation. Tempest had been furious before. Where was the fury now, the need to push Claire into filing a report?

Instead, the sisters were chatting softly and eating pizza. *That just wasn't normal.*

Eunice had said that Tempest was a metal sculptor, and he'd seen some of her small unusual pieces in Claire's home. *Were Tempest's hands scarred so badly by her torch and hot metal that she didn't want them seen? Maybe nerve damage that required a heavier protective fabric?*

After hugging and whispering to Claire, and eating a slice of pizza, the next thing Tempest had done was to take off one glove and extend her hand to Neil. He'd expected the calluses, the strength of a sculptor's hand; but she held the handshake a fraction too long, looking up at his eyes. "I'm so sorry," she whispered sincerely. "But you've done everything you could."

"Your sister should have been seen by a doctor—"

"Oh, yes, *that*, of course."

That, of course, as if Claire's attack took second place to another disaster. . . .

The women's stares locked, and both nodded at the same time. Then Tempest's glove was back on and they were chatting about hummingbird feeders as if the attack hadn't happened.

For the first time, Claire visibly seemed to relax, soothed by her sister, her expression softening.

Neil knew that to catch the man who had attacked Claire, time was essential, and the sisters were wasting it. He began to state his case, "Don't you think that how to mix food for hummingbirds could wait? Claire needs to report—"

"We'll take care of this. Thanks, Neil," Tempest stated smoothly.

He settled back in his chair and crossed his arms. He wasn't going anywhere until he understood these women and that Claire was safe. "Okay, what's going on?"

Their raised eyebrows and expressions were too innocent. Both women stopped eating at the same time, then swallowed hard as Neil continued, "Okay, then I'll tell you what's *not* right here: First of all, Claire doesn't want to report this, and she could be saving other women from the same thing."

"You're not in this, Neil," Claire stated firmly.

"The hell I'm not. How are you women going to take care of this? You said you didn't know this guy. He's probably still out there and waiting for a repeat performance. You didn't want to call the delivery service and ask about who was driving that van. Just how are you going to find him?" Neil's patience was running out. He wasn't about to let the women step out into a possibly dangerous situation.

Tempest wiped her lips with a napkin. She scrubbed at a spot on her gloves. "We just will. And Claire is right. The guy probably stole the van from the shipping company's parking lot."

Neil dug in to challenge that point. "They'd know if they were missing a van."

Tempest's shielded look at him was bland. "Not always."

Claire winced slightly, and Tempest instantly looked worried. Then, as if forcing herself to do so, her expression cleared, and she smiled blandly. "It's so peaceful here."

Neil tried to adjust to the shifting conversation. It seemed to ping-pong around him; the sisters were playing one game, and he was standing still in the middle of it, without a paddle. And from Tempest's competent, worldly look, he was certain that if anyone would know how to steal a vehicle without raising problems, it would be her. "You two women are something. Then, how does Claire know which one of you will be calling before the telephone rings?"

Tempest stretched her arms up high and rotated her shoulders in the way of an active woman who has been traveling and confined too long. She stood to do a few slow, expert tai chi exercises. "Triplets are linked just like twins. There have been whole studies on this, Neil. It's not uncommon."

"I need to do that, stretch out a bit and focus," Claire stated as she rose to match her sister's precise movements.

"She has two sisters. Claire hasn't made a mistake yet in who's calling. Perfect name, every time, before the phone rings. I just can't wait until your mother calls. With daughters like you three, she must be real special."

Claire held the pose, knee lifted, arms extended, hands and fingers elegantly poised. "Join us? Tai chi is good exercise."

"No. We have a problem here. Are we going to work with it, or not?" The women's poised and weaving movements were making Neil nervous. He stood and walked to the doorway, then leaned a shoulder against it.

The women shared a guarded look, then Claire's tone was cool, dismissive. "I'm sure you have work to do, Neil. Tempest is here now, and—"

Despite what the women said, there was no way they could handle this. As yet, Claire hadn't shown any real anger at the man, and that seemed unusual. But maybe locked in a trauma, she wasn't thinking logically. He directed his question to Tempest, who had been infuriated when Claire had been hurt. "If you think that nifty little knife you're carrying is going to stop a maniac, like the one who just attacked Claire, you may need a little help."

Claire inhaled abruptly. "You're flexing your muscles, Neil. This isn't necessarily 'man's' work. But you're not giving up, are you?"

Tempest's assessment of Neil was quiet. "No, he's not. He's the protector type. He'll see this through."

"I know, dammit," Claire stated as if she were doomed. "He can be trusted in every way, but—"

Neil noted her wary glance at him, a woman on the run from a man who might desire her. Hell, what was he thinking? Of course, his mind ran along that line, but now wasn't the time.

"We can help him later, don't you think?" Tempest asked.

"I thought maybe so. We can try."

Neil leaned against the living-room doorframe, his arms crossed. "I'm standing right here. What's going on? Help me do what?"

The women stared at each other again, then, as if in agreement, nodded.

"Just watch. Pay close attention." Claire retrieved the torn blouse and handed it to Tempest. "The man touched the door, too, shoved it open. Neil is the only one who has been in here, except you, Mom, and Leona. You know Eunice's touch. Neil cleaned up—after."

"Good." Tempest moved swiftly to the door, opened it, and removed one glove. She ran her bare hand over the door. Then her body tensed as she stepped back. "Not good."

Her hands shook as she handled the delivery package, and Claire asked, "Rage, isn't it?"

"You're right. It's way past just plain mad or just wanting to hit back at someone because his world wasn't right. This guy wanted to do some serious damage."

Neil settled into the shadows of the house and watched. The two women were evidently hunting and working together, and they were excluding him.

After a moment, Claire seemed to consider him, then moved close. She looked up at him. "Yes," she stated quietly. "We know what to do."

He hadn't said anything . . . maybe his expression . . .

"No, it's in your mind. I'm picking up your thoughts, and you're interfering with what Tempest is doing. It's not something I usually do, get so many clear thoughts, but your field of energies seem extraordinarily strong to me. I think we could be connected somehow through feelings we had—have for Eunice. You're also anxious and frustrated, of course, and really angry with whoever attacked me."

" 'Picking up my thoughts? Field of energies?' Of course I'd like to get my hands on the guy. Listen, Claire, you just took some pretty hard knocks, maybe you—" Neil watched Tempest's hands move slowly over the package wrapping that Claire had saved. Tempest seemed to go inside herself; it was as if she were looking for something, trying to feel something not visually apparent. If the women changed their minds, and Claire filed a report, the man's fingerprints on the paper would be ruined by Tempest's. But they weren't filing a report, and focused on various parts of the paper, Tempest was definitely probing something.

And Neil was standing there, wearing goddamn pink

shorts under his jeans and feeling as if he were floating away from the closest spaceship. "*What* is your sister doing?"

"Things. She uses her ability sometimes, more than I. Tempest has always been more—impulsive. When she took off her glove and shook your hand, she was getting to know your touch, familiarizing herself with you so that she would know what you touched."

Claire seemed to shut down, sealing away more information about Tempest. Then she said slowly, "Tempest feels things through her hands. What I feel by being close to someone, emotions and sensations—heat, cold, fear, anger, heartache, loneliness, that sort of thing. Everyone has an energy field, and I can tap into it, understand what that person is experiencing, mind and body. I don't want to, but I just do. It's natural, it's innate. Tempest can feel the history of objects. Like Mom, Leona dreams, or has flashes about things that haven't happened yet. We don't want these things. They're just there—inside us."

"Just call us clairvoyants," Tempest said in a distracted tone.

"Holy—!"

"No, we're not witches, and we're not fruitcakes. You're quite safe."

Neil shook his head. He was too far from that intergalactic spaceship to pull his lifeline back to safety; it had just snapped. He was drifting out in the surreal. "Wait a minute. Get back to the part about you. You 'feel' thoughts and emotions?"

"I absorb them. They can become my own." Claire took her time, carefully framing her words as she explained. "I'm untrained and can't fully control what—what can come into me, into my senses when I'm disturbed. Some people call us 'intuitives.' It's hard to describe, possibly because we prefer not to discuss what we are. I run more to sensing emotions, feelings, aversions, sometimes memories . . . add in body reactions like pain and fatigue. I'm not a pure telepath, but sometimes I receive straight thoughts, almost like words—like I get sometimes from you. Most people tend to put definite labels on this, all one thing or another, but it doesn't work that way. We're a mix—hybrids, if you will. But we are *not* witches, or shape shifters, or vampires, if there is such a thing. There's a difference. No spells or eye of newt or bat tails for us, no spells or boiling cauldrons. What we can do—if we want, or don't want—is called psychic phenomena or powers . . . or sixth sense . . . sometimes clairvoyance, or just plain old extrasensory perception—ESP."

Neil decided he needed a good stiff drink. "Oh, brother. You really believe this stuff, huh?"

"They say DNA doesn't lie, and ours comes from ancient times. It's something that doesn't let you forget it altogether, and Mom is a combination of everything that we are individually. The only 'plus' I can think of is that none of us are mediums for the dead. I don't think I could bear that. And so far, no telekinesis has appeared in our family, the ability to move things or get them to respond. We only inherited clairvoyance, precognition, that sort of thing."

" 'Only . . . that sort of thing.' " Neil repeated dully. Maybe he wasn't hearing right—he had been up all night, after all. And it had been a very unusual few hours.

Claire studied Tempest, her counterpart, but in a different way. "I don't like being able to sense what others feel, and I've never tried to develop. Isolation makes life easier for me—this house and the way I live are designed to keep me calm. There was a time when I wasn't and I—I don't want to be like that again. Tempest hunts antiquities, and she uses her hands at times to discover their history—like the Viking *fibula* she was hunting in Canada."

Neil sat abruptly in the nearest chair. He tried to digest Claire's information while he rocked his body. Logic was quickly escaping him; he felt very delicate. " '*Fibula.*' Leg bones?"

"You look dazed. I knew you'd be the kind of person who couldn't easily accept psychic phenomena. You're very physical . . . you think in terms of what you can see and touch. . . . '*Fibula*' is another term of fastening. But today's term would be a safety pin or perhaps a brooch."

Claire walked to the shelf where the Celtic-designed headband and brooch lay. She removed the pin and slid it through the brooch. "The fibula acts like a pin, holding a cloak, usually at the left shoulder. See? In and out. Through the material and out again, creating a fastening. The Greeks and Romans used them, the pin fastens through the metal to make a pin. There are other styles, but our family has a thing for the Viking style . . . the invasions, I suppose."

"I suppose," Neil repeated, and wondered why he had agreed. He didn't know a damned thing about the Vikings but what he'd picked up in high-school history class.

Claire replaced the *fibula*-brooch and smiled briefly at her sister. "Unlike Leona and I, Tempest isn't above using her ability to get what she wants."

"An empath . . . psychics . . . clairvoyance . . . ESP. I've heard about that New Age stuff, but . . ." Neil thought back to warnings about thinking good thoughts around Claire. He remembered how he felt when he'd brooded about his son, and she'd touched his face, the momentary lightening of his guilt. "Holy—"

"You've already said that." Then Claire turned to Tempest, who had taken off her other glove and was holding the torn blouse, her eyes closed. She seemed focused within herself, her voice quiet, methodical. "He works with computers. And he hates you. That's all I'm getting. The rage and need to hurt you is blocking out everything else."

Tempest shivered as if cold, but beads of sweat had appeared on her forehead. Claire hurriedly took the blouse from her. "That's enough. You don't need to know what happened. Put on your gloves."

"Where was the last place you saw a man working a computer?" Tempest asked suddenly.

"There was Neil. He used mine last night. And before that only one other." Claire turned to Neil and spoke firmly. "Your need to know everything, your curiosity, is interfering—blocking me. You're feeling delicate and upset and not grounded. I can't deal with you now. Back off and move away. We'll talk with you later."

Her order grated, but Neil complied. Hell, why not give these two free range and see what they came up with? "Fine. Go right ahead, ladies, with whatever you're doing. Tempest has been driving all night, looks as if she's going to keel over any minute, and she just could be a little off-center right now. And you're just a few hours past being mauled. But oh, well. Go for it."

"Cynic." To Tempest, Claire said, "Last fall, I went to the Bliss and New Life commune to pick up some marigold seeds. It's about twenty miles north of here. A clerk seemed pleasant, and he had to look up their inventory on the computer. I went in the back room with him . . . we talked. He had been in prison, and he was rebuilding his life, honestly trying, and so frightened he'd fail. He was just one of those people who found himself with the wrong people, doing the wrong things . . . someone easily led."

She closed her eyes as if looking into herself. "Yes,

that was him last night—but he was different. I couldn't get anything from him—nothing but the need to hurt me. Everything was focused on me."

Neil shook his head. "Just like that? You remember this guy?"

"With Tempest's help. She felt him."

"'Felt him,'" Neil repeated hollowly as he struggled to find safe, logical ground. Yesterday morning, he thought he knew Claire Brown. Today, he wasn't certain he'd met her at all. And the only "plus" in this surreal scenario was that these sisters said they weren't mediums for the dead and didn't move objects or bend spoons.

"Tell him the rest," Tempest stated with a grin.

Claire's eyebrows rose. "I'd really prefer not to."

"Oh, come on, let me have it," Neil stated. "Tell me whatever it is. It couldn't be any more weird than what you've just said."

Claire turned to him and smiled just that bit, as if she knew something that would shock him. The hair on the back of his neck lifted. "We're connected—linked, Olafson. I don't like it, but we are. It goes like this: In addition to both of us mourning Eunice, we're connected in another way. We were somewhat connected before last night, and maybe my irritation with you opened me up too much. But then, you found me at my most vulnerable time. I couldn't block you totally, and now, I'm really sensitive to everything you feel and think."

Neil stared at her, his mind churning, remembering her appearance in the shop, how she'd seemed to know what he was thinking. "I don't believe in this stuff."

"It doesn't matter if you do, or if you don't."

Neil moved through the times Claire had seemed to pick up on his thoughts: *You want to make love to me,* Claire had said earlier, and she'd been right. There had been other times, like when they were walking and she'd noted his need for Sammy—he hadn't said anything, but Claire had reached right inside him somehow and softened that ache for his son. . . .

Neil scratched his head and stared at the women. He came up with something that was based on logic, and what he understood. "I need to eat a solid meal. Maybe steak and potatoes, and a lot of pie. Berry, maybe. Apple would be okay."

"No time for comfort food. Where is the commune?" Tempest glanced at her big complicated wristwatch, the silver band woven into a Celtic design. "It's only eleven o'clock now. We can make twenty miles on open road in a few minutes. But the only thing I could find to rent—after the snowplow and the gravel truck gave out—was a compact car. It's almost shot—didn't like the rough roads under construction, and it's not going to like potholes. If the road to the commune is bad, we'll need something heavier."

Neil stared at Tempest. "You drove a snowplow?"

"Big sucker. Had to get here, didn't I? I wasn't letting a little blizzard stop me."

"Tempest's specific ability to get insights into what happened to an object, or who owned it, is called psychometry," Claire stated absently as she drew on her cape. Neil stood to test his ability to fasten her cape with the silver *fibula*-brooch-thingie; he inserted the pin through the material and back out again. Tempest's work might look delicate, but it was weighty and strong.

He studied Claire; after another man's attack, she didn't seem to mind his touch. The bruises on her throat were fading fast—unusually fast. But then, she'd taken a shower and a very long bath and probably had used some miracle women's reparative remedy. Words like "empath" . . . "ESP" . . . "psychic phenomena" tumbled through his mind.

Was she really all right or running on temporary energy? Was Tempest just humoring Claire, or did she really believe in all this?

Claire held very still and scanned his face. For some unknown reason, tiny little prickles ran over Neil's skin as she spoke: "Don't worry about me. I'm fine. Tempest just connected the blouse to the hand on the door. The road to the commune was dry last fall and with the snow and rain, the dirt road could be bad. She's right about needing a sturdier vehicle. We'll need to borrow your four-wheel pickup—please."

Outer-world stuff was one thing, but his pickup something else. He'd spent hours on Jessica, repairing the brake pads and the clutch. She was a finely tuned instrument, and she responded to his touch perfectly. In some ways, Jessica was better than a woman, and she definitely did not talk back. Jessica was logical and real. All her parts matched perfectly. But these women were a mismatch to any others he'd known. "No. She's not driving my truck. Not a woman who ran through a snowplow and a gravel truck."

"I know. You love it. It's your toy. You love to spend time under the hood. But you really should fix that muffler. It's too loud."

Claire's assessment of Neil's beloved pickup caused his hackles to rise. But one look at Claire and Tempest, and Neil knew they were going, with or without him. He struggled to find logic in pieces that didn't fit. "My pickup is *not* a toy. It's a finely tuned machine. You're telling me that Tempest took off her glove to shake my hand—and *she read me, like you say you can do?*"

"No, Tempest can only 'read' objects. She just wanted the contact with you, because—"

"Why, dammit? Because she needed to compare my touch against your attacker's? Because she wasn't certain that I might be holding out something I knew about it?"

Claire looked away and folded her arms, but Tempest answered quietly, "Years ago, I misjudged a man badly. To protect myself from that happening again, I've practiced just enough to detect certain vibes from touching human hands—when I have to. By touching yours, I could not only identify your touch, but tell that you could be trusted. You will protect what is yours, and right now, you consider Claire to be yours. You are her protector, and for that my family is grateful."

Neil shook his head. Tempest's label of him sounded noble—and embarrassing. "Anyone would have done the same. I'd really like to get my hands on that guy."

"He's embarrassed," Claire stated quietly.

Her sister agreed. "That's so—cute. And he is adorable."

He was a man, dammit, and the women were making him feel like a high-school kid. "Yeah, that's me. Adorable and cute."

The women studied Neil, and, to his horror, his face felt hot. He had to establish some sort of control. "You're not going without me, and that's that."

Tempest shook her head. "How they struggle. . . . He's adopted you, Claire, and he doesn't want anything more happening to you."

"I've got news for you, Tempest. He thinks we both need him to see that we don't completely fly off whatever sanity ledges we now have."

"Let's just get the hell on the road," Neil muttered. "There's no way I'm going to pass up seeing if all this malarkey is possible."

In his truck, Neil glanced at the profiles of both women. Claire sat next to him on the bench seat, Tempest near the passenger door. Alike and separate, they were focused on a hunt without real forensic evidence. No lab equipment had set them on this journey, but they were as certain of it as they were of him—cute, adorable Neil Olafson. All he needed were pink slippers and that feather boa around his neck.

And what the hell was that about Claire linking to him? Reading his feelings and his thoughts? Now that was freaky . . . a little terrifying. A man's thoughts and emotions should be private, and here was a woman—stepping right into the middle of them. What was he, a goddamn living diary?

"You shouldn't be frightened, Neil. All of this is difficult to understand, and it's a matter of experience and seeing what works best. I might not be so sensitive to you if the distance were extended. Unfortunately, since you had to drive and couldn't let us just borrow Jessica . . ."

Neil stared at her. He'd never told Jessica's name to anyone. It was a very private romance.

"Okay, I'm sorry I intruded into your 'romance.'"

Neil looked out at the rolling fields of winter wheat and settled in to brood. Planted early last September, the farm's two thousand acres of green shoots would be gold and ready to harvest in August. By that time, he might understand what he had just experienced. He was pretty certain that either the women were playing him somehow—or he was just plain going nuts.

As he shifted gears, Claire's breast had just brushed his arm, and the softness alerted his body. He looked down at her thigh beside his. Sex was something that could bring him back to reality but fast. Pale and long, she'd be—

Beneath those huge sunglasses, Claire's cheeks suddenly flushed. "Can you please think about something else?"

"I was just wondering how your bruises are doing."

Claire's "Uh-huh" was flat and disbelieving.

Tempest's tone was dryly amused as she studied a stand of cottonwood trees where a large flock of starlings had settled. "Give the guy a break. He's probably never had this experience before. Men revert to what they understand. Or *think* they know."

Neil shifted down, preparing for a sharp curve in the road. "You've got some opinion of men, don't you? I'm still wading through this—out-of-body experience."

Claire sighed deeply and spoke in an aside to Tempest. "He's feeling fragile."

Tempest grinned. "Men. Dontcha love 'em. Give them a mountain to conquer, an alligator to wrestle, a spittoon to hit, something personal to scratch, competition for the loudest burp—and they're okay. Give them something a little mental and emotional and sensitive, and they turn into real sissies."

"I resent that." The women's superior attitude grated on Neil. "Okay, refresh me. Exactly why didn't you want Leona on board? Why didn't you want her 'disturbed'?"

"She doesn't want the dreams, daytime or at night. She's trying so hard to be normal and not like Mom. If Leona gets stirred up, she'll be open and never be able to close that door. Like me, she doesn't want this thing. We've been trying to push it away, to deny it, since we were children and fully realized what we really were."

Neil glanced at a passing farm truck, laden with bags of feed, and tried to feel his way through this reality. It was eleven-thirty in the morning on the second of May and two sisters who claimed to be psychics were sitting next to him. Add the third triplet and their mother, and he wasn't certain of anything. "So you're protecting Leona, then, by not involving her? From herself?"

Tempest glanced at Neil. "Leona and Mom can't be around Claire now. They're too upset, and she's just developing. Trauma does that, flips over on psychics, changes them unpredictably. If Claire is linked—connected—to you so strongly, that means she's increasing her powers, and she's going to have to learn to protect herself better. Right now, the way she is, shaken by that bastard, she'd be even more vulnerable. Mom is very strong, and she could disturb Claire too much, overwhelm her with protective motherly instincts."

"So that's what you meant by 'disturb.' They're actually protecting Claire from themselves."

"Horrible, isn't it? That Mom and Leona can't be here for Claire now? That just leaves you and me, chum." Then Tempest's expression was grim, and she leaned slightly forward, a coldly determined, hard-eyed hunter locked onto her goal.

Beside her, Claire was silent, staring stonily at the road leading up to the commune. "That's it. Turn in."

Neil was no mind reader, but he understood Claire's fear at seeing the man who had harmed her. He took her hand and placed it on his thigh with his. She wasn't going anywhere without him—The Protector. He smiled briefly at the image. It wasn't the usual good-guy label women applied to him. "The Protector" smacked of a centurion, complete with sword and shield, standing at the ready. The label was a lot better than cute and adorable.

Hell, he could be wearing one of those *fibula*-brooch things himself. Oh, well. Might as well enjoy this trip to the other side of the real world, he decided cheerfully. Neil eased his arm a little closer to Claire's. Just an inch or so over was that soft breast. On an adventure like this, soaring down some muddy Montana road to find a supposed villain, The Protector should be able to have a soft breast up against him, or maybe two.

Claire quickly turned to frown at him. "Don't even think about it."

"I was just thinking how crowded it was in here." He

linked his fingers with Claire's softer ones. They felt good, feminine, strong . . . like her body would feel.

Claire turned to frown at him again and retrieved her hand, sliding it back under that voluminous cape. "Mary Jane? Your girlfriend? I suppose you're thinking about her just now?"

Neil smiled blandly. Mary Jane and he were just friends now, not lovers. "Nice day for this. I haven't played cops and robbers for years."

The Bliss and New Life commune lay amid wheat-fields. A pink angular building stood in the center of gardens; people in blue robes were evidently planting crops. Claire was right, the unpaved road was bad, and a delivery van was stuck up to its hubcaps in mud. "That's the van," she said.

Neil tensed; this day-lark was becoming weirder than ever. If Claire was right, these two women might just find her attacker. Hey. No way.

"Oh, yes, we will," Claire stated quietly.

Inside the Welcome Guests house, the visitor "greeter" seemed confused. He slid his hands inside the long, pink gown's sleeves and the beads around his throat rattled slightly as if he had trembled. "I'm afraid it's not possible to see John. He's—"

Beside Neil, Claire shivered. "John," she whispered. "That was his name. John."

"Do you have a picture of him?" Neil asked curtly because as just a plain, nonpsychic guy, he preferred Claire's visual identification.

The greeter handed a framed picture to Neil, who held it for Claire's viewing. She nodded and shivered as the greeter continued, "John was his new 'given' name. He was trying so hard to start over, to—"

Neil tossed the picture aside and locked onto one word, repeating it, " 'Was?' "

Behind the thick lenses, the man's watery blue eyes

flickered warily as Claire moved close to study him. "He was doing so well, then he went into town and stole a delivery van. You may have passed it. He drove back last night, quite agitated, but we didn't think that— Our telephone lines had been cut somehow, and we didn't have communication to report it. We are all trying to avoid the excesses of the outer world, the stress and—"

"And John shot himself. He came back here last night and committed suicide," Claire whispered, her face pale as she moved away from the man.

Neil shifted restlessly. There was no way that Claire could have known exactly what had happened to John—unless this whole surreal chunk of life was actually true, and that psychic ability really existed. He stared out the window to the acres of wheatland, anchoring himself to the real world.

The greeter stared warily at Claire. "Why, yes, that's exactly what happened. I was just getting ready to say that. We don't understand it. The council has all agreed that John had refocused and was trying to recover. And then, he destroyed the thing he seemed to love the most. He'd spent hours with that computer—searching for ways to help us. We survive by donations, you know. Would you like to look around and see the good work we do?"

"The computer room. We'd like to see that, please," Tempest stated tightly, her expression determined.

Claire took a softer approach. "I came to see John last year, and he was such a lovely man. We talked about our flower gardens, the right mulch and fertilizer. I'd really like to have a moment in the same room where he passed—to say good-bye to him."

Neil took out his billfold and tossed some bills into the collection basket. "We're in a hurry. Could you just show the lady what she wants?"

"But it's such a mess. Last night, John must have been demented, tearing things apart, breaking the screen—so much violence—we'll have to replace everything. All of our records are gone. He's destroyed them. We found him early this morning when a deputy stopped to pick up seeds. After that, the coroner arrived and investigated the room and took John's body away. With his latest history of tantrums and problems, they didn't seem to question his actions, or his death. Would you like to say good-bye to him? We could send you notification of his celebration of life."

Neil inhaled abruptly, impatiently. "No."

The greeter looked at the collection plate, then glanced at Claire's brooch, which was obviously hand-crafted and expensive. He looked at Tempest's leather jacket and boots, the big arty belt buckle. "Ah, did I say that we survived by donations?"

"You did. Look, buddy, just show the ladies what they want." Neil had had a bad day and wasn't in a mood to let some pink-robe-and-bead-wearing oddball, who evidently had lost a little of his brain cells, stop him from helping Claire and Tempest.

Neil wasn't too certain about the women now. Half of Neil believed this whole thing was a wild-goose chase. The other half said that the women were hunters on track, and it was best to let them do their jobs.

Inside the ransacked room, Claire turned to the greeter. "Thank you. Would it be possible for us to be alone now, to say a private good-bye to his spirit, here in this place that John loved so much?"

When the door closed behind the man, Tempest took off her gloves. She placed her hands on the computer's keyboard and her body bent suddenly as if taking a blow. Claire's hand opened on Tempest's back, as if to steady her sister.

Neil understood the comfort Claire could give, and

that on some silent level, the women communicated. Linked since birth was a definite possibility; linked triplets seemed logical. He stood with his back against the door, preventing an interruption; he crossed his arms and let the sisters do their work.

Amid the tumbled, broken mess of records and computer ware, Tempest shook her head as if struggling with an unseen drama. "I'm okay. He hated you so much, Claire. He thought you deserved to die. But first you needed to be hurt. I can't get anything past that."

She took a deep breath as if to steady herself, then touched the broken monitor carefully. She ran both hands over it, then looked at Claire. "It's a point of contact. Something really bad got to this guy, through his computer. It owned him. It wanted you dead. And now it's gone, wiping out its tracks."

The two women looked at each other, then Claire whispered softly, "He was so afraid he'd fail."

"Fear can make people vulnerable."

"Yes, I know what fear can do."

Tempest took Claire's hand. "Of course you'd know."

Neil didn't know if he'd accept what he'd just heard about "something" owning John, but he worried about Claire, her bruises still slightly visible. She seemed to be so fragile, and this savaged room wasn't helping. "Are you finished? Let's get out of here, shall we, ladies?" Neil asked quietly.

On her way out of the computer room, Claire glanced at Neil. "After this, Olafson, try to keep the male posturing and intimidation level down. You scared that poor man, the greeter."

"He was holding us up. And I need food . . . it's way past noon." His arm looped around Claire's waist as they walked, and the set of his jaw matched his dark, glowering mood. When she moved away from him, he tugged her back.

Claire studied Neil's grim expression and sifted through his feelings. He only wanted her to be safe and close to him. And he was angry—he was thinking about how the attacker got off too easy. He was thinking he didn't know what to do with the two women, how to handle them—they couldn't just go tromping off on Montana's countryside to catch some mental-case jerk.

When she turned to frown at him, Neil frowned back, then lifted her bodily and put her into the pickup as if she were a child; he used his body to nudge her to the middle of the bench seat. He lowered his jaw into the collar of his flannel-lined denim coat and brooded about the women. The triplets were odd, and he must be a little weird, too, because he was starting to believe them. He'd heard about this stuff before and had dismissed it. *Still, they'd run down this John-guy, and Claire had identified him. The pieces only fit one way, and that's the way the women explained. Maybe . . .*

On the way back to her home, Claire spoke to Tempest. "He's in a snit."

"I noticed, but men are like that. He wanted to handle this, take the guy out, a little repayment for what he did to you, and now his thunder is stolen. He'll deal with it, after he eats. Feed him and keep him pacified."

Neil dismissed the women's discussion of him; he had better things to sort out. "I've been thinking. Let's go back to reality and hard facts. That stuff about the computer getting to the man is possible. Chat rooms, e-mail, all are ways for a stronger personality to get to a weaker one, seducing them. I get that. There are on-line predators, slick ones. If someone wanted this John-guy to attack you, they might have worked him into thinking you were some kind of home breaker, destroying families, whatever. The question is: Who would want this freak to jump you? Who might have a grudge against you?"

He stroked Jessica's steering wheel; she was dependable and understandable. "The next question is, just how did you two *really* figure out where to go? And that brings us back to: You must have known the guy. Okay, maybe you'd forgotten him, but then something clicked, and you remembered. And that might take us back to your ex-husband and those scars on your wrists."

In an effort to control her temper, Claire tried to breathe in the good air, the positive, and exhale her negative feelings. The technique didn't calm her; neither did counting to twenty. Neil was determined to put everything Tempest had said into a here-now reality logic he could understand, and Claire was getting irritated with him. With little effort, she could work up into anger, an emotion she hadn't experienced within herself until Neil. It had nothing to do with John's residual anger, which flickered now and then within her. And Tempest knew it, hiding her impish grin. She probably couldn't wait to tell Leona that Claire, the quiet, serene, controlled sister was getting angry, her switches tripped by her next-door neighbor.

Claire turned to Neil and caught the flexing of his hands on the steering wheel, the big knuckles turning white before releasing, then tightening again. He could hold on to that steering wheel until forever, using it as an anchor because he didn't want to believe the truth that psychic powers existed. "The only reason we allowed you to come with us is that you wouldn't let us borrow your pickup—Jessica—without your driving. We did not bring you along for muscle, or to challenge us."

"I lied about Tempest driving my truck. I'd say she could handle anything she wanted. I was afraid you might want to drive my pickup. You could have torn my stick shift into hell, and I just put in a new clutch."

"That isn't true, and you know it. You wanted to come along for the experience of chasing over Montana with two—"

Claire stared pointedly at him, and continued. "Which word should I use? 'Psychics' or 'nutcases'? You actually wanted to prove to us that we couldn't possibly dig up anything that wasn't physical evidence. You wanted to see us fail. You think we need 'keepers,' isn't that right?"

She'd caught him, and silence was his best protection.

"Okay," she continued jauntily. "Sometimes, when you're proven wrong, silence is the best protection. And I . . . have . . . a Volkswagen Super Beetle, Olafson, a '74. I can drive anything you can, even Jessica." Claire sniffed, glared at him, and the rest of the trip was silent.

But Neil was busy filtering through the evident proof of the sisters' abilities: *They hadn't missed any clues yet, and "John" had been "owned." Owned by what? By whom? One sister could tell the history of an object, one could see into the future, and their mother was reported to be the head guru. And Claire was catching his thoughts pretty regularly, and her calls were very accurate and an "invasion of privacy."* Neil hadn't realized he'd muttered anything until both women stared at him.

Now, all that—plus the fact that Claire admitted being "linked" and "connected" to him—could make a man really uneasy.

"How is Mother, Leona?" Tempest had been the first to pick up Claire's telephone. As usual, it hadn't actually rung. Neil removed his jacket, tossed it to the couch, and sprawled there to contemplate the past few hours; he struggled with logic and the reality that the women had actually found Claire's attacker.

His stomach growled, and he said, "It's after lunch. I'm hungry."

The women weren't listening. The fact that the sisters could pick up the telephone before it rang and correctly identify the caller no longer astounded Neil. He tried to center on bits of reality, rather than on Tempest's claim to psychometry-handling stuff, Claire as an empath-feeler, and Leona, who could see into the future. Psychic phenomena weren't Neil's usual experience. He wondered when spoons were going to start bending and if the women could levitate him. He placed his work boots firmly on the floor and stared at them. That was where he wanted them to be, not inches above the floor.

When Claire removed her cape, Neil's mind swung to other things, like the twin nubs beneath her blue sweater and the way she filled out her jeans. . . .

Claire hung up her cape, which presented him with a fine view of her curved bottom in its tight jeans. She turned to glare at him, and Neil pushed an innocent bland smile onto his face, just in case she could really "read" him.

Tempest grinned as she spoke on the telephone to Leona. "Mom isn't happy, is she? And you argued? So what else is new?"

Tempest handed the phone to Claire. "She wants to talk with you."

Neil watched Claire move away from her sister, into her workroom. She shut the door with a firm snap.

"I'll just go home and recover." Then Neil called to the woman holed up in her workroom, "I'm leaving, honey. Don't you want to see me off?"

He shrugged at Claire's stony silence, then met Tempest's grin. "You know how to get to her, don't you?" she asked. "You know how to take her mind off what happened. Thanks, guy."

"If you decide to leave, I'll check back in, keep an eye on her, whatever."

Tempest yawned and stretched, the all-night travel weighing on her. "We know. Figures."

Neil didn't understand Tempest's statement, or maybe he didn't want to. Unnerved by the discovery of what the women could do, Neil needed the distance between himself and them. And he needed food, something in his stomach that was real and could anchor him. He retreated to his home, ate a couple of sandwiches and a package of cookies, checked the business messages, and went to work on his new camper.

Sheet metal, rivets, power saws, and welding were a lot safer than Claire's ability to sense his feelings.

One of which was the strong urge to protect her. Neil flipped that thought: He wanted to protect *and* make love to her.

Maybe this link-connection thing was working both ways.

Neil rubbed his forehead, where a nagging doubt remained. Psychics were the only avenue they had not used to find Sammy—and maybe that was a mistake.

Seven

GREER STARED OUT AT THE GRAY SWELLS OF THE PACIFIC
Ocean and smoothed the wolf's-head brooch that
matched her daughters'. Only a good-luck piece, styled
by Tempest to match the original Viking brooch, it
served to connect her family, a reminder of an ancient
heritage, passed down by their Celtic seer ancestor,
Aisling.

It was a good name, one Greer had taken for herself,
for protection and strength, after her husband, Daniel
Bartel, had died. Claire would have named her daughter Aisling.

And Greer suspected that this recent attack was not
the first time.

"It's only a suspicion, but I'm certain I sensed utter
evil and control when I spoke to Claire's doctor and
nurse, just after she lost her baby. Chock-full with lust
and greed and every evil emotion, I'm certain that exposure to them could have caused Claire to overload—
especially after walking into that holdup. No telling
what had happened to her in the hospital before we got
there. Both that doctor and the nurse had been lately
addicted to computers, just like Claire's attacker."

Greer shivered and drew her shawl around her. The

last case had been exhausting, and, restless with the nagging aftermath, she needed the night to soothe her, and she needed to think clearly, to fit the uneasy pieces together.

She remembered her research on the doctor and the nurse. Until the incident with Claire, they'd been friends, both gentle, caring people. The doctor was recently divorced and the nurse's husband had just died, and they would have been vulnerable . . . and then they'd changed. *Why? Was Claire safe now?*

"Of course she's safe. She's been practicing blocking, and from what Tempest said, Neil Olafson isn't going to let anything happen to Claire. I can't tell her what I don't know. I need more, but something caused three gentle people to change violently. Unfortunately, Claire was in their line of fire. Was that an accident, or—?"

The wind lifted Greer's hair and took it away from her face; but she held tight to the brooch and wished for the original, the one she saw in her dreams, the one the Viking conquerer wore centuries before.

The salt-scented wind whipped through the pines around Greer, the trees warped and eerie from the force. Shadows slipped around Greer, and she felt them, brought them into her, tried to see past them.

Was there really a connection between the doctor and nurse and Claire's attacker? Or were Greer's cases causing a suspicious reaction in a protective mother? "I can't let any of them know that I suspect there is a link between both traumas to Claire. Not without proof."

Greer didn't trust the absolute stillness, as if it waited, . . . For what?

"Blood of my blood, Aisling-the-seer, the wise, tell me what I need to know, tell me why I dream of a Viking warrior, why I see the brooch, why I need to hold it so I'll know the answers I seek," Greer whispered softly as the wind played in her hair, like the caress of a lover's hand.

She closed her eyes and saw Claire, her long red hair flowing around her, her skin pale, her eyes as green as Greer's own. "She's found a man of Viking blood, and if they are a match, drawn to each other, she'll become even stronger. I have to believe in that."

"Neil?" Claire knocked on the small metal camper inside Neil's shop. It had taken her until the morning of the fourth day since she'd last seen him to work up enough courage to approach him; the time had come to break the connection between them. She'd make it clear that they could be neighbors but that she did not intend to foster any growing closeness.

Neil was inside the teardrop-shaped camper, apparently lying down with one leg extended out of the doorway; he wouldn't be able to escape her chat with him.

Never one to stay long, and assured that Claire was feeling much better, Tempest had left the morning after her arrival. She had come to say good-bye to Neil; Claire expected that they'd probably exchanged telephone numbers, keeping each other apprised of Claire's safety. In short, Neil would probably be acting as the Aisling family's watchdog—for a time, until Claire was able to assure everyone that she was just fine. She intended to do that quickly. Whatever had happened to John was probably a fluke and wouldn't happen again. However, from now on, Claire had promised to be very cautious.

In the airy shop, the camper was only four feet high and maybe ten feet long. From the side, the metal camper was shaped like a teardrop, taller at one end where it attached to a vehicle, then rounded and slanted downward over the rear axle. There, a tailgating-type back door had been popped upward, opening up to a rear kitchenette—a small stove and sink and unfinished cabinets.

In the three days since she'd seen him, the only contact Claire had with Neil was regularly to e-mail him that she was sleeping and recovering and didn't wish to be disturbed. He hadn't answered, but she sensed that he watched over her home. Since he hadn't pressed visiting her in person, Claire supposed the time had come for a final closure; they were neighbors, she wasn't happy about the workshop, but she could manage. To date, he'd respected her privacy, in fact he had for five years. She would approach him with confidence and try not to remember that he'd seen her only in her bra and panties—and that he knew her whole family were psychics.

Since Neil seemed unaware of her presence, Claire took time to look around the shop. Along the shop's walls, boxes of supplies were stacked neatly on the spacious racks, a small corner of the area obviously serving as a rough office, blueprints tacked to the wall. Benches that looked as if they'd come from a school bus were piled with newspapers. A stack of small new tires that matched the ones on the camper stood nearby. A ladder led up to a big loft, where lengths of pipe and boxes had been stored.

Claire would prefer that her family not become too friendly with Neil. Polite distance was difficult to maintain in a family mix. She'd thank Neil with the gingerbread she'd just baked; it would serve to clarify that she needed her privacy and gently remind him of the promise he'd made to be quieter.

The rhythmic tap of Neil's boot on the stool beside the camper indicated he might be listening to music.

Claire looked inside the small sliding window to see him lying on his back, working on the interior's imitation-wood ceiling. Above him, a bookcase-type shelf held an assortment of tools and a small electric lamp. He wore earphones that ran down to the pocket of his flannel shirt; a small toolbox sat open beside him.

She traced the red suspenders down to his jeans, then back up to Neil's opened shirt collar, and glimpsed that dark hair curling on his chest. She remembered his tanned body sprawled in her workroom, the way the light hit his broad shoulders, the muscular bulky shape of his slightly hairy legs.

And then, despite hours of preparing herself for this meeting, she remembered that in caring for her, Neil Olafson had seen her almost naked.

Bracing herself for the inevitable encounter she had decided to precipitate, Claire rapped on the side of the camper again. Neil's boot kept tapping the stool, but he glanced at her, then returned to working his electric screwdriver.

The camper was small, and Neil was big, almost filling it. He was close enough that Claire could reach inside the camper and remove his earphones. He tossed them aside and scowled at her; then he returned to working, the screwdriver buzzing loudly.

Determined to have this conversation, Claire lifted his boot by the laces and placed it inside the camper. The screwdriver sound paused, but Neil kept working. Bracing herself, Claire eased inside the camper and sat with her legs crossed, facing him. "I know you can hear me."

"That better be food I smell, Brown."

She held out the plate of freshly baked gingerbread, perfectly acceptable bait for the conversation she wanted to have with Neil. The man was still banging away in his shop, still packing his backyard with friends and an overnight camper that had left just this morning.

Claire braced herself for her mission: a proper thank-you, and closure, tossing in some nice things about getting along. Tempest's admonishment, an older sister chastising a younger one, still echoed in Claire's mind: "You really didn't thank him properly? Just an offhand 'appreciation'? After all he did, taking care of you? You should really do something nice for him, with the thank-you to go along with it, Claire Bear."

Her senses had tuned to him during that ride, probably flipped on to a full current connection because he was the first one to find her—at her most vulnerable. All she had to do was to find a way to disconnect from Neil Olafson.

Claire took her time studying the interior of the camper. Still lying on his back, Neil filled most of it; he reached for the plate and set it on his chest. As he lifted one of the gingerbread squares, a crumb fell into the patch of hair on his chest.

He smelled like soap and lime and man; those smoky eyes were slitted, considering her, and Claire's senses went a little off-kilter.

She realized that Neil was concentrating very hard—on his camper plans. He was looking at her and thinking about specifications for his campers!

Since emotions and sensations endangered her clear thinking and her purpose for sitting in this camper, too close to Neil, Claire focused on her mission. "I suppose by now, you've had time to adjust—to recover."

"From what?" He frowned slightly and took another square of gingerbread, the little boy in him enjoying the taste and the memory of Eunice.

"Our recent—encounter. The details of which, I hope you'll keep to yourself." She hadn't meant to sound abrupt, but the one time she wanted to get inside his senses, all she was absorbing was the smell of gingerbread and camper plans. Suddenly hungry for gingerbread, Claire took a piece.

Neil looked steadily at her, his expression impassive. "Boy, this is good. I haven't had anything like this since—"

"It's Eunice's recipe," Claire stated patiently when she finished the gingerbread. She dusted her hands, brushed a crumb from her chest, and decided to continue her mission. Then, it was true: The way to reach men was through their stomachs. Everything was going well on her plotted course to make Neil see that even though he'd invaded her sanctuary, she was ready to work with him on a solution. After all, it was only logical that he would want to live in Eunice's house and that he needed to be near his business—perhaps it might not be as bad as she first experienced, now that the shop was built. Somehow, she'd manage to slip a thank-you in there—because she really did appreciate his help and care.

However, there were other disturbing qualities about Neil she did not appreciate. He was tenacious, and she wanted to make certain that his protective "adoption" of her was at an end.

"How are you feeling? Still bruised and sore?"

He was too intent upon her, and she didn't have time to shield herself, her uncertainty of him setting her off course. "I'm fine. I came over to—"

"Yes, your sister came over to ask me to keep an eye on you. You don't want that, do you?"

The statement jarred her, and Claire blinked.

Neil grinned and licked a crumb from his top lip; he glanced at her throat where the bruises had faded. "You don't have to be psychic to know that an older sister— by three minutes—would want her sister to have someone check on her. She didn't stay very long, did she?"

"No . . . oh . . . uh-huh . . . I guess that would make sense, that my family would want you to . . . I . . . I'm fine." Her mission waylaid by him, Claire struggled for balance and focus. Neil apparently enjoyed watching her struggle.

He reached for a third piece and studied it before taking a bite. "Can't wait to meet the rest of the family."

Claire's overwhelming desire for more gingerbread caused her to reach for another piece; she noted that Neil was studying her carefully, those gray eyes shielded. She licked a crumb from her lips. "What?"

"You think we have a connection, do you?"

As she enjoyed the spicy dessert, Claire was surprised by Neil's sudden question. "Yes. But only if we're close. A few feet away, and—"

"Nothing? And what happens when we're this close?" He raised slightly, leaned closer and stroked his fingertip down her cheek, then under her chin to lift it. "Tell me about how I 'mess up your reads.'"

He came closer until his face was inches from hers, and Claire's senses leaped into sensuality. Her body warmed, and she *wanted* to kiss him. Instead, her hand lifted to his hair to toy with the crisp texture, tracing those lighter sun streaks. Her body relaxed slightly, shifting from sensuality, and Claire momentarily drifted into security and peace.

Her comfort zone dissolved when Neil's eyes narrowed, and he lifted to brush his lips across hers. He leaned back and watched her reaction. Thoughts tumbled through Claire. She was definitely an oddity, and Neil could just be experimenting. . . . She vaguely remembered that she had a mission today. She longed to have that wide-open, exhausting, summit-building sex. But the warning that as a psychic, she could be feeding off *his* desire for her, building it into her own hunger, startled her.

"Boy, you're easy to read," Neil murmured as he drew her head down for a long, slow, deep, sweet kiss that stirred her way down deep inside.

She tried to shake free of the sensual tug; but with Neil near her, she realized that lovemaking had been too long ago. The surprising heat stirring inside her had awakened the need for return performances.

Neil toyed with her hair, taking his time as if the braid fascinated him. Then he was loosening it, spreading her hair through his fingers, studying it against his skin as leisurely as if he had all the time in the world. "A woman shouldn't ever be hurt like that. I'm really sorry, Claire. Are you going to be all right?"

Neil's statement was too sincere to be discarded, his expression sympathetic. The moment was too jarring, too intimate, too terrifying. Claire eased away and sat, with her arms folded around her knees. She looked around the camper interior to avoid looking at Neil's body, the heavy rise of desire against his jeans. "I'm just fine."

"Sure. Just days after an attack like that, you're just fine. You're used to hiding yourself and your feelings, aren't you? But then, I guess you'd have to, wouldn't you?" He lay down again, propped his head on his hand, and studied her. "Tell me about it—what it's like to be psychic. Tell me about how trauma can cause it to kick into high gear. Tell me about how it works."

Painful. . . . *Invasive.* . . . *Unwanted.* . . . *A curse, as if she stood exposed, in the center of a mind-blowing storm of every possible emotion and physical pain.* . . . Claire inhaled slowly and bent her forehead to her knees. She was still shaken by his tenderness and her own surprising hunger. "I wondered how long it would take you to get to that."

Neil's brief smile was a silent admission. "Okay, Claire Bear. You came over here with Eunice's gingerbread recipe for a purpose, right? You want to make sure I won't tell anyone about you or your family. You want your privacy. I can understand that, Claire Bear. You can trust me."

"I already know that."

"I imagine you do. You felt it right? What am I thinking now?"

Neil wasn't just curious. He was dead serious and cautious, wading through his lifetime disbelief in psychic phenomena and the reality that he had seen them in action. "You want to know if I can help you find Sammy."

"Maybe. We tried everything else. I've been going over everything that I saw happen after your attack, and I have to wonder if there isn't some truth in this psychic stuff. I've heard of lost kids being found that way."

Claire nodded slowly. Her mother often found missing people, alive—or what had happened to them.

His frustration and anger shook the air between them. "Do you know how many nuts turned up after Sammy was taken? Most of them claiming to be psychics?"

He frowned at Claire who was unable to keep from shivering—the violence within Neil had just burned her. Suddenly, he took her hand, and his fingers laced with hers. His other hand curved around her nape, drawing her to him. "Come here. Relax."

Neil's forehead rested against hers, his eyes closed, and the burning sensation eased. An image of a clear mountain stream, rippling, flowing through a forest appeared in her mind.

When the tension within Claire eased, she opened her eyes to Neil's shielded expression. "You don't want to believe that it exists, what isn't visible—tangible in your reality, yet it is very real in mine. I'm sorry you were put through so much."

"I think you'd better go now, Claire Bear," Neil stated quietly. The need of a man needing comfort, someone to hold him, to be a part of him, slid over Claire. That sense blended with another deeper, sexual need that suddenly simmered inside her.

Her senses humming, Claire hurried out of the camper. She stood at the camper's doorway and rubbed her hands quickly against her thighs, trying to push away the need to hold him. She backed away those cautious three feet and still felt the remnants of that attraction cling to her. "Yes, you're right. I'd better go."

But that night, when Claire started to walk, to work off her frustration, she found Neil's big silhouette yards behind her, keeping his distance, her protector. He followed her on the return trip, watched her enter her home, and stood outside, waiting for her to click her porch light on and off—a sign for him to leave.

Only then did he walk to his own home.

Claire leaned against her door. Neil evidently didn't think the danger to Claire was past, and neither did she, despite what she had said. Neil's question about who might drive John to attack her was logical. Tempest had tracked the connection from the computer, but it could have come from anywhere.

Not a pleasant thought.

Neither was the fact that Neil and she were definitely linked, in a way very different from her family's. When he started thinking about how he'd like to kiss her—or make love to her—her needs absorbed his. She'd caught the soothing woodland image, and it had to have come from Neil. She was so sensitive to him that he could stop her from blocking, from protecting herself from him.

Claire tested the heat of her cheeks. Neil was definitely too potent to handle.

* * *

"Two busy days of showing off this place and promoting a new solar panel line to my best customers, and not a word from Claire."

Neil released the sheer curtain he'd been holding to view that very quiet house next door. He took a bracing sip of coffee and thought about how much he wanted to see Claire—on her terms. He reached for the telephone to call her, his hand hovering above the receiver, and thought of how she had picked up her phone—before it rang.

In tracking down the man who had broken into Claire's home and hurt her, there were just too many coincidences. Neil circled what he knew. Tempest wore gloves to protect herself, Claire had said she was connected to Neil—because she was too vulnerable when he found her? So how did she protect herself at other times?

Neil thought about her sunglasses that day in the blizzard, the way she wore them inside the shop later. They might be one protection, the earmuffs another. "Then, all of a sudden, I find her almost unconscious, take care of her, and suddenly we're connected somehow? I just don't believe this psychic stuff is possible, let alone that it could help find Sammy. I can't go through that again, hopes up with every tiny lead, then wrung inside out when they didn't pan out."

At ten in the morning, Neil finished ordering the materials for a return customer who wanted that 1950 wood-panel look, a sun tarp, and a bicycle rack for two. He sat back from his computer, put his hands behind his head and tried unsuccessfully to settle the restless sexual desire in his body.

The screen's cursor blinked steadily at him, and Neil remembered the broken computer, the shattered screen at the Bliss and New Life commune. Someone had a whole lot of hate to do that—and to attack Claire. Yet her impression of John had been that he was sincere in rebuilding his life, that he was basically a gentle man who'd gotten in with the wrong crowd. Tempest had said something had gotten to the man, had filled him with rage—through the computer. What could possibly slide through a computer and cause a man to go haywire?

The answer had to lie in reality—a stronger personality gradually overtaking a weaker one, using e-mail and chats, a seduction of sorts. But who would want to hurt Claire? Why?

If Neil hadn't seen how the sisters worked through finding the jerk, he wouldn't have believed it. He didn't know that he believed it now. Or Claire's ability to sense feelings—but she had caught his accurately. *Could you please think pleasant thoughts now? For me? You're upsetting me. Think about being a boy and Eunice's gingerbread. You liked it, didn't you?*

How the hell could she pick up—from him—how much he wanted to get his hands on the bastard who attacked her? How the hell could Tempest "feel" things about the attacker, by taking off those gloves and touching the door and Claire's blouse?

Neil's computer screen continued blinking, his spreadsheet waiting to be fed, but he was locked in thought. None of what had happened in the past few days was in his understanding. He'd been too busy to really sort out details, more than what he'd gotten from the sisters. Eunice would have told Claire a certain amount, but there was no way one person could pick up that much. Neil put his fingers on the keyboard and typed in an online search for "empath."

He continued researching empath, clairvoyance, psychometry, and precognition, the sisters' admitted abilities. Then he searched for extrasensory perception, sixth sense, and psychic energy. An old newspaper photo jumped onto the screen—a woman with three daughters. The girls were young, but their features were an exact match to the woman's. The headlines read *World Famous Psychic Sues ESP Clinic and Others.*

Neil sat back, sipped his coffee to steady himself and slowly absorbed every word in the news article. It wasn't pleasant.

> Greer Aisling, a world-famous psychic, residing in an undisclosed location on the Northwest coast, has filed kidnapping and other charges against the Blair Institute for Parapsychology. Aisling, a widow, had been called in to work with a Canadian police force to find a missing boy. Her triplets, aged ten years old, had been left in the Aisling estate under the care of their long-term guardian and housekeeper.
>
> Reportedly, Ms. Aisling had refused the institute's efforts to test the home-schooled children, whose last name is different from hers. On the suspected charge of abuse and without the mother's knowledge and consent, the triplets had been extracted from their home. They were placed in the care of the Blair Institute Child Studies Program for testing.
>
> The children are back now in the care of their mother, who has already filed several lawsuits and promises more. Observers note that the triplets seem to be well cared for and strangely gifted.

Neil released the breath he had been holding and sat back to absorb the rest of the articles. As time had passed, the triplets had moved apart, and an occasional reporter tried to liven up interest by researching them.

However, all three seemed to be leading ordinary lives.

In Neil's brief experience, the Aisling-Bartel triplets weren't ordinary women. "If the past few days are any indication of this whole family, I'd say 'gifted' isn't the name for it. Can't wait to meet the rest of them, Claire Bear."

He rubbed his chest where the ache for his son rested. Claire had said that they were connected, and she'd definitely responded to his simple test of tasting the gingerbread. Claire definitely could anticipate Neil's feelings, and he'd seen the sisters work together. If they could track down her attacker, could they find his son?

He shook his head, uncomfortable with his thoughts, and fearing more raised and dashed hopes. Psychic phenomena were something for the fringe crowd; they didn't exist.

Or did they?

Eight

NEIL REALLY WASN'T IN THE MOOD FOR HIS ABRASIVE OLDER brother, who appeared later that morning.

Bruce had been twenty years old to Neil's sixteen when their parents' home had gone up in flames, and they'd both been killed. Underage, Neil had spent a couple years in Eunice's care, while Bruce had run through his inheritance—never forgetting for a moment that the bulk of their parents' estate had gone to his younger brother.

Neil studied the loan papers Bruce had placed in front of him; it wasn't the first time his brother had wanted loans, and Neil braced himself for his brother's bitterness.

With a list of failed business and life ventures behind Bruce, he wasn't a good loan candidate. Life was always the bad guy in Bruce's reasoning book; his logic said that it wasn't his fault that he couldn't stick to anything, work hard enough at it to be a success—and that included his three marriages.

At the bottom of the reasons Bruce resented Neil was his belief that their parents had favored their younger son.

"You're the only family I've got," Bruce was saying

as he picked up the framed picture of the two young brothers and their parents. It had been taken on a camping trip, and Bruce had always hated his parents' love of being outdoors, making no effort to participate in family activities.

Neil studied his older brother, noted their familiar features, and a slight softness curled around him as he thought of their father, bent over his worktable, carefully building the model sailing ships inside bottles. In a temper, Bruce had smashed those bottles and ships, a lost legacy that Neil mourned.

He looked at Bruce, seated beside him. Though the brothers resembled each other, Bruce was heavier around the jowls and softer in the midsection, his hard lifestyle had cut deep into the lines of his face, but still there was that bonding call of family, the only one Neil had.

"I'd think you'd want to help me out. You're successful. You've got all this—" Bruce stood and indicated Eunice's home. "And you got most of what the folks had when they died."

Neil sat back in his home office and again skimmed the figures for the loan Bruce wanted. "This Alaskan trawler has a hefty price to start with, then you'll need start-up capital. You'll need a crew. It takes a while to learn and make connections and—"

Bruce turned to frown at Neil, and his fist locked around the black coffee mug. "I'm not stupid. I know all that. Are you going to give me that loan or not?"

Neil took a deep breath, fought the love tangling with logic that had been proven, and shook his head. "No."

"Why not? Have I got 'Loser' written on my forehead? You've got all this, and you won't help me out? You've always had it all, haven't you, Mom and Dad's favorite baby? The way you can get people to like you?

Easygoing Neil, then there's the older brother who just can't quite get it together," Bruce added sarcastically.

Neil carefully placed the trawler's data back into the portfolio Bruce had given him. He loved his brother, but he also knew that Bruce lacked the ability to stick with a project when problems occurred, and the downsides were big. Love and memories tangled with reality. "Were you planning to work on the trawler yourself?"

"It's only a start, and I'll—"

"Bruce, were you going to actually work on that trawler? To go out on it?" Neil pressed and hoped that for once, his brother would actually want to put back and spirit into one of his moneymaking deals.

"Dammit, Neil. You just said I'd have to hire a crew. I wouldn't actually have to do anything but the business end. But from just this one boat, I can set up a fleet of them and make big money." As usual, Bruce jumped over the minor details and hard work that first step in business would include and leaped right into his usual fantasies of "big money."

"What do you know about the commercial fishing business?" Neil persisted, because he was pretty certain that his brother had no intention of actually laboring to build a business.

Bruce threw up his hands. "I'll learn. You're making this difficult because you like to see me squirm. Hell, you've got most of the folks' money after their accident, and you got all of Aunt Eunice's. You're sitting pretty with this business, and you won't spare a dime to help me."

Neil had spent plenty of "dimes" on Bruce's "big money" ventures. And from experience, he knew that working together with Bruce on any project would be a disaster. In the end, Neil would be left trying to untangle a mountain of debt and problems. "You quit your job in advertising, didn't you?"

Bruce eyed him defiantly. "I had better opportunities. They didn't work out."

"Okay. I've got some connections. I could see about getting you a position—"

"I'm asking for a loan, not a job, Neily-boy."

When Bruce started toward him, Neil stood slowly. Eye to eye, the brothers were an even match as adults, but work and clean living had hardened Neil's body. "Those times were over a long time ago," Neil warned very quietly.

After Bruce had cursed, scooped up his portfolio, and slammed out of the house, Neil sat down to brood. The only family he had in the world hated him—and always would.

"You called to ask if I wanted the handbag I made Eunice? I would . . . something to remember her by. Thank you. . . . I saw that you were probably finished for the day and were settling down for the evening. I hope I'm not interrupting any—ah . . . plans for the night?"

As she stood under Neil's front porch light that night, Claire watched Neil's expression close. The first sensations coming from him had been surprise, pleasure, in that order—then he was shutting down, suddenly annoyed at her unexpected appearance. "I could have brought it over. I'll get it."

Claire sensed that something was very wrong, disturbing Neil. His expression was hard, much the same as when she'd spoken to him in the snowstorm. Claire decided instantly that she wasn't leaving him now. She handed Neil the pan of freshly baked gingerbread, and said, "It's a small thank-you for what you've done. Aren't you going to invite me in?"

Everything about him was restless and unfinished, and he was brooding now. She could feel the empty holes inside him, the ache and old wounds that needed healing.

As his scent and that of soap curled around her, Claire noticed that his hair was damp from a shower—and, stunned momentarily, she stared overlong at his bare chest. She wanted to taste the drops of water on his tanned shoulders and wanted to slide her hands into his jeans.

Startled by her own sensuality, Claire hauled herself back to the reason she'd come to his home: The ginger-bread was excuse, because she really needed to test herself, to know that she was stronger. She'd have to focus, to work on her ability, when she'd always tried to shove it away.

Neil was going to be difficult—that much she got from his scowl. "I've had a hard day, Brown. I'm not in the mood to play. Thanks for the cake. Good-bye."

She'd come for one reason—to test her connection with Neil and discover how to sever it. And she was staying for another: Neil's dark emotions had just circled her, a sense of aching loneliness that she couldn't ignore. Claire stuck her boot into the doorway, blocking the door Neil was about to close. "Afraid? I do that to men—make them afraid. Are you afraid of me, Olafson?"

He opened the door fully, motioning her inside with his hand. That hand reached past her to close the door with an unfriendly click. Near her now, his look challenged her—the intruder into his private pain.

Neil was fighting a deep sadness—and visions of a fire. "I know about the fire that took your parents," Claire said.

He straightened away, drawing back from her. "Yeah, that's right. You're a psychic-intuitive-empath-telepath hybrid, aren't you? But then, Eunice would have told you about her only sister dying, and keeping me for a couple of years until I turned eighteen, wouldn't she?"

Claire felt the searing heat of the flames, felt the young teenager's terror. "Yes, Eunice told me, but now I feel it from you. Do you want to tell me about it?"

His "No, I don't" was too abrupt, marking that open wound with a big BACK OFF sign.

So much sadness. Claire wanted to move against him, to hold him. But after a brief searching look that had to do with how much he wanted to make love with her right now, a brief respite from his dark emotions, Neil turned and carried the gingerbread to the kitchen. Left to follow and determined to make her offer, Claire took note of the changes in the house. Mementoes of family and Eunice remained, mixed with sturdier furniture in brown leather and a massive television set. The lacy curtains and Eunice's tea set still marked her passing; from the hallway, one bedroom was definitely feminine and neat, the other filled with a king-size bed and rumpled sheets, men's clothing tossed everywhere.

Claire thought of the activity that had probably taken place on that bed and moved quickly toward the kitchen. As she passed through the dining room, she noted the big sturdy table that had replaced Eunice's antique spool leg set; the chairs were an odd assortment, built plain and strong. The house still carried Eunice's light fragrance, but underlined by the bite of lime aftershave coming from the tiny bathroom.

"Stay right where you are. Don't come any closer," Neil ordered, when Claire entered the spacious kitchen. He'd already dug into the gingerbread, eating a slice of it as he leaned back against the counter.

As Claire noted the changes in the kitchen, sounds of a washer and a dryer came from the small side room. Eunice's apple-shaped cookie jar was all that remained of her, her tiny refrigerator replaced with a big side-by-side freezer model. In the bright light, Neil's broad, tanned shoulders and chest contrasted his aunt's delicate collection of "kitty" knickknacks running across the windowsill behind him.

The kitchen, a domestic setting, did nothing to calm Claire's nerves; she felt as if she were standing in a minefield.

Neil's slow look took in Claire's face, her jacket and jeans, right down to her boots. "How close do you have to be to do this mind-reading thing? How many feet?"

"I'm not a mind reader. I tried to explain that. This stuff doesn't always come packaged into one label. Different people have different sensitivities and sometimes a blend. I 'feel' more than receive thoughts. I admit that lately ... maybe only with you ... I suppose that because of the attack, the trauma of it, I may be picking up more pure words. I don't know. But the distance is maybe two–three feet. I've never wanted this thing, or tried to develop it. In fact, I've fought it. I wanted to be like any other woman. I found that wasn't possible. It's in me, no matter how I try to push it away."

And she couldn't tell him that every time his senses were tuned to her—sensually—her own psychic sense, and her body went all haywire. And the connection-attraction between Neil and herself wasn't going away, and wouldn't allow her to block it.

"That's why you're living out here. People upset you," Neil probed slowly. She sensed that he was testing her, wanting to know more, moving cautiously through what his mind did not want to believe.

"Psychic abilities can be opened—or closed—by traumatic events. So far, I've had three, and with each one, I've become stronger, though I would have preferred the reverse."

"Being put through a battery of tests as a ten-year-old could have been one terrifying event. You're Greer

Aisling's daughter, aren't you? One of the Aisling-Bartel triplets?"

"I expected you to research my family." After adjusting to the sudden question, Claire waited for the scoffing, the teasing, the label of a "freak."

Instead, Neil took another piece of gingerbread. "Good," he said, nodding, those shielded silvery eyes still on her. "How are you feeling?"

"I'm fine. There's no need for you to follow me when I walk at night."

"You're really certain that this won't happen again? That some other jerk won't try the same thing?"

"I'm feeling very safe, unlike I was before. And I should have expected you'd try to research us, so here's a little more information to add to your list: I was more affected than the others. Mom had protected us, then suddenly—I still have nightmares about the doctors, the tests, and the electrodes. Suddenly, I was stronger than before, and I didn't like it. I resented everything I was. But I learned a little on how to defend myself, to block the emotions of others from me, enough to pass for 'normal' with a few oddities."

She ran her fingertip over the old apple cookie jar that had been Eunice's; it was smooth, cool, and familiar, unlike sharing herself with someone outside her family. "The day I lost my baby. We'd—Paul and I— lived in the country, so I didn't have that much contact. My family had always been very selective about our doctors and dentists, and I'd felt very safe. I guess I'd been pretty good at insulating myself, pushing the sensations back until then. Then, that day, I walked in on a bank robbery, got hit by the fear and greed of the people—and that overload put me in the hospital. And from then, it got bad."

As she explained, Claire stared at the floor; she felt as worn as the yellow roses on the linoleum there. "Everything in me spiked—went to full overdrive, taking me to the next level. I was very open—my senses receptive to everything around me—physical pain, dark emotions. Everything possible in the scope of human experience washed over me, swallowed me. I guess I was weaker then, more exposed. I couldn't defend myself, and everything came at me at once. A replay of what happened when I was a child, only stronger—because I was stronger and more receptive."

"Too many people, all their thoughts and feelings?"

Claire thought back to that nightmare; it was still too potent, ripping into her. "Mmm. It took a while for my family to get to me—they understood. My husband didn't. I lost my baby because I couldn't hold the crowd's at the bank, or the hospital staff's emotions apart from my own. In simple terms, I broke down. It took months to recover, shutting down completely and rebuilding with stronger blocking techniques—stronger, because *I* was stronger. Mom stayed with me not far from here. That's how we found this place, by driving around the countryside."

"And that is why your family didn't want you going to a hospital, right? A replay?" Neil probed gently.

"It wasn't pretty. Then the third time, when you found me, has shifted me again into something else, a 'hybrid.' With you, I'm changing, becoming more telepathic, in short, in this dimension—with you—I'm too open—vulnerable and receptive. And I do not want any of it. Somehow I've got to get back what I lost in that hospital. I have to prove that I'm stronger than whatever is inside me. I was ashamed of how I was, out of control. I feel like something was taken away from me—my ability to cope—and I want it back. I *have* to get it back somehow."

Neil shook his head. "I've never believed in this stuff. It's hard to accept. I read that your mother has recovered missing people—or at least has found out what happened to them."

"She's very strong. She's worked at it, helped me to learn how to block—to protect myself. But she says that in order to be truly successful at protecting myself, I need to open myself, to learn more about it and what I can do, by stepping into it, understanding it. I don't want to. I've been trying to block, but not to give in to it."

Neil stared at her, his voice deep and uneven. "Do you—do you think there's a chance you could find my son? What happened to Sammy?"

"Me? Oh, no. I'm not strong enough. I have no idea where to begin. I—You need someone like my mother—not me."

"Okay, you're afraid. I get that part. So am I." Neil looked at the linoleum between them. "It was a nightmare, Claire. Every kook came out of the woodwork, detectives, police, people wondering if we were good parents, our friends interrogated. . . . You said we were connected. Maybe because—if that's true—maybe you could get a lead about Sammy from me. Like a biological link somehow."

"Oh, Neil. I couldn't. But I can only imagine how you feel. I think of how my mother would have felt if she'd lost any of us. But that has nothing to do with psychic ability, Neil. I've lost a baby who's not coming back—but to know that Sammy could be out there and you can't find him, would be horrible. I can't give you closure, Neil. It would be like stepping into everything I've fought all my life."

He looked at her, his expression vulnerable, wistful, uncertain. "Far out, huh? Me believing—trusting you, enough to ask that you step into what you obviously don't want?"

"I don't think I can do what you want. You need someone you can—"

Those gray eyes pinned her. "Trust. The someone I trust is you, Claire. I know you'll do your best. You'll try. I need to know what happened to my son, good or bad—I need to know."

"I don't know how—"

"You'll learn. I'll protect you, Claire. Just try. . . . Please. Find out what happened to Sammy. I'll do anything you want—including moving out of here. You said you needed to redeem yourself, or your pride, whichever. This would be a way. And then, I'm asking you. . . . Just try."

Claire took off her jacket. She was getting too warm, and she needed to concentrate. She rubbed her face with her palms and found them damp. From her mother's work, she knew that not all missing children were found safe—and she couldn't bear to step inside another emotional trauma. "The answer is no."

She looked up suddenly to find Neil studying her violet cardigan sweater and jeans. Neil was seriously feeling her out—studying her expression and her body language, and he was trying to "read" her!

At a distance of ten feet, her senses weren't picking up anything, but the visuals of Neil's frown, his body rigid, the bright light catching on those drops of water on his shoulders, the flex of those muscles beneath that tanned skin, and that taut six-pack stomach. She shifted uneasily, aware of his body, and remembered her own in the camper.

Neil suddenly picked up a pint jar sitting next to a wine bottle. He studied the dark red liquid of the jar, then his tight, dark expression locked on to her. "What's the matter, Claire? Don't you like being on the other side of this 'reading' business?"

He lifted the jar and drank heavily, then sat it down on the counter with a thud. "Okay, I've had a hard day and I'm feeling nasty and you're just the one in the line of fire. I apologize. If you help me or don't, you may actually want to hear more details from me, so here they are. My son disappeared while we were camping, and Sammy was only six months old. We were up from Casper at a campground, holding a rally—we'd set a time and place to meet. Some RVers—recreational vehicle—people were there. Others were tent-camping, and I was doing a little business while relaxing, showing off my new son. And someone just took him. . . ."

Neil closed his eyes as if stepping back into the past, the lines between his brows and bracketing his lips deepening. "Jan—my ex-wife now—was right there outside the trailer, while Sammy was napping inside. We'd set up camp a little away from the rest, so that the baby could sleep better. When I came back, Jan was sleeping too hard in the lounger—she'd been drugged, and we never found out how. Like most campers, we had our things on the picnic table, the iced tea and water in coolers. Anyone could have put something into them. They tested clean, though. She'd gone to sleep before she could crawl in with our son. And Sammy was gone, just like that."

Neil looked at the worn flooring as if remembering. "Everyone at the rally was questioned. No one was missing. Sammy was just gone. He'd disappeared."

Those hard silvery eyes leveled at her, his tone frustrated; he ran his hands through his hair. "Now how in hell can I be standing here and asking you to pick up a trail that is eight years old? When every possible lead has been researched over and over until it was nothing but a dead end?"

Neil wasn't going to make anything easy when he added, "I don't even know if I really want to go through that again, even if your mother is a world-famous psychic who works with police. Why didn't she come when you were attacked? And I don't believe that malarkey about her upsetting you. If she took care of you while you were 'healing,' then it was okay to be near you."

She'd been expecting the question. "It's true. We're not a normal family. . . . We—upset—each other. That's why we live so far apart. My mother is very strong. She blocked her emotions during the time I healed, not far from here. I know that it cost her. But this time, her instincts as a mother might have been too easily detected—because I've changed, once again—I'm stronger, more receptive now. Tempest came because she is different—she's more hands-on—and she can move between us. You don't really want me involved, Neil. You've already been through hell, the hopes that were cruelly smashed. What if I put you through more?"

"I'll take my chances. The question is: Will you? Will you trust me enough to help you do whatever it is you do—and to protect you?"

"I—I'll think about it. I do understand how awful it would be to lose a child, how painful—without knowing what had happened to him. It must be horrible. It must haunt you every minute."

"Every . . . single . . . minute."

Tension simmered in the kitchen, skittered across the yellow rosebuds on the old linoleum flooring and wrapped around Claire. She couldn't move, pinned by the stark heat of Neil's stare. Then he said quietly, "Your husband couldn't handle whatever you are, Claire. That was his problem, not yours. He shouldn't have walked away, not when you needed him most."

Danger warnings prickled at the back of Claire's neck. Neil had just jumped from asking for her help to questioning her trust of men. "I trust you, Neil."

"Do you? Come here and tell me that."

His challenge hung in the air; he was pushing because

he needed her to hold him, to touch him. Claire wasn't one to take unwise challenges, but somehow Neil understood just how to reach her touch points.

"Closer," Neil whispered, as Claire stood within five feet of him, and the tension between them tightened and sizzled.

She slowly moved to within two feet of him. Sexual need ran molten between them, and she couldn't determine if it was Neil's or hers. But there was something else underlying Neil's, an aching need for comforting, for a softer touch. He was so tired and alone, and those he loved were gone. . . .

Claire intended to place her hands on him, to soothe those lonely aching edges with a gift and a curse she'd never wanted. Her ability to heal was undeveloped, but to lessen his pain, she would try. Neil hadn't moved, his hands braced on the countertop behind him. He stood watching her, his eyes silver slits in that dark frame of eyelashes. The bright kitchen light cut shadows and harsh planes into his face, every angle of his body challenging her. "Go ahead, touch me. That's what you want to do, isn't it? Feel around inside me, take away the pain of a lost child? Then do it."

She braced for the contact, caught slices of frustration and darkness and heartache between the fiery sensual need. If she could just reach through that raw hunger to the ache beneath.

When her fingers touched his cheeks, her palms locked to his rough, weathered skin, everything about Neil seemed to stop. He turned slightly, his lips brushing her hand. She hadn't expected the tenderness, or her reaction to it, opening her palm to those lips, her own emotions tangling with her gift. She could give his body relief, soothe him as a woman could, or she could—

Neil's lips brushed hers lightly. Then again, seeking,

asking. He tasted of hunger and pleasure, of the wine he'd drunk, of a challenge Claire had to take.

Deep inside her, she knew that truth, but she was afraid. Once that line was breached, she'd be vulnerable again— The heated ache of her body clashed with her fears for only a heartbeat, then she was opening to him, lifting up to meet that tender temptation.

That darkening of his eyes, the flare of his nostrils, the heat coming from him told her that Neil wasn't immune. Yet Neil held still, letting her set the pace, her lips softly exploring his lips, that hard edge of his jaw. He breathed harshly, his body tense, that vein in his throat pounding slowly. . . .

Claire placed her lips precisely over that vein, and Neil's head jerked back; a muscle quivered near his cheekbone, the half-moon scar a lighter shade against his tanned skin. "If this is about sympathy—"

She had to know. "Was she in your bed?"

He looked puzzled. "Who?"

"Your girlfriend. The one who stays here sometimes. I saw you together that morning—"

Neil's hands slid to Claire's hips, drawing her tight against his hard body. Then one hand slid up to her hair, toying with it, wrapping his fingers in it. "I wondered how this would feel—warm, alive. . . . Mary Jane stayed in Eunice's room. She had plans—I didn't. We went through all that years ago and a few times between."

"She jumped on you. You carried and kissed her. That doesn't sound as if it's over."

"I thought that was a nice touch. I couldn't resist putting on a show for the peeking lady next door, and told her you were watching. Got to you, did it?"

"Of course not," she lied. His hand smoothed her hair, and Claire couldn't separate the pleasure wrapping around her. *Was it hers? Or was it his?*

The pleasure deepened as Neil's lips prowled her throat, heating her as he unbuttoned her sweater and cupped her breasts. Claire held her breath, the cords within her tightening as his hands caressed her, soothing away her bra and moving downward to unzip her jeans. She held on to his shoulders as his hand found her, and the first riveting contraction shot through her body. Claire leaned against him, snuggled in deep and close and drew his scent into her. The hunger within her was savage enough to nip at his throat, to draw her nails down that powerful back.

Neil tensed, but quickly slid his hands along her hips, easing down her jeans and briefs. Then he picked her up, carried her down the hallway to his bedroom and dumped her on the bed. He lifted her boots, tugged them off, and slid away her clothing. He took a moment to study her as she drew up the sheet to shield herself and tried to adapt to how quickly he had moved. Neil's grin flashed in the shadows as he lowered himself upon her. "Make yourself comfortable. You're going to be here for a while, Claire Bear."

"What makes you think so?" But deep inside, she knew she could trust Neil. She wasn't frightened or irritated that he'd assumed they'd make love. She only wanted to match whatever he did, to challenge, to win, to pleasure and be pleasured.

Playing wasn't something she let herself do easily, but Claire struggled against him, enjoying herself a woman for a bit, testing an age-old womanly inst Neil laughed and held her wrists beside her head grip was loose, and she understood that if she w to be free, one word, just one "No" would stop He nuzzled her throat, chuckling as he rubbed hi against hers, then impatiently drew away the sheet ering her body.

She shivered as his hands ran over her body, inspecting the areas where she had been bruised. Then he lowered to kiss her throat, where the cord had drawn tight, choking her. "I'm sorry that happened to you."

"I lived."

Then, skin to skin, pulses running together, heating, Claire and Neil stared at each other, recognized what would come—and time stopped. Neil released her wrists and as she smoothed his chest and shoulders, he slid away his jeans. "I'll take care of you," he whispered rawly.

"I know." In that instant, Claire understood that Neil would move slowly, carefully tending her.

On the other hand, that wasn't what she wanted, that fierce hunger raging inside her. She moved quickly, noted his surprise, then pleasure as he slid deeply within her to set off a storm of heat that built too quickly, devouring her. . . .

When Claire opened her eyes, Neil was frowning down at her, even as his body was quivering with its last release. "Oh, no," he stated rawly. "You're not getting away with that."

She was already drifting into sleep, when Neil's lips and hands started their magic again.

But before she gave herself fully, she felt that tiny ache inside him, and knew she would— "I'll try to find what happened to Sammy, Neil. But I don't make any promises."

Neil braced himself to lift the brass Celtic-styled door knocker on Claire's front door.

At eight o'clock in the morning, the twin rottweilers showed their metal fangs, and Neil wasn't feeling that friendly himself. In fact, he was feeling pretty raw. Or else, he just needed more sex. Since meeting Claire and gaining an insight into her family, his sure-of-anything level had dropped. While Claire dealt with her supposed connection with him, Neil's link to Claire was definitely more—hungry.

He pounded the door knocker harder than necessary, just in case Claire had gone to sleep. The door opened, and Claire looked drowsy. Beneath the shade of her hand against the bright sunlight, she frowned up at him. "I *was* sleeping."

She was still scented of lovemaking and woman, and Neil wanted to remove the flannel shirt over her large T-shirt and make love to her again— That would be five times, if he counted correctly, and he still hadn't had enough. The woman knew how to get under his skin. She wasn't sweet, and she wasn't timid, and what man wouldn't want a lady in public and a sexy woman in bed?

He muscled Claire inside and shut the door after him. "So you just get up and leave before I'm awake? What kind of manners is that?"

She yawned and blinked drowsily up at him. "I'm tired. I'm usually up at night, remember? I sleep during the day."

"Yeah, well, *someone's* schedule is going to have to change. You can make purses anytime. The people I do business with are usually *day* people."

While he was set to argue with Claire, she left him standing in her shadowy living room and padded off toward the bathroom. The door clicked shut, and there Neil was, set to lay down some morning-after etiquette rules, and Claire had left him to stew while she showered. *Women.*

The telephone rang, and Neil picked it up. Distracted, he answered as if he would his business calls. "Ola here."

"What have you done with my sister? She hasn't be

home all night, and we're worried," Tempest began hotly. "You know she can't get upset, and—"

Neil thought of Claire in that shower—naked, wet, sweet-smelling, hot inside, and moist and slick. He abruptly finished the call with: "I'll tell Claire you called. She's fine."

Neil studied the little hummingbird hanging from Claire's kitchen window. If the sisters were so much in tune with each other— A little chill ran up his nape. If they were so connected, and the mother aware of everything going on, would the women know about last night?

A little unnerved that lovemaking to Claire could be intricate and not exactly private, it took Neil just two heartbeats to muscle open the locked bathroom door. He stepped into the small steamy room and pulled open the shower curtain.

Long waving strands framed Claire's face and ran down her shoulders, dark against her pale body. Those big green eyes were wide and stunned as he reached past her to turn off the shower. Determined to focus, Neil tried to ignore the water streaming down her body, those drops clinging to the tips of her breasts, the mauve dark nubs.

She was all long and pale and sweetly curved. His mind went blank for a time while his body took over, hardening. . . . Somehow, Neil managed to drag up a rough, "You agreed to find out what happened to Sammy. Where do we start?"

"We should start at the place where your son was taken. With the same people. But sleep would be nice. I need sleep to focus, Neil." Claire reached for a bath towel and wrapped it around her before stepping out of hower. "I told you that I'm untrained—I've never ted to do more than block sensations—and you someone stronger."

"Don't try to back out now. I'm counting on you to try, and that's all I'm asking." Neil grabbed another towel and tossed it over her head. He rubbed it briskly, towel-drying her hair.

Claire fought her way free and stood facing him, her face flushed; those eyes were bright and angry, that odd shade of gold. "Stop it."

Neil reached for a brush and slapped it into her hand. "Okay."

Then he made the mistake of looking down to where those pale breasts were tightly wrapped in her body towel, and his body hardened painfully. Claire's defiant look held as she quickly brushed her hair, then tossed the brush to the counter. "So you've got a little problem. You actually think that you can come over here and start demanding that I change my schedule—to accommodate you? You remember that I was here first, don't you?"

"Purses are a lot easier to make than campers, Brown."

"*Bags,* Olafson. *Handbags.*" Claire moved by him and into the bedroom.

"What's fair is fair—" Neil followed and grabbed her towel, jerking it away from her. He was feeling raw and uneasy about Claire. She wasn't an ordinary woman. On the other hand, she was *all* woman, quite the little surprise package, and she'd winded him. He felt vulnerable and unsteady, not a good "man place" to be. He hurled the towel into the tiny chair he'd used when tending her just eleven days ago. Women should be as they appear—fragile in Claire's case.

Neil considered Claire. She was packaged all wrong. Claire was like a Trojan horse, deceiving—she wasn't fragile and sweet at all. After a night of loving, she'd merely reclaimed herself as if nothing had happened.

While he was dealing with that and thinking of how

she'd feel beneath him—agile, hot, demanding—Claire dressed quickly in a man's flannel shirt and black leggings. She wrapped that towel around her head, turban-style, got into bed and tugged the covers up to her throat. Her arms crossed over them, and those gold-green eyes defied him to make just one move.

"What are you going to do, call your mommy and sisters on me?" he asked nastily, because that was just how he felt.

"I'm sure they already know about last night."

Neil took a moment to adjust; he guessed that the Aisling-Bartel family link included knowledge when one of them had sex. Good sex, Neil corrected, and he wasn't finished, hadn't had enough of Claire.

"What about last night, Claire Bear?" he asked, be-cause he wanted to hear her acknowledge that they'd actually made love. It was a real point with him not to be ignored as she picked up a book and began to read.

"I'm sure you're going to tell me," she said in a bored tone, and flipped the page.

Neil reached to take the book and placed it back in her hands, right side up. Claire stared at him, her lips pressed together. He understood that she was fright-ened of revealing too much—but then, it was too late, wasn't it? He bent to take her chin in his hand, his thumb tracing that soft bottom lip. He didn't have to be a psychic to feel the tension between them tighten, the heat of her face between this fingers.

"You're afraid of me, aren't you? Of getting tangled up with me? Why?"

Claire shook her head, obviously wary of him as she looked away. But Neil understood. She'd loved her hus-band, given her heart, but in the time of her worst trial, he'd forsaken her. She'd said she needed to redeem her-self, and maybe she did need to face her past and cleanse herself somehow.

Maybe Claire was reason enough for Neil to reopen the guilt he would carry forever—that of not keeping Sammy safe.

Neil didn't fully believe in the experiences of the past few days, but still . . . To keep himself from moving into that bed with Claire, he stood and folded his arms. "Back to the place where Sammy disappeared, huh?"

"And Neil? There's one more thing."

He was busy considering the curves beneath the covers and how great she smelled, how she'd felt against him. "Mmm?"

"I have to focus on what I'm doing. . . . You'll have to stop thinking about making love with me. It's confusing—blurring my reads. I'm too sensitive to you."

Neil's expression was pure satisfied, smug male, a man who knew that his woman responded to his touch. "I know."

"I mean it. You're going to have to watch that when we're together."

"That's not going to be easy," Neil stated grimly.

Claire leveled a look at him. "I'm really too tired. If I'm going to help you, I need my sleep, Neil."

"Okay," he said too softly.

After he had left, the back door clicking shut, Claire closed her eyes. She didn't trust how easily he left.

Nine

___

"I'VE HAD LESS THAN ONE HOUR OF SLEEP, NEIL."

Claire stared at the driver of the pickup. He was downright evil and determined to see that she *never* had any sleep. He smiled briefly, the day-person awake and thrusting his biological up-time upon Claire, torturing her.

Yet Claire sensed the tense anticipation within him, shielded by his apparent good mood.

"Uh-huh. I thought you could use that hour of sleep, while I got ready." Neil glanced in the rearview mirror to check the teardrop-shaped camper attached to his pickup. "You can sleep on the way. The motor home show is at a fairgrounds, near Great Falls, a whole day from here. It's not the same place, but several of the same crowd will be there. They've opened the grandstands, and I'll display inside it. We should have left sooner, but I needed to pack the camper, make sure I had all the sales stuff updated in my laptop, and grab some more business cards. I usually do pretty well at these shows. We can pick up a few groceries along the way."

"Mmm. You did all that, did you? In less than an hour?" she muttered.

He smiled again and patted her knee. "And I needed to pack you, Claire Bear. Boy, you're nasty in the morning."

"I have work to do, you know. I can't just pack up and run around the countryside with you."

"I'll explain to Leona why the purses are late . . . that you needed a little break."

"*Handbags*, Neil. Oh, my gosh. Why do I even try?"

After Neil lifted and wiggled his eyebrows, and she realized that he was teasing her, Claire closed her eyes against the sunlight. According to the radio's weather forecast, the weather would warm—but Claire didn't intend to. "You carried me out of my bed, wrapped up in my blankets, and stuffed me into this pickup."

"I didn't want you to catch cold, honey bun." Neil reached to tug her big floppy straw hat, then his hand slid down to caress her thigh, inching up her long skirt. She tugged it down again and found her hand captured by his large one. "You weren't waking up, and the morning was almost over—"

"Yeah. Sure. Ten o'clock, and the morning is almost over. I am usually sound asleep by this time." Claire turned to look at the rolling acres of wheatland, the shoots of winter wheat creating green lines against the brown earth. Beside her, Neil looked tough and lean in his black sweatshirt, denim jeans worn in just the right places, and those heavy-duty work boots. The bite of his aftershave and the smooth gleam of his cheek and jaw said he'd taken time to shave.

She removed the two bits of toilet paper on that tense jaw, placed over new shaving nicks, and sensed that his hands had shaken slightly when the nicks had occurred.

Claire studied Neil's profile, that line beside his mouth that had just deepened. Then she knew he was acting, bracing himself for another disappointment.

She snuggled down into his denim jacket, lined with flannel. It was oddly comfortable, as though he were holding her. Neil braked carefully as several white tail deer leaped across the road in front of them. He followed them with the eye of a hunter taking aim.

But apparently, Neil could multitask; his finger-walking on her thigh was taking her skirt higher. "Want to pull the camper over and sleep a little while?"

He was back to teasing her, shielding deeper emotions. He was expecting her to respond, and she might as well be truthful; light and reassuring wouldn't do now, and would likely only deepen his apprehension.

Claire decided not to hide her original late-night person versus an early-morning jovial resentment. "Thank you for letting me dress in the camper, all four feet high of it, while you were gassing up the truck. And washing my face and brushing my teeth in that station's disgusting, dirty bathroom just started the day off perfectly."

She settled in to brood about how Neil was changing her life; sarcasm and dark moods weren't like her at all. But then, she was running on little sleep and feeling argumentative. And arguing wasn't normal for her either; she'd always been quiet, placid by nature, soothing to others—and now that was all disappearing. Neil was bringing out qualities in herself that she didn't trust.

And she'd snagged some of his anxiety. He could keep up the cheerful act, but inside, he was afraid. . . .

"We'll get you some woman-camping stuff, those face wipes. They have those at the shows, for women who forget their stuff. We'll be all snug by tonight," Neil stated cheerfully.

"I didn't 'forget' anything. I was dragged from my bed—"

"Uh-huh, you've already said that ten times."

She leveled a cold stare at him. Neil needed to know

there were boundaries, and he was probably the first person, other than her sisters, from whose teasing she'd had to defend herself. She was irritated, an emotion she hadn't allowed herself, and somehow, she trusted Neil enough not to protect herself with mental walls. He caused her to want to move right through any walls and shake him; it was a truly natural, unsettling emotion that she'd seen in other women.

Claire looked out of the window and wondered where her protection against Neil had gone; she wanted it back. "You're hopeless. I am not talking to you."

"That's okay. I can't believe that your family lets you get away with pouting. I thought I did a pretty good job of packing for you while you were sleeping. I brought your earmuffs and relaxing CDs with those earphones, chamomile tea, that sort of thing—even stuck in some purse-making stuff."

Claire thought of the paper sack crammed with buttons, feathers, and handles; nothing would match and Neil hadn't included any scissors, needles, or thread. But he had put an apple on top of it—a nice afterthought.

Then Neil focused on the road, and his tension and memories wrapped around Claire. His son had been a part of him, small, warm, a link to his heart.

Neil's fear washed over her—fear that he was pushing Claire into another trauma by asking her to help. His fear for his son, and wary hopes of actually finding Sammy ran like a stream between all of the past disappointments. In the quiet layers, his trust in Claire remained steadfast, a quiet strength flowed from him to her.

Without hesitating, she placed her hand over his aching heart and concentrated on placing it in sync with her own.

Neil's hand covered hers. "I know what you're doing, honey," he said quietly. "Thanks."

Their liaison was temporary, based on hunger and need, on the unresolved loss of a child. What if she were wrong? What if they couldn't pick up the trail? Wasn't reopening Neil's hopes worse than leaving that wound alone?

Neil lifted her fingers to his lips. He was taking a dangerous chance, based on what? On her? On a psychic power she hadn't wanted and hadn't nurtured?

"I'm not promising results, Neil. All I can do is to try."

He nodded grimly. "I appreciate anything you can do. Anything."

"What if—?"

"Nothing turns up? I'll be glad we tried. I'll never stop looking for Sammy. I see him in every little boy. I—"

The ache was there, the emptiness of a parent without his child in his arms. And she could be raising Neil's hopes, only to fail.

Suddenly her mind turned, shifted, went into a sort of fuzzy disoriented pleasure—but then, the hot moist, rhythmic suction of Neil's lips around her finger had already started her body heating.

"And you know exactly what you're doing now," Claire accused carefully, and clasped that hand with the other, holding them in her lap. She was too aware, too linked with him now, and she could miss the signals she needed. Neil was wary of psychic phenomena, but he trusted her to try. Try? To strengthen a "gift" that had ruined every portion of her life? To really open herself? To purposefully walk into something she'd never wanted?

"I want you to promise me that if this gets too deep, and you might get hurt—just anything that might be bad for you—that you'll back off, that you'll tell me. I don't want you hurt, Claire. I don't know how this ESP business works, but from what you've said, it can really damage you. Just promise me—"

When Claire didn't answer, Neil turned to study her. Those big sunglasses, shaded by the hat's floppy brim, were facing the road, not him. Claire's expression was set, a hunter on the trail, and she wasn't stopping. "I want your promise, Claire."

"I can't give that."

Inside the huge fairgrounds arena, Neil braced himself for the familiar setting. This spring get-together served many purposes: some campers making plans to rendez-vous later in the year, some trying out new motor homes before making a long haul elsewhere, and others coming to do business—trading in older models, getting custom ideas, and selling. In the adjacent campground, friends had gathered in a "rally," a place they'd agreed to meet. Neil knew most of the crowd at the fairgrounds and doubted that any of them had anything to do with the disappearance of his son.

Sammy. That sweet ache curled around Neil as he remembered cuddling that small body in his arms. Eight years ago, the campers had set up in a primitive campground along the Missouri River, but many of these people were the regular weekend bunch, some retirees in motor homes, some newlyweds using the big fancy display fifth-wheeler, equipped to the hilt. Several big brand-name companies were already set up, handing out brochures and outlining specifications to potential customers. Because Neil's teardrop trailer was small and also on display, he was allowed to pull it inside the enclosed grandstands arena with the other small units.

Children raced around the displays, and a steady flow of people moved in and out of the arena's bathrooms and to the outdoor camping area. In the late afternoon, the concession stands had set up, and the smell of chili dogs and fries mixed with the potluck buffet set up by old friends.

When Neil looked up from his display table, Claire was standing against his teardrop, huddled inside his jacket, her face pale; her sunglasses faced the crowd, and her teeth caught her bottom lip. "Excuse me," he said to a man who was only browsing and wouldn't buy. Contacts were important in sales, and Neil handed the man his business card. "Let me know if you might want a used model. I hear about them sometimes."

As he came closer to Claire, he understood her tense expression beneath those mirrored sunglasses. With reason to be terrified of crowds, Claire was a loner, and she was overwhelmed. Neil damned himself for asking Claire to help. "We can leave."

"There are so many people." Her voice was breathless, uneven, as if terror ran like a chilling river inside her. Her hand slid inside her jacket, where Neil had seen that wolf's-head pin. Touching it seemed to be a habit and a nervous reaction, as if it were a good-luck piece. If the slight scars at her wrists were any indication, she'd need every advantage; they were treading on dangerous ground, where she could be overloaded and injured.

"They're getting ready for summer camping. These rallies and shows give them a chance to look at innovations, like solar panels, and new camping gear." Neil took her cold hands and warmed them between his. "I think this is a mistake, Claire. Maybe we should leave. It hasn't been that long since you were attacked. Maybe you're not up for this."

A man stopped at the table Neil had spread with brochures and photos, and Claire tensed. A woman came to stand beside him and looked at Neil. He recognized Brenda's silent invitation, a woman with an older husband, on the make for some fun. Neil caught Claire's searching look up at him and the tight set of her lips. He just had to bend down to kiss those lips before walking to talk with Brenda's older husband.

When the couple wandered off to another display, Neil noted Claire's folded arms, her stare at him. "Okay. A long time ago, before they were married," he explained uneasily as a trickle of guilt moved up his nape.

Her "Sure" was tight and unwelcoming as she settled into the lawn chair and dragged a thick RV magazine onto her lap.

In the next two hours, Neil watched her reaction to the crowd very closely. Claire was nervous and pale, tensing when someone passed too close. *What had he been thinking by asking her to help him?* "Look, honey. Maybe this wasn't a good idea. I think we should leave."

Dan Moriority passed close, and glanced at Neil. Neil stared back at him with the understanding of men who didn't want each other's company.

Claire tensed. "It's horrible. That man who just passed here."

Neil watched Moriority as he moved toward the fast-food concession stands. A seasoned camper and hunter, he usually wore the smell of liquor. "What about him?"

"He was abused as a child. He needs to hurt someone. He's jealous of you."

Neil remembered when he'd fought Dan, taking away his hunting knife. "I guess."

"You *know* he's dangerous."

He drew away her sunglasses and scanned her face. Her eyes were bright, looking out at the milling crowd. Neil turned her face up to his, but her gaze was reluctant to leave the crowd. "What?" she asked, slowly looking up at him.

"You know what. You're pushing, aren't you? Testing yourself? Dammit, Claire, this is costing you too much. You're too pale, and you've just gotten over that attack."

"Were all of these people around when your son was taken?"

Neil glanced out at the crowd, considering the faces. "Most of them. A few are missing. They'll probably be at the primitive campground later."

She started walking toward the display circle. "I'm going for a walk."

"Not without me, you're not," Neil stated grimly as he moved beside her.

His arm circled her as they walked around the various displays. Well-known in these circles, Neil easily turned down the usual good-natured invitations: "Hey, Neil, anytime you want to come work for Design Campers, let me know. . . . Ready for that buyout, Neil?. . . . Hey, Neil, we've got a new line of solar panels. Check 'em out. . . ."

Aware of Neil's arm around her, marking her as his "lady," Claire focused on the kindly faces in the busy crowd. She absorbed their good thoughts and the warmth flowing from them. Neil chatted easily with them, introducing her simply as "Claire." The grandmother rocking a new baby was happy for him, her feelings reaching warmly around Claire, like a hug.

One woman's jealousy, poorly hidden, nicked at Claire. Petite and shapely in a red sweater and jeans, the woman invited Neil over to see her newest display

RV. "Later on—when you're free," she added seductively. "This model has lots of extras."

"I'm tied up, Rose Marie," Neil answered lightly, and kissed Claire's forehead. Rose Marie's eyes flashed dangerously at Claire.

Claire's smile at the woman was a little too sweet. As they moved away, she said tightly, "Those extras were pretty obvious. And you're all but saying that we're living together."

Neil's grin flashed down at her. "Well, honey bun, we are."

She stopped and turned to him. "I—"

A sudden hot, savage wave of anger hit her, and she turned slowly to the man nearby. Neil was quick to catch her reaction. "What?"

The man's hatred burned her and tears came to her eyes. Neil drew her closer as he nodded at the man. "Race."

Race Chilton leered as he studied Claire from her long braid and sunglasses down to Neil's denim jacket and her long skirt and motorcycle boots. "Not your usual, is she, Neil? Since when did you start sashaying around with women hippies?"

A wave of angry tension—masculine, hard, abrasive—hit Claire. The force was enough to cause her to shiver. Neil glanced at her, then edged Claire slightly aside and behind him. "What's on your mind, Race?"

But Claire already knew: Race hated Neil, and if he could hurt him, he would. When Race walked off without speaking, Neil's terse explanation was hard. "His wife had a thing for me. He thinks I played her behind his back. I didn't."

Another man with a big wide smile came to shake Neil's hand. "Howdy, there, buckaroo. How's business?"

Obviously friendly with the man, Neil introduced Claire. "Business is good, Fred. Customers lined up, making a little profit. I just moved into my aunt's old place. I'm setting up business there . . . a lot more space, and cheaper than in Great Falls. Come see the new shop."

"That's good, that's real good. We could have been something, old buddy."

Neil smiled and nodded. "I like the slower pace."

"Yeah, right. Nice meeting you, Claire."

She had sensed that Fred wasn't Neil's friend. He was jealous of Neil's success and wished that he'd fail—she sucked in her breath, and Neil turned suddenly to her. One look at her face, the way her hand clutched his, and he hurried her into a quiet spot in front of the grandstands. "What is it?"

"I—I don't think he's your friend, Neil."

Neil studied Fred for a moment. "He was. But maybe not now. We both started out in Casper, where I'd grown up. Jan and I were married, and I was working full-time. But, on the side, I'd converted our garage into a shop and was making a few sales and moving into a real business. He tried to start a competing business, but used cheaper material. Fred turned out too many, too fast, without the quality. . . . You can't do good custom work that way. Then he wanted to go in with me, but I didn't think that would work, and he's selling for the big brands now. I guess he could resent me not going his way. Are you okay?"

"Let's just do this. Take me around to the people that were here eight years ago."

"This is all so useless. I've been over every one of them, including my friends."

"I'm sorry that this is painful to you." But there was something else disturbing Neil, something that had happened a long time ago. And he'd never forgiven himself.

"You're just endangering yourself, and I don't think you're going to find anything—"

She had to face what she was; it was time. "Let me deal with what I have to."

"I thought you didn't want to open yourself to more—now, goddammit, you're walking straight into a certain hell. I saw how that guy got to you, how you were after the attack. I don't want you going down on my account. I should never have gotten you into this."

Claire placed her hands along Neil's jawline. Her thumbs traced those new shaving nicks, and she thought of how his big steady safe hands had shaken, thinking about this moment, fearing it. "Just let me try. Please?"

"This whole thing is—Okay, you're doing that to me again, softening me up. Just do your stuff."

With Neil at her side, Claire moved into the sensations around her. A woman compared Neil's easygoing friendliness to her dull, bookish husband. . . . Then, a browsing couple wondered how they could afford a new camper, dreaming of the exhibit they had just passed through. . . . As they moved through the displays, Neil explained the various recreational vehicles, the converted van-style, the pop-up trailers that traveled flat and could be heightened for room, the pickup campers, and the exclusive RVs as big as a bus with the accommodations of a home. Neil pointed out the class "C" units, where a sleeping or storage compartment extended over the cab and the dining setup could be converted into a bed.

The range of sensations and emotions plummeted Claire, and she tried to focus on those happier energies. By the time she and Neil reached their display area, Claire was exhausted. Neil studied her face, took in the shadows beneath her eyes, and shook his head. "This isn't good for you, Claire. Why don't you go lie down in the camper and rest? I'll make some excuse and finish up the business I've started. If anyone wants to look inside the camper, I'll show them pictures. We'll leave in the morning."

"Neil? There's no one here who has any energy that feels like they might have taken your son. I'm sorry."

"Yeah. So am I."

"Forget about delivering the bags. I'm worried about you, Claire," Leona stated the next evening.

In the quiet of her home, Claire pulled the pieces of herself together; the crowd had exhausted her, their emotions hitting her constantly, tearing at her. She found it difficult even to sit and eat with the others; their troubled lives battered her. Only when Neil held her that night, and she'd curled into him, did her mind rest. He had been troubled, worried for her, drawing her in close and protectively.

And he had been missing his son, remembering that warm chubby body in his arms. "I've got to do this, Leona."

"You'll be risking yourself, Claire Bear. You've never wanted this—none of us have, but if you develop it, push yourself, you could be—"

Claire considered the light scars that the straps had made on her wrists. "In a straitjacket again? Drugged? That's exactly why I need to do this. I want to learn how to protect myself. Don't you see? I lost control. I've got to redeem myself, Leona. I've got to know that I can manage without my family posse being dragged through hell to help me. I know how you suffered after that, and Mom, too."

"Okay, so we were open for a time, vulnerable. That didn't matter."

"It would be horrible for any parent to lose a child, to wonder constantly what would have happened to him. Think of how Mom would have felt if anything had happened to us. A part of her would have been gone forever. If there is a chance that I can help Neil find Sammy, or find what happened to him, I have to."

Claire could almost feel Leona shudder, and added, "I need to help him, Leona. He trusts me. Neil isn't like Paul."

"Sex. You've had sex, Claire. Separate that from the reality that you could be stepping into hell." Then Leona's tone changed to a sister's teasing one. "Was it good? The sex?"

Like being consumed and lifted and being amid fireworks and floating like a feather down to earth. . . . Or like feeding a hunger that pleasured and burned and pounded until her heart raced with Neil's. . . . Early that morning, Claire had wondered if the camper-trailer would bounce as Neil moved over her, his lips sealing her shuddering cry. Later as he rested against her, his lips moved in a smile against her throat, his hands stroking her body. "I love those sounds you make. . . . But no, honey, nothing was rocking, but us."

While their first night was hot and hungry, last night had been slower, sweeter, and even more terrifying.

Leona's laughter finally died, remnants of it in her last words, "He's good for you, Claire Bear."

"You weren't supposed to catch that, Leona."

Leona laughed again. "You were fairly sizzling. How could I miss all that heat and energy?" she said before the call ended.

Claire watched Neil walk from his house to hers, the sunset sliding through the trees to outline his body. He stood looking up at the old oak, and Claire knew that he was thinking about Sammy swinging there.

As he looked down, a man deep in thought, aching for his son, and blaming himself for the boy's disappearance, Neil's hands were in his pockets.

Claire let the heavy curtain fall and wrapped her arms around herself. Neil seemed so alone. Was she just deepening his pain? If she pushed to develop her ability to sense people's emotions, was she endangering herself forever? And did all that really matter when a child could be found after eight years?

Was it wise to reopen the wounds of the man and perhaps unravel a child's life?

Claire studied "Date Night" beneath its plastic cover. She knew that she wouldn't be able to work well and create while nagged by the possibility that Neil's son could be found. Neil had said, "What if I missed the only ransom note from a kidnapper, and Sammy paid for it?" *Paid for it?* Was the child even alive?

She reached for the telephone. It was unusual for her mother to call. "Hi, Mom. And no one is here, so I can answer the telephone before it rings," she teased.

"Darling, I couldn't call—"

"I know. I'm glad you didn't, and I understood. I remember what it cost you to block everything, to heal me after the hospital. You were afraid that this time you couldn't block the emotions of a mother. You remembered how your anger at the hospital sent me into a panic. I know you didn't mean to do that, or my sisters. But I'm fine now."

Greer's fear vibrated across the lines. "Don't do this, Claire. I'm afraid for you."

"I have to. I have to do this for Neil, but for myself, too." Claire felt her way through the layers of her mother's protective instincts, how she must have felt when her triplets were taken, and later, her anger at seeing Claire's state in the hospital. Greer was powerful enough to— "Mom, I know that the doctor and nurse who attended me in the hospital were killed in an auto accident later. Did you—?"

Greer was silent for a moment, her answer guarded. "Have a hand in that? No. But there was something strange about it. Almost as strange as that man suddenly going berserk and attacking you. I've wondered— never mind."

"You wondered what?"

"Oh, I'm just too tired, and this case of a missing teenager I'm working on is looking bad. I really need to prepare her parents for the worst, and it's weighing on me."

At the sound of a brisk knock, Claire walked to open the door to Neil. He lifted a pot, indicating that he'd brought food. Still holding the telephone, she motioned him to come in and walk to the kitchen; the sounds indicated that he was turning on the stove, stirring something in the pot, tapping a spoon before laying it down. He returned to take off his light jacket, his eyes never leaving her, fierce hunger stirring—

Which, of course, Greer Aisling could detect easily, but she had to hear the words from her daughter. "He's nice then, this Neil Olafson? Do you want me to try to find his son? I—I'm worried that you, if you develop past a certain point, there's no going back."

Claire understood; to reassure her mother that she would be safe, she reached for Neil's hand, felt the warmth and security of it. The link of their hands traveled over the telephone lines to Greer. "Yes, I feel him. Tempest called him The Protector. He feels like that," she murmured. "Thank you, Claire."

"We'll find his son. I'm stronger with him."

"But I felt— Mm. A combination of you both, two hunters on a trail, one enhancing the other, could be powerful. . . . Did you ever think that—?"

Greer paused and something shimmered inside Claire, before her mother continued with, "Did you ever think this is what a family does? Taking care of each other?"

"Yes, of course." Claire frowned. *Did you ever think that* had begun as one thought and had ended as another. Greer had intended to say something else, but she'd forced herself to stop and successfully block Claire. But in that heartbeat before her mother swerved away into her family-mode, Claire caught something dark, evil, and suspicious. "What were you intending to say, Mom? Did I ever think that—what?"

A professional psychic and much stronger than Claire, Greer must have sensed the probe. She spoke cautiously, "Did you ever think that if you take this step, trying to find Neil's son, you might never be able to protect yourself, block out other people entirely."

"I know I'm on a ledge. But it's something I have to do. But if there is anything I can do to give Neil closure, I have to do it—for him, and for myself."

Greer was silent for a moment. "Well, then. I did something like that long ago. It was a journey I had to make alone, somewhat like yours. It's settled then. Our family has always been hunters, of one thing or another. I wondered when your time would come. I love you, Claire."

Claire frowned slightly; she didn't like the sensation she'd just gotten from her mother. *Did you ever think that?* "What's wrong, Mom?"

The hesitation was there, too strong to be ignored, and just a sliver of fear soon concealed before Greer murmured, "Just missing my daughters, dear. And I must prepare the teenager's parents for an outcome that will shatter them. I stood where she was last seen and saw it all. I don't know where her body is now, but if they catch the man from my description, I'll want to talk with him—then I'll know. Have to go. Love . . . and good hunting."

Claire held the telephone receiver for a moment after the call ended. Her mother had mentioned "hunters" and "hunting." Was that what Claire had become after a reclusive life? The image of herself, focused, tracking through a forest of details shocked her.

She turned to smile at Neil, to tell him of that image, then she frowned. She lifted his bandaged hand, then a closer look at his face caused her to lift the hair away from his forehead. The dark bruise surrounding a cut he'd closed with butterfly bandages looked serious. "What happened?"

Neil shrugged and placed his cheek against hers. He eased his body against her and his hands caressed her body. "I was thinking about getting over here and not paying attention when I went up into the shop's storage loft. The ladder slipped just as I was coming down with a couple of support rods, then part of the loft broke, and—"

Claire leaned back to look at him, fear leaping through her. "All that stuff stored up there, the pipes and rods and—"

"A regular metal rainfall. I jumped to the side, but it's a real mess. One of the tire rims almost—"

Claire gripped his face between her hands, and dove inside his memories. She caught a flash of a metal shaft falling downward, just missing Neil; she felt the painful sear on her forehead, just where Neil's injury had occurred. "I've seen that pile of metal. You could have been killed."

Neil's lips were working his way down her throat. His hands were working their way up her body. "Accidents happen in a shop, honey bun. I misjudged the weight of the rods and rims and sheet metal, or I'd have supported that storage loft better. I'm just grateful no one else was around to get hurt, especially you."

When she shuddered and held him tight, Neil added softly, "I'm a workingman, honey. Things happen, especially when you get careless."

Claire wanted to gather him close, to ease away every scar. But then, with Neil sliding his hands under her bottom and carrying her to the bed, Claire had no time to think at all—only to feel.

This kind of feeling was good, the kind of enveloping, sweet-hunger kind.

But Neil wouldn't be happy with what she planned next.

"This is it?" Neil asked the next morning as he stared at Claire's bright yellow Volkswagen Super Beetle. "You actually drive this?"

Her garage doors were open, the "Bug's" big glass headlamps catching the cold morning's sunlight. "If you could just jump-start it, I'm certain it will work. I haven't driven it for a while, and I need to go into town. I'll get a new battery there."

Neil circled the VW and popped open the back to look at the motor. He bent to test the aged belt. "Why don't you take my truck, pick up a battery and a belt for this thing, and I'll fix it for you? Better yet, Claire, you need a real vehicle out here, not a toy. I'll help you shop, if you want."

"It is not a toy. It has heart—just as much as Jessica does—and I'm not buying anything else. Oh, and by the way, I'm planning to be gone for a few days. You'll need your truck—Jessica, I mean."

She'd tossed Neil a little bait to derail him and expected some masculine grumbling about how Neil felt about his truck. But instead, Neil closed the rear hood a little too hard. "Oh, is that right? Planning a little trip, are you? Where are you going?"

Claire tried for an innocent look. "I need a few supplies."

"I thought you had those delivered at your doorstep." Neil walked toward her. He glanced at the brooch at her shoulder, then his fingertip lifted her chin, and those narrowed smoky eyes pinned hers. "You wore that pin, that *fibula* when you came to see me inside the shop. You wore it when we were at the camper show. It's a good-luck piece, or it means something to you, because you wear it during times that might be stressful to you. You're wearing it now. What's up?"

"Nothing."

"Liar."

"Okay, I need a little bit of space," Claire stated carefully. Her psychic antenna started quivering, aware of Neil close to her. Her connection with Neil was too strong, both with the psychic link and the physical one. With him beside her, her senses could be confused and distracted—it was important now to separate Neil's sensations from her own. She moved away from him, those careful three feet, then back just another foot.

Neil frowned at her. "You need space? From me?"

"Yes. I—I'm not used to sharing my life, my space with anyone. I thought I'd go to a craft shop, pick up buttons, things like that. I'll call you."

"You'd better."

Neil's dark mood didn't sweeten when the VW reared into life. He grimly removed the jumper cables as if resenting setting her free, and Claire drove away. In the rearview mirror, Neil stood in the middle of the road with his legs spread, his hands on his hips; he wasn't exactly waving a friendly good-bye. . . .

"I have to do this, Neil. And you'd only be in the way—rather your emotions would be in the way. You—you interfere with my senses, and I need total control to focus on what I need to do. I'm so sorry. . . ."

When Neil was no longer in sight, Claire settled in to practice her blocking technique, concentrating on building mental walls to protect her senses. She smoothed the wolf's-head brooch at her shoulder; she would focus on that and it would keep her safe.

Ten

NEIL AWOKE SLOWLY TO THE SMELL OF PROPANE GAS.

After a hard day's work repairing the shop's loft and keeping his mind off Claire's sudden need to put "space" between them, Neil had driven into Red Dog. He missed her, and was a little uncertain of her—she was definitely up to something.

He'd had a drink or two before bed, not enough for a "buzz," and he'd fallen asleep. Now the smell of gas layered his bedroom.

In an instant, Neil was on his feet and jerking open the window. He leaned outside for a moment, taking deep, gulping breaths of fresh air. Chilled and awake, he hurried through the house, opening doors and windows.

The pilot light on Eunice's old cookstove had gone out, one burner knob turned slightly on, enough to free gas. Once the house was thoroughly aired, Neil studied that stove. He could have bumped the knob; the old house's drafts could have caused the pilot light to die.

Then he remembered. A couple of the windows had been slightly open last night; he'd noted the house's cold temperature after coming home and closed them. Funny thing though—he hadn't remembered opening them. One match, and the whole thing would have exploded. Neil rubbed his head; with his mind on Claire, he'd been having too many accidents.

Where was she?

What was she doing?

On impulse, Neil picked up the telephone and called Tempest. She answered sleepily. "Storm here. What's up?"

Neil smiled briefly. He decided for the friendly approach. "Hi, Tempest. Nice last name."

"Thanks. I picked it myself. I like to let people know I'm not sweet. Neil?"

Just "Neil,"? not "Neil, did something happen to Claire?" "I don't suppose you know where your little sister went, do you?"

"Oh, shopping. Beads. Ribbons, stuff like that." Tempest's voice was alert now, and from her too-innocent tone, she was probably covering Claire's backside. "Don't worry about her."

"She's with you, isn't she?"

"No, she isn't," Tempest answered with the ring of truth. "Look, Neil. Claire has fought this all of her life. She's trying to get a grip on how to handle it. There are some things a woman has to do for herself. It's her journey. You shouldn't want to take that away from her. And she's lost a baby . . . she has some idea of how much you need closure . . . how much you must ache for your son. In fact, through you, she's got a really good picture, and she needs closure, too."

"You're scaring me, Tempest. I keep seeing her on that floor."

Tempest's next info-bit wasn't reassuring: "We're a scary bunch, buddy."

"You went to see my ex-wife, Claire?" Neil asked five days later. Calls and e-mail from Claire weren't the same thing as holding her against him. Maybe she wasn't feeling the same need. "You drove all the way to Casper, Wyoming, in that old toy to talk with Jan?"

He tossed his welding helmet and heavy gloves aside. After Neil's hard day's work on a custom frame, Claire's appearance in his shop wasn't surprising. "This better be good. I never thought you'd be the kind to check with the ex before moving on in a relationship. Is that what we might do if I check out okay? Move on? Together? Trust each other?"

Claire didn't miss the trust issue tucked beneath those questions. It was difficult to trust Neil when she was uncertain of herself. She handed him the pizza she'd picked up in Red Dog. Little fiery ripples danced along her skin, warning her of his mood. Neil might not be so upset if he ate first. "It's almost dinnertime."

Neil studied the pizza topping. "Hmm. Lots of beef and sausage. You're almost a straight vegetarian. I'm thinking this pizza is like the gingerbread offering. Something to butter me up. Am I right?"

She felt through the ripples, pushing them, trying to gain control of them. Neil wouldn't be that easy to control, not when her body was already reacting to his heat and scent. His hair was sweaty, plastered to his forehead, a trickle of sweat gleamed on his temple. She wanted to lick it, to taste the salt of his body and—

And she was changing, becoming more sexual, more predatory—especially around Neil.

Neil's stare at her was wary. "If you're prowling around inside my brain, you can stop it."

"I wasn't." Her senses weren't working near Neil as they did with other people. Understanding the monster that had always lived inside her was difficult, and she was exhausted, which only made her more receptive to everything about him. Claire glanced at the pile of metal rods and tire rims up in the loft; there were new support posts beneath them. "How's your head and your hand?"

"Fine. You look like hell . . . big circles under your eyes. I'd think that a woman who had been attacked would be more cautious about her rest." Neil flipped open the box, selected a slice, and placed the box on his shop's desk. He took a bite, studied her as he ate, then said, "Let's hear it. How did it go? Did Jan tell you what you wanted to know about me? Compare notes, that sort of thing? And just so you know, four days of sexy telephone chitchat, and no explanation of where you were or what you were doing—until now—isn't sitting very well with me."

Claire moved slightly away; despite his dark mood, Neil was thinking of how he wanted to stretch her out and make love right on that battered old shop desk. The primitive emotion was igniting her own and would just confuse the current problem. "I just wanted to talk with her. Jan was camping with you when Sammy was taken. She feels perhaps even more guilty than you. You're still her first sweetheart, and she worries about you. Though she has a new family, she still needs closure as much as you do."

"And just how did you know where to find her? You didn't get that from me."

"You washed your clothes the morning of the attack. There was an envelope lying on the counter—you must have taken it out of your shirt—from Jan Palmer to you, and I remembered the return address in Casper. She said you keep in touch, just in case there is any news of Sammy and because you two still have good feelings for each other."

Neil stared at her and shook his head. "You got all that, did you?"

She noted the big chain saw on a worktable. The chain had broken, one end dangling over the table's edge. There was a new deep, ragged cut on the table, and Claire ran her fingers over it. She noted the pull cord torn away from the chain saw and knew that the sharp teeth could be life-threatening. Panic raced through her—if anything happened to Neil. . . . "What happened?"

"It's just old. I keep my equipment in good shape, but anything can happen. I pulled the cord a little too hard— maybe thinking about you and not paying enough attention. The cord snapped, and so did the chain."

"It cut through the wood. You could have been hurt. That might have been your leg or an eye—"

"I wasn't hurt, just irritated at myself." Neil studied her; his dark expression said he was chewing on more than the pizza. "So, did our stories agree, Jan's and mine?"

"I didn't question that."

"What were you after, Claire? What could you possibly want from Jan that you couldn't get from me?"

"A mother's instinct," she stated quietly. "The physical bond between mother and child is usually a little stronger . . . she carried Sammy for nine months. If I can help you and Jan end this, I might be able to understand myself better. But most of all, I *want* to help. You need to understand that my natural impulse as an empath is to try to help, to heal. But it's more than that— my link with you had also caused me to connect with the ache within you. In short, I need to heal—give closure to—myself, as well."

Neil shook his head. "Tempest was right—you are a scary family. Also a complicated one, and I'm not certain I believe all this yet. Jan didn't know who you were, or she would have called me."

"I know. You were her first love, and she trusts you. You're still her friend, and her support. She's never forgotten how you stood by her when people were whispering that she shouldn't have taken drugs, that she hadn't watched Sammy as she should—and even those who whispered that she might have done something with her own son."

Claire smoothed the half-moon scar on Neil's cheek and smiled slightly. "She remembers when you were a boy, and got that. We talked at the grocery store, just a passing conversation between two women. She's very nice, a good mother. She buys two gallons of milk at a time—her two little boys like to watch the swirls of chocolate when it's poured into the milk. Like you, she's missing a part of herself—her firstborn child. We were standing at the bulletin board of missing children, and she almost cried when she told me about Sammy. We went into a little bistro, and I listened. Strangers are good for that—listening."

Neil threw the pizza slice into the trash and folded his arms. "So? What did you get by 'feeling' her? That's what you were really doing, right? I would have somehow interfered with your little experiment, right?"

He was irritated. She'd pried into his life, and the pain he held inside every moment for the last eight years. Claire understood that she had gone into the area of his life where he was weakest, and Neil considered that a trespass. "Your emotions would have cluttered—I mean tangled with hers. And you definitely affect me. I lose clarity with you around. I thought it best to see her alone. I'm new at this, you know. I'm not that skilled in separating the feelings of those people within close distance of me. I have defenses, building mental walls, that sort of thing, but I needed to open, to receive. And you—we've . . . because we've made love, you can send my senses reeling every which way."

"Well, that's just great. Give me a good mark for that, if nothing else." Neil's tone was sarcastic.

Claire braced herself; she also had little experience in

dealing with brooding men, in making up. She planned to really work at the making-up part. "I'm making a rice-and-chicken casserole tonight. Are you coming over?" she asked lightly.

"What else is on the menu?" Neil wasn't asking about food. He was asking if they were going to make love.

"I'll think of something nice. I missed you, Neil—and I'm sorry I upset you."

"You'd better damn well prove it then."

"You really think there's something else we can do?" Neil's finger prowled the delicate silk Geisha on the A-shaped tote bag. His casual attitude was belied by that tense cord in his throat.

At midnight, Claire had waited until they'd made love twice and eaten again before serving Neil a beer and her next idea. The recipe to make Neil more receptive to her next move seemed to be working. "Recipe" was a much better word than "manipulation." Claire wasn't experienced at manipulation; she preferred to think of it as a timed, persuasive technique.

Neil had been using her computer to catch up on business messages. In Claire's workroom and wearing only his jeans, he seemed almost beautiful, a tall muscular male profiled against the shelves of feminine bags.

A potentially lethal male, Claire decided, as she studied the width of his shoulders, those heavily padded biceps; his chest flexed with power that ran down into that taut belly. On the delicate tote, his hands looked big and powerful. If he found that one of his friends or acquaintances had been a party to his son's disappearance, Neil was certain to react violently. He'd lost years with his son, and his tension now lay in the lock of his jaw, that cord in his throat.

"I think Jan is right, that someone you knew had

something to do with Sammy's disappearance. You said not everyone was at the fairgrounds. I'd like to meet them all," Claire began in a conversational tone.

Neil's fist gripped the black silk handle of Claire's new "Dreamscape" tote. "Everyone was investigated at the time."

"Not by me. I'm playing a little different game, wouldn't you say?" But Neil was locked in the past, prowling over dead ends and disappointments. Claire decided to press her idea anyway. . . . "Jan could be right, Neil. We should make a clean sweep of all the people who were camping with you then."

"She didn't know them. They were mostly my friends. People with families, a few retired, all good people."

"Did you have any kind of a list to make certain we don't miss anyone?"

"I had a contest for some camping gear. I think I still have the shoe box with the entries somewhere—"

Neil stood abruptly and paced the small room—his anger filling the space, shafting into her. He leaned against her cutting table, his hands spread and locked to it as he stared across it to Claire. "You really think someone I know took my son?" he asked too quietly.

"I think it's possible. The question is: Who would have motive to do such a thing?"

"Hell, I don't know." The anger vibrating off Neil had taken away her breath. His voice was too quiet, but the feather boas stirred restlessly. "There's always a rally the third weekend in May. That's in two days, and a lot of the people we missed will be there."

"Good. This time, I thought we could use a little something extra—"

Neil frowned as headlights slashed at the windows. A car motor died, a car door slammed. He pulled aside the heavy curtains to look outside. "Tempest. What is she doing here?"

When Claire was quiet, Neil turned back to her, and demanded, "Why is your sister here?"

"I—thought she'd be here tomorrow. But now she's going to stay overnight. I'm sorry—"

"You thought you'd have time to get me to see things your way first, right?"

This wasn't going to be easy. Neil was already moving to open the living-room door. He reached for Tempest's backpack. "You travel light. Going to be here long, are you?"

Tempest grinned as she looked at Neil, wearing only his jeans at one o'clock in the morning, and Claire in his T-shirt. She took off her jacket and that wolf's-head pin flashed at her shoulder. "Oh, did I interrupt? I told Mom and Leona that I'd do the big sister checking-in thing with Claire. I'm just passing through."

Neil shut the door a little too firmly and tossed her backpack to the couch. Claire noted how he crossed his arms and stared at her. That cord running down his jaw and his throat started pulsing; the hair on Claire's nape lifted. "Hi, Tempest. There's casserole in the fridge if you want some."

"Thanks, I'm famished. I'm headed for a private collection in Arizona. You'd think the guy would be into Zuni stuff and not Viking antiquities."

"Thanks for the update. I'm glad you *came to check on me*." Claire shot her sister a narrowed, meaningful look.

When Tempest walked to the kitchen, Neil continued to look at Claire. "See? Your family is worried, and so am I. You look like you've been dragged through hell."

"Thanks for the compliment, but the way I look might have something to do with the fact that we have been rather busy in the past few hours. My sister is really here to help us." Neil was right though, she was really tired. The visit to Jan had cost Claire every bit of her reserves, and she needed to wrap the peace of her home around her. And Neil didn't look peaceful.

"Help us? Do what? I want this business to stop, right now. Your family is worried, and so am I."

"I thought we could—"

Tempest returned to the living room with a plate of food. She dug into it and looked from Claire to Neil and back again. "He doesn't look happy, so I guess you told him. When do we start? I'm ready anytime you two are."

Neil's dark look pinned Claire. "Uh-huh. Just checking up on you, huh? Real nice, Claire. Nice setup, too. Start what exactly?"

Tempest grinned at him. "I'm still running on jet fumes, and it looks like you two won't be sleeping anytime soon. Get me something to feel, will you?"

"What's this? A new way of profiling?" Neil asked as he sat at Claire's kitchen table. Tempest placed eight pieces of paper in front of him; she had selected them from papers he had retrieved from his house. They had been handled by people he remembered being at the campsite eight years, those whom Claire had not yet met.

"A very, very old way of profiling. You might say, an ancient way," Claire said as Tempest drew on her gloves. After straining to pick up any indication of someone who might be capable of stealing a child—or harming one, she suddenly looked drained. "Thank you, Tempest."

Tempest nodded grimly. "I hope it helps. I think those people might be capable of taking a child. The rest is up to you, Neil. I think I'd better crash. The couch is fine."

While Claire and Tempest made up the couch, Neil stared at the slips of paper. He'd retrieved them from a drawing's shoe box; the drawing for camping gear was held at the primitive campsite eight years ago; some entries were handwritten on scraps of paper, and some were just business cards. Was it really possible that one of those people had taken Sammy?

He stared at the contest entries and tried to remember what each one had said when investigated. He knew each person well and hadn't looked past that friendship. Maybe he'd missed something—

"I'm sorry about this," Claire said quietly as she returned to the kitchen. "But Tempest is very good, maybe the best when she sets her mind to it. Like Leona and me, she's not happy about these special inheritances, but she's not afraid to use hers to get what she wants."

Neil stared at the eight slips of paper. "She thinks one of them—"

"She said they *might* be capable of a crime. Remember that when those were handled, Sammy hadn't been taken yet. She couldn't pick up future plans."

"I heard you talking. What else did she tell you while you were making up the couch?" Neil studied Claire's quick frown before she turned from him to the sink. "What else, Claire? She gave me a little rundown on each one—pretty accurate from what I know of them— but what did she tell you just now?"

When Claire shook her head, Neil stood to turn her back to him. "What else did she say, Claire?"

"She's just worried about me. I'm getting stronger, but this time, it isn't because my life wasn't in danger. It's because I'm stepping into what I am. I'm stronger, and I'm learning, so there could be consequences. It's an unstable period." Claire wrapped her arms around him. "Jan feels that Sammy is alive and out there somewhere, Neil. Hold on to that."

In his gut, he felt Sammy was alive, too. "I will, but I don't want anything happening to you, honey."

"Neil? There's something I should tell you. This connection, this link between us is very strong. I'm uncertain of it, too. I don't know how to handle that just yet. You could be in danger—from me."

"I'll take my chances."

She'd always known the time would come. . . .

Greer Aisling stood in her garden where her triplets once played. The early-morning fog hadn't lifted yet, and she could feel something. *It* was still out there, waiting. Too strong to be ignored, too elusive to catch, the darkness had already struck Claire. But why?

Greer's fingers tightened on her crossed arms. Claire was heading into the most dangerous time of her life, and she wasn't stopping. The youngest of the triplets, she was determined to find her own strengths, her own destiny. Coupled with her sensitivity to any parent who had lost a child, those needs could cause Claire to be driven. In hunting Neil's child, she would be exposed to so much.

The Pacific Ocean's gray waves pounded at the brown sand as Greer fought to catch what flitted just beyond her senses.

She inhaled the salty air and closed her eyes. "I know you want something. What is it? Who are you? Come out to me, not my daughters . . . *not my daughters.*"

She sensed a stillness and opened her eyes.

Seagulls hovered just off the shoreline, held aloft by the winds and still as death against the gray, troubled sky.

"What's this business about not being near big water?" Neil carefully eased the pickup and camper-trailer onto the off-road that would lead to the primitive campground. A stand of lodgepole pines concealed the area; cottonwoods and brush stood nearer the Missouri River.

Beside him, Claire had settled into brooding about

her overprotective family. Just yesterday, she'd argued fiercely with Tempest about going to the rally, and Greer and Leona had both called, forbidding her to take this camping trip near the Missouri River.

Still, Claire was determined. And nervous. She stared at the river and braced herself against it. Nothing happened; she felt nothing. Aware that Neil was concerned for her, she said, "We had a sailboat accident when we were young, and we sometimes have a fear of water—"

"Uh-huh. I know enough about your family that they don't spook easy. When you were attacked, I had orders not to take you to a clinic—or to let you get near 'large bodies of water.' I'd call the Missouri River pretty big, end to end."

At sunset, Claire studied the gray width of the river, filled with spring flooding and churning with power; it swept past the campground where the various recreational vehicles nestled. She knew the danger, that she was most vulnerable near water.

When suddenly she realized her fascination with the swirling, seemingly smooth surface, Claire shook herself free. Perhaps the avoidance of oceans, major lakes, and rivers had made her more susceptible. Perhaps fear from the past had suddenly gripped her, but the river was definitely calling to her. . . .

Claire smoothed the silver brooch at her shoulder and focused on her sisters and her mother, drawing their images inside her mind. She pushed away the uneasiness, but wondered at its cause. Was it really true that psychics were their most vulnerable near those waters? Or in a land of ancient Native American mystics, was it possible that she had snagged some of the psychic remnants of the earlier campers, near this same river?

Trouble was already stirring in her family—because of her. In aiding Claire, Tempest had upset Greer and Leona, and when the Aisling family was at odds, tempers flared. Claire usually smoothed her family's ruffled feathers; but this time, she was at odds with all of them. She had completely stepped away from them, ignoring the warnings, and they were worried for her.

"Claire? You're touching that brooch again, and you've been staring at that river. What's wrong?" Neil asked.

The watery swirls were so beautiful, almost like textured silk rippling, winding along shining satin. Entranced by the river, Claire came up with: "Tempest is excited about the Viking sword in the Arizona collection. She has a brooch like this one, and I was just thinking about her."

"Don't change the subject." Neil carefully eased his pickup and the trailer into a wide area and parked. As he leveled the trailer, Claire studied the varied collection of tents and motor homes that circled a main area in which folding picnic tables had been placed. In the evening hour, smoke from a big bonfire rose into the overcast sky.

She sensed Neil's tension and his fears as the campers waved at them. Claire recognized some of them from the arena; others were new to her. When Neil didn't attempt to smile, his apprehension wrapping around her, Claire placed her hand on his thigh. "I know this is difficult."

" 'Difficult?' " Neil's tone was harsh, mocking her.

"I'm so sorry. You've been through so much already. I know it's asking a lot of you."

"Just take care of yourself, will you? I'll be watching you. I don't want anything to happen to you. We can leave at any time."

If Neil only knew how frightened she was, the deadly gray currents only yards from camp. The river's water seemed to be calling her, waiting for her.

Apparently well respected and liked, Neil was greeted by the campers, and he introduced Claire, his arm firmly, protectively around her. She absorbed his strength, taking it into her, matching it with her own, latching on to the feel of that big, safe hand.

A buffet-style dinner had already been set, and the group sat around the huge campfire. Neil placed their folding chairs in the circle but sat very close, holding her hand. He was tense, alert to the people around them, despite acting calm.

As Neil talked easily with the other campers about his new shop and the installation of solar panels, Claire was aware of him studying her. He was starting to send out sexual vibrations, and she couldn't concentrate on the people. "Stop it."

"It's been a long day," Neil stated loudly as he drew Claire to her feet and folded their chairs. "We're turning in. See you in the morning."

As they walked back to the trailer, Neil placed his arm around her and kissed her cheek. "You look peeved. What's the problem?"

"Don't you think that was a little obvious?"

"What?"

"That you wanted to—"

Neil opened the trailer's door, waited until they were in, then closed it. His hands were already busy, taking off her clothes. "I do. I'm tired, you're all wound up, and maybe a little friendly activity will take the edge off the both of us."

Claire stopped his hands with her own. "Neil. No. Not tonight. Not while we're here."

He lay down, turned on his side, and braced his head on his hand. Neil had that sexy look that said he knew he would be getting his way. His finger circled her lips. "You're looking rosy, Claire Bear," he singsonged. "I know that look."

With a grin, he rolled over on her, nuzzling her throat playfully, but his hands were working their way beneath her clothing.

Claire was trembling, eager for him, when she remembered. Her voice was muffled by the sweater he was drawing away from her head. "Neil. Stop. We might not be alone."

His lips were on her breast, tugging at it, nibbling and his hand was working at her jeans zipper. "Mmm?"

She gripped his hand, and squirmed away from those lips. Neil looked all hot and disheveled and delectable, and against her thigh, he was hard and thrusting. Claire's body recognized his and started softening. "My mother and sisters. They know," she managed desperately.

"Sure, they do. You told them you were going camping with me. They can connect the dots." He wasn't listening, sitting up to take off her walking boots, then his own.

Claire sat up and pulled on her flannel pajama top. She scooted into the pajama bottoms, then into the big double sleeping bag. Neil lifted a mocking eyebrow. "You know those are just coming off in a minute, honey bun."

"I meant it, Neil. We're not exactly alone."

He blinked twice. "What do you mean, 'exactly'?"

Then as realization hit, that the triplets and their mother were extraordinarily connected, Neil hurried to zip up his jeans. "Okay, just how is your family in here with us?"

"The water. It could be a conduit for a psychic. I'm more vulnerable near large natural bodies of water. My family could pick up—"

Neil groaned painfully. "Through you? They'd get an image of what *we're doing*?"

"Maybe. I'm getting stronger. I don't really know."

Neil flopped to his back, his arms behind his head as he stared up at the ceiling. "And that's why they didn't want you near water—because you're more vulnerable. How the hell does that work?"

"It just does. It leaves me—my sisters more 'open.' It's like when people say the ocean waves relax them. While I might give off something of myself, something might come in. It's that way with my sisters, too. The ocean replenishes my mother, and it's her strength. It's our weakness. The only logical explanation is that we were sailing once with Dad and went overboard. The illogical reason could be that we're descended from sea-faring blood, from a Viking ancestor."

"I'll take the first one: All of you live away from major water, and you all went overboard and got scared. Makes sense to me. And I know how it feels to look out at the ocean. Peaceful . . . endless. I'll take your word for the rest of it, but you're definitely fascinated by that river. I've seen you staring at it." Then Neil's tone sharpened, as he demanded, "Why the hell would you want to come here? I told you this campground was by the Missouri River."

"This is important to me, Neil . . . and to you. I've got to understand what I am to control it. I don't want to go through what I did in that hospital again. And there's something else—I really feel the loss of your son, almost as if he were my own. Through your love of him and by seeing his picture, he's somehow become a part of me. I need to find what happened to him . . . I need closure."

"Because you're connected to me—linked as you said," Neil repeated slowly, as if he were trying to absorb something outside his comprehension. He stared at the teardrop's wood-grain ceiling, then slid into the sleeping bag.

Neil removed his jeans and hurled them at the end of the camper. "I don't like this at all."

"Neither did my ex-husband. I scared him."

"What kind of a man wouldn't stick by his wife when she was scared and had just lost her baby?" Neil muttered darkly.

"I don't blame him. And don't feel sorry for me. I can't stand pity." Claire came to lie beside him, her head on his shoulder. She smoothed his chest with her hand, nestling close to him, feeling for his ache and soothing it. "I'm learning about myself, Neil. I managed tonight. I'll manage tomorrow."

Neil's arm circled her, drawing her close and safe. "I know what you're doing—easing me somehow. But I'm worried about you. Promise me that if you—if things go wrong, that you'll tell me, and we'll get out of here."

Instead, Claire listened to the muffled sounds of the other campers outside. Someone was playing a guitar, and a mother called to her child. She listened to the steady beat of Neil's heart, let the warmth and safety of his body seep into hers, and let herself drift into sleep.

"We can't," Claire whispered as Neil's body pressed down on hers, and his lips started their hungry persuasion. He was still half-asleep, but his hunger simmered, warming her.

"Hmm?"

"Mom. Tempest. Leona."

Neil stilled and braced himself away from her. With his hair tousled, his eyes still drowsy, he seemed boyish. Just his face seemed boyish, Claire corrected, because the rest of him was very large and very hard. Neil's disgruntled look caused her to smile. "What's on the menu today, honey bun?" she asked, smoothing his hair.

He glanced at her and shook his head. "Real cute. Right now, I've got a little problem, and I can't think of anything past that."

"The fog is outside. I feel it. It wants to come in," she whispered after a moment, because she'd been waiting, feeling the river nearby and wondering what pulsed through it and into the fog.

"The fog? This trailer is snug. We're not getting damp." Neil smoothed her hair on the pillows, studying the silky mass against his skin. He lifted a strand to the dim light, then brought it to his lips. "I'm worried, Claire. This could be bad for you."

"Just get me close to the people Tempest identified and let me do my job."

When they had dressed and stepped outside into the cold, crisp air, Claire stood still and looked around the camping area. With the tall pines as a backdrop, the fresh morning scents blended with the smoke of last night's campfires.

Then suddenly she saw the fog curl around her, almost like a lover. Something inside her shimmered and drew her, a wave of energy passed through her, and she stood to stare at the gray churning width of the river beyond the fog. There was so much movement, almost as if the river were alive, as if she could step into it and be carried wherever she wanted to go—

Neil opened the rear of the camper to the chuckwagon-style kitchen and started water to boil on the small propane stove. The sounds distracted Claire from the river. She shook off her fascination with it; she was just overexcited and anxious to begin. Her mother's cautions about water had just stirred her imagination, and as an empath, Claire was more responsive to nature, that was all.

She turned to enjoy watching Neil in his familiar tasks. With ease, he laid out his shaving gear on their small folding table and hung a small mirror on the camper.

He glanced at Claire, and nodded, clearly approving of the way she looked in the morning, dressed in her dark green woolen cape, jeans, and boots. "I like your hair down like that. It sways around you when you walk. Very sexy. The cape brings out the forest color of your eyes. . . . Breakfast will be ready in a minute. Good old oatmeal."

As he brushed his teeth, Neil's dark, brooding look at Claire said he'd like to go back into the camper and make love. Instead, he lathered his face with foam and turned to look at her. The look softened and held and warmed as Neil bent to kiss her. " 'Morning, Claire Bear."

"Disgusting morning-person," she teased, enjoying the lingering softness between them. She held her cosmetic case in one hand, but the other lay on his chest, over the warmth and beat of his heart.

"Night owl." Neil used the end of the towel around his neck to dab away the shaving foam on her chin.

Claire leaned against the camper and settled in to enjoy the sight of Neil's shaving routine. In a red-and-black flannel shirt, rolled up at the sleeves, a worn belt around faded jeans and laced, steel-toed work boots, he seemed to be a perfect, timeless male. "Stop it. You're embarrassing me," he whispered.

She tilted her head and studied him critically. "You're really rather pretty, in a rough masculine sort of way."

His disbelieving snort caused her to grin. "We do this much, and I'm expecting you to get up early and get breakfast in the pan, woman."

"Dream on." It was all very comfortable, the teasing between a man and a woman, then something inside Claire stilled.

"Claire?" The whisper was so soft, so close and unrecognizable in the fog. She held very still, and the fog seemed to caress her face. It had come from the river—for her.

The steam of her breath mixed with the fog, and for that one heartbeat, they were one. . . .

"Claire?" Neil was saying at her side. Maybe he'd said her name that first time and— "The fog will lift after breakfast. Then I get to show off for you."

Neil nodded at a passerby, a big burly man with a beard, and spoke quietly. "That's Mac Pearson. He was there eight years ago and one of the names Tempest . . . got."

Neil was apparently finding it difficult to admit that psychic powers existed, even after firsthand demonstrations. Had he said Claire's name that first time, or had she just imagined the voice had come from the river?

"Okay." Beyond the campers who were setting up breakfast, calling out to each other, the fog was sliding back toward the river, hovering over it in layers. It seemed to be waiting. She placed her hand along her cheek, replacing the chill dampness and pushing away that unknown touch.

"Something wrong?" Neil asked as he leaned closer to her, his expression concerned; the bracing lime scent of his aftershave startled her, pulled her away from the fog's grip.

Was it true, then, that her senses were more open near water? She hadn't tested—hadn't a reason to test— Greer's warnings. After the sailboat accident, she'd been too terrified to go near major bodies of water. "I'm fine.

It's just really cold and damp. I'm going to the ladies' trailer—so nice of them to provide it."

With her cosmetic bag in hand, Claire walked to the ladies' bathroom, a larger trailer to accommodate several people. In the mirror, her face was very pale within the long red mass of her hair, her eyes shadowed, perhaps a little fear in the green shadows. Her maternal ancestor might have looked the same, mysterious, wary, uncertain. Had that ancient Aisling wanted her seer abilities, what she could feel that wasn't real?

The fog had wanted Claire, or had it? Was that real? That one moment when her breath and the fog became one?

Preparing for a day of outdoor activities, Claire wound her hair up and clamped it into a knot on top of her head. Tendrils drifted around her face, stirred by her breath, strands escaped the confinement, drifting down her nape. For luck, and perhaps for protection, Claire rubbed the silver brooch at her shoulder. It was just an artsy pin to someone not familiar with its history, but the wolf represented that Viking conqueror. The silver ring on her hand was something she'd wanted to give her daughter. "I should have done this long ago, worn things to protect me. I should have learned more about myself, to protect my baby."

She was just applying moisturizer when a woman came inside and washed her hands in the sink next to Claire's.

The woman smiled uneasily and hurried, leaving quickly. But in those few minutes, Claire had grasped the woman's fear. It vibrated from her, so vivid that it blocked all other images and emotions. For a moment after she left, Claire rummaged through that fear—it had something to do with Neil and his son.

By midmorning, with the chili cook-off scents filling the bright spring air, the lumberjack contest was also under way. Claire had met all of the people on the list, and though she sensed they were dark personalities, capable of crime, she found no attachment or guilt concerning Neil.

Then she noted the woman from the bathroom—thin, pale, with lank hair—to Neil. He identified her as Linda Baker and she'd been at the campsite eight years ago, with her husband, Roy. Neil spoke quietly as he looked at Linda. "I heard she had an operation a few years back. It changed her. She has a lot of health problems now. She used to be a little heavier and happy."

Claire mentally ran down the list of people Tempest had selected. Linda Baker's name hadn't appeared.

Married to a retired, good man, Linda was now a birdlike woman, looking this way and that, as if terrified; she kept to herself, her voice pattern abrupt and uncertain. She stayed on the edge of the crowds, always holding a little back, and her eyes would dart at Claire, then away.

Linda was standing back and alone during the wood-chopping contest. But as Claire stood apart in another direction, she caught Linda's wary glances. In a row of ten men chopping at the lengths of timber in front of them, Neil was almost beautiful, the rhythm of his body sensuous, power in each blow. The logger's ax blades looked dangerous, flashing in the midmorning light, biting savagely into the wood. Claire held her breath; one wrong move and—

Neil swung furiously as if he were fighting demons and not a block of wood. Periodically, the men rotated, chopping big wedges into the opposite sides, and when finished, they yelled as blocks of wood separated and tumbled down. Neil placed third in the contest and came swaggering back to Claire with his logger's ax over one shoulder and a small plastic trophy in one hand.

When he grinned at her, her heart skipped a beat and flipped over; it was the kind of look that a teenage boy gave his girlfriend, and Claire felt just about that young and fresh. Neil handed her the trophy and wrapped his arm around her, kissing her breathless.

"I don't ever want to see anything like that again. You could have chopped off your toes, or a leg or a hand and you could have fallen and—" Claire managed unsteadily.

But Neil was enjoying himself and knew just how to use his tongue to set her simmering. He did that playful chest-nudging thing, as if he enjoyed her softness against him, and his hand was caressing her bottom beneath her cape. He knew what he was doing, creating a little payback, getting her to respond to him before he reminded her of that moratorium on lovemaking. Claire wanted to drag him back to their camper and stretch him out and—

"Okay. You won't see that again this year, honey bun," he said cheerfully. "That contest is over. Next year I intend to get that first prize. I could have used that chain saw in the next contest."

Claire remembered that chain saw and what it could have done—kill Neil. Now here he was, testing himself against the other men, for no reason at all. "Boys and toys. This bull-of-the-woods contest stuff is lifting the testosterone level of every man here. You're competing like a bunch of—"

Just then, Neil picked a sturdy tree and hurled his ax. The blade and long handle rotated through the air, whirling, and the blade sank into the tree. Clearly in his element, Neil grinned and squeezed her next to him. "I'm better at hatchets. I've been practicing my rotations against distance. If this no-lovemaking ban holds, I might have enough energy stored up to win every contest."

"You're not doing that again, Neil. That big ax could—"

"Okay. No axes. This afternoon's contest is for hatchets anyway." His grin widened, the boy within the man teasing her.

That afternoon, the Montana sky was blue and clear above the men preparing to climb the tall, limbless trees; the trees' trunks had been scarred by previous contests. "I thought you said you weren't going to do anything dangerous again," Claire said as she gripped Neil's shirt.

He was looking up that tree, gauging it. "I said 'like that' again. Ax competition is over."

"I'd rather you wouldn't."

"Can't back down now. I put good money on the line to enter this. No refund on that." Neil kicked the tree with his boot, testing the heavy metal shank strapped to his shin and calf, the spike stabbing the wood.

"I'll—I'll repay you whatever the refund would be." Claire looked up the length of the trees. They seemed to stretch into the blue sky, the sunlight flashing through the foliage at the tops. If Neil fell—

"Claire, what kind of a guy would I be if I took your purse money?"

"Designer handbags, Neil!" Claire realized she had yelled. Yelled. Calm, serene, quiet Claire Brown had lost it. People were looking at her and laughing and it was Neil's fault. "Stop . . . irritating me."

"Okay, they're bags. Pretty little bags. How's that going anyway? You could sell a few here if you tried."

"Remember that designer handbags are the new shoes, Neil. Perfect, changeable accessories. Mine are very expensive, and this crowd doesn't look like they're into designer wear," Claire explained overpatiently. He knew how to push her to the limits, and he was grinning now, playing her. Neil liked to tease her just to see her light up. Claire struggled for composure. "You're trying to distract me. It won't work. And I did not come here to peddle my *designer, one-of-a-kind handbags*. And you are *not* climbing that tree."

"I'm not?" Neil looked down at her briefly, slapped a heavy-duty belt around the pole, and buckled it to himself to test the buckle's adjustment. Leaning back against the belt, he took leather gloves from his jeans back pocket. He drew the gloves on carefully, then rolled his head and rotated his shoulders, apparently loosening his body for the task.

Neil looked every inch like a man suiting up for serious business—like risking his life to win some dumb little plastic trophy. And nothing—evidently not the woman he was sleeping with—was going to stop him.

It was the first time Claire had seriously faced and opposed macho-man testosterone leaping to a challenge, despite its deadly danger. Neil looked down at her hands gripping his belt. "Let go, Claire. This is man's work. Well, except for Nelda over there. She can rip right up a tree. Her dad owns a sawmill. She runs it. I could teach you to climb, if you wanted. You'd be good at it. You're real agile and strong."

The starting call sounded, and Neil tensed, adjusted the big belt to his body and the scarred tree trunk, his hands gripping the thick, wide leather. He tugged it away from her hands. "Back off, Claire Bear."

"I—I suppose we could—you know—a distance away from here," Claire offered softly, hoping that she'd played a winning card. Inspired, she went for an image she knew would get to him. "Did you know I can put my feet behind my head?"

Distracted, Neil stared at her blankly just as the starting whistle sounded. Then recovering quickly, he shook his head and started climbing upward. He jabbed steel spikes into the wood, at the same time lifting the belt again and again, each time higher.

Claire held her breath and watched him quickly move up the tree, a rhythmic blend of moving the belt, jabbing in his spikes.

Then about forty feet from the ground, Neil had just lifted that big belt higher, preparing to move upward with his spikes. The belt snapped open, the ends flaying as it came free, and he was falling backward. He seemed to fall in slow motion, his hands reaching out to catch the branches of a nearby smaller pine. He snagged a branch, his fall slowing. He held on to the branch with both hands, working downward to the lowest branch. He hung for a moment before dropping easily into the brush.

Terrified for Neil, Claire rushed toward him. "Neil!"

Instantly, a crowd surrounded him, blocking Claire from him. Her consuming fear for Neil, isolated and protected her from the crowd's sensations. In working through the crowd, she brushed a woman's sleeve and felt trembling fear jar her. That fear was separate, very different from those of the crowd concerned about Neil. As Claire glanced at the woman, Linda Baker's panicked blue eyes stared back at her.

Claire's heartbeat seemed to still, though it was only a fraction of a second, and everything seemed to happen in slow motion. If only Claire were more experienced, she might have gotten past the wall of fear blocking her. Instead, she was absorbing Linda's fear, and it was becoming her own, shifting from her fear for Neil. She had to stop and think and focus. Claire sank into those words, giving herself to them. *Stop . . . think . . . focus. . . . Build walls, keep them outside you. . . .* The woman's look held for another heartbeat before Claire forced herself to pull away.

Ahead of her, two men waded into the brush. "Hey, Neil! Are you okay?"

"Yeah."

By the time Claire made it past the crowd, the two men had hauled him out of the brush. "I'm okay, everyone. No big deal."

When Claire managed to get near him, Neil was sucking in air, clearly steadying himself. And he wasn't happy. "I lost that one, too, dammit."

"Are you hurt?" Claire gripped his shirt with one hand and her other ran over his face. She dusted away the light debris and held his face in both hands, drawing it down to her as she inspected a small new cut and a few scratches. She was too panicked to sense anything but his irritation as she carefully lifted a small branch from his hair.

"I might have a few bruises and scratches, but the only thing hurt is my pride. I really wanted that trophy."

"You'd go through all that for a little plastic—?"

But Neil wasn't listening; he walked to where his belt had fallen and studied the belt. The leather holding the buckle had torn open. "I just oiled and worked with this not long ago. I guess I missed something."

"You seem to be having a lot of accidents, Neil," Claire stated carefully as she brushed away the debris caught on his back.

Neil turned slowly, and her hands rested on his chest—his heart was beating safe and strong. "I'm so glad that you're safe," she whispered, drawing his head down for a kiss.

It quickly changed to sensual, and Neil whispered in her ear, "What was that you were saying about putting your feet behind your head?"

Before she could answer, a prickle ran up her back; it caused Claire to turn to see Linda. Then the woman noted Claire watching her and hurried away, her thin shoulders hunched up protectively.

Something was definitely bothering Linda, and Claire intended to find out what it was. . . .

Eleven

A LITTLE APART FROM THE REST OF THE GROUP AROUND THE
evening bonfire, Linda Baker sat near her motor home,
a big tan, older homey unit. Beside her, a lighted battery-
lantern stood on a small folding table. Several small
crocheted doilies were displayed on the table, handwritten prices pinned to them. Colorful Scandinavian-
style caps with tassels lay on top of matching scarves.

When Claire entered its sensors, the plastic German
shepherd sitting on the motor home's steps sounded a
loud, realistic bark. Linda's hand moved behind it and
the artificial barking stopped. She quickly returned to
crocheting, her long metal hook flashing in and out of
the thick yarn. She didn't look up as Claire removed her
sunglasses to study the crocheted work; she wanted no
buffers between herself and what she might sense from
Linda.

"Hi, Linda. I'm Claire Brown. We haven't had a
chance to talk. I thought we could get acquainted
now. Your things are lovely," Claire said gently as she
stood near the woman who had seemed so frightened
of her.

"Prices are marked on them. Lots of folks peddle
things here. Roy and I are retired and it makes a little

extra gas money." In a defensive, protective movement, she pulled her thick shawl tightly around her shoulders.

A few yards away, couples two-stepped to a country band in the light of a bonfire, and the crowd clapped to the beat. They laughed when the rusty-voiced singer added his comments to the song.

Neil stood talking earnestly to a group of men, his boot braced on a stump. But Claire caught his glance, filled with concern, warmth, and the promise to deliver when they were alone. That special delivery simmered for a moment through the distance, because Neil's hungry growls throughout the day as he caressed her bottom said he wanted more. She smiled briefly, and, apparently reassured that she was fine, Neil turned back to the men, who were comparing a variety of wooden ax handles from a vendor.

Linda's crochet hook stopped for just a moment, then jabbed through the yarn quickly as she continued watching. She reached to pull the zigzag-pattern afghan onto her lap and tug more yarn from her basket. But her hand shook just slightly, and Claire didn't miss the quick intake of Linda's breath.

Fear pulsed from Linda as she edged slightly away from Claire. Linda's fear was powerful enough to block Claire's unskilled psychic probes, and Claire had to work hard to keep that fear apart and outside her—at a level that couldn't hurt her.

The chilly wind had picked up, playing in Linda's thin gray hair. The colorful plastic lanterns hung from the motor home's awning began to swing. As Linda watched the bonfire, firelight gleamed on the dry, weathered skin covering sharp cheekbones. She appeared to be in her fifties; her lips were thin and tight, deep lines surrounding them. The crochet hook worked faster, the woman yanking more yarn as she needed it, whipping it around her fingers. "You're with Neil Olafson. He hasn't brought a woman here for a long time."

"He brought his wife eight years ago. They had a son, just six months old. They're divorced now and neither one of them ever got over the kidnapping. But it wasn't really a kidnapping, was it? Or else there would have been a ransom note. . . . Someone just took the baby while his mother was sleeping. The baby's disappearance must have been an awful time for them both."

Linda's silence was so loud, Claire heard it instead of the warning beat of her own heart. "Did you know them?"

Flashes of burning pain, a silent scream of terror hit Claire, and she knew that the unfriendly energy was coming from Linda. . . .

Claire pushed herself to focus, to reassure herself that the emotions weren't hers. But she might never get another chance to talk privately with Linda, and she had to be very careful. Claire moved a slight distance away, just enough to rebuild her defenses.

Disturbed again by movement, the plastic dog started barking loudly. As if it startled her, Linda briskly thrust her crochet hook through the ball of yarn and hurriedly tucked the afghan into her basket. She snatched the crochet work on the table, as if she didn't want to leave any of herself behind. "I have to go fix something for tomorrow's potluck. We all have to do our share, you know."

Focus, Claire. . . . Tap into Linda's sensations, but keep them separate from your own. . . . Is Linda afraid of her husband?

Wanting to explore Linda, Claire moved closer, and tiny pinpricks of fear danced all around her. But it didn't take psychic abilities to see Linda's fear. She quickly folded her chair, placing it against her camper. "I need to neaten up before turning in. That's my husband's chair beside you."

Claire folded the chair and placed it with the other. Disturbed again, the plastic dog's barking had started the campground's other dogs barking, but Claire needed to concentrate on Linda. *Focus, Claire. . . .* "Would you tell me about the day Neil's son was taken, what you remember? Anything you know, please?"

"I know you don't belong here," Linda stated harshly, then forced a brief, tight smile. "Neil is an outdoor, common kind of guy. You don't look like you camp much, keeping to yourself. And you don't wear off-the-rack clothes and jewelry. I don't know why you're here, talking with me."

"Because I'm a very good listener, if you ever want to talk. Here's my card. Just call. I make designer bags, and maybe you might tell me a little about all the beautiful things you've made. . . . Or if you want to talk about anything—"

Linda frowned sharply. "Everyone got questioned at the time. Me and Roy, too. No one knows what happened to the boy. What are you doing here?" she demanded. "You been asking too many questions. Campers live and let live."

But Linda snatched the card Claire held out to her, then hurriedly stepped inside her camper and closed the door. Claire stood quietly, trying to feel inside; she wasn't strong enough, but even without her abilities, she could recognize that Linda was hiding something. "Oh, sure. Now you're quiet," she muttered to the dog.

The wind flirted with the tendrils along her cheek, chilled her nape, and Claire looked out at the river, wondering what it wanted from her. Uneasy without understanding why, Claire quickly walked to Neil's camper and leaned against it. She scanned the campsite and found him standing apart from the other men.

He was staring into the bonfire, the flames lighting his hard face. A fire had taken his parents, and from his expression, he appeared to be locked back in that time.

"Neil!" Claire called out to him; she wanted him safe and away from that darkness. She watched Neil walk toward her, his body silhouetted by the flames behind him; he seemed to walk through the fire, a terrifying image that clung to Claire. A man of fire, a man in the fire.

Claire shook free of the image she didn't understand—unless it was related to the way Neil's parent's had died. Her instincts told her that Linda knew something about Neil's son. But should she tell him?

When he tugged her long braid and kissed her, she held him tightly. "Neil?"

"Mmm?"

Claire waded through the sensuality stirring between them and braced herself to tell Neil of what she had just felt, while near Linda. "I think I picked up something about Sammy."

Instantly, Neil stepped back and frowned. "What? You mean, you felt something from someone?" he clarified.

"Yes. I think Linda Baker could know something. She's terrified and nervous. I couldn't get past that. Mom could, but I'm not strong enough . . . I think Linda's fear blocked me."

"Linda? You think she might know something about Sammy? But she's happily married, Claire, with four grown kids and grandchildren. She and Roy were questioned back then, but they had just retired and were glad to be away from their family for a while. They had no reason— No, Claire. You're wrong on this one. Linda may seem a little odd at times, but she's okay.

Her health has really gone downhill since I first met her."

"She's terribly afraid of something, Neil. I think someone has abused her . . . she feels pressure from something—and horrible fear."

Neil shook his head. "Roy? No. He's a gentle guy. He's protective of her."

"Cosseting women closely could be a sign of an abuser, cutting off her ties to other people—"

"She's in a lot of charity organizations, a member of this and that, always hitting us up for donations. She's not cut off from anything. She has to take medicine for her nerves sometimes . . . maybe that's not working." Neil turned to the man who had just called him. "Just a minute, Ollie. Okay, I'll bring that price list. I'll be right over."

When Neil walked toward the man's motor home, Claire stared at the river, a wide silver ribbon in the moonlight. Replaying her time with Linda and Neil's denial of possible involvement with the disappearance of his son, Claire inhaled the chilly damp mist and slowly walked to the riverbank.

In a land where Native American spirituality still hovered nearby, the river had known so much. Beneath the smooth, swirling surface, the currents were deadly and waiting.

Claire had to test herself against the water, to see if it truly could act as a portal through which she could reach others—and they could reach her.

If she could just stand near the river and not feel anything. To protect herself in that first link against whatever wanted her, Claire focused on a new design: horizontal swirls of color, layered in oranges, yellows, and browns, crossed by vertical striations of black—

From the campground, a man yelled at her. "You, there! Claire! I want to talk with you."

She turned suddenly to Linda's husband, Roy. Burning red flashes leaped at Claire as he came near, leaning down toward her. Anger had changed his usually round, jovial face into a mask of fury. "Why are you bothering my wife? Linda is all upset and crying, because she thinks you're after her for something—asking her questions about Neil's baby. She didn't have anything to do with that ugly business. We've got kids of our own—grandkids. She's a mother, for God's sakes. I want you to leave her alone—"

Claire struggled to remain calm. The man's anger burned her, but the river behind her seemed to be getting closer. . . . She reached for the brooch, gripped it tightly, found that sharp point, and mentally repeated the blocking phrases she'd practiced: *Stop . . . think . . . focus. . . .*

She forced herself to imagine a wall, brick by brick, circling her, keeping herself separate from everything else around her. She stopped the uncertainty and fear circling her, found inner calm and centered on that.

"Claire?" someone called to her. Neil was probably looking for her. But she had no time to answer; she had to focus on Roy's anger, to push it away. It wasn't her own. It wasn't coming into her. "I'm sorry if I've upset Linda—"

"Upset her? She thinks you're accusing her of taking Neil's baby. My wife would not do a thing like that."

Emotions were pulsing around her—fear, worry, anger . . . and love. Roy deeply loved his wife; he only wanted to protect her.

A healer, descended from a seer, Claire instinctively started to place her hand on his face, to calm him, but Roy shoved it away.

To the man behind Roy, his action could have looked like a slap. "Don't do that again, Roy," Neil advised as he came closer to put his arm around Claire. His glance noted her fist wrapped around the brooch, a sign of her distress and anger flared in his eyes. "What's this about?"

"I—" Claire turned to the river. It seemed to be tugging at her, wanting her to know its secrets. . . . But to know them, she'd have to step into the water, to go under it. . . .

"Claire?" Neil was worried about her. Had he called her before—or was it something, someone else?

She could be picking up Roy's anger and it was weakening her defenses.

She laced her fingers with Neil's and an instant surge of power and warmth ran up her arm.

Roy set into furiously defending his wife against Claire's "lies." Neil glanced at Claire, who stood bound by the men's emotions. Unable to move, she could only hold her brooch tightly and silently ask him to help her. She looked at the river, then at him, her lips moving—

In that heartbeat, Neil understood. He hurried to draw Claire away from the river and Roy's anger. "Claire isn't accusing anyone of anything. She just knows how important closure is for me. We're all just a little tired, Roy. That's all this is."

"Your girl better not come around my Linda again," Roy yelled from behind them.

"Come on, Claire. Come back to me," Neil urged, as they walked toward their campsite, his arm around her.

"It's true about the water. I was vulnerable, and I felt something from it," she managed. "And Roy was so furious. He was only protecting his wife. He loves her very much, and he loves children. He's a good man."

Neil glanced around the campground; people had stopped to watch the scene. "He's really protective of Linda, and if he thought you upset her, he probably wanted to push you in it. You need some rest. This whole thing isn't good for you. We should leave in the morning."

Claire stopped walking; she turned to him. "Wait a minute. Are you worried about protecting me? Or are you worried that I'm upsetting your friends? You're not happy about me talking to Linda either, are you? You don't believe me about Linda knowing something, do you? I was getting a reading from her, Neil. You weren't around to interfere, and I'm certain I caught something. Do you believe that?"

"I . . . think that she's obviously ill, a nervous person, and anyone who doesn't know her might look at her and get the impression that she's—"

"Is that what you *really* think? True . . . sometimes visuals and feelings go together, but I *was* getting a read from her, Neil. I'm positive. Her energy was too strong. But you can't handle that, or believe it, can you?" she demanded, her temper rising. But then, it wasn't Neil's fault, was it? It was her DNA's fault, her damned inherited seer's blood.

Her anger might not really be hers at all. Maybe she was still experiencing Roy's, a backlash of some sort. After her attack, bits of the man's rage had lingered, disturbing her. Separating her own emotions from those of others was a skill Claire badly needed to practice.

"You asked me to help you. I'm trying. I'm learning. And right now, I'm not exactly certain of myself or what I can do. But I felt something in Linda's energy. Do you believe that? Or are you just going to explain it away, so that you don't have to deal with something you can't physically experience?"

When Neil hesitated, Claire knew she had to have some time apart—from everyone. "I know this is hard to accept easily, Neil. I'm not blaming you. I didn't blame my ex-husband. It's *my* problem. But I can't walk away from what I'm feeling. In fact, there is *no* ignoring what I am. I know that now. I'm taking a walk. Alone."

Neil wasn't happy with Claire, but then he *couldn't* fully understand, could he? How could anyone, when she didn't entirely understand herself?

At this point, she could only pick up energy from other people, their emotions and just a tinge of words; she wasn't a true telepath, she couldn't get exact thoughts— except she had been receiving Neil's pretty accurately. She could be wrong about Linda; Claire's perception could have been based on the simple visuals of a nervous person.

Claire wrapped her cape around her and walked up the trail to the dirt access road. The moon slid through the pines above, animals rustling in the underbrush. A few deer crossed the road ahead of her, moving toward the river.

The river. Her mother's warnings were true then, that there was real danger in the water. But then, her own fear was a danger, throwing her into a panic. In just a few heartbeats, Claire had felt herself opening, transmitting, communicating. Empaths connected with nature easily, but a river? What had she sensed coming from it? A psychic connection to her family? A link with Sammy?

But then, maybe she was too curious, also a trait of empaths. Maybe she was picking up fragments that didn't mean anything— Or maybe it did. Maybe she was picking up something left behind by Sammy, or communicated by him.

Greer Aisling could sometimes stand in the room where a person had last been and catch flashes of what had happened to them. Neither Claire nor her sisters had ever received such insights. Was it possible that

Sammy was out there somewhere, alive and linked to this area, thinking about it?

Claire abruptly inhaled the pine-scented air, holding it inside her before releasing it. But then, she didn't really know herself yet, did she? Was Neil's son actually calling out to her, using the river as a psychic connection?

Linda had snatched the business card from Claire. But would she make contact? What did she know?

Locked in thought, considering Linda's unusual behavior, the fear apparently riding her, Claire suddenly heard pounding footsteps behind her. She turned slightly to find Neil charging her, his body slamming into her as a vehicle drove past them.

Startled and off-balance, Claire momentarily faced the big pickup bearing down on them. The headlamps weren't on, but she caught a glimpse of the driver. Caught in that rectangle of glass and moonlight, his face was hard and fierce and determined—

Then the force of Neil's body took them both tumbling into the ditch; rocks crunched beneath the tires, and dirt billowed into the air as the big pickup sped by them. Only then did the headlights turn on, too late to see the vehicle's color or the license plate.

"Are you all right? Hurt anywhere? I didn't think you heard that truck coming up behind you," Neil stated unevenly as he pulled Claire to her feet and scanned her face.

"I'm fine," she whispered unevenly. Neil tugged her into his arms and held her shaking body tight against him. *That driver had intended to hit her.*

"The guy should be using his headlights. He should have honked. He could have hit you—it even looked like he was aiming for you. You could have been killed, dammit."

*She'd seen the driver's rage-filled expression on an-
other man; the man who had attacked her at her
home—*

Neil looked at the direction of the road from where
the pickup had come. "There's a few old shacks down
there, past the entrance to the campground. They're
mostly used by winter hunters to warm up. I'll go down
there in the morning and see what I can find out. I
know the pickup's make and model. And then, we're
heading for home—you need some rest, that's all."

"I saw his face—the driver. It was just a flashing impression, but I think he wanted to do just that—hit *and*
kill me."

"I didn't get his license plate. Did you see him? Who
was it? Do you know him?"

Beneath her cheek, Neil's heart was pounding, his
breath harsh against her cheek as he cradled her close.
To push her terror away, Claire focused on that slowing
heartbeat, pacing her own with it, until they seemed to
beat as one. "I don't know. I've never seen him before.
If you hadn't been walking behind me— Why were you
there? Roy surely wouldn't—"

"No, he wouldn't. That's twice you've almost been
killed, Claire."

"No, three times," Claire corrected softly. "There
was another time, when I lost my baby. If my family
hadn't come when they did, there would have been
nothing left of my mind. . . . Neil? Show me the picture
of Sammy again?"

Claire stood apart as Neil retrieved Sammy's picture
from his wallet. Before he handed it to her, there was
just that sweep of Neil's big thumb across the photo,
the caress of a father longing for his child.

Claire held the photo between her two hands and
tried to picture the child, safely asleep in the camper.
She was stronger now, perhaps. . . .

But no images appeared in her mind, and Claire shook her head. She gave the photograph back to Neil. "I don't know what I am yet. I don't know what I can do. I did sense something from Linda, and when I stood between Roy's anger and the river, I was able to protect myself. I did it, Neil. I panicked, but I actually stood still and built a wall around myself, blocking everything else out."

She smoothed the brooch, remembering how just gripping it had stopped the panic. "There's something else. I saw something—I saw a man in a fire. It has something to do with you. I've never actually *seen* images, never— And I know it has something to do with Sammy. I know it! I feel it!"

"Take it easy. You were almost killed just now, and you're shaking. You'll be okay."

But Claire wanted more than "okay." She wanted to find Sammy.

In his home office the next evening, Neil stopped working on his estimates of a new camper order he'd taken at the rally.

He'd pulled into his driveway a couple of hours earlier and walked Claire to her door. After he'd insisted on going into Claire's home to check it, she'd been very clear that she needed to rest—without him. But first, she needed to return the calls to her family; they were worried about her. And he wasn't? Okay. Fine.

Neil almost regretted asking Claire to help him; the dimensions within her were changing, elements growing and shifting, and he couldn't help her. *I saw something—I saw a man in a fire. . . . It has something to do with you. . . . I've never actually seen images, never. . . .*

Before entering his house, Neil had spent a couple hours going over his inventory in the shop—and cooling down. Little had kept him from walking to Claire's door and— He'd made a bad mistake by not supporting her at a time when she needed him.

Neil turned off his calculator and tossed his pencil to the yellow pad. He leaned back in his desk chair and considered the windows of the little house next door. The little off-limits house, he corrected darkly—and that was Claire's decision.

Since he'd known her, she could have died the second time, because that truck was aimed right for her. The red brake lights had lit just once in the night's shadows, the lights turned on too late for a description. But that driver had to know he'd almost hit someone—someone who wasn't paying attention. If Neil hadn't followed Claire, he didn't want to think what might have happened.

Neil looked down at the scratch pad where he'd been tracing Sammy's name over and over again. Claire seemed obsessed by Sammy's disappearance, and there was no way that Linda Baker could be involved. Neil had seen her with her own children and grandchildren and was positive that whatever Claire had sensed, Linda Baker wouldn't have taken his son.

Neil picked up the framed picture of Sammy. He traced the baby's round, happy face. His son might be out there somewhere. He'd be eight and a half now, playing ball, running with other boys. . . .

Was Claire so deeply involved because she'd lost her own baby? Had she really transferred that ache, and absorbed his own need for closure, into the search for Sammy?

Did she sense somehow that Sammy had gone into that water? Was that why she seemed drawn to that wide gray river, staring at it?

Was that how Sammy had disappeared, into the river? Had someone taken his son and thrown him

*into those deadly gray currents? Was that why Claire
needed to take her walk "alone"? Because she had to
frame her words to tell him what she suspected?*

After the pickup had nearly hit her, Claire had withdrawn from Neil. She was over there now, all tucked
into her little house, away from him. While Claire
clearly needed to recover, Neil needed to hold her, to
make love to her, to reassure himself that she was safe.

With his mind on Claire, and Sammy's disappearance, Neil walked into the bedroom and tried not to
look at the bed where they'd made love; he picked up a
basket of dirty clothes and walked into the back utility
room. Neil didn't notice the trickle of water at his bare
feet.

Electricity sizzled and held him only for a minute,
throwing him backward—

"Yes, I felt it. The river wanted me. It drew me, or I
thought it did. But I'm back home and safe now," Claire
told her mother over the telephone. "But I'm certain
this woman knew something about Neil's baby. I'm
positive of it. She was too nervous of me."

"Mmm. Probably has a touch of the psychic herself . . .
she could have sensed you. Psychics are often nervous
of each other. You were too open by that water, Claire.
I warned you."

Claire decided not to tell her mother of the near hit-
and-run. She had seen the driver's face clearly, and he
wasn't any of the campers. Neil had said the truck was
headed for her, as if it meant to hit her. "Or maybe I
was just reading Linda's body language, the shift of her
eyes."

"It all goes together sometimes. I'm just glad you're
safe. Your sisters and I were worried, Claire Bear. I
know they've called. Leona has been restless, not a
good sign for someone with unwanted precognition."

Claire focused, trying to make a stronger psychic connection with her mother. "There's something else, isn't there, Mom? What is it?"

"Okay, honey. You've been avoiding telling me about the near accident you almost had with a vehicle—a truck? A big pickup?"

The trickle at the back of Claire's neck warned her to be cautious. She focused on her "Imagine" bag, methodically checking each individual, intricate stitch, following them as they sank into the fabric and appeared again. "I was saving that. You said you'd had a restless night."

"No, I didn't. But that was a really good blocking technique and a good probe, Claire Bear. You're uneasy, aren't you? We're connected, you know," Greer reminded her. "Did you remember to focus, Claire? Did you keep her outside of you?"

"I wanted to know what she was feeling."

"You called her in, didn't you? That's so dangerous for you now, Claire. You're still learning," Greer warned.

Claire probed again, testing her strengths, and her mother's smooth voice chided her lightly. "Naughty, naughty, honey. I've been 'probed' before, by experts. But that was a good try for a beginner."

"Something is really bothering you, isn't it? And it has nothing to do with me or my sisters. Are you feeling all right?" She could feel Greer closing up, backing away.

"I'm always 'feeling,' dear. I'm fine. I'd really rather we didn't talk about this. It's a new case I'm working on, and you certainly don't need the overload. . . ."

"I wasn't expecting to be so attracted to the river. It had something to tell me. Is that possible?" The fog had also seemed to reach out to her, the layers tangling around her legs, almost like tentacles. And she could feel it waiting outside the camper.

"Very possible. Empaths are connected to nature and very curious. You were attracted to it, were you?"

"Fascinated. It seemed—" The fog had seemed like the arms of the river . . . wanting her, beckoning her. . . .

"To grip you? That's dangerous, Claire. You were too open to nature and what it could do. That's why you've got to stay away from large bodies of water. They have the potential to leave you vulnerable and open to anyone with psychic powers. And that could have been the woman you spoke to. I could help you, honey—"

"Thank you, but this is my journey. It's time I met this demon, isn't it? Learned how to control it? Or, rather, control myself? Isn't that what you had to do?"

After a long hesitation in which her mother weighed a protective instinct against the reality that her daughter must live her own life, Greer agreed. "I'd rather you didn't go through what I did. Our special gifts came down through my mother, and she refused to admit it. I think she knew what I was but thought she could take it out of me. Not good at all. Not when you can't help what you are, when you're a child who doesn't understand yourself, or the adult's frustration with you, the reflection of everything she doesn't want. I know now that it was actually her own desperate frustration with herself."

When the call ended, Claire shook her head. Whatever was bothering Greer had been there for some time, and she was hoarding it. "Naughty, naughty, Mom."

Claire tried to focus on her new "Imagine," methodically sewing the beads on with silk thread, using yarn to outline the big vivid silk flowers. . . . But her mind was on Linda and the nearby river.

Leona was uneasy now. . . . Greer wasn't revealing whatever was bothering her. And that made two restless clairvoyants. *Add them together, and what do you get? What do you get?*

Then there was Neil, who made no effort to shield Claire from his dark mood. He wanted to help her, to protect her. But what was happening to her would be difficult for anyone to understand.

This wasn't her journey alone; she'd asked him to open up a painful wound— Claire looked at Neil's house and at one o'clock in the morning the lights were still on, unusual for an early-morning person. She sipped her tea and relaxed in a warm, scented bath, and let the stressful events and problems drain out of her. The water lapped around her body, and suddenly Claire remembered the river's call to her. Shaken, she hurried out of the bath to dry.

With her eyes closed, her hair piled on top of her head, Claire listened to the soft strains of calming music—and thought of Neil. Anyone lacking psychic ability could easily get the point of his brooding silence and clipped, sarcastic, "Okay, if that's the way you want it. Fine, be by yourself. You have my number— and know how to use my mailbox. Let me know when you're ready to chat."

"I can do better than that, honey bun," Claire murmured, using Neil's nickname for her, tit for tat. "I just needed a little calming space, that's all."

A half hour later, Claire walked toward Neil's dark home. She tested the front doorknob and when the door swung open easily, she knew he was expecting her.

In his bed, Neil knew it would be a long, wakeful night: He was missing Claire's warm softness, and the painful electric shock had shaken him—he was lucky to be alive.

He heard the light footsteps pass through his house,

slowing at his bedroom door. Claire appeared, silhouetted by the dim light behind her. The long coat she was
wearing slid slowly to the floor to reveal her curved
body. She shook loose the hair piled on top of her head,
and it spilled around her.

As she moved slowly, sensuously toward him, the
moonlight passing through the window appeared in
pale strips on her body. Her eyes gleamed, her scent
feminine and arousing as she moved over him, found
him, gloved him moistly, tightly. .

Her body tensed suddenly, and the hiss of her breath
brushed his skin—Claire raised slightly to frown down
at him. She seemed wary and puzzled. "Neil?"

"What took you so long?" he whispered against her
lips, as his hands slid down her body. . . .

"Business can wait," Neil stated softly as he gathered
Claire against him in the early morning. Outside, in the
fourth week of May, the birds chirped and the world
seemed right again. In the aftermath of lovemaking, his
voice was lazy, relaxed, his body hard and safe against
hers. "I missed you."

"I missed you, too."

He toyed with her hair, spreading the dark red strands
across his chest and studying the effect. He wiggled the
end of one strand beneath her nose. "Liar. You were on
the telephone with your family, discussing this whole
thing with them."

Claire smoothed his shin with her insole, enjoying
the contrasting textures. "Only Mom. I'm a learner, and
learners need to talk. I didn't think you'd want to listen."

"I'm listening now."

"I went out to the kitchen to get a drink of water last
night. There wasn't any electricity. The utility room's
window is broken . . . cardboard duct-taped over it.

The washer is pulled free of its pipes in the utility room, and there are tools everywhere. What happened?"

Neil was too still, then he said, "There was a water leak—"

Claire raised up to look down at him. He was hiding something. In last night's initial lock of their bodies, she'd been stunned by a powerful jolt—but then with Neil deep inside her, hitting all the right spots, pleasure jolts usually happened. This one was different, painful and riveting for just that heartbeat. "What else?"

"I got a little shock, just enough to stun me." Neil stroked her hair, easing it away from her face. "You've got the cutest ears."

"You were standing in water when it happened?"

Neil eased her over him. His hands moved to grip her hips, as he studied the length of her pale body against his own. He breathed slowly as he moved her against his hardness, probing gently. "Mmm. I wasn't hurt—just took a pretty big jolt. I had to step up on a chair, walk across the kitchen cabinet to the window. The utility-room window was stuck, and I had to break it, to get in and turn off the breakers."

"The washer or plumbing leaked . . . but what else?"

Neil was nudging her intimately, watching— Claire shook him. "Stop that, Neil."

"Honey bun, I haven't started yet."

She braced away slightly. "The electricity. That's what I felt last night. It hurt—"

At that, Neil scanned her face and frowned. "I never thought— I'm sorry."

"Only a little, at first. It held me. And I knew something was wrong, but we were already—"

"It's an old house, Claire. The ground on the hot water heater had come undone, and there was a nick in the 'hot' wires off the breaker. The ground should have tripped the breaker, but it didn't. The washer had been leaking a little from the tub, but I've been so busy that I—"

Claire seemed to leap from the bed, tearing away the blanket and sheet from him. Her hands traveled all over his body. Neil held his breath as those agile fingers explored him intimately. He allowed himself a pleased smirk; his girl really knew how to investigate.

"Turn over," she ordered briskly.

"Could you just feel around a little more where it counts?"

"Shut up. Just do it." Her hands slid down his shoulders and back, over his butt and down each arm and leg. Her hands stopped at his feet and slowly, carefully went over them. "Details, Neil."

It was going to be difficult to keep secrets from a "feeling" woman, of both kinds, mental and physical. Neil turned over and tugged her over him.

Claire frowned down at him; her fingers dug into his shoulders. "I knew something was wrong. I knew something had happened to you. You should have told me."

"I didn't have time. It was nothing, Claire. I'm just glad you weren't here to get hurt." Neil held his breath as those green eyes darkened and slid into that dark gold color. They seemed to devour him—something he was hoping her body might do in a moment.

Her anger seemed to crackle around her, her hair draped around her face, running in red waves across her pale shoulders. The strands caught sparks from the dim morning light, the tips seeming to lift and curl at the ends.

Neil sensed that he was going to get a real wake-up jolt; he settled in to enjoy Claire's mood—she looked fierce and determined. He could only hope.

Her body tensed beneath his roaming hands—he especially liked the way her butt curved right there, before it slid into that long thigh, down to the soft back of her knee, and the way he could circle that butt to come up inside that dampness.

He didn't have time for a slow exploration because Claire took away his breath, diving into him, demanding everything. . . .

Twelve

FROM HER HOME, CLAIRE WATCHED THE ELECTRICAL service truck pull into Neil's driveway. After her terrifying discovery this morning, his house was going to get a thorough going-over, plumbing and electrical, or she wasn't visiting him again.

Neil's casual "Don't worry, honey bun. Stuff like this happens all the time," and his attitude that her fear for him was just feminine whimsy had set her off. Unusual for a peaceful woman who didn't like conflict, Claire had taken a fierce stand on his safety, and Neil had promised to redo the electrical and plumbing in the old house.

She wrapped her arms around herself as she looked out the window and remembered how she'd put every bit of whatever power she might have into making Neil understand that "everyday accidents" weren't acceptable. Neil was far too important to her, a part of her right now and on this journey. Correction: He was necessary to her on *every* level.

A pickup truck with two more men pulled into the driveway. Neil greeted them. He took time to grin at her window and give the thumbs-up sign that said his house would be safe enough for her to come back soon.

That relaxed look Neil wore this morning suited him, and pleasure washed over Claire. "Sexual" suited her; she'd done a fine job on him, from head to toe—but then the favor had been returned, primitive, demanding, and satisfying after their abstinence at the campground.

Claire shivered restlessly; her hunger for Neil was growing and she wasn't certain she liked the emerging, possessive, demanding Claire—a woman who knew just how to take what she wanted in her own hands.

This new physical Claire wasn't at all calm when it came to Neil. Her own anger, the way he could set her off, was too primitive, something she had never appreciated in other women. *Was she like other women, after all? When it came to one special man?*

Claire tucked those questions away in her mental to-do-later box. But one thing, she knew for certain, she had changed. The old Claire would have never zapped, reached in, and demanded everything in lovemaking.

When the men weren't looking, Neil turned toward her house. Though Claire was several yards away and viewing him through the window, she could easily see his playful kiss, followed by his teasing grin. She caught herself smiling back, feeling light and easy, and playful, too. Neil could make her feel like a young girl with her first boyfriend. After returning the air-kiss, she closed the curtain because she wanted him to know that her terms stood. Neil had to be more careful.

She could have killed him for not telling her about the electical jolt—until after they'd made love. At first touch, she'd felt it inside her, sizzling just that moment, then it was gone; she'd caught the remnants of the electricity from Neil.

Claire closed her eyes and remembered Neil tumbling through the air into that brush. "Big idiot. You don't have to go out and *find* accidents. They seem to find you."

Possessive? For the moment she was invested in Neil's welfare on a very personal, basic, feminine level.

That he hadn't told her of last night's accident nettled. And she'd made him pay to the fullest, prolonging every minute of his passion. Tempest was right: Men had to be tamed and trained. They were ignorant of some relationship necessities.

Her first experience with a full-blown snit had been exhausting. Claire yawned and tried to concentrate on fitting "Imagine's" tortoise-tone handle to the bag. She'd missed sleep during her days and nights with Neil. Somehow she was turning into a daytime-person. That was irritating, or maybe it was just because she didn't know what else to do to give Neil—or herself—closure.

Claire recounted her time with Linda. If Linda did have psychic powers, Claire could have just picked up her energy. Maybe the river had embellished either one's powers to the point of—

Distracted and tired, Claire reached for the telephone. It had actually rung this time, and it wasn't her family.

The woman's voice was thin and uneven, hushed. "I've only got a minute. This is Linda Baker. Could we meet? I don't want Roy to know I've called you."

Claire's heart started pounding fiercely as she picked up a pen. "Yes. Just tell me where and when. I'll be there."

"Alone?" Linda pressed desperately.

"Neil won't know, or anyone else. I'll come alone. Two days, then. Yes, the day after tomorrow, at the old barn."

After the disconnect, Claire continued holding the telephone receiver. Curiosity demanded that she try to feel out Linda. But nothing remained except the terror echoing in the woman's voice.

And the uneasy certainty that while Claire had asked for Neil's trust, she wasn't returning the favor—not this time.

Keeping her rendezvous with Linda from Neil wouldn't be easy.

Weather-beaten and airy, surrounded by discarded and rusted farm machinery, the old barn stood amid acres of land that would be gold with wheat in late summer, the wind creating waves over it. The singular paddle of the old windmill caught the sweeping wind and turned slowly, creating a slight rhythmic whoosh.

It matched the slow beat of Claire's heart. She could be creating problems for everyone, including herself. She was still a novice, but her psychic ability was growing and changing its dimensions.

Three crows sat on the windmill's weathered gray scaffolding, watching her. The morning sun caught their feathers in shades of blue-black, their beaks gleaming as they tilted their heads. Suddenly, all three cawed and swooped to the ground, strutting and pecking at it.

To Claire, the birds seemed like miniature guards, marching their rounds, but then, as an empath, she was sensitized to nature, wasn't she?

Claire watched that single blade turn, its shadow touching her again and again. Wind lifted the tendrils around her face and chilled her. In pursuing what she guessed might be a lead to Sammy, she was taking a big chance that could affect several people, perhaps harm them. Yet, as her experienced mother had warned: The curiosity of an empath, the knowledge that there would always be answers to questions wouldn't let her rest. "And they say that curiosity killed the cat," Claire reminded herself.

Bracing herself with a deep breath, Claire forced open the big doors of the barn and drove her Beetle into it. Linda had been adamant about hiding their vehicles during their rendezvous, and the old barn was big enough for both.

Claire stepped into the barn's cold shadows. Slices of daylight laid strips in the darkness; disturbed, mice scurried to hide from the intruder.

The late-May wind slid through the places where the boards were missing, and doves dipped in and out of the spaces, perching momentarily on the old rafters. As Claire thought of Neil, a pale feather spiraled down through the shadows. Her path to find Neil's son was much like that feather, uncertain of the end, where the final answers lay in the shadows of time.

The feather landed on a large pale shape in the shadows, and Claire came closer to find a buffalo skull staring back at her with hollow eyes.

She shuddered, but remembered that the Blackfeet once hunted these lands. Someone had collected a skull to be forgotten later. Recovering, Claire forced herself to think of Neil.

He'd needed repair and business supplies in Great Falls, and he'd be gone all day. She'd said that she needed to rest, then wait for the deliveryman to pick up the bags for Leona. At first, he was determined to wait with her; but early that morning, she'd convinced him that together, they weren't likely to rest. . . .

It was only a little lie, but Claire felt guilty. She'd dropped off the bags at Red Dog's commercial mailing depot before coming to the old wheat "ranch."

Would Linda come? Claire listened to the loud sound of an approaching vehicle; the Bakers' big powerful pickup had seen better days, its muffler needed replacement. She remembered Roy's anger, and grimly tightened Neil's denim jacket around her.

The loud truck died, backfired, then Claire heard only the beat of her heart and the wind sweeping through the cracks and missing boards. Had Linda changed her mind?

The pickup started again and moved slowly into the barn. When the driver got out, a sliver of daylight outlined Linda's thin figure. "I'm here, Linda," Claire called as she walked out of the shadows.

Linda pushed the barn doors closed, and as Claire came closer, she could feel horrible fear pounding at her. It wasn't hers, it wasn't hers—it was Linda's energy, not hers. "Please don't be frightened of me, Linda. I only want to give Neil closure. It's so awful to lose a child and not know what happened to him. Neil needs closure so badly—and so does Sammy's mother. If you can help give them that."

Linda moved away from Claire and hunched into the shadows; her voice was thin, hesitant. "You scare me."

"I'm sorry. I only want to help. I know this isn't easy." *Be patient, Claire. Focus. . . . Focus on Linda. . . . Open. . . .*

"I'm supposed to be shopping for a present. Roy's birthday is coming up. The kids and me went in on a new recliner for him."

"That's wonderful. I know you love him very much—and he loves you. You're so lucky to have your children and grandchildren—"

Tears gleamed on Linda's pale, thin face. "That's why I know I have to do this. You can't tell anyone. I have to trust someone or I'll—I'll just go crazy with what I did. You're—different—aren't you?"

Different? Was that the label of what she was, what ran inside her, the gift of that ancient Celtic mystic? "Now you know my secret, Linda. Yes, I'm very different. I just feel things, and what I feel from you is that you want to help."

"Oh, God help me!" Linda cried out, and startled birds fluttered up off the rafters and flew into those slices of clear Montana sky. "I've carried this for so long. It's eating at me."

As a compassionate woman who wanted to help another—and as a woman determined to help Neil, Claire moved instinctively to hold Linda tight.

Images flashed at Claire, fragments of blurred memories sailed by her. There were sponge-like layers upon layers of memories, repressed and quivering, little holes where scenes had slipped through. Certain that Linda might not consciously remember specifics, that to survive she had probably worked to forget her living nightmare, Claire worked to open those holes, pushing through the levels of darkness and deprivation. A young Linda amid other young people, frightened and alone, seeking shelter, seeking oneness. . . . A dictatorial leader, demanding sexual favors for himself and others, painted faces, drugs . . . spiders crawling on faces. "You were a part of a cult, Linda?"

Wrapped in her own memories, Linda didn't question Claire's assumption. She nodded and pressed her face against Claire's shoulder, and gripped her as if holding onto a lifeline. "A long time ago. I got out of it and married Roy. I blocked most of it away. I can't remember the faces, some of the details. I don't want to. I was a misled kid, who looked for love in the wrong places and made a bad mistake. Everything was good until *he* saw me in Great Falls. And then, it started. I have a family, and he was going to ruin everything, tell them about when I was younger, the things I did, if I didn't—"

A flash of Linda taking the baby leaped into Claire's mind, but she needed to hear the words. "And you took the baby."

Linda's sobbing had leaped into wild cries. "Yes, yes! I took that baby and I gave the boy to him. He promised the boy would be treated well, and I—I thought maybe some nice couple needed a baby and that Neil and Jan would have more. I know it wasn't right, but I was so scared!"

Forcing herself to focus and put Linda's emotions outside her own, Claire held the woman tightly. "Do you know where the boy is now?"

"No. I've lived with this for years. I've gone over it and over it, what I could have done—should have done. I can't sleep—I've been so sick, and I can't sleep, haunted by it all. Jan came to visit our site, and she was going to put the baby down for a nap. We had a cup of tea and—I used Roy's slow-acting sleeping pills in her cup! I didn't want to do it! I didn't! I have children, and I knew what it would mean to lose one of them, but—"

Despite her own stunned emotions, Claire knew Linda had paid terribly in those eight years, her health suffering. She would carry this guilt for the rest of her life. Untrained in perceiving illnesses, Claire sensed a large dark spot, then several spots throughout Linda's body. The disease would take her painfully, and she didn't have much time—she shouldn't have to live the rest of her life in shame.

Shaken by the knowledge that her abilities were moving beyond what she had expected or what she could control, Claire forced herself to remain calm. She stroked Linda's back and comforted her. "I know you didn't want to do it. You were protecting yourself and the life that you had, your children. You were so afraid. Don't be, Linda. You have me to help now. Do you know the name of the man who made you do this?"

Linda spat the name like a curse, "John. He was 'John' in the commune, but in private, he made me call him 'Master.' "

John? The name of the man who had attacked Claire?

*Before the attack, he had been trying so hard to build a
new life. But if he was the same man, she might never
find the boy. . . .*

"Do you remember what John looked like, Linda?"

"I told you—I tried to block all that out!"

Afraid to push Linda too much, Claire focused on
spreading a calm, soft glow in the other woman's mind,
pushing away the darkness. "You have a beautiful family, Linda, and Roy loves you so much. Think of how
the wind flows over the wheatfields, like waves on the
water. . . ."

After a moment, Linda's panic eased somewhat and
she straightened.

"You're going to find the boy?" Linda asked cautiously as she moved away. She trembled and wrapped
her arms around herself. "I need to tell Neil, don't I? I
should, shouldn't I? Now?"

"Let's wait, shall we? Neil has been through so much.
I would like to see if I can find more information before
getting his hopes up, okay?"

Linda sniffed and dried her tears on her sleeve. She
seemed lighter, more at ease, but now Claire shared her
burden, didn't she? Linda peered at Claire. "You look
so tired. You're exhausted, aren't you? What are you? I
mean, how do you know so much?"

"I feel things. Don't you? Just a little?" Claire asked
cautiously.

Linda shook her head. "No. I don't have the 'sight.'
I've heard about it, but just thought it was weirdo stuff.
But now— You *do* have it, don't you?"

"A little, maybe." Claire tried a light probe into Linda's psyche and found only distress, fear, and hope
that Claire could help her. She found relief and love,
but nothing that was strong enough to affect her, to
draw her to the river. Whatever connection had been
there wasn't through Linda's psychic ability. "I'm a good

listener, Linda. Anytime you want to talk, you can call me. I know what it is to hide a secret, a big one that you don't want."

As Linda hurried away, Claire stood very still inside the barn. The windmill's paddle whooshed rhythmically to that slow, fearful beat of her heart.

Would the trail end with John's death? Was the boy alive? Where was he?

As Claire put the key into her home's new dead bolt, she recognized the heavy footsteps coming up her porch steps. She didn't turn; she was exhausted and too vulnerable, and needed time to protect and shield her emotions. "Hi, Neil."

Anger shimmered in his tight words. "Had a nice outing today, did you?"

She nodded and turned the key to open the door. "It was a beautiful day for a drive."

Neil turned her quickly and shoved open the door behind her. "Get in."

He leaned down to study her face. "You look like hell. Where were you, and what happened to you?"

When Claire braced, preparing what she should say, Neil simply wrapped both arms around her, picked her up, and walked inside her house. He put her down and closed the door behind them. "Now. Explain. I came over to—well, never mind. But you weren't in the house when I came in. I was going to check on you. I called a few times and left e-mail for you. I called the delivery company and checked about the pickup—"

"How did you get in? I locked everything. I've been very careful."

"The dead bolts came with two keys, and it wasn't difficult to open the others with a credit card. We're going to change those, honey bun, aren't we?" His "aren't we?" was a statement of fact, not a question.

He started unbuttoning her jacket, and his tone was tight, sarcastic. "This jacket is mine. That's real sweet. You thought of me. Or did you? A pickup for your bags wasn't scheduled for here—today, honey bun. But they're gone—I checked. So that means you probably dropped them off somewhere. I called the place in Red Dog. They said you'd shipped your bags."

"I didn't want to wait. I didn't have enough packaging material for shipping and thought—"

"I want you to live *with* me. The electric and the plumbing are almost fixed now. What do you think?"

It wasn't the way Neil wanted to ask Claire to be a part of his life, but there it was, a bald, demanding statement.

Neil could feel Claire slipping away from him. Today, she'd gone somewhere and had come back looking as if she'd been through hell. Whatever she was up to, Neil wanted to help.

Clearly stunned by his lovers-living-together plan, her lips moved without sound.

"Gotcha, didn't I? Surprised you?" he asked gently as he drew her into his arms. "I just don't want to worry about some freak busting in here and hurting you."

Claire eased away. She wasn't looking at him; the prospect of moving in with him didn't seem to be appealing to her. "You could still use this house as a workshop," he added as an incentive.

Raw and vulnerable weren't emotions that Neil wanted to feel. He'd lived with women a couple of times, with Jan and one other. He'd learned a few things.

"Okay, I promise to leave the toilet seat down," he offered for a lighter feel, because Claire didn't look overjoyed. He followed her into the kitchen, where she filled the teakettle and put it on the stove. Clearly, Claire was taking her time before giving an answer. The big romantic moment, complete with candles, and his home-cooked dinner, might not happen. *What the hell was wrong with him? Where was she today? Why did she feel the need to lie?*

Neil was certain of one thing above all others: They were definitely, well and good, lovers. And lovers shouldn't lie.

Claire turned to him, her hands braced back against the counter, her face in shadow. The dark circles beneath her eyes alarmed him and she was looking at the floorboards between them. For Neil, that space was far too wide. "Okay, Claire. You could have gone with me, or sent the bags with me to be mailed. But you wanted—"

"I wanted some time alone."

Those words cut through him. "Is that right? What about a little honesty, Claire?"

Her head lifted and her eyes locked with his. "Okay. Here it is: You wouldn't like life with me, Neil. I'm not your usual."

"I haven't had a lot of 'usuals.' And I'm not going to walk out on you when things get rough."

Sunlight caught on her hair, circling her head in a ring of fire. "You think I'm comparing you to my ex-husband? Maybe I am."

"Strange. I've thought of you as a fair person."

"Paul didn't know what he was getting into either. But since—since the hospital, I've changed. I'm more sensitive, but now I'm becoming stronger." Then Claire turned to the steaming kettle and poured hot water into the teapot. "Tea?"

"Sure. Fine. Fix me a cup. Let's chat."

In the living room, Claire curled her legs beneath her and sat in an oversized chair—apparently putting distance between them. Neil sat on the couch and waited until she was ready to talk—one of the longest moments in his life.

Then Claire seemed to sink into the past; she spoke

of her childhood, how she'd been terrorized by the studies in the parapsychology clinic. She spoke of the bank robbery, of others' emotions storming over her, of blacking out. She'd awakened in the hospital, stunned by the loss of her baby and under the care of an angry, bitter nurse and a greedy, lust-filled doctor.

She spoke of her sisters, Tempest, who could feel the history of an object through her hands, and Leona, who was the most like the triplets' mother, possibly the strongest of the triplets, and that was what she detested about herself.

"Leona had flashes of the future, premonitions that her husband would be killed, and she didn't want her legacy. She's always detested it. Her husband did die in that avalanche, and Leona has never recovered from realizing that she can't change what she is. She doesn't want to 'dream,' as she calls it. My entering this search for Sammy is disturbing her. . . . We're linked, remember? That old family-tie thing?" Claire smiled softly, as if mocking herself.

Neil understood that Claire wasn't only giving explanations. She was walking down a trail she hadn't verbalized before and aligning herself with the reality that it was her individual passage—one that could not be denied. He waited for her to continue.

"Mom is restless, too. We all are stirred, uneasy. It happens that way—one becomes a little off-center and draws the rest with her. Distance helps, and Tempest isn't quite as sensitive as the rest of us. That's why she can move between us more easily."

Claire took a deep breath and inhaled as if bracing herself. "I'm afraid we come as a package, Neil. We're all very different . . . but my mother has it all, the combination of what my sisters and I have—and more. My ex wasn't up to dealing with that, and I wasn't turning my back on my family. I couldn't. But I loved Paul, and he loved me. He's a craftsman, too—woodworking. I guess our common ground was creating beautiful things and appreciating nature. He was a quiet, gentle, good man, a recluse like me. I loved him in that way—quiet and good. For a time, our lives were idyllic. He knew I had nightmares about the testing when I was ten, but after—"

She shivered as if chilled and rubbed her wrists. "That's where I got these marks, from the hospital—the nurse forgot to check on the padding of the restraints. After I lost our baby, after my—losing control—in the hospital, he saw what I really was. Ever hear of the words, 'run, don't walk'? That's what Paul did as soon as he could."

Neil ached for her, for what she was going through even now. "The guy was a jerk. I understand."

Claire stopped to sip her tea, then she spoke very quietly. "I don't think you do—just yet. Our baby would have been beautiful . . . a girl. Her name would have been Aisling, and we were already connected by more than my body. She would have had my seer blood, this ancient gift, in one form or another. I don't think Paul could have withstood that, either. Or that's what he said—he said, 'Maybe it was for the best,' when I lost the baby."

"Bastard."

Still locked back in that time, Claire wrapped her arms around herself and rocked her body. " 'For the best,' as if my daughter—our daughter—Aisling would have been a freak. I've been called a freak, you know. I couldn't hide it as well as my sisters. I'm more . . . open. I'm working with that now. I was successful at the river, when Roy was so angry. I'm learning to manage better, to block better, to build those walls and protect myself. I'd better, because I'm getting stronger, but I'm still terrorized by the thought of a repeat performance in some hospital. And I am never, ever getting pregnant again. You've got to understand that part, Neil, because you're a man who should have a family, a normal family. And it won't be with me."

"Honey—" Neil ached for what had happened to Claire, the ten-year-old child picked to pieces by the doctors and scientists studying her, the woman who had lost her baby and was terrorized, who had struggled against the restraints hard enough to leave scars on her wrists and ankles.

Claire looked at him, and Neil held his breath. From her expression, whatever she said next was very important and had to be said. "Today, I held a woman in my arms, and I knew she was going to die painfully. She doesn't know it yet. She's a good woman, one who has done her best in her marriage and with her family. She has adult children and grandchildren, and they love her. I didn't know I could feel disease—it just leaped upon me, and I knew."

She breathed slowly and licked her dry lips as she stared down at her open hands. "It's said that empaths can heal, but I don't know. I only know that I can ease heartache, and sometimes it becomes my own. I just knew that she would die. But there was a way I could help her, to relieve her of her burden before she passed. . . . Neil, she wanted to see me alone today. She's afraid of you."

Claire trembled slightly as if remembering the experience, then placed her cup into the saucer too precisely. She turned it slowly, studying it, and Neil shook his head. "I don't understand. Why would she be afraid of me?"

Claire stood and walked to him. She stood between his knees and placed her hands on his shoulders. A little gentle wave ran through him, and her eyes were soft and shadowed. "Neil, it's even difficult for me to understand.

But this is what I know. This woman—who is going to die painfully—took your baby. She gave it—"

Neil gripped Claire's wrists and stood to face her. Everything in him had gone stone-cold, then shock mixed with rage. Claire had gone out and discovered something that he hadn't been able to in eight solid years. And she hadn't told him she was on to anything, until now. "*What?*"

"She's dying, Neil. I won't give you her name. But I am going to find your son. I am asking you to trust me."

"That's a hell of a lot to ask since you've been able to keep your meeting with her from me. What's her name?" Neil realized that his grip on Claire was too tight, and he released her. He stood back and shoved his hands in his back pockets. "What's her name? *Linda?* You said something like this at the campground, and I didn't think it was possible. Roy called me later. Linda was still upset when they got home. She was being secretive with him—not like herself."

Claire's quick, confused frown and the way she turned from him gave Neil the answer. *Linda was involved in Sammy's disappearance*. "You didn't have to tell me her name. It wasn't difficult to guess . . . it was Linda Baker, wasn't it? So maybe I'm psychic, too," he added sarcastically.

"Everyone is a little. They just don't explore it, and you haven't. I'd know. Our link is of a different nature. You're just very quick and tuned to me now."

Neil sat down and put his face in his hands. The enormity of how anyone he knew—how anyone, he corrected—could have taken his son, overwhelmed him. But to let the years pass, see him and not feel his pain? He shook his head, as the discovery slowly sank into him. "All this time . . . Linda Baker took Sammy. What did she do with him?"

"She gave him to a man named John."

That brought Neil to his feet again. "John? The guy who committed suicide? Who attacked you?"

"I don't know. John's a very common name, and she can't remember what he looked like. But I intend to find out. She's started to remember now, and she could call at any time. She's shared a horrible secret with me. She's held it for years, and now she might remember more. Talking to me might open her memory."

Neil rammed his hand through his hair, his energy crackling around her in fierce, angry, anxious waves. "We should go see her, ask her—"

"Linda is dying, Neil. She's had eight years of stress that's taken its toll on her body and her nerves. And the legacy of taking a baby from its parents isn't one to leave to her family; they love her. She was forced . . ."

As Claire described her time with Linda, Neil felt as if his blood had stopped running through his body. He held Claire's hands and drew her down on his lap, close against him. She seemed warm and soft against the chill enveloping him. "Stop that. I know what you're doing—you're trying to calm me. Claire, there is no staying calm after this news. I hunted for Sammy for years. I still try, and nothing has turned up. I've seen the Bakers over those years, and they were investigated. Surely, something would have turned up."

"Roy's contest entry wouldn't have been caught by Tempest. He didn't know anything about the threat to Linda or what she felt she had to do. And Linda didn't enter the contest."

Then Neil remembered how Linda had changed, had seemed more withdrawn; he had supposed that was because of her various illnesses. *Clearly it was caused by the stress of taking Sammy!* He wanted to go to Linda, to force her to admit everything. "What's next?"

"We wait. You're still uncertain of all this, aren't you?"

"It's too much of a coincidence—the name John—the man who attacked you and the one who took my son. He must have known you were living next to me. Maybe he knew Linda was weakening and that he had to—"

Claire stroked his hair and kissed his forehead. "Before Linda, I'd get impressions, sensations—flashes . . . insights—from the others. But that is the first time I've sensed a disease from anyone. I guess it happened because it was so strong, and I had opened myself. . . . Are you mad at me?"

"Yes. Definitely. Okay. Maybe. It's a lot to take in. My son—"

Claire turned his face to hers. "We can't take away the rest of Linda's life with this. I think she'll call soon, with what else she can remember. Promise me you won't say anything to upset her? If you do, she might never remember. Please?"

"All I can think about now is that she took my son," Neil stated truthfully. But he wanted to trust Claire's instincts, gifts, whatever. It wouldn't be easy to wait.

"Then, for now, why don't you think about me moving in with you?"

"Keeping tabs on me, are you? Afraid I'll go over there and bully Linda?"

Claire answered honestly. "Yes. If I were you, I just might."

After all these years—*Sammy*. . . . "You think he's alive, Claire? Do you think Sammy is alive?"

"Yes, I do."

"Why?" he demanded, needing more.

"Because you and I are connected, and because he's a part of you, and because I *feel* him. I wouldn't feel him if he were dead—or at least I don't think so. Our seer blood doesn't include mediums for the dead. I think that maybe I felt him calling me at the river, I don't know. It was definitely calling to me. Neil, we have to give Linda time to remember what she can—"

Claire moved from him to walk to the telephone. Her eyes never left him as she picked it up. "Hi, Tempest."

Neil sat back to absorb Claire's discovery. The ache to hold his child was so fierce that tears burned his eyes. He'd be eight and a half now. Eight long years. . . . *Sammy.* . . .

Clearly, Claire was worried about how he would react, and if he would try to contact Linda.

She wasn't the only one to be worried. If the way she looked now, tired and wrung out emotionally, was any indication of what one meeting would do, how much more could she take?

Finding Sammy could cost Claire too much.

But Neil knew that they weren't turning back now, no matter what.

Thirteen

LINDA BAKER, A LONGTIME FRIEND, HAD TAKEN SAMMY.
The thought invaded his sleep and jolted him awake. Furious, Neil slid from Claire's bed. In the cool, feminine-scented shadows, he stood still; he listened for the slight sounds that indicated her presence, then jerked on his undershorts and walked to her workroom. At two o'clock in the morning, Claire didn't look up from cutting the fabric on her worktable. "Can't you sleep? No, I guess not."

"Could you?" Neil's tone carried the sarcastic bite of his frustration, and he resented how easily Claire could focus on her work.

The strategically placed lamps glowed around her softly, but one was angled high and bright over her cutting board. The folds of her overlarge white shirt lay in shadow, the fabric smooth where it touched her body. The sleeves had been rolled up, her right forearm flexing with the snip of the scissors while her left hand steadied the material. Neil tilted his head, studying those arms; Claire was stronger than she looked, and she knew how to keep secrets—but this time, she'd kept an important one, and she'd lied to him.

She leaned slightly over, the vee of the worn shirt revealing one breast, and Neil settled in to watch her work. The lamplight caught sparks in her hair; that long braid curved down her chest, dark red against the thin white fabric. The braid's tip brushed the worktable as she bent, angling for a better cut. It slid almost sensually along the cool white squares, used as cutting markers—and Neil recognized the tug of his body, because he knew how her hair felt in his hands, silky as it dragged across his skin.

Her intent expression, the methodical snip of those scissors following that rose pattern, seemed almost mechanical, as if nothing else existed—including him.

Neil remembered the day he came into this same room, the way the pearls and red beads caught in the loose strands that had spread away from her head. Her attacker's name was John and that was the name of the man who took Sammy—were they the same man? If John-in-the-same had died, would the trail to Sammy end?

Neil leaned against the doorframe, studying the graceful movements of Claire's hands, carefully cutting the material. Claire moved expertly, comfortable in the small neat area, the brightly colored boas shimmering with her movements. Neil blew gently and stirred them. "You need to play fair, honey bun. This is the second time you've given me a little something extra in our lovemaking."

Her scissors stopped flashing momentarily. "I don't know what you mean."

"You know, that little something to take the edge off, to calm me."

The scissors started cutting again. "Oh, that."

"Yes, that. After a hard day like yesterday, that secret spy meeting with Linda, you still had enough energy left to zap me, slide right in and smooth me down? That little mind and body tranquilizer?"

Claire wasn't admitting that she'd used her ability on Neil. She carefully removed the pins from the pattern and stuck them in her pincushion. She folded the pattern neatly, put it into a large envelope, and placed that in her file cabinet. Every movement seemed calculated to give herself time, then she returned to smooth the bag's red rose fabric. "I'm going to sew vertical braids on this, like a trellis, maybe puffing up the roses a bit . . . Dupioni silk and black braid, good sturdy handles . . . maybe a little pocket on the side for sunglasses. I'll make a sash to go with it, and Leona can put that around a wide-brimmed hat. Perfect for the horse-racing crowd, don't you think?"

"I think you're tired and should be in bed. All your spy work should have made you tired." Neil resented the nip of his words, his dark, brooding mood, and, most of all, the sensual light stroke of her fingers on that silk. It reminded him of her touch on his body.

Claire's soft smile mocked him. This time she looked at him, slowly taking in his body with the appraising ease of a woman who had made thorough love to him. "I'm a night owl, remember. My biological time isn't flipping over that easily, Mr. Daytime Person."

"I don't know if I can wait for Linda to call," Neil stated bluntly. He needed to do something, anything, and recognized the illogical transfer of his frustration to Claire. His raw emotions erupted suddenly. "And I don't know that I like the way you can pull that psychic business out of a drawer and use me as a guinea pig. You're busy here, and we both have work to do. I'm going to go over to my house and work on my accounts. At least that will keep me busy."

Her hand slid to take his. It was cool and soft and feminine and dangerous. "You can't keep this up, Neil. It will devour you. Give Linda time to—"

"She's had a full eight years." Neil studied those slender fingers lying on his larger hand and frowned; a wave of soft feathers seemed to be enfolding him, a euphoric fatigue. Neil slid his hands away. "Not this time, Claire Bear. Back off."

Her quick frown said she wasn't used to verbal slaps. She moved past him, that big shirt swaying at her hips and revealing long legs. "It's time for my walk. Are you coming?"

"Not this time." Neil moved quickly toward her and tugged her into his arms. He lifted her until their eyes were level. Hers narrowed and darkened into gold, his reflection in the irises; the lady was wearing a bit of temper herself. "Maybe there are other things we could do."

She wasn't backing up, and she wasn't giving in. "Maybe. You're feeling raw and anxious and frustrated, and you're looking for an argument. I'm not playing that game."

As always, Claire had exactly pinpointed his current mood. And that was very irritating. Claire could be nasty and irritating—and she was right about everything. Neil caught her braid and gently pulled it, angling her face closer to his. "Why not? So what if I want a little reality in what we're doing? Men and women argue, sweetheart. It's natural—it brings out the truth, levels the playing field. And don't try that feel-good stuff on me this time. I'm not in the mood to be babied."

" 'Playing field.' How typical." She caught his hair with both hands, pulling it just that bit for equal opportunity. "And I thought you were so easygoing, too. Don't worry, I won't 'baby' you."

Claire leaned closer and rubbed her lips against his, then the nip of her teeth surprised him. "Let's play. You want dominance, don't you? In one way, or another? To make me see how right you are? That we should just charge right in and get answers from Linda? Well, Neil-sweetheart, that's not going to work. She needs time, and you're not bullying me to get your way."

She was right again, dammit. Neil leaned Claire against the wall, let her feet touch the ground, and braced his arms on either side of her head. He took a hard, deep kiss, which Claire returned, locking her body against his. "You're irritating, Claire-sweetheart. And you're pushing. I'm an easygoing guy, but you reach right in there and go for it, don't you?"

This time, she nipped his earlobe, and whispered. "You know, I'm a little irritated with you, too. Until I met you, my life was pretty well calm and packaged. Now it's all over the place. I think I just may be in a snit, and you're the reason. I've only had one other snit, and you were the reason for that, too. I don't like to be in snits, honey bun."

Neil leaned down to rub that soft cheek with his own. He appreciated the steel and the focus beneath all that softness. "Yeah? What happens now?"

Her hands slid down his body to his shorts, then inside. "Guess."

"Hi, Leona," Claire said as she picked up the telephone. Through her window, she watched Neil walk to his pickup and get in. The last bit of the repairs and minor remodeling had just been completed that morning, so he probably wasn't running into town for supplies. He'd planned to catch up for lost time, working in his shop.

Yet he sat with both hands on the steering wheel, staring into space. Then he turned to her, his face harsh behind the tinted windshield. Very little was keeping him from driving to confront Linda Baker.

Claire listened to the sound of paper and plastic and Leona's excited "Oh! Oh!" and smiled. The eldest of the triplets and the most able to cover her emotions, Leona simply stated, "I love you. And I love these bags!"

"I'm glad. What's going on with Mom? She hasn't called." Neil was just sitting staring into space. Would he turn the pickup's key? Would he drive to Linda's?

Their primitive lovemaking had ended with her sprawled over him, panting for breath. Beneath her, Neil's heart was pounding, his body slick with sweat. "Think that did it, do you?" he asked rawly. "Well, think again."

A slight hot quiver ran through Claire's body, a remnant of their high-voltage lovemaking as she leaned against her workroom's wall, her knees weak. She remembered how they'd made love, almost like a battle for supremacy, each pushing the other until they both lay exhausted in the dawn, staring at each other.

Then Neil had pushed from the mussed bed and walked from the bedroom without looking back at her. He'd taken his shower and left her house without a word. When the door closed, the quiet deadly click echoed in Claire's heart, and she had drawn the pillow scented of Neil to her body. Tears had burned her eyes, spilling onto the pillow. She was asking him to wait for Linda's response, and that was probably the most difficult thing in Neil's life—other than losing Sammy.

Leona's voice brought Claire back to the present. "The bags are super. Every one. I'm unpacking them now and cannot wait to display them. I'm going to call my best customers right away for first pick. Oh, look!" Leona exclaimed as the bags' packaging crackled over the telephone line. "Let me see if—oh, you did! Your 'Claire's Bags' label is in every one. You're a genius, a real creative genius, Claire. These are going to cost a fortune. Profit, profit, profit. I'll work these up and get a check to you right away."

She paused, then offered a reminder, "Claire Bear,

you really shouldn't think about making love while we're connected. Especially the really hot, passionate kind. You could spare me that. I was getting a little embarrassed. . . . But I love these bags!"

Leona's excitement over the shipment gave Claire the opportunity to ask questions. "When Mom doesn't call, it usually means problems, and she hasn't called."

"Mom and I don't do well in conversation, Claire Bear, but I have no idea why she hasn't contacted you. I think I'll call Olivia Tremble first. She'll bring her friends to the shop. I bet these sell out in the next few days. Are you working on anything new now?"

Just getting answers from you, Leona. "One called 'Imagine'. . . . And I'm moving in with Neil."

Leona's pause said too much; she was concerned and holding back. "The Protector. It isn't all about hot sex. You're with him, then. Linked? Bonded in something other that sex?"

"I am—for a time. I want to see this through, to help him find his son."

"You care for him, and you're just afraid. Of him, and yourself. It's okay to feel like a woman, Claire Bear, to have all those natural emotions. You feel lighter, by the way, when we talk, so he's good for you. But there's more to it than his son. You actually *feel* his son, don't you? Through Neil? Oh, Claire. That could be so dangerous." Leona's uneasiness quivered over the phone lines. "Claire, be careful, will you? You're so—"

"Delicate?" Claire supplied. Her terror in the hospital flashed back at her. It was a place she never wanted to be again—terrified, losing control. She had to make this journey, not only for Neil, but to test herself.

"You're changing, becoming stronger. That could be a good thing—"

"Or a bad one? I know what I'm risking, Leona. I'm stepping into areas where I've never been. But I have to do this, balance my life, and I never want to be that exposed again."

"Mmm. And you're thinking that if anything had happened to us at the parapsychology clinic, or during our lives, that our mother would have felt the same loss as Neil—pure devastation. You're thinking that as closely as we're linked, that if something happened to any one of us—you, Tempest, or me, the rest would never recover."

"I think it's possible to find Sammy—alive. Do you?" Claire had resisted asking her sister's help, because for years Leona had pushed away her clairvoyance, had buried it as much as she could. Asking Leona to open, to penetrate reality, could be dangerous.

The prickle rising up Claire's nape told her that Leona was deep in thought and watching her words. "This 'Dreamscape' bag is gorgeous. . . ."

Leona inhaled sharply, and Claire's heart started pounding wildly—because she'd felt the words, got their impression, before her sister actually spoke. "I . . . think . . . he's okay. The boy. But don't count on me. I don't want to ever— Claire, be careful. I feel as if something is moving out there. It's hunting, and it's hungry for something. . . . No, don't listen to me. I got upset because you were hurt, that's all. I wanted to be with you and knew I couldn't. That's rough enough to upset any sister, right? Forget I said anything. Just be careful, love."

Claire hung up the telephone and watched Neil get out of the pickup and walk into his workshop. For a time at least, he wouldn't be going after Linda, but he was frustrated and uncertain, fearing that he would never learn more about Sammy.

She closed her eyes and leaned back against the wall. All she could do was wait.

But Leona was obviously upset. Her perceptions were

the same as Claire had felt by the river: *Something is moving out there. It's hunting.* What was it? What did it want?

The river and the fog had seemed to be calling to Claire, wanting her. Why?

Disturbed, Claire settled into working on "Imagine," forcing herself to focus on the design. It was late when Neil came to her house. Beneath her porch light, the lines around his face were grim, his eyes shadowed, and he looked too tired. She shook her head at his silent question. Linda hadn't called.

"The house is almost ready. You can bring over what you need. I'm not holding you to any live-in deal."

But the night's cold mist layered her backyard, and it curled around Neil's work boots, almost as if it wanted to drag him back into— "Claire?" He asked cautiously and dragged his hand through his hair. "I understand if you want to change your mind—after last night."

Fear raced through her. Whatever was lurking outside, wanted Neil— But there was nothing there. Nature had always been comforting, and now it frightened her. "Please come in, Neil."

"You've just turned white—you're too tired. I'll—"

"I said, *get in here.*"

"A nap in the morning and one in the early afternoon doesn't cut it for a nighttime person," Claire mused the next day as she looked around at Neil's living room.

She sipped tea from Eunice's china cup and smoothed the matching gold-trimmed teapot, squat and splashed with African violets. At the windows, Eunice's lacy curtains softened the bright late-afternoon sunlight and laid dainty feminine patterns on Neil's computer and desk.

In spite of worrying about Sammy, Neil was anxious that Claire be comfortable in his home; he wanted to keep their living arrangements adaptable to her needs, a come-and-go, back-and-forth relationship. And he wanted to protect her. But there were some things she needed to do herself, to test and strengthen herself. She shuddered lightly as she remembered sensing the big dark masses in Linda's body—something Claire preferred not to experience again.

She called her message machine next door and checked to see if Linda had called; she hadn't. *Come on, Linda. . . . Remember more. . . .*

Claire leaned back in Neil's desk chair, studying the neat desk and the pictures across the top. Eunice had showed her the pictures years ago, and now Claire studied them carefully. She touched the framed picture of Sammy, then the one of Neil's family—ordinary parents, a proud mother, two teenage boys, both of them looking like their father—big, Nordic-looking. The next picture was of the two brothers as twentysomething adults, each holding up a fish. The photo was a little off, as if a self-timer might have been used, the camera propped upon something.

Click. Neil's brother was a little too familiar, but she hadn't met him before— Claire picked up another framed photograph of Bruce as an adult. She turned it to the light. Traces of a hard lifestyle lined Bruce's face. The eyes were more fierce, a cold blue to Neil's gray shade.

Claire held her breath as she studied the photograph. She had seen the man before, and recently! Just a slice of moonlight had caught those same eyes . . . Bruce was the driver of the truck that had almost hit her!

Her heart pounding, Claire replaced the photograph; she sat back in Neil's big desk chair, gripped the armrests to anchor her, and stared at the photograph. *Bruce, Neil's brother, had driven that truck without lights, aimed straight for her—*

Or—if Neil had been following her, maybe she wasn't the target. . . . Surely not— Bruce wouldn't want to kill his only family.

She heard Neil's special rap on the back door, a signal used for her safety. Water ran in the bathroom as he washed his hands and face, then his footsteps came through the hallway to her. He stood behind her, his hands on her shoulders, and bent for a lingering kiss.

Claire smiled and said, "Nice-looking family. Is that your brother?"

Neil crouched at her side, looking up at her as his open hand rubbed her back. Claire leaned back slightly, studying her reaction to the easy, affectionate caress. "Uh-huh. Bruce is coming here in an hour or so. He usually picks times that suit his own schedule, and comes when he wants something—like money. This time it's a loan. I'm not giving it to him, and he can get pretty upset. Maybe you'd like to leave before he gets here?"

Money would be a big reason for murder, especially if Bruce were Neil's only heir. . . . Only heir—because Neil's son wasn't around. . . . Stunned by the photograph, Claire waded through the implications of one man killing his brother. If Bruce was there, that meant he had to be circling Neil—and Neil had been having so many potentially deadly accidents. *Could Bruce want money badly enough to kill Neil?* As Neil's only heir, Bruce was likely to inherit everything of Neil's.

Claire couldn't tell Neil any of this until she'd had time to think it through.

Still. She was certain that Bruce was the driver of that truck. "You won't tell him about Linda, will you?"

"Bruce isn't the kind of guy that you let know anything potentially dangerous. I'd rather you . . . maybe take another nap? You look like you could use one—at your house? Bruce isn't always quiet, or nice." As gravel crunched in Neil's driveway, he stood up, looked out of the window, and cursed. "That's him. You should leave now."

If she could just meet Bruce, she could sense if he wanted to harm Neil or her. She wasn't going anywhere until she had actually met Bruce and sifted through his personality, getting impressions of his dangerous potential to Neil.

"I'm not going anywhere, sugarplum. Don't you want to introduce me to your brother?" Claire asked with a flirty look.

Neil stared blankly at her for a moment, then said, "That 'sugarplum' remark is a real surprise, right up there with when you said you could put your feet behind your head. You do that on purpose, don't you? You know that it stops me in my tracks."

"Hell, yes." Claire stood on tiptoe to kiss him briefly.

The kiss was impulsive, teasing, and Neil savored this playful new side of Claire. Things were definitely looking up. "So can you? Put your feet behind your head?"

Claire's cheeky grin was more devastating than her flirtation mode, and Neil struggled to where he was going with whatever argument they had been having. He ran both hands through his hair; Neil was clearly not prepared to meet his brother and had been caught by Claire's wish to be introduced. "Okay, have it your way. Everything else has been."

Claire realized the dark, underlying message: He wanted to push Linda, and waiting wasn't easy for him. Then she stood slowly and braced herself to meet a brother whom Neil evidently loved, but who could cause trouble—and who had driven the pickup that had almost hit her.

Bruce was no sweetheart. The impact of hatred hit Claire the moment Neil's brother stepped inside the door. When they were introduced and shook hands, Bruce held hers a little longer than necessary—but then, she wanted the contact, too. She wanted to know if this was a man who could want to kill his only brother. A fiery jolt mixed with primitive sexual desire and hatred ran up her arm, taking away her breath. Bruce's crude, sexually appraising look took in her entire body; he leered as he looked at her breasts.

His sexual hunger wrapped around her; it was selfish, dominating, cruel. Claire braced herself, using her mental walls to repel the crude sensations. The brothers were Night and Day, she thought, Good and Evil, yet there was an undercurrent between them, a family link too strong to be ignored. The darkness she felt within Bruce could destory.

She held her breath as fire burned a path up her arm and when she closed her eyes, she saw the man of the fire—the man in the fire. . . .

Neil's hand on her wrist, drawing her hand away from Bruce's, could have been taken for proprietary. Or he could have seen that she was momentarily shook-up and unable to conceal her aversion.

Claire had thought she'd been prepared, her defenses high. But the churning mix of greed and self-indulgence and hatred had penetrated her mental walls, leaving her exposed.

On the pretense of straightening a curtain, Claire quickly moved away, her fingers shaking as she rearranged the old lace. "Neil, thank you for helping me with—who I should call to help with my electricity. But I'd better go home now."

"Sure." Neil seemed to understand; he knew his brother well, and he knew what she could be sensing—and that wasn't pleasant. Bristling, protective warnings shimmered within Claire, and she understood that Neil wanted her away and safe from whatever Bruce might say or do. Neil concealed that reassuring squeeze to her hand from his brother.

As she stepped outside the door, Claire heard Bruce say, "That's a nice piece. Doing her?"

Neil's deep voice was indistinguishable, but curt. As Claire walked to her home, she thought about Bruce's touch. *Electric . . . riveting . . . a painful jolt of dark desires.*

She entered her home and, to calm herself, moved automatically to make tea and cook—but her mind was on the driver of that truck; that slash of moonlight on the windshield had framed Bruce's hard features.

But then, she'd been falling, tumbling into the ditch with Neil. She could be wrong, but inside, Claire recognized that the sensations she'd gotten from Bruce could suit a man who wanted to commit murder.

If money was the motive and Bruce had the potential to kill, he also had the potential to kidnap a baby—and Sammy would be Neil's direct heir. . . .

On the other hand . . . on the other hand, if Bruce were circling Neil, he just might want to hurt anyone close to his brother. The Ifs were big and bad as Claire considered them. And there was no easy way to tell Neil of her suspicions.

By the time she had prepared a pasta salad, Bruce's big Lincoln was revving; his tires spewed the driveway's gravel as he spun onto the dirt road. One look at Neil walking on the path to her home, and Claire knew the brothers were at odds.

Because she wasn't entirely certain of her ability or its strength, and because if she were right about Bruce, Neil could be deeply hurt, Claire called Tempest. "I need you."

Then suddenly, Neil turned and walked toward his shop, and Claire understood the buffer of time he needed to deal with his emotions. Neil still loved his brother, but Bruce lacked that emotion for anyone except himself.

The light on the shop burned for another hour while Claire waited anxiously. This was Neil's journey, and all she could do was wait. When the light turned off, Claire walked to the old oak tree and waited.

She ached for Neil—he seemed so tormented, so drained.

"You're tired," Claire stated simply as she took his hand, lacing her fingers with his and sweeping his hair back from his forehead. It was damp with sweat, his face shadowed.

"Dealing with Bruce is never easy," Neil explained carefully. "He's got a little problem with me. I'm sorry if he insulted you. He won't again."

She suspected that Neil was wrong about his brother insulting her again—because men like Bruce rarely changed.

"You don't believe me?" Neil asked sadly as he wound her hair around his hand, studying the contrast of textures. "He won't, or I'll cut him off completely. He needs me to get him out of the messes he makes. He's never been able to handle money or work."

Claire wrapped her arms around him and wished she could ease the pain within him. "You can't fix him, Neil."

"I try periodically," he said with a sad smile. "He's all the family I've got. Wouldn't you try, in my place?"

He looked up at the old tree, and Claire caught the sensation of falling and of pain. She traced the crescent-shaped scar on his cheekbone. "You got that from falling from a tree like that, didn't you?"

"Uh-huh. Can't hide anything from you, can I? I broke an arm and a collarbone, and was pretty messed up. After I got better, Dad really laid into me, up one side and down the other. He said that going out on that limb was a fool thing to do. He was right. . . . Mom just cried." Neil was remembering his boyhood: riding bicycles, sneaking a smoke behind a building, playing ball, learning how to drive too early—all with an older brother.

Claire looked up at the tall tree, her hand still linked with Neil's, and closed her eyes. She saw a young Bruce high in that tree, grinning down as Neil-the-boy plummeted to the ground. Neil had seen Bruce just that way, and he'd lied to protect his brother. The image sickened her. "Did you have many accidents as a boy?"

"Probably no more than normal. I was pretty active and doing everything. I got chewed out a lot from the folks. I miss them. I guess I picked up where Dad left off when it comes to Bruce—arguing with him, trying to help him get his life on track. The folks tried to help by getting stricter with him. I know it was rough for him."

As a man who loved his brother, Neil was probably trying to justify Bruce's resentment. Claire wondered about the rest of Neil's accidents—the metal pipes falling from the shop's loft, a carefully built structure, the perfectly tuned chain saw that had gone wrong and could have killed him. The trouble with old electrical wiring and the leaky washing machine . . .

All of the accidents could have been explained, but the supports had given way in the loft, even though Neil had been very careful about its construction and the weight it would hold. The image of that pipe shafting down toward Neil chilled her.

Everything could have been accidental—except the incidents occurred *after* Neil had been away, leaving his place unguarded. Since she had been with Neil, Claire wouldn't have been home to notice anything, either. Brothers would let each other know their whereabouts, wouldn't they? Bruce would know exactly when

Neil wasn't home. *And Bruce had definitely driven that truck, almost running them down.*

"But you're still in touch. Maybe things will change between you."

"Nice of you to say that, honey bun. I know you're trying to offer hope, but that's not likely. He's a part of my parents, and I can't forget that, no matter what. We e-mail pretty regularly, keeping track of each other. He knows that if ever the bottom really falls through on him, he can come here—" Neil turned suddenly, bent, and lifted her into his arms. "I don't want you in this, Claire. It's been going on a long time. Just—watch out for him, okay?"

"I know. He wants what you have, doesn't he? And you have me?"

"I'm afraid it's an old story. But with you around, I'm changing my locks. If Bruce hasn't lost them, he has the keys."

As Neil walked with her to his home, Claire wondered about the locks. "What about the shop's keys?"

He kissed her forehead. "Okay, if you're worried about that, I'll change those locks, too."

As Neil slept restlessly beside her, Claire focused on Bruce. Neil could be wrong: If her suspicions were right, Bruce didn't have a *little* problem with his younger, successful brother. He had a *big* one.

"Neil is in Great Falls for the day, helping someone install solar panels in his camper and getting my car's fan belt. I said I needed to rest." The first week of June was bright and warm as Claire unlocked Neil's back door. Tempest stepped into the utility room that led to the kitchen.

"So the coast is clear, huh?" Tempest glanced at the washer, at the floor, then moved into the renovated kitchen. "No problem at all. You let me know when

Neil wouldn't be around, and I was all set up to travel. It's only a hop and a skip, a plane ride and a rental car, to you from Scottsdale. I can't believe you actually sawed through that fan belt."

"Not all the way. Just partially, and it was weathered already. It snapped perfectly, when I started the motor." Claire opened a kitchen cabinet and reached into a deep bowl. She retrieved a big black modern mug, then led the way to Neil's desk. "I got this mug just after Bruce left two days ago. He handled it."

Tempest paused in the hallway by the bathroom. She glanced at the mix of Claire's feminine articles with Neil's. "Aha. Thought so. He's not the kind of guy to let you brush him off. Told you. And you're different with him—lighter, happier. And definitely sexier—it's in the way you move, Claire Bear. Slinky."

Claire told herself that she was above Tempest's teasing. At the same time, she played to her sister's appraisal by sexily flipping her hair and slowly licking her lips. When Tempest's eyes widened, and she blinked as if stunned, Claire smiled and winked. It felt so good to be at the other end of the teasing business. "Got you, didn't I? We're just working things out now. Don't get all excited, and you really should work on your own love life."

"It's crummy. Some men like women to wear high heels when they make love—jewelry, whatever. But ever tried making love with your gloves on?"

When Claire laughed suddenly, Tempest stated quietly, "Neil really is good for you, Claire Bear."

"I know. I feel good when I'm with him. Lighter, as you said. And stronger." Claire managed to focus on what Tempest needed for a good hands-on scan. "Here is the portfolio of the brochures and paperwork that Bruce touched. I'm certain about that. Let's see . . . This mug was on the desk beside Neil's favorite one. And

Neil said that Bruce had brought that ship in a bottle. Apparently, it was meant to soften Neil up for a loan. Bruce once smashed their father's collection when he was in a rage."

Tempest slowly withdrew a glove from one hand as she studied Claire. "Nothing better happen to you, Claire. You're locked into this thing—finding Neil's son—and you could get hurt. If this guy, Bruce, is what you think he is, he—"

"I went all over this, once I recognized him as the driver of the pickup. I wondered if he could have gotten control of John. He'd definitely be a stronger personality, perhaps even charismatic and charming when he wanted, seducing and driving a weaker person. He's apparently good enough to deceive quite a few business partners, if not his own brother. But I can't find a real connection why he would have John attack me. Feel this."

Tempest stared at the cup Claire had just placed in her naked hand. Tempest tensed, her breath catching in her lungs as she closed her eyes, focusing on the cup. "Not good."

She shuddered and placed the cup aside, then ran her hand over the ship's bottle. "Not good at all."

Tempest removed the other glove and ran her open hands over the brochures and paperwork that Claire had spread on Neil's desk. "There's Neil. I know him. But the other is darker. . . . And you were right. Neil's brother is very dangerous. He's capable of doing anything to get what he wants, without regrets."

Claire asked carefully, "Do you think he could actually hurt Neil?"

A man of fire, a man in the fire. . . . She'd seen that image when Neil had walked to her at the campground. Had Claire gotten a preview of what Bruce had planned for Neil? Was her psychic element reshaping into seeing flashes of the future?

"I think Bruce could really hurt Neil, and from what you've said, he already has when they were boys." Tempest walked back to the washer and studied it. "So this thing leaked, huh? You say there were workmen here, right? I'll have to wade through them."

She ran her open hands over the washer and grimaced. "Sex and plenty of unprotected sex and beef—rare and thick cut. Motors and parts. Beer. More big breasts and sex. Mmm. Odd sex—heard of that, but can't imagine. . . . Deer seasons. Pioneer parents. Old cowboy songs where the dog died. This guy kissed his horse. Recovered alcoholics. . . . Well, no wonder Santa Claus didn't fill this guy's stockings—he was wearing them and a bra. . . . Okay, here. I found something."

Tempest crouched down, her hands sliding over the washer. Then she angled around and ran her hands over the exposed pipes and wall near the electrical outlet. She closed her eyes and concentrated. "He was here . . . messing around . . . and wanting Neil dead."

"I was afraid of that. Apparently the bulk of their parents' estate went to Neil. Bruce never got over that. Then Eunice named Neil as her only heir. It's not only an inheritance, it's jealousy and revenge, isn't it?"

"Pretty dark stuff. This guy has done a lot of bad things." Tempest straightened and drew on the gloves that Claire handed her. "Are you going to tell Neil that his brother wants to kill him? Are you going to tell Neil that Bruce was driving that pickup?"

"I can't do that to him just now. Thanks for the backup. My feelings for Neil could be interfering with how I'm absorbing sensations, I don't know."

"The guy is bad, Claire. No ifs about it." Tempest studied Claire. "We need you, you know. You balance us, bring us together, solve all our family problems. You're our own little therapeutic peacemaker. If anything happened to you—"

"I know. I'm developing, and there's no going back. I'll be careful. I'm focusing better, protecting myself better under stress. I have to. So while I'm glad you came, I hope your report to Mom and Leona will be reassuring," Claire added with a teasing smile.

But Tempest didn't return the smile or her usual flip remark. "You haven't been the same since you camped beside that river. There's something bothering you— and it's not light and easy as you are with Neil. Are you sure you're okay? Nothing unusual?"

At her back porch, the fog had seemed to linger around Neil's boots as if it wanted to suck him into its depths— "No, everything is just fine, except what we know of Bruce, and of Neil's son."

"Liar. Pants on fire. We're three minutes apart, and while I'm not up to mind-speed like you and Leona and Mom, we are linked. You'll have to do better than that, little sister."

Claire spoke carefully. "Tempest? There's one thing more—"

Tempest's green eyes widened and blinked. "Jeez, Claire Bear, what else could there be?"

"I think it might be possible that Bruce was involved in abducting Neil's baby."

Fourteen

NEIL TOSSED THE NEW FAN BELT ONTO CLAIRE'S WORKROOM desk. "It's a good thing you carry a spare fan belt in your trunk. If I'd actually gone to Great Falls to help Tinker with his solar panels and pick up a new belt for you, I would have missed seeing Tempest's visit. It's pretty hard to miss that snazzy little rental car out here in the country."

Just inches away from him, Claire sat at her portable sewing machine. Filtered by sheer curtains, the late-morning sun came through the windows, lighting the loosely tied knot on top of her head, those spiraling tendrils down her nape. He'd given a signal knock, and she'd obviously heard him come through her house, yet Claire hadn't turned to him. And there was probably a good reason why.

Neil moved around the table in the center of the room to see her better. He leaned against her work counter and crossed his arms. "Okay, Claire. You've been watching me to see that I didn't go have that little chat with Linda. Then, all of a sudden, you break a fan belt on a car you never drive. What's up? Other than now you're working by day."

"I couldn't sleep." Claire took her time setting her

sewing machine's needle into the free-motion embellishment pattern she was creating with the tiny black braid on the big red flowers. The sewing machine's light swept up to her profile, her throat, and the quick nervous swallow. "I could say I'd forgotten about the spare fan belt."

"You could." That was as far as Neil was going. She'd have to come the rest of the way.

The very careful way Claire removed the material from the machine and folded it said she was pacing her answer. "I *could* say that Tempest just dropped in."

"You could. But then, it's pretty amazing that she just 'happened' to drop in—especially when I wasn't supposed to be here, isn't it? Come on, Claire, you can do better than that. Give me some credit—you've been deceptive before, like when you went to see Jan, then Linda. What were you two doing in my house?"

Claire shifted slightly, just enough to tell Neil that she really was hiding something. Then she seemed to brace herself as she studied him; that dark red hair took fire beneath the sunlight, and her eyes had just turned that dark shade of gold. Claire's eyes were better than a lie detector, and certain that she was holding something big, Neil wasn't backing off.

Claire wasn't making it easy. "So, you parked down the road and waited to see what happened?"

"Offense is always a good defense. But yes, it seemed like a good idea." Neil shrugged; a man ought to be able to trust the woman living with him. But Claire was up to something; she'd called in her "feeler" sister to help, and she wasn't sharing why. Now that grated, and Neil pushed for the truth, lining up the facts: "I thought maybe Linda might have decided to show up. I decided that I wanted to be here when she did. Instead, here comes Tempest, doing maybe sixty on a rough road, moon roof open on a flashy red sports car. She had on a black scarf and big sunglasses—some fancy disguise, by the way, in rural Montana—and Linda wouldn't be up to handling a dandy little stick shift like a professional racer."

He didn't miss the protective body language as Claire crossed her arms and sat back in her chair. "I think that you're sparring, asking for a fight. I'm not giving you one. If my sister wants to see where I'm staying my nights—sometimes, and if I wish—that shouldn't be a problem. Is it?"

"I don't buy that." Claire's ability to remind Neil that theirs was a temporary relationship, some tenuous bond until she finished her "redemption" and her "journey," and helped give him closure, grated. But she was right; he was set to find out what she was hiding.

"Did I ask you to?"

"You're stonewalling, honey bun. You're trying to make me think you're angry—but then your eyes are still green and not that mad-gold. So I know you're playacting. Whatever you're hiding must really be good."

Neil was getting too good at reading her, and that was a little irritating. Claire stood and faced him. "There goes all my womanly mystique. Okay, I think I'm losing it. At least with you. I think that whatever is happening—has happened—between us has made me lose whatever strength I've gained to protect myself—against you."

"Now, that's news. You mean we actually could be dealing with each other just on a plain old man-woman level?" Her diversion was enough to let Tempest's impromptu visit go—for the moment.

He noted her eyes, their cool forest green sliding into dark gold color as she said, "Here's some other news.

While I was at your house, your girlfriend called. Mary Jane wants you to return the call. She seems to be missing you."

"Okay, I will." He should have already made it very clear to Mary Jane that he was involved with Claire, highly involved. But then keeping close to Claire was keeping him busy. Her eyes were still that dark gold and flashing at him; Claire was definitely in a snit, and just maybe that was good.

Neil decided to push that snit into anger and get what he wanted—just how Claire really felt about their relationship. "Let's see. I think I'm reading this right: You're probably peeved about Mary Jane. I'm sorry about that. I should have already taken care of telling her that we're in a *relationship in which trust is a big issue.*"

The drawer of beads that Claire was sliding into the cabinet closed; the snap echoed sharply in the tension-filled room. She turned to stare at him as if ready to say something, but her lips tightened just that bit, and her eyes were still that flashing dark gold color.

She seemed determined not to argue with him. Claire suddenly began clearing away her scissors and threads and ribbons. And that meant Neil had hit a nerve. She was either really jealous, which apparently, as a male, he needed to reassure himself that she—dammit, where Claire was concerned, he was too delicate. Neil shifted uneasily; he didn't like the latter idea. "That still leaves us with Tempest and the real reason she was here."

Claire tilted her head and studied him again, then she frowned as if perturbed. "I was wondering if I could use Eunice's tea set. I'm having a guest this afternoon. I think she'd be more comfortable here—and so would I. I don't want any interference when we chat. I'll need everything I can get from Linda. And I do not want your girlfriend to call here—while I'm talking to Linda Baker—so maybe you just better go home and check in with her."

"Linda Baker is coming here? She called?" For a moment, Neil's heart leaped, pounded so hard he couldn't catch his breath. He'd barely kept from going to Linda's and now she'd called. . . . *Sammy!*

Claire came close to him, her expression concerned and earnest. "This is what we've been waiting for. She's ready. She told Roy that she's going to come talk with me, and she's bringing pictures of her family. Somehow she's talked Roy into thinking that we—she and I—just got off to a bad start and that I'm going to give her a designer bag, which I am . . . one with pictures of her family on it, that she can take with her through her— whatever is left of her life."

When Neil shook his head and thought of all the years he'd missed with his son, Claire took his face in her hands. "You have to promise me that you won't do more harm to Linda than what she already feels now. Her guilt has eaten away her life, Neil. That's a big punishment. Her husband and family still don't know. And she's got such a short time left."

Neil didn't know how he would react. "Just find out what happened to my son."

"And Neil? You're not invited."

As Claire prepared chamomile tea, she glanced at Neil's home to find him staring back at her through the kitchen window. His face was hard and shadowed, fierce with emotion. To wait for her to link with Linda was eating at him, but the moments with Linda were tenuous. They could be gone forever if pushed too hard, if Neil became impatient. And when it came to his son, Neil wouldn't be patient.

Claire carried the tea tray into her workroom, the perfect setting to relate to a woman who enjoyed handcrafts. In the filtered light, Linda sat in a small comfortable chair; she seemed even more frail and pale, her thin hands knotted together on her lap. "Thank you for the fresh hen's eggs, and this crocheted cap. It's really lovely. I love the Celtic design, and I love that shade of green."

"To match your eyes. . . . When I saw that skein at the crafts store, I thought of your eyes, the shade of forests and grass. I can't forget how you looked at me by the river. I saw your ring and just copied the design. I saw more of that design on your door knocker. That wolf's head was a little scary . . . it matched the pin you wore at the campground."

"My sister likes to incorporate it into her designs. I wanted my daughter to have that ring, but I lost my baby before she was born. Her name would have been Aisling. It's an old family name—very old. My mother took it for her surname when my father died; it helped her survive very tough times." That tender hook snagged Claire's heart; her baby had shared more than her body. They had been already connected in a way that every mother had been connected to every daughter since the first Aisling and before her.

The doctors had called Claire's terrifying aftermath a "depression." But she and her unborn child had already been relating.

Linda studied the wall, filled with different photographs of Claire's bags. "I never imagined. Very expensive, probably, those designer bags. I usually get mine at the discount store."

"One of my sisters sells them for me and makes a hefty profit, so I am able to make a living out here. Leona runs a vintage clothing store in Lexington, Kentucky." Claire poured the tea and on impulse put on the cap; handcrafters were usually pleased when someone chose to wear their work. "How do I look?"

They were just two women, enjoying the colors and the skill of each other's crafts, but Claire sensed that Linda was uneasy; she needed to know more about the woman who had uncovered her horrible secret. "Pretty. You look Irish with that red hair tumbling around your face and shoulders. You come from those people, then?"

From a long, long line, before the invasions of the Norsemen—but then, she carried their blood, too. "Basically, yes."

"The blood runs strong in you, doesn't it? You see things, don't you?" Linda pressed as she held the cup and saucer Claire had handed her.

"Not really. I just get impressions—from people. Very strong ones. . . . That brand of tea is really very good. Chamomile. . . . very relaxing. Try it?" Claire sat in her desk chair near Linda and sipped her tea.

Linda slowly tasted the tea, but tuned to the other woman, Claire sensed that Linda was circling how to start. The room was quiet, early-afternoon sunlight filtering through the curtains. Time had seemed to stop; the world was quiet and very still, and Claire knew it was time to begin. "What I feel sometimes is my secret, Linda. And now, other than my family and one other, you're the only one to know."

"And Neil knows? He's your man now, isn't he?"

Claire thought of how Paul had been—uneasy with her and finally wanting a life with a normal woman. Somehow she had linked with Neil, a physical bond, but life paths changed and lives flowed apart. "For now."

Tears welled in Linda's eyes as she met Claire's. "You were right. I am remembering. I'd closed that door to what I'd done long ago. It was the only way I could live with myself. Opening it hurt. Sometimes now, when I close my eyes, I see John's face."

Claire held Linda's hand. If Linda's "John" was the same man who attacked Claire, the trail could be a dead end. "Could you think about him now? Just try to remember? Please?"

Linda closed her eyes and Claire locked into focus, closing her own. Tiny streams came winding around Claire, and formed into a tall, thin blond man. Icy blue eyes set in a narrow, hawkish face looked back at her. A small spider tattoo lay on his cheek. Linda's fear prickled around her, and Claire shook her head clearing it. "John" wasn't the same man who had attacked her.

Claire stroked Linda's hair, easing her after a long hard journey. "Don't be afraid, Linda. I'm here with you."

"But I didn't say anything—" Then suddenly Linda relaxed, her expression accepting and sad. "I don't have long to live. I just found out. And I need to tell Neil before I can't anymore."

"I'll call him to come over. And Linda? I'll have your bag done very soon."

"'I'm sorry' doesn't cut it, Claire." Neil turned to Claire, who was stirring spaghetti sauce in his kitchen. The fiery sunset lit her hair, wound into a knot high on her head.

She noted the heft of the bourbon bottle in his hand for a third time. "I wish you wouldn't."

Linda had been so frail and hysterical that Neil couldn't help feeling sorry for her. Facing those two women in that tiny workroom had been one of the most difficult things he'd ever done.

In his kitchen three hours later, Neil looked across to Claire's home, the path that he had taken to meet Linda.

Him? Grounded? After he'd just listened to a dying woman confess to taking Sammy because she was being blackmailed?

Clearly protective, Claire's hand had rested on Linda's shoulders, and Neil understood how that slender feminine hand could give comfort. He managed to listen to Linda, when with every heartbeat he wanted to know Sammy's location. Claire had said it was very important to let whatever Linda said stream out of her, without interruption.

He poured the bourbon slowly into the glass, just a little defiance because he was really feeling nasty. Linda had given Sammy to a man she'd known from some cult, and he'd said the boy would be well loved. Maybe Neil should be grateful for that pitiful bit of information, but he wasn't. At least not right now. "Another dead end. She doesn't know anything more about the guy . . . hasn't seen him since. Dammit."

When his fist hit the counter, Claire tensed; the wooden spoon she was using to stir paused. Neil poured the drink down the sink. "Okay, let's have it. You've been chopping vegetables, and that spoon is stirring a mile a minute, and something is bothering you. Linda gave me her 'I'm sorry' routine and she went home to her husband and family. So everything is just peachy? Sammy is still gone, Claire."

Neil looked out the window toward the old oak tree—almost as if he imagined his son swinging there. Then he turned back to Claire. "We should go to the police now. She's commited a crime. She's confessed to you. They'll get the rest out of her."

Claire shook her head. "Do you honestly think as panicked as she is, that tossing her into an even more dangerous situation, where she exposes her family to all kinds of gossip and the media, Linda is going to remember more? I don't think so. She's buried details of that time in her life, just to survive. As frightened as she is, those repressed memories could sink even deeper and we might never get the details we need to find Sammy. We're not pushing her over that edge, Neil. Linda is trying very hard and it has to be painful."

He sucked in his breath and held it as he weighed his impatience against Linda's terror and the chance that what lay trapped inside her mind might be lost forever. "Okay, you're right," he agreed reluctantly.

Neil looked outside to the wind moving through the brush between their homes, to the deer sliding through it on their way to graze in the meadow. *Oh, Sammy. . . . Where are you?*

Claire methodically turned off the stove; she washed and dried her hands. "I don't think it's quite the dead end that you think, Neil. Linda is remembering more . . . she's blocked this out a long time. She'll call again. You did a wonderful thing today, by just listening. I know how difficult it was for you."

"Great. My son was taken. He may or may not be out there, alive. I listen to a woman confess, and you're rewarding her with a designer bag. She gave you a pretty cap. That makes everything just fine, doesn't it?" Restless and unable to think about anything but Sammy, Neil walked out of the house.

He had to do something, anything, and walked to Claire's garage, carrying his toolkit. He dug into the chore of replacing her fan belt and cleaning up the tiny motor, but his mind was on his son.

Claire moved in the garage doorway, just that long slender silhouette in the sunset behind her. Neil braced his open hands on the car in an attempt to anchor his unsteady emotions, and shook his head. "I miss him, Claire. I miss all the things we could have done together."

When she came close, Neil tugged her into his arms and held her tight. Her body flowed into his, her fingers smoothing his hair, her face tucked against his throat. He wondered then, how a woman could feel so safe to a man larger and stronger than her.

Suddenly, tension ran through her body and her lips moved against his throat. "Neil? Do you know of anyone with a small spider tattooed on his face?"

Neil held very still, then moved away. He tried to remember and shook his head. "No. I don't think so. Why?"

"Linda remembered that John had a spider on his cheek. It's a small identification, but it's something. A tall thin blond man with a spider tattoo might be somewhere to start. We need to find out more about that cult—Neil? Are you okay?"

Neil was thinking back to when he'd met Bruce and another man at a roadside cafe near Billings. Clearly friends, they were hungover and nasty. The man was tall, too thin, a blond with ice blue eyes, even when he leered at the waitress. When a state patrolman came into the cafe, he'd tensed and quieted, slinking down in the booth a bit; he'd used the shade of his Western hat to conceal his face.

Neil had understood immediately. In his deals, Bruce usually had someone who knew how to get things done—outside of the law, and under the ethics bar. And he had introduced the man as "Lanky."

But just as Neil had stood to leave the men, "Lanky" had smirked up at him. It was as if he knew something about Neil—and the sunlight had lit that spider on his cheekbone. . . .

"I may know someone like that. I think he's a friend of Bruce's. Or was. That would have been about a year after Sammy disappeared."

* * *

When he asked Bruce about the man with the spider on his cheek, Neil wanted to see his brother's face. A call, asking to talk with Bruce about business, was sure to bring him running. At noon the day after Linda's visit, Neil sat in that same booth, in that same Billings roadside cafe, and waited for his brother.

He didn't want Claire with him; she was safer away from both brothers . . . because Neil wasn't certain of what *he* would do. His emotions and Bruce's could terrify a sensitive woman, let alone a sensitive psychic, and Neil was set to go to war to find his son. If Bruce had anything to do with Sammy's disappearance, that would be the end of any family ties and the beginning of trouble that just might end one way. Claire was better off away from this moment, and from the look of her this morning—the shadows under her eyes—she badly needed rest.

Neil spooned ice cubes into his steaming coffee and stirred it slowly, tapping his spoon on the edge of the heavy porcelain cup. The cafe was typically Western— good food, men sitting on the counter stools, a few couples in the booths, a kid wanting chocolate ice cream instead of green beans.

The setting wasn't what he wanted; Neil would have preferred a back-alley brawl. Frustrated, he wanted nothing more than to pin Bruce against the wall and make him tell everything he knew about Sammy. But he wanted Bruce to feel comfortable with this particular meeting. He intended to keep it casual . . . then ask about the man, "Lanky."

Claire was probably right: If Bruce became suspicious, little Sammy could pay—if he was still alive.

Bruce came in the door, wearing that expectant, excited expression of someone about to get a lot of money handed to him. Once more, Neil saw their father in the familiar features, a good man who loved his sons. But Bruce never saw that he was equally loved, just that Neil was getting preference.

His brother grinned and made for the booth, sliding into it. Neil forced a smile and a calm, everyday invitation. "Want something to eat? The pie is good. Remember the apple ones Mom used to make? These are like hers. The burgers remind me of Dad's on the campfire."

"I'll take a burger and fries. Coffee," Bruce stated briskly to the waitress who had come to take his order. He seemed eager and cheerful, but Neil couldn't find anything of a fond memory touching his brother's expression.

He struggled to leash himself from what he had to know. "Nice weather. Warm for the first of June."

In the red vinyl booth, Bruce sat less than three feet opposite Neil, and he looked so much like their father. . . . They ate, discussed the weather, then Bruce leaned back, his arm running across the back of the booth; Neil recognized his brother's narrowed expression—it was "business time." Bruce apparently thought that Neil had reconsidered his loan for the trawler.

But this time, Neil wasn't that easy; he wasn't launching into a discussion about financing Bruce's latest big-money deal. Neil wanted information about his son—and the man Linda had identified. "You know, the last time we were in here, you were with a guy with a tattoo on his cheek. A spider? Yeah, that's what it was, a spider . . . unusual. I've been thinking I might want something like that."

Bruce frowned slightly. "You? 'Health boy'? A tattoo?"

"Things I haven't tried." Neil wondered how long he

could circle what he really wanted to know. "I thought he might come with you today, and I'd ask him."

"He's dead."

Neil stirred the "warmer" the waitress had just poured into his coffee cup. *If the man who took Sammy was dead, he might never be found. . . .* He managed to shrug and speak normally, when his throat had gone dry and tight. "Huh. Too bad. I was going to ask him about that tattoo."

Bruce's smile wasn't sweet. "Topper got that spider when he was in some cult, Neily-boy. That wouldn't do for you, buttercup."

Linda had been in a cult. . . . "His name wasn't 'Lanky'?"

"He was just using it at the time. His name was Topper." Then Bruce leaned forward, his elbows on the table, his expression eager. "You've been thinking about that trawler deal, haven't you? About how we could make some money on it? You could be a silent partner, Neil. You wouldn't have to do anything but put your part of the money into the bank. It would pay a lot better than working day and night on those campers. The old man worked too hard to enjoy life, and it's no way to go. You need to enjoy life while you can. Well, what do you think? Think you'd want to go in on that deal?"

Another dead end. Family memories and love warred with suspicions as Neil took the waitress's check. It was just possible that Topper had acted on his own, without Bruce's knowledge. Sammy was Bruce's nephew, after all. Bruce could have been showing off his nephew's picture to Topper. And Topper just could have been looking for a black-market baby.

On the other hand, Bruce wasn't exactly a model family member. He'd never taken notice of Sammy.

He *could* be involved. The thought settled uneasily in Neil.

Neil realized that his fist was gripping the cup too hard, his knuckles white beneath the tanned skin. He forced his hand to relax, and said, "I'm thinking about your trawler deal, punching some keys to see how much I can handle. I just started the shop, and it hasn't started paying out just yet, so I'm being careful."

Bruce shook his head and scowled. "This deal won't be on the table forever, Neil."

"I just wanted to let you know that I'm working on it. I'd been thinking about that tattoo and thought maybe the guy might be with you. I can't remember his last name. What was it? I seem to remember 'Lanky' Reed? Topper Reed?"

When Bruce stood suddenly, he bumped the table, and the dishes shook. "I thought you came here to give me that bankroll. You're wasting my time. I just might get the money from someone else."

"Don't let me stop you." Neil stood slowly. An even match for size, Neil wasn't the little brother taking any more falls and broken bones because of his older brother. And he wasn't done with Bruce and what he might know. A business deal was the best way to keep Bruce close and talkative. "Don't push me, Bruce. I said I was thinking about it."

For an instant, Bruce's expression turned ugly, but Neil forced himself to smile. "I'll call when I've got those numbers lined up. Keep in touch. We're all the family we have, you know."

The probe to find a family tie, some love deep down inside his brother, failed.

And so did Neil's effort to find the man with a spider on his cheek.

But he had the unusual name of Topper and he'd

remembered the last name—Reed—and that was something.

Sammy. . . . Let me find you. . . .

Neil returned home at dusk to find Mary Jane's red pickup parked in his driveway. After a confrontation with Bruce and a visit with an old friend in Billings—someone who could tap into police records—Neil braced himself to meet Mary Jane. They'd been lovers and friends; he wanted to keep the "friends" part, but she wasn't taking "No" easily. He should have returned Mary Jane's call because she wasn't one to wait before taking what she wanted.

Neil entered his quiet house and prayed that Mary Jane wasn't in his bed. She wasn't. He walked to the workshop and it had remained locked. The third place she just might be was—Neil sucked in his breath and braced himself as he started toward Claire's home.

A sense of doom weighed on him as he used that ornate Celtic door knocker. The twin rottweilers seemed almost sympathetic as Neil braced himself to meet both women—together, in the same room.

Okay, he'd handled Bruce carefully, no easy matter when he wanted to directly question his brother about Sammy's disappearance. Okay, Bruce was probably much easier than these two women—one of whom could tap into everything that was going on between him and Mary Jane. *He had to get Mary Jane out of Claire's sensing distance, and fast!*

Neil was still trying to come up with a plan when Claire suddenly opened the door. Her "Oh, I'm so glad you're home. We've been waiting for you," was too sweet . . . so was her bright, cheery smile.

Goose bumps leaped on Neil's body; his mind waded through big warning signs as Claire led the way to her workroom. He wondered briefly why the meeting had to occur in a place that favored the women and made him uncomfortable.

Mary Jane was inspecting material spread from a roll onto the cutting table. Claire had been using Eunice's tea set, and even without ESP, Neil knew that he was in trouble. "Mary Jane. I meant to return your call."

Claire was standing to one side, her arms crossed as she studied him. Neil checked the color of her eyes. Uh-oh. . . . They were that dark gold color—

Mary Jane wasn't hesitating in the awkward situation. Instead, she moved to him and wrapped her arms around his shoulders. "Hello, lover."

"You might want to take this over to your house, Neil. Or, I could just leave," Claire warned very coolly.

One look at her set face, and Neil eased away from Mary Jane's clinging arms. "Claire needs to work. Let's go to my place."

Later, in his living room, Mary Jane didn't like what Neil had to say. "So you're in a relationship with Miss Classy, all polished and cool and nice. She's got money, doesn't she? What's she doing out here anyway? And I don't see what she's got that I don't."

Neil had to clear Mary Jane's misconceptions about their current relationship. "You and I haven't been lovers for years, Mary Jane. But I like to think that we're good friends now."

"We were lovers! We were! Then you go off and move to Casper, Wyoming, and marry someone else and leave me with egg on my face."

Neil frowned, remembering how Mary Jane had cried when he called to tell her that he'd married Jan. "I'm sorry. But you had been seeing other men by then—"

Mary Jane put her hands on her waist, her expression furious. "Only to make you jealous, Neil. Then, when you split with your wife, moved to Great Falls, and who did you come running to? Me, that's who."

He thought of the few times Mary Jane had come after him—and he hadn't refused. "I was lonely, I guess. I'm sorry I gave you the impression—"

Her hand swept out, cutting off the rest of his sentence. "That's what they all say. We should have gotten married, that should have been *my* son, and *I* should be living here, right now—not that woman. She is living here, isn't she?"

Mary Jane moved close, latching her arms around his neck, though Neil tried to hold her away. "Come on, honey. I can give you more kids. That's what really changed you, wasn't it? Losing your boy?"

The thought of having children with Mary Jane stunned Neil, and he eased her away. "I guess I never thought of you that way."

Her hands went to her hips, and she was angry again. "You mean that I've waited for you to realize that I'm the one for you—the woman who should be the mother of your kids—then you start up with that woman next door? *I* should have been the mother of your baby, Neil, not that other woman. I thought that once he was gone and you were divorced that we'd get back together again—"

Neil caught her wrist as her hand moved to stroke his cheek; keeping up with Mary Jane wasn't easy. "Wait a minute. I never gave you any reason to think that."

Mary Jane threw back her long black hair, her expression hard, as she said, "You owe me, Neil. You owe me a wedding ring and a baby for all those years I waited for you."

"'*Owe* you a baby?'" Neil stood back and took a realistic look at the woman he'd thought had been his friend.

Her anger shifted into uncertainty; she shifted uneasily. "Well, yes. With your baby gone, that would leave an empty spot, wouldn't it? You'd want more? That's what your brother said."

"*My brother?*" Neil remembered how Bruce had looked at Mary Jane the time they'd met for drinks, with just that heartbeat of recognition that he'd soon shielded. "How well do you know Bruce?"

She shifted uneasily, her head up and her eyes challenging Neil. "He comes around sometimes, asking about you. He gives me things . . . he calls once in a while. He's been very nice to me."

"I'll bet." *Bruce had always wanted anything that was Neil's, and that would include women. . . .* It took all of Neil's control to say quietly, "Get out, Mary Jane. And don't come back."

After Mary Jane's pickup spun out of his driveway, Neil sat at his desk. He felt as if he'd taken a body blow. Not only would Bruce have contact with him through e-mail and calls, but through Mary Jane he'd know even more about Neil's whereabouts—like his being at a campground with his son.

Neil studied the framed picture of the brothers and their father. In his mind, he saw the flames licking at the glass. He felt the helplessness of a sixteen-year-old boy, prevented by others from entering the burning house. He'd cried out for his parents, begging them to escape.

Aware now that Claire was entering the house, Neil didn't look up from the picture.

Claire's hand rested on his arm. "From the way Mary Jane's pickup took off out of here, I'd say she wasn't happy. You said she was your friend, and that must bother you. Want to tell me about it?" she asked softly.

"I've known her a long time. We were kids and had issues and maybe we helped each other, I don't know. Not for a long time. . . ."

Neil was locked in the disaster that had changed his

life. He replaced the framed photograph and stared at the lacy curtains. He'd seen other curtains go up in flames. . . . "I was on Casper's football team and after the Friday night game, I'd stopped for a burger with the rest of the kids. The folks had gone on ahead. There was this girl . . . we spent some time in the backseat. Then I heard the sirens and someone was yelling, 'It's your folks' house.' By the time I got there, it was too late. An electrical fire they said . . . started in the garage, where Dad had his workshop. A spark hit some old rags near a gas can. They found him there. Mom was caught in their bedroom bathroom, and it didn't have a window. I should have gone home sooner. I should have gotten them out. I said I'd be home in a couple of hours. It was more like midnight. . . ."

He shook his head and sat in the desk chair. "I've never forgiven myself for being late."

Claire's hand remained on his shoulder as she asked quietly, "And where was Bruce?"

"He was in Cheyenne, but coming home for the weekend. We couldn't locate him that night . . . he was out partying. He turned up Saturday morning—with a hangover—but there wasn't a home left." Neil frowned suddenly, and stared up at Claire. "What do you mean, 'where was Bruce?'"

Claire shook her head and didn't answer. Her silence underlined her question. *Just where was Bruce when the fire started?* Neil cursed darkly and stood. "You think my own brother would have anything to do with my parents' deaths? My own brother? Claire, you're really off base on this one. Back off."

She inhaled, held that breath, and nodded. "Okay. Good night."

And with that cool final note, Claire walked out of his home.

Neil ran his hands through his hair. Claire knew something, and she was keeping it to herself.

Either that, or Mary Jane had made quite the point with her.

But her question remained, circling him: *Just where was Bruce when the fire started?*

Fifteen

CLAIRE HAD ALMOST REACHED HER BACK DOORSTEP WHEN
Neil caught up with her. His hand locked on to her
forearm and spun her around. "Mary Jane and I were
really over a long time ago. I just found out that she's
been seeing Bruce. Whatever she told you, I'm asking
you to take my word, she hasn't been anything but a
friend, for a long time—or so I thought."

Claire stood back and folded her arms. Neil's pain
vibrated around her. He struggled with the past and
with what could be uncovered. "I never thought anything different. I would have known. She did care for
you though. She wanted children with you."

She remembered the other woman's violence. It had
crackled, burning, pricking, but Claire had focused
on her own energy and protected herself. Yet Mary
Jane's fierce claim on Neil circled her: *You can't have
him. He's always been mine. He's always come back
to me.*

Neil stuck his hands in his back pockets, his face cut
with grim lines. "I'd like us to see this through—to try
to find Sammy. I've turned up a mug shot of Topper
Reed. He's dead now, but he had that spider tattoo that
Linda described. I thought maybe we could show the

photo to her and see what she says. Are you game for that?"

That pulse of Neil's energy told Claire that he was also asking another question: *Was she staying in her home or in his for the night?*

Claire wanted any doubt of another woman put behind them before they moved on. She tilted up her face and moved close to Neil; she studied his wary expression, a doomed man waiting for his exile. "Don't you want to know what Mary Jane said to me?"

"The usual things, I suppose. I never asked her to marry me, Claire. After that first heat when we were kids, it was just now and then and when she came after me. Not the other way around, and not for a long time before I moved here. After Sammy—I had my low moments . . . I needed someone. I guess we both did."

"You don't actually have any idea, do you?" Claire thought back to Mary Jane's threat, that she'd waited for years for Neil, and Claire would never have him.

Neil shifted restlessly. In the shadows, he seemed uncertain. "I've made mistakes in my life, Claire. Are we going to get past this?"

Claire tried to ignore her jealousy as she thought of Mary Jane in Neil's arms. At first, she'd absorbed the other woman's anger, then she'd focused on her own. Maybe she was human after all, with all the full-blown emotions of a woman wanting to mark a man as her own. Stepping off her protected isolated platform and into everyday human emotions concerning her own real life wasn't that easy. "I thought I'd work really hard tonight and finish Linda's bag. You can show her the photograph when she comes to collect it."

Neil nodded and studied her. "Are you coming to my place later?"

"I don't know. But don't wait up for me."

"Okay." Neil didn't move. "Are *we* okay?"

"I don't know that either."

Neil stared at her and stated firmly, "I didn't lie to you about having other women. There weren't that many."

"Oh, well, yes. I could tell you weren't a novice."

"You're really burned, aren't you? That gives me hope that you may not be able to walk away from me as easily as you just did. Just maybe you're a little jealous, Claire."

"And you have a big fat ego. You're just a new experience, that's all. I seem to be racking up new experiences with you." *Was this what it was all about? Feeling frustrated and jealous and wanting to pit herself against another woman?*

Or were her emotions more centered on fear for Neil, for what he might discover about his own brother?

"You're holding all sorts of things, aren't you? Want to tell me what they are?" Neil asked curtly.

Claire shook her head. She had no hard proof, nothing but that extra, very perceptive sense.

After a hard stare and a deep breath, Neil turned and stood with his back to her, his hands on his hips. Then he walked away.

Chilled by how easily he could turn from her, Claire wrapped her arms around herself and watched Neil enter his home. She longed to go to him, to ease him, but she was set on her course—Linda would be coming for her bag in the morning, and she might identify the man with the spider tattoo.

Claire inhaled when she heard the sound of Neil's pickup passing her home; she prayed he wasn't going to see Linda or Bruce, but she could only wait. . . .

From a dark corner, Neil watched Mary Jane enter her home in Red Dog. She dropped her keys onto a table as she weaved unsteadily past him. When he clicked on the lamp, she spun to look at him. "Neil!"

"Hi, Mary Jane. I thought we'd finish our earlier conversation."

She shook her head as if to clear it. "About what? And how did you get in here?"

Neil held up the key he'd found under her front door-mat. "Let's talk about Bruce. You know, my brother? You were playing us both?"

"Oh, no, Neil. There's only been you. I swear."

Neil stood and walked to where Mary Jane was cowering against the wall. She smelled of alcohol and heavy perfume, her lipstick glossy and smeared. "Let's get back to the part where you thought you would be the mother of my baby. . . . And where once my son was gone, Bruce had said I would want more children—with you."

Fear ran across her face, quivered in her body. "You took that woman, that Claire to meet everyone at the fairgrounds, didn't you? And camping? People told me that you did."

"I'm not denying that."

Mary Jane's fist hit his chest. "*I'm* the one you should have taken. Not her. People expect us to be together, Neil. Then you show up with her. It's embarrassing, Neil."

Neil held her hand away from him, then released it. He remembered a girl long ago, trying to escape a bad family relationship; he remembered the comfort she'd given him. "I'm sorry that you feel that way. I never made any promises to you, Mary Jane. I thought we'd become good friends over the years."

"Everyone thought we might get married—until she came along, that weirdo next door to you. No one knows much about her except that Eunice liked her and she orders things sent to her house. What kind of a woman doesn't get out and do her own shopping all the time? She never goes to the dress stores or beauty shop in Red Dog. I'd know."

Mary Jane's measure of a woman and a relationship was different from his own. In Claire he'd found more woman than any other, some integral completion of his life.

Neil clicked on the bright overhead light to see Mary Jane's expression more clearly. He paced his words carefully, making certain that she understood his questions. "Do you know anything about my son's disappearance? And do you know Topper Reed?"

Her eyes widened, the drunken fog replaced by fear. "No, Neil. I'd tell you if I knew anything at all. Who's Topper Reed?"

Neil was losing patience. Her reaction suggested that she knew something. "A dead man. A man with a spider tattoo on his cheek. Ever see anyone like that?"

Mary Jane shook her head. "No. It's that woman, isn't it? That weird one living next to you. She's put all sorts of ideas into your head. Just because you're messing with her doesn't mean that you can come in here and accuse me of all sorts of things."

"I haven't accused you of anything. I've just asked a few questions, Mary Jane. And by the way, whoever killed Topper Reed might want to finish anyone who could identify him."

She paled, a thin sheen of sweat covering her forehead. "I don't know that guy—Topper Someone."

Neil didn't believe her, but he had no proof that she was lying. "According to police files, he's a guy who ended up dead—murdered. See you around, Mary Jane. We're not finished. And if I were you, I wouldn't tell Bruce about our little meeting. I've got an idea that he wouldn't be happy with you telling me about your little spy act."

Her hand went to her throat; her eyes filled with fear. "Neil, he can be real mean."

Neil nodded; after a lifetime of dealing with Bruce,

the composite picture of his brother wasn't good. He left Mary Jane with this advice: "Take care, Mary Jane. We'll be talking. Meanwhile, I want you to do the same for me as you did for Bruce—I want you to let me know every move he makes. Keep in touch."

An hour later, Neil sat on his back porch, considering his recent accidents. In every case, they occurred after he and Claire—a next-door neighbor, who might have noticed anything suspicious—had been gone. Bruce would have had an opportunity to tamper with the chain saw, the gas stove, and the electrical ground in the house, to weaken the supports on the shop's loft. He would have had the opportunity to damage a perfectly good climbing belt. "If he did all that, he's gotten a lot better than when we were kids."

And Bruce couldn't be found on the night of their parents' fire.

Neil remembered the furious argument Bruce had had with their father the week before. Dan Olafson had refused to pay any more of Bruce's debts and ordered him to start supporting himself; their father had stated that he was cutting Bruce out of any funds or inheritance until he changed his lifestyle. . . .

Neil shook his head. Motive . . . opportunity . . . Bruce had it all—with Mary Jane's help. . . .

Claire's house was dark, except for the slight glow from her workroom window. He reached for his cell phone and dialed Claire's number. Neil frowned when she picked up so quickly. "Did it ring?"

"I—no, I guess not. I just knew you were calling."

Neil let that sink in. Claire might think she was tied to him for this journey, to redeem herself and to find his son, but their link might be stronger than she supposed. He intended to strengthen it more, and that would require her trust.

"I went to see Mary Jane. She's involved in this

somehow—maybe feeding Bruce information about where I'm at and what I'm doing. They've probably been involved for years. What I want to know is why you and Tempest were in my house that day? Was she feeling around? And if so, what was she touching—without her gloves? Did it have anything to do with my brother trying to kill me?"

When Claire didn't answer immediately, Neil came up with his own conclusion. "I thought so. Get back to work, honey. Mary Jane probably called Bruce right away, but he won't dare show up here tonight. Or rather, he'd better not," he added grimly.

As badly as he needed to see Claire and hold her, Neil understood that his tumultuous, savage emotions now were too violent for her to be near.

After Sammy had been abducted and Neil's marriage had dissolved, he'd simply removed Jan's name from his will. He'd known that eventually, he'd have to make different arrangements, but he couldn't bear to remove his son's name; it would have been like cutting the last tie to Sammy. With Neil's parents dead, with Neil dead and without an heir, Bruce was primed to inherit everything. . . . A perfect motive.

The enormity of Bruce's guilt—without solid proof—was overwhelming, and waiting to confront his brother would be the most difficult thing Neil had done in his life.

Claire worked feverishly, scanning the Baker family photographs and creating the tote bag; she was drained and tired when it was finished. Claire stretched, noted the two o'clock hour, and realized that the steady beat inside her head was actually coming from Neil's back-yard.

Drawing aside the curtain, Claire saw the bright spotlight. In its beam, a big, powerful man methodically swung a logger's ax against the old oak tree. "That's one way of working out problems, I guess."

She walked to the shadows, beyond the spotlight, and stood watching Neil. His hair was damp and plastered to his head, his chest and powerful arms gleaming with sweat, his body braced against each blow. His fierce expression told her everything: Neil wasn't chopping down a tree; he was fighting his demons.

Suddenly, he sank the ax into the wood and turned, finding her in the shadows. "Finished?"

With him? Or with the bag? Claire didn't have time to answer, before Neil reached her, his expression savage, his fist wrapping around the length of her hair, drawing her face up to his.

She wasn't frightened; her hands braced on his chest, her eyes locked with his. Somewhere back in time, another man had taken another woman, just like this. The other woman wasn't frightened either—because she wanted the primitive taste of him, the even match for the savagery that ran beneath her smooth, calm manners, her quiet soothing voice. The man, this man, stirred her blood, heated it, as no other, and she would fight to hold him.

Claire drew her nails lightly down Neil's chest, letting him know that she was no easy fare to be taken lightly, that they were an even match.

She'd expected that fist locked in her big shirt to tear it away. She'd expected the primitive glitter of his eyes raking the length of her body. "You're really like this, aren't you?" he asked fiercely. "Beneath those cool looks, you're like this, fire and silk, aren't you."

"I'm what you think I am, and yes," she answered to the question he didn't need to ask, that of making love to her in a new way, that of claiming each other. Neil had discovered what no one else knew, not even Claire's family. He'd stirred her savage blood, the need to capture and hold him captive, and she instinctively knew how to fight, on her own terms. . . .

It was just a heartbeat, flowing between them, but Claire knew this time would be different, more consuming. His hand covered her breast, not with a caress, but with possession, fingers spread, the capture light, but firm. His other hand drew her head back, his eyes silvery slits in the shadows as he studied her, his breath harsh upon her skin. "I know what you can do, like making me pay for not telling you about that electrical accident. Do your damndest now," Neil challenged quietly.

"I will. Will you?"

For an answer, he swung her up in his arms and carried her to his bed. The claiming was what she had to have, the truth of it, his possession and hers, burning away any other woman.

Still pulsing inside her after a feverish, primitive lovemaking, Neil held her wrists beside her head. She could have freed herself easily, but instead, she stretched and luxuriated in Neil's weight, the passion and hunger only slightly eased. When she could speak, Claire said, "You didn't hurt me. I took what I wanted, too."

Neil frowned slightly, his gaze moving down to where they were still joined, male and female, where pleasure still quivered and where new life could begin. "She said she wanted my baby."

"I know." Claire smoothed his hair, but something inside her grew momentarily cold and flew from his grasp.

Neil understood that for just that heartbeat, Claire thought of her own unborn child and longed for her. "You know who tried to run you down at the campground, too, don't you? Was it Bruce?"

When she didn't answer, Neil shook his head and lowered to rest his cheek against hers. He eased to her side, holding her close against him. "I'm sorry, Claire. You shouldn't be in this."

She held Neil close, giving him comfort as women had done for men through the ages. Brother against brother could lead to murder, and she wanted to protect Neil. "I want to be with you when you talk to Bruce next time."

"No. I don't want you there. It won't be pretty."

Claire sat up, her arms around her knees. She looked over her bare shoulder to Neil as he toyed with her hair. "Neil, be careful. Bruce has to be approached carefully. Right now, he's the only lead to where Sammy might be."

"I love your hair." Neil sat up behind her, slowly braiding her hair.

He'd changed the subject too quickly. "Neil. You have to be very careful now."

"Mmm. So you said."

And then Claire knew that Neil had plans that did not include her.

Greer Aisling stood in the night, watching the Pacific Ocean, where her daughters had once played so freely.

Her blood was churning, stirred by theirs. Claire had stepped into what she was, a psychic, purposefully absorbing sensations and energy and emotions from others, with a slight telepathic twist. And Claire was afraid.

Her emotions had set Leona's and Greer's dreams tumbling within them.

A sudden gust of wind, a tightening within her, and she knew that it was coming, always the same. Greer closed her eyes and went into herself to see the two men, pitted against each other for a Celtic female slave: The bold Viking lord, wearing little but his thick fur cape and soft leather breeches, his strong legs bound in cord and fur-trimmed leather, stood beside her. The long blade in his hand was stained with blood, the victory had been his band's. He stared down at the seer, smoke of the ruined Celt village curling around them. He'd taken her bound hands, freeing them.

The Viking lord had wrapped a cloak around her ruined shift, and fastened it with a *fibula*, shaped like a wolf's head. "Mine . . . she will be my woman," he stated as he searched his band for those who would challenge him.

One man stood forth, the smoke curling around his feet. Cruelty lay in his eyes and mouth, and his surly study of her. "I would have her. Show her to me, what I would have when you are dead, Thorgood."

"I have said, she is mine, Borg. She wears my mark, the fastening of her cloak is that of the wolf, my mark."

"She is a slave, Thorgood, not a Viking woman with rights and choices, and I would fight you for her." The man came close, smelling of sweet oils and incense, his black eyes sly upon her. She sensed his powerful evil; it pulsed around him. As tall as the blond Viking beside her, this man smiled cunningly. He lifted a long strand of her bright red hair and spoke to her, "Pretty. Strong. I would give you freedom, woman—if you chose me. You would have slaves of your own."

For an answer, she placed her hand over the wolf *fibula*, and in an instant, Thorgood's blade rose even as he pushed her behind him. Sparks flew as blade clashed with blade, and the men moved in to fight.

Borg's curse rose over the melee, silenced by the ocean's tides crashing against the rocks below Greer's Pacific home.

Chilled by the dream that had come through the years, Greer wished she had never told her daughters of the original wolf *fibula*, of the curse and the promise it held, because that was what Tempest hunted now. . . .

Greer smoothed the endless, winding Celtic carvings along her garden doorway and feared for her daughters. The first had started her journey; Claire was opening herself and discovering what she was and how to deal with what she had been given.

She had chosen a warrior, and now they were on the hunt for his son.

"Claire?"

Was the whisper real or in her head? Claire stood in Neil's backyard, the fog curling around her feet and winding up her body. It had called to her, the same as that day beside the river, and had drawn her from Neil's bed. What did it want?

In the gray hours before dawn, the world seemed to stand still. The only sound was that of her heart, the snap of a small branch as the deer slid by into the meadow, and the steady drip from the leaves.

An empath and in tune with nature, Claire waited for someone to step from the fog, to speak her name again. A few birds prepared for their day, rustling in the trees' leaves, but she was alone. Her skin was damp from the mist, her nightshirt cold and clinging to her body. "Who are you?"

Only the steady drip from the leaves sounded, matching that of her heart because nothing was there, only her sense that she was being touched and explored.

Claire shivered and wrapped her arms around herself. She heard the scrape of a door, then Neil's body pressed against her back, warming her. His arms drew her in close, his cheek rough with stubble, resting against hers. "What's wrong?"

Everything. Nothing. She leaned back against him. "I guess I'm uneasy, that's all."

"I'm sorry that you're in this. I know it can't be easy. You're too cold, honey. Come back to bed."

"You can't sleep either."

"No," Neil agreed grimly. "I keep remembering how my parents' died . . . how little emotion Bruce showed, until the will was read. He was furious then—my own brother, Claire. And to set up the abduction of a baby. . . . If he did that, I can't promise that I won't kill him."

A man of fire, a man in the fire. . . . Was that how Bruce intended to kill his brother?

"You won't kill Bruce. You're not a killer." The fog moved closer, circling Neil, and Claire felt as though it were sensing him through her. "Let's go inside, shall we?" Claire asked.

Neil turned her to him. "You're shaking. What's going on?"

The fog slid between them, a sly mist that frightened her. "I—I don't know."

"Honey?" he asked, concerned.

"Get me inside," she whispered desperately.

In the kitchen, Neil drew her close again. "You're freezing—shaking. Do you think Bruce is out there? Do you? Mary Jane would have called him, and this whole thing might be taking off real fast. If he thinks he can come here and scare you—"

Claire wrapped her arms tight around Neil, her face against the warmth of his throat. "Don't go out there. Please don't."

"I know what Bruce is capable of now, honey. I'll be careful."

"Bruce isn't out there. I would have known. It was something else."

"Something else? What?"

Claire shook her head; she didn't understand the unknown, only that it wanted her. "Nothing. Nothing else."

She drew back and through the kitchen window watched the sunrise eat through the fog. Why did it want her?

And now it wanted Neil.

Neil was watching her. She'd seen that puzzled expression before—on her ex-husband when he was just discovering what she really was. "You know, this would be a lot easier if we involved my mother. She's been through these cases before, helping find the lost."

His answer seemed to take forever. "Maybe. But this is more important to you, isn't it? You're in this now, and you need to finish it. You're a fighter, Claire, and you're tougher than you know."

Claire hadn't thought of herself as a fighter or tough, the thought surprising. She'd always been the one who needed protection, the baby under the care of her family. Now, suddenly, she stood apart and strong. But was she strong enough?

"There's too much at risk. I could make a mistake. Yesterday, with Mary Jane, I got angry and yes, jealous, too. If I can't manage my own emotions, I'm not developed enough—centered enough to find Sammy."

He spun her around. "The hell you're not. You've gotten us this far . . . you're not backing off now. We're going the distance—to find Sammy, one way or the other. You're right about scaring off Bruce and maybe losing that link if we move too fast. You can do this, Claire. Just tell me what we do next?"

Sixteen

"WAITING FOR AN OPENING IS THE HARDEST PART," CLAIRE
stated that evening, when Neil ended his call with Mary
Jane.

"She says he's leaving soon . . . going to Alaska for
a few days. We can get into his house near Billings. He
just uses it as storage and to spend a few days when he
hasn't anywhere else to go."

"I'm sorry about Mary Jane. I know you considered
her to be a friend."

"Uh-huh." His tone closed conversation about a
trusted friend who had betrayed him. Neil leaned against
his workshop desk and studied the plate of freshly baked
gingersnaps. "Mmm. Lasagna—the meat kind—in the
oven at my place and a plate of cookies brought out to
my shop by a sexy-looking woman. . . . Add them together and I have to ask this question: What's up?"

His gaze slid down Claire's body, taking in the form-
fitting back sweater and pants, the brooch at her shoulder. Woven with Celtic designs, the thin gold headband,
circled her head; below the headband, her hair was loose,
waving softly and freshly shampooed and fragrant. Her
heavy bracelet matched the headband's design.

Claire had prepared carefully, dressing almost as if for a ceremony in which she would fully admit her heritage. The time had come to admit that blood, what ran inside her and could not be denied: She was descended from the bond of a Celtic mystic and a Viking conqueror; the seer's special abilities had been passed down to Claire and her sisters. While they struggled with that particular and unwelcome psychic strand of DNA, Claire prepared to open herself to it.

She needed every power possible to help Neil find his son.

Claire straightened her shoulders, bracing herself for what she would tell Neil. Her family, and what she truly was, had terrified another man. Would Neil turn from her after learning everything?

"Interesting getup," Neil stated. "You're dressed for business . . . from the look of you, it's something to do with your family. You're using the lasagna and cookies to soften whatever you're about to tell me. Nice bait."

Claire thought of an ancient time, when the Celtic mystic had prepared the Viking for what he had really claimed but could never conquer.

Neil reached to touch the headband circling her forehead and traced the design. "Old . . . not Tempest's work."

"It's called a 'diadem.' She discovered it while on an archaeological dig in Norway. She likes hunting for things. In that way, she's like our mother."

"And like you." Neil's gray eyes narrowed warily, and he shook his head. "Lead on. At this point, I can take anything you can hand out."

Claire fought the terror inside her. In her lifetime, she had not been so bare-bone exposed and determined to give another person the mysteries that she had so long avoided. Neil already knew portions of her family's story, but he was about to discover more. "We'll see about that. Let's go into the house, shall we?"

He lifted an eyebrow. "Boy, this is really going to be good."

On the way to Neil's back door, he walked close beside her, his arm around her protectively, that big hand straying low on her hip. Claire listened to the timeless sense inside her, that somewhere back in time, another man, a warrior like Neil, had walked with a woman into a new journey, his arm just as possessive and protective— claiming what was his.

Inside the kitchen, Neil drew her close and studied her. His finger traced a long fiery strand down her throat and to the tip of her breast. He lifted that strand to his lips, brushing it against them. "I think I'll take a shower. If you're all rigged up like this, set to do God knows what, I don't want to be sweaty and smelling like an oil rig."

"Take your time," Claire managed evenly. As she set their dinner places, she wondered how to began the ancient story, how she could explain what she and her sisters were. . . .

After dinner, Neil raised his wineglass to her in a toast. "Have I told you how great you look, all that red hair loose and that tight black outfit? The jewelry just adds a little flavor, but with that red hair and those green eyes, you look almost as if you stepped from another time."

"Part of me has. Here, have another glass of wine. And it isn't just jewelry. At least the brooch isn't. It's more for protection—and it's a replica." Claire poured the wine and stood. "Let's finish this in your office, shall we? I'm expecting a call, and we'll need the speakerphone there."

Neil shrugged and stood. Those smoky eyes ran over her body as he said, "I was hoping for the bedroom, not a telephone call."

Claire moved close to him. "Bear with me, will you? Just don't touch me."

"Honey bun, that's asking a lot. You're looking very edible."

She studied that broad face, the lines on his forehead, the way his hair waved to one side, the sturdy line of his brows, those gray eyes, and that blunt nose. Then she settled on the line of his mouth—curved at the top, a fuller bottom lip, but generally thinner and harder than her own. Near him, Claire caught the sexual waves, the heat and the hunger enclosing them.

"What are you doing, honey bun?" Neil asked warily.

"Feeling. Just feeling. When we first met, I didn't know if it was my sexual needs, or if I was absorbing yours and making it my own."

"Now that's a hell of an admission," he stated rawly. "What's your conclusion now, Doctor?"

"That now it is my own. But we are connected somehow, beyond this journey. . . . Scared yet?"

"I could have told you that. You've been picking up the phone calls from me before they rang. Let's get this show on the road." With that, Neil lifted his wineglass in a teasing toast to her, then followed Claire down the hallway.

In the living room, Neil sat at his desk. Claire leaned against the wall and studied the lacy curtains, which filtered the sunset. She waited for the right heartbeat to tell her it was time, then she began.

"You know about my family and what we are. I know it's difficult to understand, but we are as we are. I know that now. I can't pretend I'm something I'm not, not any longer. I can't hide, deny the truth."

"I know what you are, Claire. I've seen what you can do. And I know about Tempest."

She smiled softly, thinking back through the legend of the Celtic seer and the Viking conqueror. "You came from the same blood—Viking blood. Olafson . . . Olaf's son. We were probably meant to be together from the start. At least, we were probably meant to intersect, in this special time, for this one journey."

Neil's smile was all sexy, competent male. "I like to think that we have something special. And we do the 'intersect' thing pretty well."

He wasn't understanding her meaning. "Let me make it clearer. Your family liked the outdoors. Your father built sailing ships and was a woodworker. He probably descended from a line of ship makers, from seafaring men, from the Vikings."

Neil shook his head and frowned. "I never thought of it that way."

Claire touched the wolf's-head brooch. "This is like one that came from my Viking ancestor who took a Celt seer for a wife."

"Okay. I understand." Neil's tone was wary. "What's that got to do with us?"

"Everything. Nothing. Tempest is a sculptor, but she's also a hunter."

"Agreed. I've seen her work."

"For a year now, Tempest has been hunting for something that my mother dreams about. It's a link to something, and we don't know what. It's a *fibula*, the one that the Viking used to claim my ancestor. It's been lost, and we've got to find it to finish something—and we don't know what. But whatever it is, we have to find that original wolf *fibula* and claim it."

Neil nodded slowly. "I understand about wanting to keep family things. We—Bruce and I—lost everything in that fire, except the ones Eunice had."

"We're uneasy now—me, my sisters, and my mother. Leona has just had a dream about a wolf. She wouldn't tell me everything, but I'd say her dream could coincide with Mother's. Two precognitives at the same time, with the same basic dream, and I'm uneasy now, could mean trouble—bad trouble."

"Because you're trying to find out about my son. . . . The things happening to you, because of me, have upset your family. I'm sorry about that. And you're uneasy, bothered about something you can't identify. I've got that part."

Claire shook her head. "My unrest began before my attack. I sensed something in the red beads—they reminded me of blood. I'm not a precognitive, but remember that some of our abilities overlap and change . . . we're a mixed breed. My sisters admitted to being restless, too. The fact that Mom is keeping out of this says that she's also uneasy. She's blocking me when I come too close to whatever is bothering her. She's very strong, and if she can't understand it, then it's big. I think she's hunting something—she can get very secretive when she thinks it might affect one of us."

When Neil nodded solemnly, as if he were trying to understand, Claire braced herself to continue. "To recount: It has something to do with being susceptible to large bodies of water, my sisters and I. It has something to do with how I felt at the river, about how I feel sometimes about the fog. That tie could be linked to our Viking ancestor. We don't know. There is something about large bodies of water that makes us vulnerable. Our sailing accident heightened our sense of fear near water. Water is—can be a medium, a connection, a portal—for those with psychic abilities. I hadn't thought about the fog also being used as a conduit. But at times, I've felt it lurking around me—and you."

Neil rose and drew her into his arms. He sat again,

holding her on his lap. "I'm sorry you went through facing so many people all at once. That had to upset you."

Claire settled into his arms, placing her face against his throat. She inhaled his fresh, good scent, that male scent to complement her own feminine one. "I'm not sorry about that. It was a learning experience, and you were there to protect me. Opening—understanding myself, had to come sometime. Or else I would have become nothing—a shadow."

"You wouldn't have become a shadow. You're too strong," Neil stated firmly.

The room was completely dark now, and Claire focused on Neil's heartbeat, matching it with hers. "Leona is going to call soon. I told her I'd be here. I want you to talk with her."

Neil nuzzled her hair. "I've spoken with her before."

"Not like this. She's having dreams, and she doesn't want them. As a clairvoyant or a precognitive, she can be accurate, almost as accurate as Mom, when she focuses. Even as children, we knew that she could be the most powerful if she'd wanted. She's tuned to us, aware of what has been happening to me, aware of how I feel about a man who aches for his son. But something has stirred in Leona lately, and she needs to tell you herself. Because I trust you, she's agreed to do so, to help you."

Claire leaned back to look up at Neil, then she reached for the telephone. "Hi, Leona. Yes, he's right here."

As Neil listened to Leona, his eyes locked on Claire, his expression tense. His voice was coarse as he ended the call, his eyes shimmering with tears. "Thank you, Leona. Thank you."

To Claire, Neil said, "I don't know that I believe her—that Sammy is alive and well and happy. But I have to, or else—she said he looks like me."

"Well, we'll just have to believe in her, won't we?"

Claire held him tight, and understood his tears

against her throat. She couldn't tell Neil how much she feared for him, how much Leona feared that she could be wrong.

Yet, there in her vintage shop, with Claire's bags on display, Leona had images of a small boy, happy and playing, a child with silvery eyes and dark waving hair touched by the sun, a healthy sturdy boy. She'd gripped a bag that Neil had touched, "Dreamscape," and in the shop's window had seen a father bend close to his son, their features alike.

And she knew that Neil and his son would be reunited. . . .

But Leona had seen something else, an image she hadn't shared with Neil: Like Claire, she saw the fire—the man in the fire. . . .

"I hope Mary Jane is right about Bruce taking off for Alaska," Neil said three days later.

The ten o'clock hour didn't hide the poor condition of Bruce's home. Lying on the outskirts of Billings, Bruce's large, sprawling house reflected his lifestyle—the absence of responsibility.

"I ended up buying this place and paying the bills on it, to make certain that my brother had some kind of home base. This house is just another of his investments in real estate that didn't pay off when no one bought out here. The house used to be okay, and it had a woodworking shop. I had some idea Bruce might want to take that up, like Dad. Bad idea," Neil stated grimly as he looked down the deserted road bordered by natural grasses.

Claire placed her hand on Neil's, covering the big fist gripping the steering wheel. "It was one of the heart. You loved him. You were trying to give him a chance. I know this is hard for you."

"He had plenty of chances. From the folks and from

me." Neil pulled into the driveway that ran beside the house, separating it from the three-car garage. In the backyard, he parked and stepped into the night.

Claire followed him to the unlocked garage. Neil clicked on the overhead lights to reveal several motorcycles, an empty space, and a pickup truck; it was the same model as the one that had almost run Claire down. Neil's expression tightened as he stared at her. "Just couldn't tell me who you saw that night, huh? Didn't recognize my brother?"

"I wasn't certain until I saw his picture at your house. I'd seen the ones Eunice had, but you must have added that close-up when you moved in."

His "Sure" was clipped and disbelieving. At the house's back door, Neil held the flashlight while he watched Claire bend to use the pick from her brooch. "I don't want to know, but I bet you learned that from Tempest," he said, as the door swung open.

"Hey. What works, works."

Neil led the way into the house and turned on the lights as they walked through the ill-used rooms, stale with odors of cigarettes and liquor.

The rooms were cluttered with boxes and papers and garbage. Neil's distaste of his brother's lifestyle was apparent. "This used to be a nice place."

In a large ranch-style living room, a stack of boxes stood by the massive rock fireplace. Partially burned papers lay in the ashes, and Neil bent to study them. But Claire was looking at the photographs on the fireplace mantel. They were the same as Neil's, except for one, which was his high-school graduation picture. Several bullet holes had punctured Neil's photograph.

"I guess that picture says it all," Neil murmured as he shuffled through the papers and selected a box, which he placed on a battered table. "He had all these things, and didn't tell me after the fire. If Eunice hadn't made copies, I wouldn't have had any pictures of Mom and Dad, of us as kids. Let's start here. From the post-marks on the letters, this stuff is about eight years old, about the time Sammy was taken. Bruce was burning them for some reason—I can guess why."

Claire picked up a note from the fireplace. It was a man's handwriting, the words misspelled and specify-ing thousands of dollars of cash. It was signed "Top-per." She handed it to Neil, who scanned the note, his expression grim.

Neil breathed deeply and handed her a list of telephone numbers and names; Linda Baker's name was under-lined, Topper Reed's below it with the note, "Picked up delivery at the main road of the campground. Female scared and won't talk. Transported delivery to new owner. Pay me in cash."

" 'Delivery.' My son." Neil's raw, pained whisper echoed in the room, tearing at Claire's heart.

Locked in his brother's crime, the direct link to the abduction of his son, Neil's fury built, shaking Claire. "Neil, I'm so sorry."

"I . . . will . . . kill him."

Neil's violence stunned Claire, then she tensed, be-cause suddenly the house was too quiet. She turned to where she'd felt that first stab of evil. "Hello, Bruce."

The shadows moved, and Bruce, holding a revolver, stepped into the light. "I knew that when you talked to Mary Jane, and she was so eager to know about my travel plans, you were up to something, little brother. As usual, I'm smarter than you. Your little double-spy play didn't work. Kill me? I don't think so, Neil. Though I have to admit, your luck was running good—until now."

Claire stepped in front of Neil, who was set to charge his brother, to kill him. "Move out of the way, Claire."

"Sweet Claire," Bruce mused coolly. "I should have known you would be trouble."

"You set the fire that killed your parents, didn't you?" Claire asked as she tried to push away Neil's restraining hand. She looked at him, willing him to understand. "Let me go, Neil. You *know* what I have to do."

She had to get closer to Bruce, to move inside him, to know his thoughts, his feelings. . . .

Neil's hand locked tighter, and he shook his head.

"I still have it," Bruce crowed as he leered at Claire. "That old Bruce Olafson charm. I knew you'd want me, honey, from the moment I saw you."

"Now is not the time for *that*, Claire," Neil stated harshly.

Despite his warning, she pushed harder, needing Neil to understand that as a psychic, she needed to be closer to Bruce, to understand what he knew. Claire *needed* not only her psychic antenna, but the visuals that could support it. "But, darling, he's more interesting than you—right now."

Bruce's wild laughter ricocheted in the large room. "Sure. Come over here, honey. Neil, stay put, or I'll kill her right now."

Neil looked desperate enough to charge his brother, and Claire made certain she was directly between the men as she walked toward Bruce. In those few steps, her mind contained a flood of ideas. How could she get information about Sammy's whereabouts? And how could she stop Bruce from killing them?

Then— Was it true that a stronger mind could rule a weaker one, draw energy from the weaker? Was it possible that she could force Bruce, just for an instant, to put down his weapon? Did she have that ability?

Claire pushed away her fear; she needed all of her resources to face Bruce, to get what she needed. Someone had reached through the computer lines to "own" her attacker, to bend him to a superior will. Was it possible she could do the same?

*Untried, she could make a mistake that could cost
Neil's life and her own.*

"Don't move, Neil," Bruce warned again, as Claire
stood next to him.

She placed her hand on his chest, right over his heart.
It was filled with hatred, the blackness shocking her,
burning up her arm. But she was stronger, forcing it
back down her arm and into a tiny warm corner of
Bruce's heart. "You set the fire that killed your parents,
didn't you, Bruce?" she asked quietly.

His eyes flickered, and a trickle of energy shifted inside him, greed eating at the dim remainder of family
love. "Yes. Dad wouldn't give me any more money. He
wanted me to straighten out and get a job. I owed bills.
The sharks were coming after me, and they were going
to let the folks know soon. I had to do something.
Then the major share of everything they had went to
my little, sweet brother. *Everything* was always for Neil,
not me."

"Bruce, the folks did provide for you. You went
through your inheritance in no time," Neil stated softly.

Bruce's handgun jerked to Neil. "Shut up!"

Claire tried not to feel Neil's pain, the link between
them strong and quivering. She focused on Bruce.
"You're right, Bruce. They weren't fair to you. You had
to do what you did."

His eyes moved from Neil to her, and Claire hoped
she was gaining more control, feeding on his energy,
becoming stronger as he weakened. . . .

"What are you doing? Why are you looking at me
like that? All I can see is those eyes, and you're doing
something. What is it?" he asked suddenly, as the handgun returned to press hard against her stomach.

"Knowing you. You'd like me to know you, wouldn't
you?" She was looking inside him, getting images, just
flashes skipping from Bruce to her.

"No tricks," Bruce ordered uneasily.

"Of course not." Claire kept her voice calm, pushing her strength, wanting more, sucking more from Bruce, working fiercely inside him, where the past lurked dark and strong.

She'd made contact with something deep inside Bruce, linking to it, making it her own. Just as she had with Neil, Claire focused on his heartbeat, placing it in rhythm with hers.

The connection jolted her, and Bruce stared at her, mesmerized; she was the stronger now, holding him in her power.

Claire listened to the beat of their hearts, then she spoke soothingly, "Everything will work out for the best, Bruce."

"I'll kill Neil, and then you and I will go places." His voice wavered uncertainly, the gun aimed at Neil now.

But Neil wasn't standing where he had been. Claire smiled, drawing Bruce's attention to her, her strength ruling his. "I don't think so, Bruce. Because Neil is right beside you, and he's taking that gun now."

Drained with the effort of focusing on Bruce and controlling her own terror that Neil would be hurt, Claire quickly stepped away, breaking the psychic link to Bruce.

Surprised and surfacing to the danger of Neil closing in on him, Bruce started to fight, but it was too late.

Neil's fist slammed into Bruce's jaw, and he sprawled on the floor. Neil kicked away the discarded gun; his hands gripped Bruce's shirt and hauled him upright. He shoved Bruce against the wall hard—once, twice, so hard the windows rattled. "Where's my son? What did you do with him? Tell me, or I'll—"

Bruce managed to leer at Neil. "You'll never know where your kid is."

"Won't I?" he asked too softly, violence pulsing from

him. "Remember all those times my big brother taught me about fighting? Let's just see what you remember."

Using every bit of her strength, Claire moved to circle Neil with her arms, holding him tight. She pressed her face against his back, felt the killing strength there, and pitted herself against him. "There's no need for that. Don't lower yourself to what he is. You don't want to come to your son with his blood on your hands. . . . I have what you want. . . . I know where Sammy is."

Seventeen

"ARE YOU SURE YOU GOT IT? WHERE SAMMY IS?" NEIL asked unevenly as he shoved Bruce against the wall.

"I got enough." Exhausted, Claire nodded and closed her eyes. In that connection with Bruce, when she became the stronger, she had gathered the crimes he had committed. They weighed upon her now, dark, evil flashes of his past, and in the center stood a little boy, aged eight and half who resembled the Olafson men.

Bruce sneered. "There's no way she could get anything from me. You want news of your kid, little brother? Then you're going to have to be very nice to me. You want to trade? Fine. I'll give you what you want, and you give me money. I'll be out of the country before you can find that kid."

Neil's fist cocked back, poised to strike Bruce, but Claire managed to hold his arm. "Neil! Don't! I have everything."

"Like what?" Bruce's taunt revealed his contempt.

Claire looked steadily at him. "Does a town with a penguin logo ring a bell?"

Bruce's surprised expression was almost comical. "There's no way. Who told you? Topper?"

"He couldn't very well do that when he was dead, could he, Bruce? You saw to that, didn't you?"

"It wasn't me. Someone did him, but not me. No—you can't lay that on me. Topper ran with the wrong people, and one of them got him."

"Maybe," Claire murmured quietly. She pressed her fingertips to her temples; she was suddenly drained and light-headed.

She had sensed that Bruce was involved, though he had not actually committed the murder. "Neil, your brother is wanted for a string of robberies he committed with Topper in Washington state. He used an alias, and no one actually knew who he was, but Topper. And that is why Topper had to die, and he wasn't pinning anything on Bruce, not anymore. And—"

Neil nodded solemnly. "What else, Claire?"

Bruce squirmed in Neil's hold, his expression that of fear. "What is it with her? How did she get that information? No one knows anything about any of that, but—"

"But you," Neil finished for his brother. "She got it from you."

He glanced at Claire. "Claire, you've turned white. Are you okay?"

Are you okay? Neil's question sounded fuzzy and slow and distant as Claire seemed to drift downward to the floor. Or did the floor move up to fold around her? she wondered distantly before she slid into the darkness.

Neil glanced at Claire as she seemed to slide to the floor. Distracted and concerned for her, he turned to her.

At the same time, he heard a scraping sound, felt his brother's body tense, and then the blow to his head.

Stunned at first, Neil could only stare at Bruce as he raised the metal lamp for the second time.

* * *

The sound of his own groan caused Neil to surface slightly. That was a mistake; his head throbbed fiercely. He opened his eyes to see Claire lying beside him. Had he been out a few seconds? Or had Bruce done something to her?

Neil closed his eyes, tried to regroup, then opened them again. The pain was still there and the crackling sound was that of fire, firelight dancing on the wall. Flames filled the fireplace and had spread to the boxes of papers and those scattered on the floor. The drapes had ignited, and one had been torn free; smoke filled the room.

Bruce was screaming in pain from somewhere down the hallway.

Beside him, Claire lay too quietly, her face pale. Was she already overcome by smoke?

Fear raced through Neil as he slowly forced himself to his knees and tried to draw her upward, to wake her. "Claire, wake up. We've got to get out of here."

Claire's lids fluttered open. "I'm so sorry. I just felt this wave of utter—"

"Evil. We've got to get out of here." Neil supported Claire as she tried to stand, and she began coughing.

Neil began moving them carefully, quickly, through the heavy layer of smoke. The front door was blocked by flames, the back way would be faster; he had to get Claire to safety . . . just a few feet more, past the hallway and out the back door.

Suddenly Bruce appeared in the hallway. Flames were coming from the old drapes twisted around him. Neil pushed Claire back. "Get out of here."

"You're hurt. I'm not—" Neil's rough shove sent Claire stumbling toward the kitchen, already filled by smoke. Neil turned to Bruce. "Hold still, let me get those off you."

Bruce's face held terror as he stopped for just that one instant and stared at Neil. "Dad? Dad, I'm sorry! I'm sorry, Dad!"

Shielding his face against the flames rising around Bruce, Neil moved toward his brother. "I'm Neil, Bruce . . . hold still. You're tangled in the drapes."

With a scream of horror, his clothing on fire, Bruce chose the wrong direction to run for safety; he turned and ran back down the hallway.

Neil glanced at the living room, in flames, the papers igniting. With no time to lose, Neil turned and found Claire huddled nearby. She stared at him, her whisper almost covered by the roar of the fire. "A man of the fire, a man in the fire. . . . A man of the fire, a man in the fire. . . ."

He hurried to her, grabbed her, and put her over his shoulder. Neil didn't stop running until they were outside and a safe distance away. He placed Claire on the ground and bent to her. She was still coughing, tears streaking the smudges on her face. "Breathe deeply, Claire. Come on, honey."

Claire gulped in air and clung to him. "Are you all right, Neil?"

He turned her face up to his, searched it, and kissed her briefly. He pressed his cell phone into her hand. Neil was already moving toward the house when he called back to her, "Stay put. Call for help."

Claire watched Neil enter the house and quickly dialed 9-1-1. When Neil appeared at the back doorway, flames behind him, she whispered, "Man in the fire. . . . Oh, Neil, don't let it be you. . . ."

But Neil wasn't in the fire, he was running away from it—to her, and he was alive. Relieved, Claire ran to meet him. He was coughing, and they moved back from the house.

But Neil had to try to find his brother. Still coughing, he circled the house with Claire; they found no sign of Bruce. There was nothing they could do, but stand back and watch the house burn. Neil held Claire tightly against him. "He was using lighter fluid to start the fire. I saw the can. It must have gotten on his clothes, and he got tangled in that drape. . . ."

"He's gone, Neil."

Neil didn't answer, the lines on his face deepening as he remembered another fire in which his parents had died. "I guess that part is over," he said finally, in a tired tone that said he'd had years of dealing with Bruce's hatred and shady life. "He thought I was Dad and ran from me."

Claire held Neil tight as the sirens began to whine in the distance. "You did what you could, Neil."

It was almost dawn the next morning when Claire stood naked in the center of Neil's bedroom. The effort of making a connection with Bruce, of absorbing the flashes of his life and finding information about Sammy had exhausted her. Freshly showered and shampooed by Neil, Claire stood still, childlike, as he slid a T-shirt over her head. "You're going to rest now, Claire."

He should have taken her to a hospital emergency room and had her checked for smoke inhalation. When the firemen had arrived, Claire had been adamant about refusing the paramedic's care, her expression frantic. Neil had remembered Claire's trauma when she'd lost her baby and the warnings from her family. He'd spoken quietly to the paramedic. "She's still terrified. Tell me what to do. I'll help her."

Above the oxygen mask he held to her face, Claire's eyes had held gratitude.

Neil had automatically moved in to protect her, holding her closely while answering the coroner's questions about the fire in which Bruce had died. "We were a little late, but we were close, and he said to stop by anyway, that it was a little chilly, and he'd lit a fire. The house was already burning when we arrived. I tried to go in, bumped my head, and couldn't find my brother. I saw him inside and tried to—then I didn't see him anymore."

Following routine procedure, the coroner had the body sent for forensic examination in Billings. "You've already identified him, but we'll need more—dental records, that sort of thing. Routine for this kind of death by thermal injury. . . . Give you a call when we're done."

As Neil brushed Claire's hair in his bedroom, he remembered Bruce's face, a man who had killed his own parents and arranged to abduct his nephew, all out of greed and hatred. Claire turned to Neil, and her hand rose to gently smooth the lumps on his head. "How awful to lose your brother that way."

"It's been coming for a long time." Neil didn't want to think about Bruce, about how he had died. He didn't want to think about how he'd lied in the official report of the fire—that Claire and he had decided on a whim to visit Bruce and had found the house burning. He didn't want to think about funeral arrangements, but he would—because his parents had loved both their sons.

Neil only wanted to see Claire with color in her face again, those green eyes clear and bright, her body strong. In the past few hours, he'd felt her cold hand in his, the way her body leaned against him, as if her last bit of strength had been sapped from her.

He eased Claire into his bed, then undressed and slid in beside her. He gathered her into his arms and frowned. Claire seemed so lifeless and cold. Was she in shock? "I still think you should have seen a doctor."

"You didn't."

"They checked me over. I wasn't leaving you alone, and if you weren't going to an emergency room, I wasn't."

He wrapped her closer, tucking the blankets close around her. Outside, the June morning was beginning, but Neil was drained; in those few hours, he'd traveled through a lifetime. . . . Bruce had admitted to killing their parents, and his horror at seeing Neil was because he had been haunted by guilt—*Dad? I'm sorry, Dad. . . .*

Neil realized that it would take years before those words would slide away forever.

He listened to Claire's breathing, her breath slowly, rhythmically touching his throat. When she shivered, he rubbed her shoulder and drew her closer. "I don't ever want you to do something like that again. When you started feeling out Bruce, I knew exactly what you were doing, and you scared the hell out of me."

"I was afraid you would kill him, your own brother. You'd have regretted that for the rest of your life."

At the moment, Neil's anger with Bruce hadn't completely died. "Maybe. Get some rest."

"I'm too tired. I just want to lie here with you and know that you're safe. It wasn't you that I saw in the fire. At the campground, I saw the fire behind you, and I thought—"

"You can stop that, honey bun," Neil stated, as Claire's hand smoothed his arm. "I'm okay. Save your energy for yourself. You really scared me last night, going after Bruce like that, putting yourself between his gun and me. That was *not* goddamn smart, Claire. You could have been killed."

She lifted slightly above him and looked down, her face pale in the dim light, her hair flowing down to brush his face and chest. "I've never been a predator before. I realized that it is possible to take control of someone, and I did it. And I realized that was probably what had happened to my attacker—he was trying to rebuild his life. I know that he was a good man, until something, someone got to him. The power of suggestion is one thing, but bending another to your will is exhilarating. I can see how some could get addicted to it."

Neil considered the woman leaning over him as he brought a silky strand to his lips. She'd moved from exhaustion to excitement in a few minutes. She'd pushed the limits of what she could do, and she'd succeeded. He understood, but worried for her. "Take it easy, Claire. You need your rest."

"I saw everything, Neil. The city limit sign of the town, the street name, the house. Bruce had been there, checking on Sammy, and now we're going to get your son. All we have to do is find a town that uses a penguin for a logo. How difficult can that be?"

"Not that hard, I suppose, but for right now, we both need rest." Concerned for Claire, Neil hid his need to immediately start searching for a town with that penguin logo.

Claire's eyes blazed down at him, her body shivering. Neil feared for an afterreaction to the violence she'd experienced earlier. "Claire, simmer down."

In one lithe movement, she slid out of bed and turned to stare down at him. "Why? We're going to get Sammy. When Bruce's body is released, we'll take care of his burial, because that's the right thing to do. You're a man who always does the right thing, then we'll go see Sammy."

Apparently deeply in her planning-strategy mode, Claire started pacing the length of the bedroom. Suddenly, she stopped, her hair swinging out and around her head. "We've got to be careful now. We've got to do this in the right way, introducing you to Sammy. Let's see—how we knew he was there. . . . What about if someone was passing through 'penguin-town' saw this little boy and he looked like you, about the right age and you just wondered. Okay, that's a start. . . . So you call his parents—he's adopted legally, by the way, Neil. He was deserted—"

"*What?*"

"Didn't I tell you? Topper must have left Sammy in a church—I saw the white steeple. From there, Sammy went to foster care, then he was adopted legally. Somehow, Bruce knew all this . . . someone like him is likely to use whatever he can to track something. I did it! I got all that! I didn't know I could!"

She hurried to Neil and tugged his head down for a brief, hard kiss. Then she leaped back, raised her arms, and danced in a circle. "I did it . . . I did it," she sing-songed. "All we have to do is find a town with a penguin logo."

Stunned by the new twist in Sammy's journey, Neil stood and stared at her. Dawn touched Claire's hair as it spun around her, her arms and legs pale in the shadows. "What else did you get?" he asked cautiously.

"That you never stopped loving Bruce. You're like that. Solid. Good."

Neil wasn't feeling "solid"; he was feeling light-headed, overwhelmed by this fresh blast of information. He put out a hand to brace himself on the bedpost. "I need a drink."

"What about a nice big breakfast? I'm in the mood to cook, and you have a big day ahead of you. You know what? I just got the neatest idea for a new handbag. I'm going to call it 'Found.' Leona will make a mint on it." With that, Claire stopped as if in midthought. "Neil, I'm so sorry about Bruce. I don't mean to be callous, and I do know what this cost you."

"Okay. . . . Are you all right? I mean, did last night

do something to—you know? Did it change you some-how?"

"Oh, I'm just fine. Well, except, that I wish things had turned out differently. And I wish you hadn't been hurt so. . . . But we have to be very careful how we handle this now. I know that every particle of you wants to see Sammy. We don't know what kind of people have adopted him, and if notified that you may be looking, they could leave before—"

"I know that this is tricky, Claire. Everything has to be done for the sake of my son. We'll do it your way. I'm not going to endanger my son."

When Claire nodded and hurried out of the bedroom and into the kitchen, Neil stood very still. He listened to Claire singing something with a Celtic bounce to it, punctuated by the sound of pots and pans and running water. He tried to adapt to what had passed, the new information about Sammy, and Claire's reaction—setting speed records from exhaustion to full-blown energy. If Claire had tapped into whatever truth remained in Bruce correctly, Sammy would be safe for a few days longer. That moved Claire to the front of Neil's concerned list.

He shook his head, then did the only thing he could do—call her mother. "It takes one to know one. Her mother will know what to do."

The ocean sounded in the background as Greer Aisling's soothing voice answered the call. "Hello, Neil. I've been waiting for your call."

"It didn't ring, did it? The telephone?" In his bedroom, Neil spoke quietly, so Claire wouldn't hear.

"No." Greer didn't hide the humor in her tone. "A connection with one psychic can link them with others. And yours has that masculine flavor, a little woodsy, a little boyish teasing, but sturdy and good."

Neil wondered warily if Greer were probing him as they spoke. But he didn't have time to check the intricacies of connection by connection. "I'm sorry to call you this early, but I'm worried about Claire."

"Of course you are. You're The Protector." Greer's soothing tone was underlined by humor.

Neil decided to deal with The Protector business later and focused on getting Greer's help. "We've just been through a pretty bad scene with my brother. He's dead, we're home, we haven't slept all night . . . and she's really revved out there in the kitchen cooking a big breakfast at five in the morning. I'm worried about her. We've got leads on Sammy, my son, but right now, Claire needs to rest. It's almost as if she's on some high. Tell me what to do?"

"I'm glad you've got news of your son. That's wonderful, but I am sorry to hear about your brother."

For just an instant, Bruce's terrified face flashed in front of Neil. *Dad? I'm sorry.*

Greer's voice was soothing. "That nightmare will lessen as time goes on. You'll come to a point where you can forgive and remember the good times with your family. You'll have your son, and he'll fill your heart. . . . As for my daughter, the world has just opened up for her, and she's discovered that she can manage her gift, that it can't rule her, if she focuses and protects herself. She's just done the one thing that she felt she needed to do most of all, that she wished she could have done to protect her baby. This challenge has been very important to her, and she faced her fears and won. She's hid from what she is, and now she knows how to deal with her sensitivities."

Neil noted that the sounds from the kitchen had stopped. He turned to the woman in the doorway. Claire walked to take the telephone from him. She looked at him as she spoke, "Hello, Mother. . . . Yes, I know that it's possible, taking control of someone else. I found that out last night. The feeling of power is incredible. I felt so—predatory and strong. I can see how someone could have seduced John through the computer and caused him to hate me."

Claire turned from Neil to the early morning outside. A bird had perched on the windowsill and didn't move when Claire placed her open hand over the glass between them. "The river did seem to call to me. And there's something about the fog—yes, it could be an extension of the water. Yes, I'll be careful."

Claire, poised by the window, her hand almost touching the bird was a captivating scene; Neil remembered what he had read about empaths, that they were in tune with nature and disturbed by human emotions. Somehow, he had to find a way to protect Claire from the next few days, from dealing with the darkness and the end of Bruce's life. He thought of the boxes of papers that could have held more information about Sammy and how they had been used to set the fire.

They were burned and the only information they had now was Claire's psychic grasp on Bruce, a very tenuous lead involving a town with a penguin logo.

Claire turned back to Neil and smiled softly. "Yes, he's my protector. Don't worry about me. We'll find his son and start working through the best way to handle this, and later, I want you to come here—for a family reunion. Yes, Leona will be here if I have to go get her and drag her here. Yes, it is a penguin. Cute, aren't they?"

Neil sat on the edge of the bed, and Claire came to sit on his lap. She smoothed his hair and kissed his cheek, cuddling against him. "He does seem a little bewildered, and he's just adapting a little now. He'll be okay. Once he sees his son, he'll be just fine. We're going to be very careful how we handle this, so as not to disturb Sammy from any security and love he's known."

Claire yawned and slid backward, her head on the pillow. "Night, Mom."

Neil slid her feet beneath the blankets, watched her curl into a ball, and stood looking at the woman who had opened the door to his son. He stood, took the telephone from her relaxed hand, and replaced it.

He shook his head again and walked to the brightly lit kitchen. Neil placed the bowl of pancake batter into the refrigerator and studied the kitchen. In a few minutes, Claire had whipped up a gigantic breakfast and started the dishwasher. Unable to sleep, Neil wrapped a slice of toast around strips of bacon, stopped at his bedroom door to find Claire deeply asleep, then went to the living room.

For a long time he sat and stared at the picture of the brothers, trying to understand how Bruce could have killed their parents. Neil struggled with the past and proof that Bruce had tried to kill him, too. Hatred of Neil was one thing, but to take a child from his mother. . . . Driven by jealousy, determined to reclaim what he considered rightfully his, Bruce had intended to kill Claire, too.

Unable to look at the picture any longer, Neil placed it in a drawer and turned on his computer. In a few short minutes he'd located Penguin, Arkansas, a small rural town founded by an Australian with a fondness for penguins.

Neil sat back and stared at the lit screen. Claire had caught the street name and the house. Finally, after all these years, he would soon find his son.

"Leona was right. Your son does look like you."

Claire sat beside Neil in the Penguin, Arkansas cafe. By the third week of June, Neil had buried his brother's ashes and cleaned up any lingering details, such as silencing Mary Jane with a very effective threat.

Rather than fly, Neil had chosen to drive to Arkansas, because he wanted to protect Claire from the intrusions of others' emotions. In the four days of driving and the nights at the motels, he had insisted that Claire rest. And he had prepared to see his son, a boy who had been renamed Lucas Richards.

A short time spent in the backroom files of Penguin's local newspaper, on the pretense of researching Neil's family history, had produced a picture of a boy whose parents and sisters loved him. Lucas-Sammy had played ball and was in church, school, and club activities.

Hunched over the cafe's coffee cup, Neil was locked in the first sight of his son after eight years. The boy had turned toward them as they passed on the street, the same street name that Claire had gotten from Bruce; Sammy bore that same dark hair, that sturdy build. He was poised to jump onto his bike, one jean leg rolled a little higher to stay free of the chain. He had yelled and pushed his bike out onto the street sidewalk to meet another boy, decked out in skateboarding gear. The two friends stood talking as Neil and Claire had passed slowly in their pickup. When Claire had waved, Neil's son flashed a wide grin, much like his biological father's.

"I don't know what to do, Claire," Neil said, as she slid her fingers through his. His sleepless nights shadowed his eyes; his face was grim with tension.

"You'll do the right thing. You'll do whatever is best for your son's welfare. You'll be very careful to put his needs above your own."

Neil nodded. "The first thing would be to call his . . . parents and talk to them, I guess. I know—the story about someone passing through and saw him, thought he looked like me."

Claire reached for him, and he felt the silver chain slide around his neck. Neil looked down at the ring she had intended for Aisling, her own daughter. The tip of his little finger barely fit into the small Celtic-designed ring. "What's this?"

"For good luck. . . . To keep you safe in your passage."

Neil kissed the ring, then Claire. "Thanks. I'm scared, you know . . . of course, you know. I want to pick him up and run home with him, to catch up on all those lost years."

"But you won't. Because you'll put his safety and his needs above your own. You'll do everything you can to see that he isn't unduly upset, and you'll wait for years, if you have to. He's alive and safe, and to you, that's the most important thing. You're not a selfish man, Neil. This is going to work out."

"So now you can see into the future?" Neil asked quietly, his mind still on the image of his son.

Claire smiled. "No, but I have a sister who's pretty good."

When Neil called and asked for a meeting, Bill and Betty Richards were cautious and protective. Sitting beside Neil, Claire was quietly supportive, her hand in his, her voice calm. He noted the mark of her family, the wolf brooch at her vest's shoulder, a Celtic bracelet on her wrist. She'd chosen a plain white blouse and black slacks, her long hair in an elegant, shining knot at her nape. She'd chosen a bright scarlet handbag, triangles of silk, cut by black ribbon with a black, braided shoulder strap—the perfect accessory.

In their home with the children away visiting friends, the Richards were obviously upset and nervous. As former foster parents, they had adopted their son and later two young daughters. Now they feared that if proven to be Sammy's father, Neil would want the return of his son, and they were defensive. Bill Richards was fiercely protective: "He had a note on him, just a baby, about six months or so, the doctor said. The note said that a teenage girl's boyfriend had deserted her and she couldn't take care of the baby. She left him right in the church. We took him right away and went through everything legal to find the girl. . . . I want proof that you're his father—those paternity tests."

Neil nodded slowly. "I'll do whatever you want. I know this is hard for you. In no way would I want to take him from you now. I'll do whatever is in Sam—Lucas's best interests. It's important that his well-being be considered above everything—and that includes me."

Betty was close to tears. "It happens, you know. Young girls who sometimes can't take care of their babies . . . that's how his sisters came to us."

"He sure looks like you, those gray eyes, that waving hair. Lucas's is a bit lighter, but picking up the sun that way," Bill admitted reluctantly.

Sammy was the picture of the young Olafson boys . . . sturdy, a bit wild and impetuous, and those gray eyes reminded Neil of his father—and of Bruce.

"I wouldn't take him away from you, from his safety here. That would be wrong—harmful to him, and I couldn't do it," Neil stated carefully. "You've kept him safe and made a good home for him. He's happy. I wouldn't upset Sam—Lucas by telling him everything now. I just couldn't. There's no way I'd want to endanger how safe he feels now . . . he needs that, growing up, the parents he's known all his life. But if in time, he does want to know, and you feel that time is right, I'll work with you in any way I can to help him. I'll do what you say. But I'll have the tests sent to you right away."

Obviously relieved, Bill and his wife relaxed slightly, then Betty said, "Would you like to see his pictures? Our family albums?"

Neil shuddered just once, and nodded. He swallowed suddenly, his eyes shimmering with tears. He looked down at Claire's hand in his, the softness flowing from it into him. "I really would appreciate that. Thank you. And thank you for taking care of him so well."

"Sure. I know how you might feel." Apparently moved by Neil's emotion, Bill's voice was rough. "Would you like to stay and meet him? He'll be back from summer ball practice soon."

A cautious parent, Bill stood by later as Neil bent to help "Lucas" tighten his bicycle chain.

With emotion clogging his throat, Neil—as Bill's visiting friend—studied every line of the boy's face, the familiar broad cheekbones, that dark waving hair touched by sun. Lucas-Sammy didn't like haircuts, and curls were beginning to form at his nape. His striped T-shirt had been torn on the playground and a girl was bothering him and girls were disgusting—except Tracey, who could really climb the park's playground equipment.

When Lucas-Sammy stared up at Neil, his eyes were that special shade of light gray that could pick up the sky in shades of blue. "You're a lot bigger than Dad."

Beside Neil, Bill Richards shifted restlessly, a father worried about how he compared to another man—especially one that could be the biological father of his adopted son.

Neil struggled not to say the words in his heart, ones his father had told him—*I love you, son.* Instead he said, "Your dad is a special man. You're lucky to have him."

"Yeah. If they just didn't have to go and get my sisters, life would be okay. They're real pains." Lucas-Sammy glanced at the neighbor boy. "Hey, Rick! You wanna come over? My sisters are at a birthday party, and we can watch our shows on TV without them bothering us. We can set up my cars in the living room, ramps and speedways and everything."

Neil had to have just one more minute of his son. He

touched the ring at this throat and turned to Claire with a silent question. When she nodded, Neil said, "Wait, Lucas."

At his side, Bill Richards tensed protectively, and watched Neil remove the chain from his neck and slide the silver ring into his palm. He held it out to Lucas-Sammy. "Here's something that's kept someone I know safe, and me, too. I thought you might like to wear it—it's a special design."

Bill relaxed a bit as the boy considered the ring, slowly sliding it on his finger, then on his thumb. "Girl's stuff," Lucas-Sammy stated curtly.

"I was wearing it, wasn't I? It's a good-luck piece."

"I'll keep it for you, son," Bill offered, when Lucas-Sammy seemed uneasy. "You might change your mind. Mmm. It's Celtic. You like reading about the ancient, Druids and seers and magic, don't you? Well, here you have a real piece of history, and you can wear it. What do you think? Would you like to keep it?"

"Okay, but I gotta go now, Dad. Rick is waiting. Thanks, Neil. See you."

"Sure. See you," Neil returned, the ache in his throat tightening with longing to hold his son.

"He's just excited now, but I'll keep this ring safe for him when he wants it. I know it must be special to you," Bill said.

When the boy ran to his friend, Bill didn't miss the longing in Neil's expression. "If this works out, the paternity test and all, you're welcome to come back to visit, get to know Lucas and him to know you. You've made it clear that you wouldn't want to disrupt a young boy's life—by taking him out of a home and family that he loves. As a foster parent, I've seen people do that and it's heartbreaking."

"I—Thanks. You have my word that I'll always hold what is best for him above everything else. I'm just so glad that he's safe and happy." *And alive. . . . After all these years, Sammy was alive and happy and loved.*

Neil turned to see Claire's fiery hair catch the sun. Her hands covered her lips, her eyes brilliant with emotion. She had brought him this far—to his son. Neil didn't speak, but mouthed the words to her, "Thank you."

On the drive back to Montana and their nights in motels, Neil felt Claire's gentling vibrations ease his longing, troubled heart.

For once, he did not tell her to stop. . . .

Eighteen

"'FOUND.' THAT'S A GOOD NAME FOR THIS PURSE."

Neil ignored Claire's narrowed, warning look. He held the A-shaped tote bag that Claire had just finished up to the midafternoon light coming through her windows. He turned his fingertip tracing the winding ribbon that formed a turquoise path between gardens of vibrant yellow and red silk flowers. Embroidery outlined the butterflies that fluttered above the path, their tiny wings glittering with beads. They were so lifelike, they could have been alive and flying outside in the last week of June's bright, warm sunshine. At the end of the path circling the bag was a tiny stenciled heart.

He traced that heart and wondered where Claire's heart lay; he hoped it lay with him. She'd been exhausted after the fire, and the trip to Arkansas had cost her energy. They'd held and comforted each other, but they hadn't made love.

After returning to Montana three days ago, Claire had seemed distant, immersing herself in her work. Accepting that the trauma of his brother, the fire, and last week's travel could have exhausted her, Neil hadn't pushed her; he realized that Claire needed time and quiet to heal and that his uneven emotions—dealing with his brother's crimes and hatred—could upset her.

And she had led him to Sammy; that journey alone had surely cost her. But Sammy was alive and safe and best of all, loved, just as Leona and Claire had believed. His son was well and safe, and happy—Neil concentrated on that fact, grateful that the Richards were such good people with loving hearts, and that Claire's ring somehow linked him to his son. . . . "It's enough for me. Time will take care of the rest. I want whatever is best for my son . . . I'll work with the Richards, whatever they feel is right for Sammy. I trust them."

Yet the ache for his son remained, a loss that Bruce had caused. At times, Neil didn't want Claire exposed to his darker side, when he needed to be alone, to work until he could no longer think about how Bruce had killed their parents and cost him years of being a father. That deep vein of violence still ran within him, forgiveness far away, and he didn't want that touching Claire; he'd seen the aftermath of her attack.

But those times when Neil had attempted to step back into their relationship, Claire was definitely drawing up separate lives—too busy to have dinner, wanting to sleep during the day, working at night—all gradually drawing away from the lovers they had been. Her turndowns to his invitations had become routine; she was purposefully slipping away from their relationship. Neil had been patient, but now he'd decided to try one more time before confronting her.

As Claire stood in front of the window, Neil took in her big white work shirt, the way the light caught her body's silhouette within the cloth. He noted the long tight jeans down to her bare feet. Then he studied her hair, the way that thick dark red braid wound sensuously over her shoulder, the tip curved just over her breast. Neil didn't hide his hunger for her, and knew by the ripple of that long body that she had recognized his look. "We've been pretty well tied up by finding my son. Everything is going to take a long time to settle, if ever, but I can wait—now that I know he's safe and happy. But life has to go on, Claire. I learned that a long time ago. Why don't we start by going out to dinner?"

Claire tensed, as if she'd been expecting the invitation. She quickly tossed some beads into a drawer and walked to shove it into the big wooden cabinet. "I'm busy and behind. I really need to work. I hope you'll excuse me, but I really do need to start laying out another design. I'm sure you have work to do, too. This time of year, with July almost here and with good camping weather, you're probably really busy."

Neil noted the jerky movement of those slender hands as Claire straightened her scissors and threads. A spool of bright red silk seemed to dance out of her hands and tumbled to the floor. Claire disappeared a little too long behind the table, before she stood up again, carefully, thoughtfully winding the thread back on the spool.

"What's wrong, Claire?" Neil placed "Found" on her worktable, then leaned back against it. He studied Claire, who was suddenly too busy and too nervous, stirring the feather boas as she neatened her work area. She'd worked all night, and in the morning shadows of her workroom, she looked drained and pale against the vivid material she'd begun unwinding from the long roll. She placed the roll on the table, adjusted the fabric to her cutting board, and began snipping.

"So much has happened. Thank you for talking to Linda. She'll pass more easily now." Claire appeared to be in her crisp professional work mode, placing the roll back in its holder. She returned to smooth the material she had just cut, studying it. "A pouch type, I think . . . maybe a magnetic closure, a flap. . . ."

Neil wasn't letting Claire slide away from him that

easily. He wanted whatever was bothering her as defined as the brightly colored hibiscus flowers on that fabric. "Jan has agreed that we'll take it slow with Sammy. She's agreed that nothing should tear him from the love and safety he's known, and that we can all wait, placing his needs above our own. We're all going to work on this—doing what's best for Sammy. Not for anything in the world would we tear his life apart."

"That's good. I thought she might think as you do—just grateful that he's safe. She'll be very careful with him, just as you are."

Claire seemed too distant, and Neil pushed on to clear up any problems in their relationship. "We're all adults, not kids fighting over a possession. Sammy comes first. . . . If you're wondering about Mary Jane and the trouble she's caused, she's definitely out of the picture. She's left town, headed for Alaska."

Claire's hands stopped smoothing the Hawaiian print silk on her cutting board. She folded it slowly, precisely as if placing her thoughts in order. "Alaska?"

"Bruce's trawler deal would be good, done right and starting small. Mary Jane is a fast learner, and a good businesswoman when she sets her mind to it. . . . And she wouldn't want some of the evidence that she'd been connected to Topper's dealings to turn up suddenly—just a few things I found the night that I visited her—the night you were so jealous of her."

Neil smiled, appreciating the quick golden burn of Claire's eyes; he'd gotten her full attention, and to know that she didn't like another woman around him didn't hurt at all.

"You're baiting me, Neil. You came here to start something, didn't you?"

"You've got it. I thought we could have a little chat. Maybe something about our relationship? What it was, and what it's going to be?"

When she seemed to regroup and started smoothing the colorful material again, Neil flattened his hands over it and leaned in to make his point. "What's the deal, Claire? Why are you backing off from us? Just because we've found Sammy doesn't mean we're finished. I thought we had a good thing going."

"Convenient, you mean?"

Her edgy tone quickly took him around the table. Neil hauled her up to him, locking her arms between their bodies. If he couldn't get Claire's complete attention one way, he would another. "Why, exactly, are you backing off, Claire? I deserve an answer. Is it me, or is it something else? And don't try to muck up things by dragging in some malarkey about convenient sex."

Her head went up, her anger clearly visible. "We both got what we wanted, didn't we?"

"Maybe I want more . . . a whole lot more. The question is: Do you?"

Claire stared up at him, her eyes flashing a challenge at him, color rising in her cheeks. "I'd think you'd be running by now. By the way, you can have this corner of Montana. I'm moving as soon as I find a suitable place."

"Is that what this is about? Me running off from you? You think I'd do that? Why?"

When she looked away, her expression shielded, Neil understood immediately. "You're scared. You're flat-out scared that you're going to be hurt again, aren't you? I know more about you than anyone but your family. I haven't run yet, have I?"

She shook her head but didn't look at him. The trembling of her body told Neil all he needed to know. Claire might be trying to pull away emotionally and mentally, but her body still reacted to his, softening and fragrant. Neil opened his hands and slowly drew them down her sides, following the curves he wanted naked and warm and silky against him. "Okay, this may not be the right way to show you that I'm not going anywhere, but sweetheart, it's been a long, long time."

Claire's head tilted as she studied his face. Neil inhaled roughly; he admitted his humbling fear that she might turn away from him. He'd come this far, and now he braced himself to nudge Claire into making a decision about them. "You can tell me to back off. . . . Or you can undo that braid. Your choice."

When Claire didn't move away, and when her hands slid slowly to her braid, Neil didn't wait; he lifted her into his arms, carried her out of the workroom and out the back door. He relaxed just slightly when her arms went around his shoulders. All he had to do was to get Claire to his bed and show her what she meant to him. "Close it. You're not coming back for a long time," he ordered.

Claire complied with a shrug. "You'll hurt your back with all this macho stuff."

"This isn't the way I intend to use it most."

"Just down to basics? Sex?"

"And more . . . making love, is a better term, don't you think? Just until you get the idea that you're not running off just because you're scared of what we might have together."

"This may have worked centuries ago—carrying off a woman—but not now."

Neil stopped in midstride. He frowned at her. "Claire. Wake up. Here's the picture. I've got you in my arms. I'm headed for my bed. You're not objecting. It's working, isn't it?"

"Because *I'm* letting it work, snooky."

Neil stared at her blankly. "Huh?"

"Got you, didn't I?"

"Now isn't the time to get cute. I'm serious here, Claire, making a big point with you. Don't try to distract me. As for sewing your bags—ah, handbags—with noise coming from the shop, I'm thinking about what we can do there. . . . There's a big, run-down building in Red Dog, and I should be able to lease it pretty cheap—to use as a showroom, a pickup point for special orders. I could hire someone part-time to work it."

When Claire was silent, her expression unchanged, Neil started walking again.

Every step of the way toward his house, Neil feared that Claire would tell him to stop. She was taking in every one of his features as if she wanted to imprint them on her forever—which could mean Claire planned to end their relationship. He could feel her mental fingers prowling around him, trying to "read" him. Those weren't the fingers he wanted right now. He wanted real ones, reassuring him that nothing had changed between them.

Okay, so he actually was delicate where Claire was concerned.

"I think we can work through the noise part," Claire said quietly.

Neil stopped and stared at her. He wondered if he were hearing things. "You do?"

"Uh-huh."

"Just like that?"

"I imagine we'll have a few arguments. But I think I can handle you now."

Neil hurried to carry her into his house and to his bedroom. He held her aloft a moment, before dumping her onto his bed. "That is where you belong. If you've got any ideas about leaving, do it now."

Claire landed in the rumpled sheets and blankets. Out of breath and a little furious at his high-handed method of claiming her, she started to get up—he pushed her down. He stood over her, his hands on his hips and those gray eyes narrowed, clearly waiting for her next move. In a black T-shirt and worn jeans, he'd never looked more gorgeous. She'd known from the moment he'd come to her house that he was out to make a statement. The fresh comb marks in his hair, that clean-shaven jaw, and the scent of his shower said that he'd prepared to come to her. He was really quite cute in his macho-mode, dominating, laying down the law.

Neil knew what she was and yet he wanted her. He'd moved through her journey, and his, and he'd never failed. She thought of Neil as her protector, as her mate—and as a challenge she had to have. In every instance, Neil had done what he'd felt was the right thing, even to the final closure with Bruce.

She slowly unwound her braid, playing the submissive female to whatever ritualistic male role Neil needed to play. Taking her time, Claire peeled away her jeans and slowly began to unbutton her shirt. She truly enjoyed Neil's evident hunger, that tense set of his body.

"Now, who's baiting whom?" he asked roughly, as Claire sat to spread her hair around her body. Neil stripped off his clothes and stood, tall and strong and beautiful. "You're not scared of this, of me now, and you shouldn't be scared of living with me—and that's final."

"Nothing is ever final," she murmured, just to challenge him. Neil was great at taking up challenges.

"This is going to be."

Neil came down to her, his lips fused to hers, his hands already preparing her for his possession. Cradled in her body, he stretched her out, his hands holding her wrists. There was that long, searching look, the question he needed answered, despite his urgency. When Claire lifted to brush her lips with his, a silent yes, Neil began—

This time was different, she realized suddenly, her body jolted with that first deep sensation, the heated friction moving too quickly for her to control. Quaking with that first reaction, Claire stared up at Neil. In that moment, before his lips took hers again, his face was hard, the planes defined, those silver eyes burning, consuming her.

He tasted of something Claire had to have, something deep and basic and necessary. Hunger pounded through her, the need to feast and take and give, each brush of her lips, each tiny bite she placed, each draw of her nails, was meant to drive him to the edge, to the very edge, where she waited to claim him. Equal on that plane, man and woman, they fought that ancient give-and-take war.

Claire arched against him, her hips thrusting hard against his, meeting the savage, primitive challenge. This was no gentle lovemaking as before; Neil was set to make his point.

But then, so was she.

Claire wound her arms and legs around him, demanding just as much as the fire built and consumed and burst.

Barely able to move, her body heavy and sated, floating in the aftermath of their passion, Claire stroked his hair, giving him ease after that fierce journey.

Suddenly, Neil tensed and lifted. He leaned down, his kiss possessive and hot. "Oh, no. You're not getting away with that. I know what you're doing. Save it for some other time, Claire. This is the real you—strong, fierce, demanding. Okay, play your little quiet sensitive game with someone else, but I know what you are, and I'm not going anywhere. You think I'd run from this? From you? Do your damnedest, Claire. You and I aren't going anywhere until this is settled."

"And I was feeling so kindly toward you, too."

Neil grinned down at her. "Sure, you were," he taunted her. "Let's talk about this when we're finished."

Claire attempted to push Neil away; he pulled her back beneath him, and his smile challenged her.

"Okay, have it your way," she said as she pushed him away again, this time to straddle him.

"That's my girl."

Sprawled on her stomach after a night of loving, Claire was in no mood for the bright daylight. "Close the blinds, Neil."

"It's almost noon, honey bun. Time to rise and shine."

She caught the scents of his shower and aftershave. Claire turned her head and opened one eye to see Neil dressed only in jeans, broad tanned chest gleaming in the sunlight. His cheerful, knowing grin caused her to groan and close her eyes; she dug deeper into the pillow and tugged the sheet over her head.

Neil pulled it down again and kissed her bare shoulder. His tongue flicked her skin lightly, then he nuzzled the back of her neck. "Better get up, honey bun. Your family is going to turn up any minute."

"Listen, sweetie-pie, lover, macho-man . . . I'm tired. Let me sleep." Something he just said caught her. Claire blinked once and again and tried to rouse. She wasn't certain she had heard him correctly. "Ah. . . . What was that you said about my family?"

Neil's big hand was caressing her bottom. His "Hmm?" sounded distracted and sensual.

Claire flipped over, holding the sheet against her well-tended and sensitive breasts. She tucked the sheet between her thighs, just in case Neil wanted a follow-up to the night's hours of lovemaking, both intense and slow and gentle. "What was that about my family?" she asked again.

His finger prowled over the mound of her breast, his eyes following the trail. "Didn't I tell you? I invited them before we left for Arkansas, because I knew that no matter what happened, it wouldn't change things between us. And I knew that you were going to invite them sometime. I just thought I'd do it for you."

" 'For me?' I was going to do that much later, Neil."

"Honey bun, you've been busy, tied up. Okay, I wanted to meet the rest of the family. They wanted to meet me. What's the problem?"

"The problem?" Claire stared at him, this man she thought she knew and didn't.

Neil's grin was broad and boyish. "I thought they'd like to meet me in person, sort of a family affair. Your mother was really happy."

"You didn't."

"I did."

From his time spent with Claire, Neil recognized that to cement a deeper, long-term relationship, he needed to be accepted by her family; Claire was definitely a package deal, very close to them. Their shared psychic elements created an even deeper tie than usual.

Claire had been so cute, running around nervously, picking up his house. She'd run into the kitchen and stopped, staring blankly at him, as if she didn't know him. Then she'd hurried away, fussing about the house. Neil had stirred the spaghetti sauce and whistled as he'd added a dollop of wine; life was good.

Now, Neil studied the four women as they sat in his living room, relaxing a bit before the dinner he'd prepared. The bright afternoon sunlight lit their fiery hair and each woman had those unusual green eyes and pale skin, but each was clearly very much an individual and separate from the others.

After the usual family introductions, Claire's family had settled their things into the bedrooms of the two houses. Neil would sleep in his camper; he hoped he wouldn't be alone.

Neil listened to the soft tones of the women, relaxing, nice, comfortable. He would enjoy having them around.

He swirled the sauvignon blanc in his wineglass and remembered how each woman had taken in everything about him, the teardrop campers, the changes to Eunice's home, the small mementoes of her remaining, and those of his family. Greer Aisling had paused at the doorway of his bathroom and bedroom, apparently noting her daughter's presence.

Even without extrasensory perception, Neil understood that the triplets' mother was no ordinary woman. In his invitation call to her, Leona had been right in a brief, terse, and slightly bitter warning, "Our mother can see right through you, Neil, down to the bones. I hate it. It's an invasion of privacy."

Already experienced with Claire's delicate psychic probes, those intent looks, Neil wasn't surprised by Greer's. Across the space of the living room, he met her look, waited until that tingling sensation passed, and noted her small pleased smile. No words had passed between them; none had been necessary.

Claire hadn't spoken to him for hours—small price for the invitation to her family that she considered an overstep in the boundaries of their relationship.

She was clearly nervous. Neil had no idea why. He was going to be just lovely and sweet, adorable and cute. By the time her family's visit was over, he intended that any doubts Claire and her family might have about him would be ended.

Neil sipped his wine and studied the woman he considered his. Elegant even in a plain black sweater, long tight jeans, and canvas sneakers, Claire seemed to have recovered from their long, intense night of lovemaking. He mentally noted that a repeat performance was needed to remind her just what ran between them. Neil smiled briefly; from her family's thoughtful looks at him and then to Claire, they had also noted a change in her. Though she seemed the same, her hair was long and free around her face and shoulders—just the way he liked it. Others might not notice, but to Claire's intimate family and Neil, she bore the stamp of a well-loved woman.

As the women talked softly, Neil settled in to study them. He'd already met Tempest, a sharp contrast to Leona's cool, classic businesswoman. Leona's haircut, a practical smooth shoulder cut, turned under at the ends, with bangs that accentuated her eyes, framed her face. She wore light cosmetics, a navy sweater, and flowing slacks with flats. Used as a pendant, the wolf brooch lay amid the delicate crystals of the vintage necklace at her throat. Neil's impression of Leona was that beneath that smooth surface, the currents ran deep and restless. Outwardly, she seemed to be more like Greer, calm and in full possession, not as easy to laugh or show her emotions as Tempest.

Greer wore the wolf's-head brooch as a fastener to her neck scarf on her blue tunic and slacks outfit.

All of the women wore copies of the brooch tonight. Was that planned—or accidental? Other than Neil's strategy to make Claire fully his, what else was brewing?

He'd seen Tempest and Claire, just after her attack, talking calmly about everyday things, protecting her sensitized psyche. The women's voices coursed over his living room in that same calm, soothing manner. But every once in a while, Claire had shivered and tensed just enough to tell him that she sensed something from the others.

Neil noted Greer's close study of him. While her daughters talked about which of Claire's handbags they liked best, Greer lifted her wineglass in a toast, which he answered. Lifted in midair, a room's length apart, the glasses symbolized something Neil didn't fully understand . . . but he'd take it to mean that Greer approved of him.

After an early dinner, they relaxed, went to Claire's workroom to see her new bags, and gradually everyone settled into the separate houses for the night, Claire using his bed, Greer in his guest room.

Neil stepped out into the crisp night air, noted the deer moving down to graze in the meadow, the great horned owl's wings silhouetted against the moon, and then Greer joined him. She drew a dark green merino wool shawl around her. "Nice night."

"Yes. Can I get you a lawn chair? Or would you like to see my workshop?"

"Your workshop would be nice. Thank you."

Neil understood; Greer wanted to speak to him alone. At the midnight hour, she'd chosen a perfect time.

He didn't fully light the shop; Greer might feel too exposed and uncomfortable. Neil briefly outlined the creation of the teardrops, why he liked custom work, creating individual projects and tailoring them to his customers. Greer walked around the teardrop trailer that he had shared with Claire and had pulled into the shop; he wanted to create a sliding panel on the roof, that could be opened—so he and Claire could lie beneath the moonlight together—

"Lying beneath the moonlight with someone you love is very, very beautiful," Greer stated softly.

"You got that, did you? A little telepathy? I'll have to watch myself."

"I knew it right away when we spoke—how she spoke of you, how she felt about you, near you. It's there between you, just as it was between me and my husband, Daniel, the girls' father. But it's so beautiful actually to see Claire bloom and come alive as she has with you.

She's been alone for so long, maybe since . . . since she became more sensitive, and we discovered how deeply our emotions could upset each other. Tempest and Leona are somewhat affected, but not like this tie with Claire. Her sisters have other ties with me—different, of course."

"Whatever you and her sisters are—whatever Claire is—doesn't affect how I feel about her."

"Of course. We know that. But there's something I've kept from Claire." Greer turned to the woman standing in the shop's wide doorway. "Claire, perhaps it's time you knew."

"Tell me what, Mom? Just what have you kept from me?"

Greer smiled briefly. "It wasn't easy. I've had to focus very hard to block you."

As Claire came to stand near Neil, he wrapped his arm around her and drew her close. If Greer had waited this long to tell Claire, it wasn't going to be good. Greer drew a long, slow breath as if bracing herself. "This isn't easy to say, dear. I think that someone intended you to lose your baby. I think that just as the man who attacked you was motivated by someone else, I think the nurse was also sent to agitate you, to stir you. That would take someone who knew that in your weakened condition, you could be affected by those around you. This particular nurse was very upset, unusual for her, according to the staff. The doctor was also unusually upset, and for no apparent reason. Basically, five years ago, you were surrounded by emotional storms of all kinds—not good for an empath, especially one with undeveloped shields."

Greer took a deep, steadying breath and then said, "And now, all three are dead—the doctor, the nurse, and your attacker. That's too much of a coincidence. At the hospital, I was too involved with rescuing you, getting you out of there. I should have paid more attention to the doctor and nurse. Did you—can you remember anything about them? About how you felt near them?"

Claire shuddered and eased closer to Neil. She closed her eyes. "I did feel something. Rage, the same I felt with the man who hated me. I had no idea why anyone would hate me enough to harm me."

She looked at Greer. "Why are you telling me this now?"

"Because you're stronger, you're more focused, and Neil isn't letting anything happen to you. Together, you've formed a bond too strong to penetrate easily. You've grown, Claire. You'll fight with Neil, but you'll also fight for him. You weren't like that before, except maybe for your family."

Claire tensed, but Neil summed up the trauma. "I get the picture. She was ambushed. Someone chose her weakest time—just after the bank robbery—to get to her. Why?"

Claire and Greer turned to the two women standing in the shop's doorway. Neil watched Leona and Tempest enter the shop. The four red-haired women, each with those slanted mysterious green eyes, suited the midnight hour. The gathering of the clan had begun. "Come in, ladies."

Leona moved gracefully to the camper and ran her hand over it. Her long robe seemed to swirl around her body, the green shade a match to Greer's shawl. She glanced at Greer. "You wouldn't do this without us, would you, Mother Dear?"

"Take it easy, Leona." Tempest's dark green silk pajamas gleamed in the shadows. She sat on a sawhorse, and reminded Neil of a cat, twitching its tail, watching and waiting. As the one woman who could move more easily between the other psychics, Tempest clearly wanted to ensure that the meeting ran smoothly.

Neil rested his cheek against Claire's. He wanted her to know that he would take any emotional journey she needed—with her. Her hand tightened over his, accepting that anchor.

"You're starting to dream again, aren't you, Leona?" Greer asked quietly. "You saw Neil's little boy and knew he was alive. You were stirred by Claire's connection to him and how she was affected. You knew she needed closure as much as he, and you deliberately focused to give it to her."

Leona's, "You're so wise, Mother," carried just that bitter nip.

"Tell us what happened then."

Leona turned suddenly, and her hair spun out around her; the long robe rippled and settled slowly. "Okay, I am—restless, if that's the word. I wanted to help Neil and, therefore, my sister on her journey to reclaim what she felt she'd lost. I opened myself and the nightmares began—I felt crushed. But then, maybe I was affected by how my husband died in that avalanche."

A physically active woman and restless now, Tempest raised one leg and wrapped her arms around it. "And Mom is dreaming about the Viking. Sexy dreams, if I'm not mistaken. If they could get along for two minutes, it would be easier on Claire and me. What's really got Leona bugged is that she's recently had the same dream."

"I told you that in confidence," Leona stated darkly.

"He needs to know what is happening with us, Sis. Claire Bear has caught one that isn't running . . . Neil hasn't been spooked so far, and he knows what we are. So Neil is in this with us, whether you like it or not."

"Tempest. That's enough." Greer crossed her arms over her chest, and, with a tired sigh, explained, "All this started a long time ago, Neil. Leona has never forgiven me for—her genetic inheritance—or that I was away when my daughters were taken into that awful lab."

"We were used as guinea pigs at the Blair Institute of Parapsychology, Mother. Two long days and one ugly night of electrodes, blood work, hooked up to every possible meter, sleep deprivation, effects of sound loud enough to hurt eardrums. You were supposed to keep us safe—and you didn't. Remember how badly Claire suffered?"

Tears shimmered in Greer's eyes. "If I could go back in time and have prepared better, I would. I had no idea they would go to such lengths. . . ."

Claire spoke suddenly, impatiently. "She's suffered enough, Leona. Now back off. She can't help it if you're more like her than the rest of us."

The other women stared at her as if stunned. Usually calm and soft-spoken, Claire hadn't used her psychic skills to ease the tension. She had simply moved in to fiercely protect her mother. But then Neil wasn't surprised; he had more experience with this new Claire. "Go for it, Champ," he whispered.

Claire stared at him, her eyes flashing gold. "When I need a cheerleader, I'll ask for one."

Neil couldn't resist: "Now, snook-ums. You know I wouldn't look good in that short skirt and pom-poms."

Clearly stunned, Claire blinked and shook her head. Then she smiled. "Don't try to distract me, Protector. Now isn't the time."

"Hey. By the way, where is my sword and shield— uh!" Neil rubbed his side where Claire's elbow had just nudged.

"Oh, he is so cute and so much fun, Claire Bear. I love to see him with you. He absolutely knocks your socks off." Tempest's grin died as she looked at Neil. "Okay . . . on with the story: I made the replicas of the wolf's-head brooch in Mom's dreams. Since Claire's hospital nightmare, I'd been looking for some symbol to unite us. I wanted something to remind us that we are all—one, so to speak—connected. Something to give us strength in the hard times, an amulet, if you will. Oh, yeah, we believe in good-luck charms. When I find the original *fibula,* shaped like that wolf's head, we might have some answers as to what is bothering us. With Leona dreaming about being crushed, it's time to speed up the hunt."

Neil shook his head; whatever dots in a story line the women were laying out for him, he wasn't able to connect them. "But why Claire? Why would someone hurt her, Greer?"

"I don't know, but she's too strong now, and she has you. That bond is too strong."

Claire nestled closer to Neil. "That's what case you've been working on, isn't it? Mine? Trying to find out why the doctor and the nurse changed? The reason I was attacked?"

"Yes. Apparently, both the doctor and the nurse changed after coming back from a medical convention. Before that, they were calm, peaceful, centered people—then suddenly they changed—just before the bank robbery."

Neil shifted uneasily. "You're saying that the bank robbery was a setup, too?"

"Maybe. The timing was right. Again, the robbers met the same fate—they died in prison. I've been going over every case I've been involved in, trying to find a connection. I've been going over anything, anyone possibly related to psychic experience, anything that might have touched our family."

Greer smoothed the silver brooch at her shoulder, her voice almost a whisper. "I hope this isn't because of something I've done—and there have been a lot of unhappy people in my career, and a lot of threats from criminal elements. But I feel something else is hunting us; it's dark and predatory. I'd hoped that it wasn't after my daughters, but it reached Claire. Something wanted you at the river, and the fog was an extension. I've had that feeling about fog, too. Leona?"

"Count me out. I don't know what you're talking about."

"Yes, you do," Tempest murmured as she leveled a stare at Leona. "You were visiting a friend in Kentucky, and they had a small pond. You said the fog was so thick you couldn't breathe. You said you felt crushed then, too."

Neil looked at Leona, then at Tempest. Both women's eyes had flashed in the dim light, turning that same shade of gold as Claire's when she was angry.

Greer came to smooth Claire's hair and, in Neil's arms, she relaxed slightly. Experienced now, Neil understood the soothing of a psychic's touch.

Greer cradled Claire's face in her hands. "With Claire's history, she might be the weakest and the most vulnerable, a good place to start. Under the circumstances, with the battery of emotions that you had just gone through, Claire, I would have experienced trauma. Losing Aisling wasn't your fault. Stop blaming yourself, Claire Bear."

"A pretty nasty one-two punch," Neil stated quietly.

"I can tell we're going to have to get used to having a man in our family. They usually cut everything down to the basics."

Claire breathed deeply and leaned back against Neil. She shook her head. "All this time—"

"Is it over?" Neil asked cautiously.

"No." All four women had answered at the same time.

Tempest stared at Leona. "Told you that Leona felt it, whether she wants to or not. Told you."

Greer studied the moths circling the bare lightbulb

above them. "Claire may be out of danger. It's tested Claire and found her stronger than she was. I feel that about her, too, how much she's changed. And she's so much lighter, less weighed by the past, and a little bit playful—all good things, thanks to Neil."

"What do we do?" Neil asked quietly.

"We wait."

Epilogue

NEIL AWOKE TO THE SILENCE OF THE HOUSE, CLAIRE'S SPACE beside him cool to his wandering hand. "Claire?"

The house was silent. Her family had gone the day before, staying just one night. . . .

She could have gone to her house to work. Fear for Claire took Neil to his feet, and he quickly drew on his jeans. He scanned the bed and nightstand. The clock read six o'clock, and the mist at the window was keeping the dawn at bay. "There's no note—Claire!"

A quick search of the house proved it to be empty. Neil remembered how Claire had been frightened of the river's mist and in her backyard. Aware of how she could be harmed, how all the psychics were restless now, Neil hurried outside.

The fog curled around him instantly, damp upon his hair and skin. *Claire had said that it wanted her.*

Neil started toward her house, then he saw movement stir the mist, her pale face wrapped within it.

Terrified and ready to fight for her, Neil forced himself to approach Claire slowly.

Her outstretched arms were pale as she turned slowly

within the layers of mist, her long hair moving sensuously around her body. She seemed wrapped in another
world, as if she could float away.

Neil held his breath; he had to bring her back. "You
can't go anywhere without me, Claire," he stated gently, and moved closer.

She wore only the dark green shawl, her mother's
parting gift. The wolf's-head brooch gleamed eerily at
her shoulder. As she turned, her face lifted upward, a
pale curved hip and leg appeared, her feet slender and
bare upon the grass.

A thin gold band, the Celtic diadem, circled her head.
Her hair seemed to float down softly to frame her face
and throat as she found him in the mist. The shawl
pooled to her feet, leaving her body pale and curved in
the dim light.

"I know what I am now. I know that I am strong, and
I know how to protect myself. We're strong—together.
It's not coming back, Neil. It can't hurt me. I'm free.
And you know that your son is alive and safe. You have
closure. He'll come to know you and love you—when
it's time—and he'll love you more for holding his needs
above your own. . . ."

Claire didn't hide her joy, or her love, for the man
moving through the mist, coming to stand near her.

He'd come to find her, as he always would. Neil
could have been a Viking lord from long ago, straight
and tall and fierce, strength in his body and courage
and goodness in his heart.

But there was tenderness, too, in the way he picked
up the shawl and wrapped it around her, the way he
lifted her hair free and smoothed it with his fingers,
studying the texture against his skin. Then, suddenly,
as if making his claim, Neil picked her up in his arms,
and his deep, rough voice curled firmly around her,

"Whatever comes, there'll be no more of this leaving our bed without telling me, Claire Bear."

"Oh? Really?" It was an ancient man-woman game, and one she suddenly knew how to play, to love the man, to tease him just that bit into acting a dominant, macho role—a little pampering of the male ego didn't hurt at times, she decided.

The fog curled around them, damp against her skin. Claire closed her eyes and eased into the sensations, but there was nothing.

"Anything?" Neil asked warily.

Claire studied him, ran her fingertip across those fierce eyebrows, and smiled. "Nothing but you."

"Tempest is hunting this, huh?"

Seated at his desk, Neil held the new belt buckle in his hand. Celtic symbols circled the large, weighty buckle, designed for a man. He ran his thumb over the impression of a snarling wolf; the design matched the Aisling women's brooches. "It's a nice present. She does good work."

"You're just glad she didn't send you a feminine brooch. . . . It's a welcome-to-the-family, and hope-you-can-survive present. She started working on it after she got back from—from seeing us together." Standing beside him, Claire's voice was uneven, as remnants of the attack still lingered in her. She pushed them away.

Neil Olafson, Olaf's son, held that Viking blood, an enjoyment of life, a fierce fighter, when protecting his own. Was it an accident that they'd been brought together? Or was it fate, a combination of a certain heritage, coming together at just the right time?

As an empath, and as a woman, Claire preferred to think it was simply love. "You're in for some interesting experiences, buddy."

"Oh, I'm not going anywhere." Neil placed the buckle

beside the large ship-in-a-bottle building kit Greer had sent him. A Viking longship, complete with oars and sail, was featured on the box. Claire's fine handwork, a brilliant red sail with a black screen-painted wolf's-head design and Celtic symbols lay over the box.

Claire rested her hand on his shoulder. "The sail is red, because Vikings wanted their enemies to be afraid—it symbolizes blood. That's how I feel about protecting you . . . if anyone—anything—came to harm you. The brooch, the replicas, were intended as reminders of our family's unity, a good-luck protection."

"My little Viking sweetheart." Neil's tone was smug, but then, he'd already seen how Claire would give her life to protect him.

"Just don't push your luck too much with me, Olafson. . . . Tempest is working very hard to find the original brooch. It could be lost for all time. Or perhaps the dreams of Leona and Mom are wrong—dreams can be misinterpreted. Perhaps it never existed at all. Perhaps the wolf insignia symbolizes danger."

"Mmm. . . . What do you think? Do you think there really is an original?"

Claire hesitated. "I can't see into the future, or into the past, Neil. I can only feel—toss in a little telepathy with you."

"Stop the cautious stalling, sweetheart. I've been through enough with you and your family to know that you have certain takes. Well, do you think there is an original Viking brooch?" Neil pushed.

Then he picked up the buckle and held it in both hands, running his thumbs over the buckle's design. "Do you think that Greer can get anything by just holding it?"

Claire didn't hesitate this time. "If she holds the original, she'll know why and what caused a normally placid personality to attack me without cause. She'll know what came through his computer to change him, to create his rage. With Leona and Mom both dreaming about that brooch, I have no doubt that it is real, and that it is connected somehow to this feeling we all have—that of being stalked. Somehow, that brooch holds the answers we need to deal with this sense of danger."

"Predators have existed since forever, a weaker mind seduced by a stronger one. The guy who attacked you is an example of someone—"

"Taking his energy? Redirecting it to harm me? Why me specifically? It's because as an empath, I'm the most vulnerable. We're dealing on another level, that of extra senses and psychic portals, like the river that day and its energy's extension—the fog. We have to find that brooch, Neil, and Tempest will—if it's not lost forever."

Neil drew her down to his lap and held her close. "I hope she finds it soon. I want this over."

Claire snuggled closer to him but looked at the box of the Viking longship, the red flag draped across it. Centuries ago, a Viking chieftain had captured a Celtic seer. He'd worn the wolf's-head brooch at his shoulder. Then she studied Neil, born of Viking blood, her protector, her strength, the man she loved, just as Aisling had come to love her Viking. "It won't harm me now because with you and our bond, I'm stronger."

"You're worried about your family, who might be next, aren't you?"

"Yes, I am. Whatever energy is out there, it's not going away."

Next month, don't miss these exciting new love stories only from Avon Books

How to Engage an Earl by Kathryn Caskie

An Avon Romantic Treasure

When middle sister Anne Royle is caught in Allan, Earl MacLaren's bedchamber, she does the only thing possible—she declares that she and the earl are engaged! Allan and Anne's lives will never be the same...and they're beginning to realize that may not be such a bad thing after all.

When She Was Bad by Cindy Kirk

An Avon Contemporary Romance

Sick of her squeaky-clean image, Jenny Carman decides to let her inner bad girl out. When unexpected feelings arise from a one night stand, Jenny knows she'll have to come clean, but will it mean the end of the one good thing to come out of her bad lie?

A Warrior's Taking by Margo Maguire

An Avon Romance

Danger besets Brogan Mac Lochlainn and threatens both his quest and his chance at love in Margo Maguire's magical new series about time-traveling warriors who search throughout the world and the ages for a missing sacred object—and for their one true love.

The Highlander's Bride by Donna Fletcher

An Avon Romance

Sara McHern is praying for a husband when Highlander Cullen Longton appears. With Cullen desperate to find his lost son, Sara proposes a bargain—marriage in exchange for information. It starts as a business arrangement, but as they struggle to escape from an evil earl who would see them dead, love may be the only thing that will save them.